MISSILE

PARADISE

MISSILE PARADISE

A NOVEL

RON TANNER

NEW YORK, NEW YORK

Printed in the United States
First Edition
10 9 8 7 6 5 4 3 2 1

Ig Publishing
Box 2547
New York, NY 10163
www.igpub.com

This is a work of fiction.
Any similarities to persons living or dead is purely coincidental. The Marshall Islands do exist, however, and Kwajalein is real. Americans do live there and their work is indeed top secret, though their presence is not. As those who have lived there may notice, I have taken some liberties with some details of daily life and with some facts having to do with the region. For those few readers who catch me taking such liberties, I ask your indulgence.

ISBN: 978-1-63246-009-7 (paperback)

To Newton Lajuan

America's greatest strength, and its greatest weakness, is our belief in second chances, our belief that we can always start over, that things can be made betteer.

—*Anthony Walton*

The problem is, we don't know how contaminated we are. We found out the Americans had been dropping bombs east of us which were never recorded. They could have irradiated the whole damn area. The Americans says Kwajalein is helping in the prevention of nuclear warfare. That's the biggest joke we ever heard.

—*King Amata Kabua*

PART I

ONE

Cooper anchors a good hundred yards from the pilings—because he doesn't have the strength to tie up, much less negotiate the breakers. The island looks like an accident of nature, a thicket of palm trees on a hump of sand, hazy in the distance. Cooper can't be sure how much of the haze is due to heat and salt spray and how much is a product of his alarming fever: 104 by the thermometer's last warning. His right leg looks like a broiled side of beef, yellow-brown and bloated, a crusty custard of puss attracting all manner of flies on this windless afternoon.

His pain is a hot and humming thing, as if it had a life of its own. Like a teeming colony of red ants: always busy, always chewing.

Ahead he sees only a single, aged pier, which suggests that the island has few inhabitants and receives fewer visitors. He's not completely ignorant about the mid-Pacific. He's done some reading. He knows that these atolls are crowns of coral left by sunken volcanoes a million years ago. Some come and go with the surge of storms. Many have never been visited or have been visited only long enough to be deemed uninhabitable because there's little fresh water out here. It's tropical, yes, just north of the equator, but not rain-forest tropical. The rainy season crashes through every summer, sometimes a typhoon in the spring, but most storms are squalls, abrupt and short-lived, the sun breaking through to bake things dry within the hour. Always the relentless sun.

This afternoon's squall won't even reach him: he sees sky-scraping thunderheads thresh the water a mile away. The clouds are trundling north, black as a nasty bruise. Behind him lies a silver gleaming, endless horizon. No wind today, so he couldn't sail even if he had the strength. Which is why he put into this lagoon two days ago to find a landing. Since then he has been congratulating himself for this show of prudence.

The atoll's name, he thinks, is Lili. Or, rather, he wishes it were Lili because the name reminds him of his ex-finacée, Lillian. Orange-haired Lillian, three inches taller than he (which accounts for her slight stoop); green-eyed Lillian, a collector of vintage pottery, which she displays on shelves and tables throughout her A-frame in Montara, just south of San Francisco; swan-necked Lillian, who leotards her yoga in front of the CD-player, with its music of Zen garden gongs, the A-frame resounding with eerily sonorous notes at eerie intervals: bong . . . bong . . . bong; cinnamon-scented Lillian, who bakes oatmeal-cinnamon-coconut-raisin granola for breakfast; speech-impeded Lillian, whose stutter makes even her anger sound charming.

"Must have been destiny," she claimed of their first meeting. She was selling plants at the Saturday flea market in the sandy lot near the Half Moon Bay marina, where he moored his boat. He was living over the mountain in Palo Alto, spending every free hour—and every dollar he made—on rehabbing the Alberg 35, which was in the water but hardly ready to sail.

"Think I could use one of these on my boat?" he asked, raising a potted spider plant for an appraisal.

"You'd kill it," she said. Not a criticism exactly, just flat fact.

The way she looked at him from her lawn chair behind the plant-ladened card table, her narrowed eyes peering over her wire-rim sunglasses, made it clear that she knew he was flirting. Because he was still sweaty, and his hands greasy, from a hard day of engine work; because his hair was flattened from leaning into tight places; because he needed a shave and was wearing his worst work clothes, paint-splattered and ragged, he thought he had nothing to lose.

It seemed she didn't either. She was pretty—maybe too pretty for him—and had an oddly defensive manner, as if she were out to prove herself, though a woman over thirty shouldn't have that need.

She put him on edge.

It didn't help that to her right, in the shade of a pink-striped sunbrella, sat her thirteen-year-old daughter, eyeing him curiously—a squinting, shorter replica of her mother, except the girl was wearing a black loose-collared man's shirt over a baggy black T-shirt that fell to her black-stockinged knees. She wore black Birkenstocks and her hair was dyed black-black and tied off in a dozen angry little knots as if to announce a protest.

What are you supposed to be? Cooper wanted to ask the girl, who now had his full attention.

Too predictably she was plugged into an iPod, nodding her head ever-so-slowly to a dirge-like noise that was hissing from her earbuds.

"Her name's Bailey," Lillian announced as if in warning. "She's thirteen."

Cooper was immediately embarrassed because he wasn't looking at the girl that way. Anybody could plainly see he was simply put out by the pair, the stereotypical alien daughter and the slim, lovely youngish mother who could have been a Marin county debutante down on her luck.

But then, turning his stare again to the woman's barely perceptible smile, he realized that her last comment was more bait, challenging him to make a come-back. And he did want to come back.

His thoughts scrambling like pilots for their grounded jets, he heard sirens wailing in the distance—fire trucks roaring past on Highway 1—and he was suddenly as nervous as he had been at his last job interview, which he thought would change his life. It did change his life, bringing him from the Baltimore-Washington corridor to sunny Palo Alto. He now belonged to a thirty-person team developing a 200 million dollar video game called Stone Deaf Death Rangers. It was the highest level work he'd ever done. And more money than he'd ever imagine making, which had enabled him to buy and rehab the vintage Alberg 35. Who'd have thought that he—a Chesapeake Bay skiff sailor— would become a Pacific blue water freak? Much had changed in two years.

So, facing down this attractive mom and her daughter, he was on: "This pot looks vintage, maybe the 1940s?" he said, hefting the blue-glazed thing in his hand.

"Good eye," Lillian said. "Can you tell me the maker?"

"Without looking," the daughter added, her eyes seeming to mock him: geek!

He said the only old pottery name he could think of—something he'd come across while searching for boat parts online: "McCoy?"

Lillian smiled her approval. "You w-w-win," she said, betraying her stutter for the first time. Which made her more interesting because he could see that, like her daughter, she was defensive mostly because she wasn't wholly sure of herself.

"Does this mean I can treat you both to an early dinner?" he asked, surprising himself.

"Get a life," Bailey said.

It was nearly five on a Saturday afternoon, tourists crowding the nearby beach, the bay popcorned with sailboats, Highway 1 slow with traffic, and the sun hot on his already peeling forehead. Briefly he surveyed the table of plants. On the one hand it was touching that mother and daughter were spending time together; on the other hand it seemed sad that this was the best they could do. Did they need the money?

He said: "Bailey, you wouldn't have to do anything but sit politely while we grown-ups conversed. What do you say?"

"Assuming that her m-m-mother has a-accepted the invitation," Lillian answered.

"Which came first," he asked to put her off her guard, "the

old pots or the plants?"

"The p-p-plants aren't old," she said. "And the pots came first."

"She's a pot hag," Bailey said.

"I bet you're listening to Ozzie Osborn," he said. It was almost a taunt.

"James Taylor," the girl replied with a smirk. "Only the early stuff."

"But she's so Goth!" he said to Lillian in jest. "What's the deal?"

Lillian smiled. "It's a complicated world, isn't it?"

He told them his name and Lillian surrendered her own. He helped them load the plants into the back of her Honda Element. Lillian said she'd be happy to meet him at the Pelican in Montara an hour later.

"You live in Montara, then?" he asked.

"Does it matter?" Bailey said before her mother could answer.

"Remember what I said about polite?" he reminded her.

"She's not yours to correct," Lillian reminded him.

This gave him a pause, like a spark of static at a light switch.

He said: "If she's in the world, she's subject to correction." Then to Bailey with a wink: "Be sure to bring 'Fire and Rain' with you. Maybe we'll have a sing-along."

"You shouldn't taunt her," Lillian warned at dinner while Bailey was in the bathroom. "She's at that age."

Lillian was wearing an airy blue blouse with the same faded blue jeans she'd worn at the flea market, but also he detected a trace of fresh lip gloss and subtle eye-liner. For his benefit or was this simply her going-out face?

Her protectiveness of her daughter was a good trait, he decided. But he wasn't about to let a thirteen-year-old dictate the terms of his engagement. He'd heard too many stories about failed relationships involving children from a previous marriage.

"I remember that age," he said. "A little challenge builds

character." He didn't like that this echoed his own father's platitudes.

"You don't remember that age as a girl, Cooper. It's very d-d-different for girls." Lillian forked her grilled tuna tentatively. She seemed alternately shy and petulant, as though she were fighting with herself over some difficult question. She said: "You don't have children, I take it."

This made the heat rise to his cheeks—it felt like sunburn. So she was interested in him, and already he was into *the Interview*?

"You assume I've been married," he said.

"Hasn't everybody our age been married? You're what, thirty-five?"

"Four. And, yes, I was married. No kids."

"Was that part of the problem?"

This was like getting caught sideways in a trough, the waves raking in one after the other. A little scary, a little exhilarating.

"There were many problems," he said. "We were together for seven unlucky years. The child question was a topic of conversation but not the issue."

"So you don't blame her for the failure?"

"We both made our mistakes," he said. "But she was the bigger fuck-up."

Carefully, with a furtive glance, she asked: "Infidelity?"

Immediately he took the hint: "Your ex was unfaithful?"

"Very." She reached for her white wine.

"But she still works for the bastard," Bailey interjected, dropping herself into the chair between them.

Lillian frowned at her daughter. "Since when have you started calling your father a bastard?"

"I'm just channeling your anger, mom."

"How long has it been?" Cooper asked.

"Two years and counting," chirped Bailey.

"*You work for your ex?*" Cooper asked, this fact just now hitting home.

"I hardly ever see him," Lillian said dismissively. "I work in the greenhouse. He's in the field."

"He owns Trumaine's Nurseries and Landscaping," Bailey explained, popping a French fry into her mouth. "You've seen the trucks."

"No, I haven't." Maybe Bailey was warning him off—but this only made him more curious.

"Very classy trucks," Bailey continued. "He makes tons of money."

"Don't eat with your mouth open, Bailey."

Bailey grinned, potato mash on her teeth.

"I *own* the greenhouse," Lillian said, her eyes now fixed on Cooper as if to assure him that she was no patsy, that she had her life well in hand.

"She owns *one* of the greenhouses," Bailey corrected, her pretty eyes glinting at her mother. "Dad owns three."

"Then why don't you start your own business?" Cooper asked—because he wanted Lillian to be unencumbered and unbeholden.

"My ex's business is too well established, the clientele too firmly tied to him," she said. "If I were on my own, he'd put me out of business."

Cooper shook his head in sympathy. *Not healthy*, he was thinking. Maybe this family was too tied up with itself and there would be no room for him. "I guess that's the prudent thing to do then," he said, feeling oppressed by the story.

"Sometimes I don't like being prudent," Lillian said, almost angrily. "But I've got a daughter to raise and a mortgage to pay."

"That's me," said Bailey, "her ball and chain."

"You know I don't mean it that way, Bailey."

"So you collect pots," he said. "And you raise plants."

"Ornamental bushes, actually."

"Rhododendrons, philodendrons, tetrahedrons," Bailey said in sing-song.

"Do you even know what a tetrahedron is?" Cooper asked.

"That's right, he's a programmer, Bailey, he knows all about math."

"If you start dating my mother does that mean you'll do my math homework?"

Lillian laughed nervously. And so it began for the three of them. Eight months of courtship, then the proposal—which Lillian made and Cooper, flattered and abashed, accepted. And then he moved into her Montara A-frame for a year's trial run. During that year, he landed the job he's headed for now, a job so prestigious, he felt obliged to take it after he passed the many interviews, and security clearances. It's a 12-month contract to help study missile re-entries at the Ronald Reagan Test Site in the Kwajalein atoll. It became for him a challenge, a grand adventure. And Lillian was going to sail the 4500 miles with him, stay for a month on Kwajalein, then fly back to the States, while Bailey stayed with her father. But Bailey betrayed them, undermining their intimacy at every turn and ultimately finding ways to discredit Cooper until Lillian gave him up, refusing finally to go through with the trip whose highlight would have been their wedding in Honolulu.

Life is full of surprises, isn't it? Today Cooper is surprised and a little frightened at his uncharacteristic fumbling as he tries to untether the yellow rubber dinghy from the back of the Lickety Split—the boat Lillian herself named. Once he gets the dinghy overboard, he falls flat-backed into it, his impact raising a splash that soaks his right shoulder. Upended, wallowing in the raft as if it were a hammock, his injured leg extended up and over the side, he watches the sky rocking in big see-saw swings.

He recalls how he was so lucky as a boy because motion never made him woozy, much less sick. Happily, triumphantly, he rode the local amusement park's octopus, its swing ring, its rocket rocker while Teddy, his younger brother, watched with grave envy from a nearby bench.

And, later, as a teenager, Teddy stood on the shore and watched as Cooper skippered his 16-foot single-sail skiff into the choppy shallows of Baltimore's back bay, dropping cages to catch crabs. It would take Cooper years to understand the difference between those who love land and those who love water. He, Cooper, belongs on water.

He sits up slowly, carefully, thankful that he hasn't hit his throbbing leg. It takes great concentration to wrap the outboard's nylon cord around his right hand, great focus to marshal strength in his biceps and steady himself with his left hand, then great effort to yank that cord decisively. But he does. And immediately the motor sputters, then whines its eagerness, the air abruptly smoky with gas fumes. *Yes, this is good.* Cooper drops the hand-sized prop into the water, which churns and bubbles. Then he is off, skittering over the surface, the swell of growing breakers propelling the raft, a hot wind in his face—the kind of breeze any sailor would welcome. It never ceases to surprise him how long it takes to arrive at landfall after the first sighting. There's no sense of scale out here. The island, he assumes, is or was a coconut plantation, like so many of the outlying atolls. Which is to say that a hundred years ago the Marshallese—directed by their German conquerors—cleared the scrub away and planted trees. Harvesters visit once or twice a season to gather the fruit; a few rusted tin-roofed shacks stand at the island's edge to house the harvest. What other industry the island offers Cooper can only guess. He tried to radio earlier but got only static. He was too embarrassed to send an S.O.S.

He would like to imagine the islanders crowding around him, rejoicing at his visit: *What has this handsome stranger brought from the great world?*

But only a shirtless boy, wearing denim shorts, watches him from the beach.

"*Yokwe yuk,*" Cooper calls. *Greetings!*

The boy arches his eyebrows in wonder and continues to stare.

As soon as the dinghy butts the sand, Cooper lurches forward and vomits, everything going yellow-green, his head tightening as if his scalp would pop. He feels better after he clears his mouth. Then he looks up at the boy, who must be about seven, skinny, missing a few teeth up front. The boy says, "You sick?"

Cooper hauls himself out of the dinghy, bad leg first—he feels his wound bubble and ooze: the bloody pus looks like hot wax. The boy gapes at his leg, which makes Cooper feel worse. Angry at himself, Cooper swats the flies away. "I need a doctor," he says. Some small part of him—a penitent monk—sits in a dark cell and prays fervently for a miracle. The prayer includes a promise, *I will never make this mistake again!*

He sees the boy nodding his head yes, yes. The boy says, "We got a doctor."

Cooper can hardly believe his luck. He hobbles after the kid. The palm-tops hover and bob over him, their frond-clatter like applause. Cooper knows this is a beautiful place but none of it registers—not the turquoise crescent of the lagoon, not the blinding white sand, not the mermaids singing from the tide pools. It is all he can do to will himself to keep moving. Stay conscious. He leans into the boy, who allows the sudden intimacy without a hint of distaste or discomfort. He imagines the boy sleeps in a shack with a mob of brothers and sisters.

The settlement is a clutter of unpainted hovels with corrugated tin roofs and, incongruously, late model Japanese motorcycles parked out front. Skinny dogs, whipping their tails and trotting a few paces behind, bark at Cooper gleefully. Other children crowd around, calling, "Hey, what-sup, man? What-sup!" Half delirious, stumping along on his hot ice-pick pain, the children's chatter piercing to his ears, Cooper feels surly, stupid, and much too white. He's tempted to fling a handful of change over the sandy road, let the children dive for it like pigeons after popcorn. But all he has in his pocket are keys to his boat. And a penknife.

Where are the adults on this island?

"Town meeting," the boy says, as if reading his mind. He is pointing to a single-story, whitewashed cinderblock building that looks to Cooper like a run-down Laundromat. From here, he can see the outer edge of the island, the oceanside, where the swells are breaking with frothy crashes, having traveled thousands of Pacific miles unimpeded. Blacktip sharks are gliding in with the tide. Soon they'll be dancing on the reef. With the mermaids.

It's chaos out there.

Wouldn't Lillian be sorry now, to see him like this? Wouldn't she fold him in her arms and make up at last?

Maybe not. Didn't she warn him? Didn't she say, "You don't know your limits—that's why I'm scared."

The whitewashed building *is* a Laundromat, Cooper discovers. And air conditioned. As cold as an ice chest. Six washers on one side of the room, six dryers on the other, none of them going. At the center of the room is a long, uncovered plastic table, the portable kind you might find at a bake sale. Around it sit the adults, who regard Cooper with mild surprise. These are short people of dark brown complexion, with broad noses and curly black hair, though their race has been diluted for a century by foreigners: first the Spanish, then the Germans, then the Japanese, and then the Americans. The men wear T-shirts, American baseball caps, baggy trousers and *zori*, rubber flip-flops. The women wear flowered, cotton shifts, no head covering. They are smiling reassuringly in his direction but not quite at him. A bashful people.

Curiously, a number of them have pinkish welts on their foreheads and forearms. Some kind of disease? Or more of Cooper's hallucinations?

Just beyond the table, on the dirty, gold indoor-outdoor carpet, sits a craggy boulder as big as a bean bag chair. It must have taken five men to carry it. A rock of historical significance?

The room smells of . . . French fries, he decides. But the table is empty of food.

Suddenly the men, five to seven of them, are at his side, grinning and shaking his hand limply. They smell sweetly of coconut oil, their hair wet with pomade. It seems they have been expecting him. "Welcome," they are telling him, "sit, please, we have brought it for you, over here." They are gesturing to the boulder, everyone excited. The women chatter among themselves in Marshallese. It is a language that comes from the back of the throat and resonates through the nose, high-pitched, adenoidal, filigreed with trilling r's.

Painfully, Cooper sits, and yet no one remarks upon his leg. "I need help," he says. "My little friend said there is a doctor here." The children, he sees, are outside, peering through the Laundromat's filmy plastic windows, hands cupped over their eyes.

"*You* are a doctor," one of the men says. It's not a question.

This man—is this the chief?—looks about Cooper's age, has poor posture and a small bowl of a belly, his Diet Pepsi T-shirt stained from recent meals. He's smiling, showing off a silver tooth up front, but the Marshallese always smile, Cooper has read. It is their heritage to be pleasant, anything to keep the peace on their tiny atolls.

"Are you the boss?" Cooper asks.

"I am the *mayor*," the little man says. "Harold Van Horn the third." The others look at him with admiration. He speaks English very well; only his staccato delivery and especially his elaborately rolled "r's" betray his mother tongue.

"You're kidding," says Cooper.

"It's Dutch."

"Dutch," someone echoes.

Cooper nods his understanding. "I'm *not* a doctor," he tells them. "I *need* a doctor for my leg."

It should be simple, he thinks. Surely, even a remote islet like this has penicillin.

Harold-the-mayor gazes down at his leg and shakes his head with concern. "It looks infected, your leg!"

Somebody places a plastic tumbler of orangeade in front of Cooper. Without thinking, he drinks it down. Its warmth and sweetness nearly make him gag. But he wants more of it. His ears are burning.

"You have a doctor?" he asks. *Is there an ice machine nearby?* he wonders.

"You mean Dr. Thomas, the American?" Harold-the-mayor says.

American! Cooper has never considered himself patriotic or chauvinistic or jingoistic—he's been indifferent to America's power and prestige. He's not political. He's never been political. Geeks don't care about such things. Or so he has joked. But lately he has been feeling increasingly—and grudgingly—political, now that America has invaded Iraq and too many Americans are insisting that this is payback for 9/11, even though it's clear—and has been clear—that Saddam had nothing to do with 9/11. Cooper feels pained by the spectacle, like a hapless witness to a playground fight where the bully punches the wrong kid in the nose. And it's looking bad: last year's supposed end to the invasion ("Mission accomplished!" the president boasted from the deck of an aircraft carrier) has devolved into an agonizing, bloody, embarrassing war. It could drag on for years. Another Vietnam!

Whenever Cooper explains his work—anti-ballistic missile defense—nobody hears anything but "missile": *you make missiles?* Cooper makes missiles that shoot down other missiles. Actually, he doesn't even make missiles, he makes guidance systems. Actually, not the guidance systems themselves but the programs that constitute the brains of those systems. See how complicated this is? His is a necessary, a *useful*, job. He agrees that tyranny must be defeated. But he's not fighting tyranny exactly. He's not fighting at all.

And he's not a "patriot." It's not like he has an American flag sewn onto his windbreaker or blazoned on the bow of his boat. Still, when he hears this Pacific islander say the word "American,"

Cooper shudders with a chill of excitement and surging pride because, out here in the doctorless swelter of sandspeck islands, Americans are a godsend: Americans get things done! If you're in trouble, you want the Americans on your side.

Without Americans, the world would not have become the big, beautiful modern mess that it is, with movie stars and rock and roll and men on the moon and V-8-propelled sports cars and brick-thick hamburgers and super-sized milkshakes and 120-channel TV and air conditioning in every room and cloud-piercing skyscrapers and all-night supermarkets and 3-D monster movies and virtual reality video games. It's junk, most of it. But it's also an expression of an irrepressible will to do better. It's a celebration too of a restless, reckless drive to live fully. Isn't that why Cooper took the risk to sail all this way alone? He was restless and wanted to feel things he could feel only if he were reckless.

Now, surrounded by the enthusiastic chatter of the dusky wide-eyed people, he is overwhelmed by the sweet scent of their coconut oil, overwhelmed by the impossible remoteness of their tiny island, overwhelmed by the fact that here, in the middle of nowhere, he will see another American.

Tears burn at the corners of his eyes. America, the beautiful, land of the free, home of the . . . . "Dr. Thomas, an American?" Cooper gasps.

"That would be me."

Cooper turns to see the American's approach from a room in the rear, which must be a kitchen because the man carries a platter of steaming French fries.

They must have seen Cooper coming! They must have set up all of this for his welcome!

The American is a big bearded man with a sunburnt face and black plastic-rimmed glasses. He wears a T-shirt that says, across the chest in multi-colored block print, "Fruit of the Loom." His Bermuda shorts look like they could use a good wash.

As soon as he sets down the platter of fries, a flock of brown hands flutters to them.

"Marvin Thomas," he says. He sits heavily across the table from Cooper. As formidable as a bull walrus, though far from obese, he's one of those guys who looks big and fit but has never jogged a block or lifted a five-pound dumbbell. "Everybody here calls me Thomas." He extends his paw, which Cooper tries to shake but ends up squeezing only two fat fingers. "I used to be with the Corps."

"Marine?"

"Peace."

"You're a doctor?" Cooper asks.

"Of American literature. A Melville man, to be exact. I hope you like Melville."

Cooper wants to groan in dismay but, instead, he hears himself asking, "Can you help me with my leg?"

Thomas glances over the table, arches his brows at Cooper's leg, then says, "It's infected."

"I need penicillin."

Cooper tells him about the 45-pound bluefin. It pissed him off, how the blue refused to succumb after he'd fought the thing for a good half hour, after he'd played and pulled it to the boat finally, after he'd hauled it on deck and hammered it with his Louisville slugger. After all that, the beautiful bastard bucked, gills yawning, dorsal fins arcing at him, sun glinting from the yellow-blue of its gorgeous scales. It spooked Cooper, the life in the thing, and for a moment he wondered if he should kick it overboard because sometimes it's better that way. Letting it go would have been a sign of respect.

At that moment, his heel on the blue's bloody gills, the gaff got him and tore a searing thirteen-inch gash down the calf of his right leg. He can't remember if it was the tuna that slammed it home or his own carelessness as he dodged the fish's formidable tail. In anger, he batted the tuna until his forearms ached. Then, disgusted with himself, and disappointed that a great catch had become so ugly, he dragged the bludgeoned blue into the cooler below, then he tended his bleeding wound, flushing it first with peroxide. He dressed it with anti-bacterial salve and sterile gauze. He knew it'd be inflamed for a few days but he didn't imagine it'd get like this. He used three bottles of peroxide on it, wasted his one bottle of rubbing alcohol, then his last bottle of vodka, but the gash only got worse.

"It's the polyps," Thomas says. "Coral's in the air. Everything gets infected if you don't soak it in hot salts."

For three days Cooper debated whether or not to put in at the nearest lagoon. He's five days east of the International Date Line—not more than a week from Kwajalein Atoll, where he's supposed to start work in 15 days. Brad, his former supervisor, told him it was a stupid idea, sailing the Pacific alone like this, especially since Cooper knew only coastal sailing: "Doesn't matter how much time you've logged in a boat, Cooper, it's a whole other world once you lose sight of land, for pity's sake—and you've got a new job to think about."

There is some similarity between sailing and the work he does, computing alone in a cubicle: the necessary self-absorption, the surrounding emptiness, the charting of a course among the known variables. The major difference is that computing can't kill you. Even a bayshore weekender like Brad could appreciate that much. Cooper assured him that as long as the mast holds, a sailor can tie off the wheel, flag the staysail, trawl a storm drogue, then go below, batten the hatch and ride it out. Cooper has done just that twice already, tossed and tumbled like a sock in a washing machine. Something to be proud of.

But now to have fucked up while fishing, on a calm day, so close to his destination? It's too ironic.

Thomas looks at him with some concern, though Cooper isn't convinced this is for his sake. The big man says, "You're not our geologist then?"

This question sounds more like an announcement. It puts an

abrupt halt to the others' robust eating of the fries. The Marshallese now stare expectantly at Cooper.

Cooper sees that he is about to disappoint them all. "You were expecting a geologist?"

"To examine the meteorite," says Thomas, nodding to the big rock.

"Meteorite," a few of the others repeat.

"Biggest in the world!" says Harold-the-mayor, and this starts all of them talking excitedly in Marshallese.

"Probably among the biggest in the world," Thomas corrects. His boom-box voice silences the others. Then he explains: last week there was a meteor shower, thousands of tiny stones raining from the early morning sky while the men were out fishing. This accounts for the small welts on their foreheads and forearms.

The rain of rocks was preceded by an immense white flash.

"Like a million camera lights," Harold-the-mayor says. "Dorean thought it was another bomb." He points to Dorean, a young man wearing a T-shirt that says "The Rolling Stones," it tongue-and-lips logo faded to a pale pink. "His grandfather was burned by fallout in nineteen fifty-four."

Dorean nods gravely.

"Then we hear the rocks falling. Like fish."

Someone makes a rapid slapping noise that truly sounds like fish hitting water.

"It was two-ten AM," Harold-the-mayor says. "Benjamin was wearing his chronometer."

"Rocks falling all over, man."

"Scared me shitless."

Laughter.

"Meteor shower!"

"More likely a comet or piece of comet," Thomas says. He radioed the tracking station at Kwajalein, which would neither confirm nor deny his conjecture. "They don't care shit about anything but spying on the Chinese, the Russians, and the towel-heads. You know they got a radar on Roi-Namur so big it can track a wrench floating away from the space shuttle?"

"Yes, I know!" Cooper says—because, by God, he's going to be among them shortly, the most elite group of civilian programmers and engineers in the world.

"Helene found the meteor yesterday when she was collecting ni," Harold-the-mayor continues. He looks with pride to the small stout woman with a streak of gray at her right temple.

Helene smiles all around, then says quietly, "I thought it was a egg."

The others laugh. "Egg!"

Cooper regards the black-brown boulder beyond the table's end and thinks of the egg of the Roc, the house-sized bird-beast from the tale of Sinbad the sailor. Anything seems possible out here.

He struggles to his feet, wavers a moment in the tight grasp of pain, then declares: "I've got a fever. I've got an infection!" He hears his voice crack. "I'm asking for *help*!"

Only now does he realize how desperate he has become. The next inhabited island, with or without a doctor, could be days away. His leg has been oozing pus for two. How soon before gangrene?

The islanders stare kindly at him, nodding agreeably as if encouraging him to make a speech.

"Why don't you lie down and we'll see what we can do," Thomas says. He motions for someone to clear away the empty fry platter.

"You can do something?" Cooper asks.

"I don't know." Thomas shrugs. "Maybe cast a spell, say a prayer, cut off your leg."

"Not funny," Cooper says with a croak of weariness.

"Sorry." Thomas grins at him and Cooper sees for the first time that the man has nearly no teeth. This appalls Cooper. What doesn't rot out here?

* * *

In the month before he set sail, he lived on his boat, moored at the Half Moon Bay marina, where anchorage was more than he liked to pay. Lillian wouldn't see him, wouldn't even let him in the house. So, twice a week, he drove south to see his therapist, a woman who might once have been a hippie. Though homey and hempy, she asked hard questions, which gratified Cooper because they made him feel he was getting somewhere, doing something concrete to win Lillian back and get his life in order.

Nobody's life is in order, he has decided. Most people are simply good at hiding their private chaos. The biggest surprise of his growing older—and now, at 36, he feels he can say he is "older"—the biggest surprise is this: most people don't really get wiser or more mature with age. Meredith, his ex-wife, is a stunningly beautiful and fucked-up example. Lillian seemed the exception.

"Still no traction?" his therapist asked. She was old enough to be his mother—Cooper liked that—but she was much tougher than his mother. And, better still, Sarah was a sailor. Her office was the front room of her houseboat.

With a sigh, Cooper dropped himself into his usual seat, the bulky leather chair near the window. "She must have been really frightened," he said.

"Nice of you to be so understanding." Sarah's smile was cautionary. Sitting cross-legged on her battered sofa, she wore a bulky sweatshirt, paint-spattered jeans, and no shoes. Her toenails were painted pink.

"Oh, I understand," said Cooper. He heard the teakettle beginning to hiss in the galley behind Sarah. "Bailey could have drowned!"

"But she didn't."

"You don't sound so understanding," he joked.

"Didn't you say that Bailey made all of this happen? That she was a conniving little brat who manipulated her mother?"

"She's just a kid."

"Fifteen." Sarah got up to fetch the tea. "Stay put," she said when Cooper rose to help. "You've got three weeks before you're supposed to set sail and Lillian's not talking to you, so what do you think will happen?"

He glanced out the window. The boat bobbed gently on the wake of a passing cabin cruiser. A 5,000-gallon tank of diesel will take you across the Pacific. Cooper could think of nothing more boring than chugging through the chop in a boat like that. Sailing, on the other hand, was a head-spinning thrill because it was all about problem-solving, looking for wind, then making the most of what you could catch.

He had learned this as a boy. By the time he was fifteen, he owned a gorgeous little 13-foot skiff made of cedar, with a mahogany backbone and a 24-inch steel centerboard. It had cedar spars and a single sail. As he fished and crabbed in the shallow backwaters of the Chesapeake, he learned about wind and waves but it never occurred to him that he should try deeper waters. He loved the fishy stink of the tidelands, the clouded view to the sandy bottom, the buck and roll of waves as he set his line and angled for stripers. The fight to reel fish into his boat often humbled him and the time alone, the waiting and watching, made him extremely patient.

But the roots of his passion for deep-water sailing predate his teen years on the water. It goes back to a game he played by himself as a child. He'd lay a blanket on the floor, then with a tiny plastic man in a tiny boat made of Legos, he'd set off across that fabric ocean. Every wrinkle of the blanket offered a new dilemma, another potential calamity. Again and again, he found his way through the trouble. As much as anything, it was this solitary pursuit that gave him practice for the programming he would enjoy years later and then, to his surprise, prepare him for deep-water sailing.

When he looked back to Sarah, she was smiling, handing him a mug of green tea. He thanked her, then blew across the steamy surface and thought of mist rising from morning water. "What will happen, you ask? I expect Lillian will snap out of it. Our little accident triggered something—some issue about safety and I don't know, it really threw her."

"Is that what she said—it threw her? "

"She's not talking to me, remember?" He took a sip and winced as he burned his tongue. Again he glanced out the window. Sarah's boat was charming, as far as houseboats go, a two-story cabin painted moss green, with a striped canvas awning over the portside deck, potted ferns and lots of sunlight in the front room, a creaky cedar floor with a rosy patina, a stained glass transom over the front door—a tidy, arty little house, not really a boat. He preferred his Alberg with its aged, amber-colored paneling, its graceful lines, its readiness for sea. There was nothing ready about Sarah's old boat.

What do you need to be ready for? Lillian had teased him more than once. He tried to explain: you can't take good weather for granted, not when you're on water. You owe it to your boat to keep it always in top form. If a storm blows in suddenly, you can get away from the dock quickly and moor in open water.

Oh, my sweet pea, Lillian said, *I didn't realize Meredith had damaged you that much! You're so cautious!*

Was he so cautious, he who would sail the Pacific alone? He who nearly drowned Bailey?

"Why don't you like Lillian?" he asked Sarah.

"I've never met her, how could I dislike her?" She cupped her steamy mug with both weathered hands. Cooper liked that Sarah was always working on her boat.

"It seems you're pushing me to get angry at her."

Sarah arched her bushy eyebrows. "You're not angry?"

"I'm frustrated. I'm confused. I'm hurt," he said. "I don't know that anger is part of it."

"Not even when you recall Lillian blaming your for the fiasco with Bailey?"

Cooper slouched in his chair and tried to let the gentle bob and rock of Sarah's house sooth him.

What about pirates? Lillian had asked him.

Pirates?

I've been doing research on line. They say you should travel with a grenade launcher to ward off any approaching boats in the open seas.

We're not going to see any pirates, Lil, not where we're going.

But there are pirates!

Well, sure, and sharks too. And water spouts. And giant squids.

Are you trying to scare me?

Come on, you're pulling my leg, right?

Then Lillian laughed and he was relieved. She said, *If any brigands board, I'll cut their gizzards out with me kitchen knife!* He loved her for that.

Was it all an act, playing brave because that's what you do in love until intimacy or circumstance outs you and, at last, you're exposed for the coward you know you've always been?

"I thought she was excited about our adventure," Cooper said. "But now I'm not so sure. Maybe it's just cold feet?"

"It's your adventure, Cooper, not hers, isn't it?"

"Yes, but she loves me and wants to share it. I've got a twelve month contract. Then I'm back stateside. Sailing out there isn't really a big deal."

"For you."

"I *signed a contract*," he said. "I can't break it. This is the chance of a lifetime."

"Taking the trip or taking the work?"

"Both!"

"You could take the work without sailing out there, couldn't you?"

"Oh, I see," he said. "Lillian wants to dump the sailing adventure and jet out there?"

"No, I don't think that's it," Sarah said. "It sounds like she wants to dump you."

"Whoa! How'd you come to that?"

"You leave in three weeks and she's not talking to you? She says you nearly drowned her daughter? She says you don't know your limits—isn't that how she put it?"

"She was angry when she said those things." Cooper set down his tea. He was sweating, trickles streaming down his spine and rib cage. "She loves me!"

Sarah nodded an irritating, knowing nod, as if to say, *What does anybody truly know of love?*

"What the fuck, Sarah?"

* * *

"We'll call the Army," Thomas says.

"You mean on Kwajalein?"

Kwajalein, a three-mile crescent with an airfield at one end: it took the Marines four days of bloody hand-to-hand combat to wrest the Island from the Japs in 1945. Now it's home to a civilian community of engineers and programmers like Cooper, all of them working on missile defense systems.

"The U.S. Army controls everything out this way," Thomas is saying. "I imagine they can do a difficult rescue."

Rescue? Only now in this unreal world, as the Marshallese stare at him curiously, is Cooper's humiliation becoming real to him. Eventually Lillian will hear of his failure, his need of rescue, and she'll shake her head in dismay and perhaps pity too, reassured that she made the right choice in dumping him.

And Cooper, well, he had no choice but to sail without her. But it was for the wrong reasons—he sailed away with anger and bitterness and the selfish satisfaction of leaving her behind. By the second week, far from landfall, the Lickety Split roller-coasting on twenty-foot swells, nothing in sight but a silver-blue sky, he heard himself whimpering like a wounded animal.

He longed for the chatter and crowd of people in his daily life: he missed humanity, and Lillian most of all. He was no recluse! Already he was talking to himself nonstop—loudly and with great animation, as if he were on stage. Surely somebody was watching, the sky nothing more than the single open eye of God. It was too easy to see how a lone sailor could go mad. You had to be careful. You had to ration your interior resources. Don't panic! That was the first thing he told himself. It rang in his head like a mantra.

From the footlocker in his cabin, he fished out one of his T-shirts that Lillian had worn. Burying his face in it, he could smell her honeysuckle perfume and the mild mushroomy odor of her sweat. It was like dope! He tied the T-shirt around his neck and wore it day and night, wiping his face with it, weeping into it, kissing it, clutching it, until it was in tatters and still he wouldn't let it go.

Occasionally he would spy a ship plying the horizon: a delicate, white miniature that looked like a cake decoration. The sight of it would make him catch and hold his breath and stifle the urge to wave and yell.

When seven birds, small as tea cups, found him and roosted for two days on the wire lifeline, he sat near them and derived some comfort from their clucks and yawning trills. One afternoon he fed a gull his dinner of ramen just to keep the creature near. It flew off when he tried to talk to it.

But he didn't panic. No, he didn't panic! He sailed on, he sailed hard, alternately terrified and exhilarated, and the farther he sailed, the bolder he grew because, after the third week, a dizzying kind of fatalism took over. He saw himself as a mote of dust carried on the wind. It made him feel that he fit in somehow. At night the canyon of the cosmos wheeled over him and he was stunned by its depth and light. And below, the ocean was another sky, riven by luminescent whitecaps and surprised by blue-flamed fields of tiny fish and constellations of jellyfish that floated by like ghostly green nebulae.

At some point he threw off Lillian's tattered T-shirt and settled in at last to the rhythm of long days. The noise of waves and wind drove mainland thoughts from his head. His charted trajectory, and his minute adjustments to stay within one degree of that line, became his obsession. The horizon fascinated him: he couldn't stop staring into the distance because he knew that, eventually, he'd see *something*.

All that changed when he injured his leg. Close now to his destination and threatened by an imminent illness, maybe even death, he was disgusted with himself and took to calling himself "asshole": *What is it now, asshole? Is the pain inconvenient?*

"It won't be cheap," Thomas says.

Cooper wakes abruptly from his thoughts. "Cheap?"

It feels like he's grilling his leg over white-hot coals.

"They'll charge you, you know, for the rescue. Are you rich, Cooper?"

Cooper notices the islanders watching him with renewed interest. A rich American might buy their meteorite.

"No," he says. "I'm not rich. Everything I have is in that boat."

"Don't worry about your boat," says Thomas. "I'll take care of that."

"I'm not leaving my boat!" says Cooper.

"You'll leave your boat or you'll die," says Thomas. "The choice is yours."

"I don't want to die!" says Cooper, sounding like a petulant child.

"Then let's go make that call."

It seems the entire village follows them to Thomas's shack. Two men help Cooper make the short walk.

There is little inside the pandanus-leaf hut to distinguish this as the American's place except a GE refrigerator crowded with books. Cooper notices the books when Thomas opens the fridge for a beer.

"It's the only place they don't mildew," Thomas explains. He hands Cooper an Olympia in a can. "This is my Melville collection. What's left of it."

Cooper drinks down his beer in two long draughts. Then he sits wearily on a plastic milk crate, sucking air through his teeth, willing himself to abandon the pain, just leave it behind like a bad thought.

The islanders crowd at the open door, whispering and smiling and nodding among themselves, as if they were preparing to vote on something.

"Doesn't anybody have work to do around here?" Cooper says in exasperation.

"That sounds like a complaint." Thomas is fiddling with a shortwave that sits on a rusted oil drum in one corner of the shack. The place is no bigger than Lillian's kitchen. Doorless. A dirt floor. A translucent green rectangle of corrugated fiberglass for a roof. A rickety cot. A netted hammock full of clothes.

In the confined space, Cooper can smell the big man's sweat: like a wet wool blanket.

Every time Cooper opens his eyes and looks to the door, he sees the islanders smiling encouragement and kindness.

"They want to know who you are," Thomas says. He's wearing a headset. His glasses are nearly opaque with dust and salt spray.

"Who?" Cooper asks.

"I got the Army on the line, man." Thomas sounds irritated. "They need some info."

"I've got papers," Cooper says. "Tell them I'm a DataCell programmer—I've got *clearance*."

Cooper turns and says to one of the nearby children—the boy who met him on the beach: "Do you know how hard it is to get clearance in the post 9/11 world?"

The boy flashes the peace sign.

"Yeah, that's right," says Cooper.

"I've got one of your people here," Thomas says into his rusted microphone. "A programmer. Cooper Davies. He'll die for sure if you don't pick him up."

Then: "It's his leg. Looks like gangrene."

Then: "I know gangrene when I see it. I said he's one of yours—he's got clearance. If you leave him here, we're just gonna dump the body in the *lagoon.* . . . I said the *lagoon.*"

Thomas turns to wink at Cooper. "I'm exaggerating."

Then Thomas nods some more at the radio. "Let me read you the coordinates. We can't waste any time."

"Do they know who I am?" Cooper asks.

Thomas sets down the microphone, then swivels to Cooper: "How do you like that? They're on their way!"

Some of the onlookers repeat the announcement like momentous news: "They're on their way!"

"A big helicopter!" Thomas crows. Then he grins, showing off his few brown teeth.

The onlookers repeat the magic word: helicopter!

"Holy shit," Cooper gasps. "I'm gonna be saved?"

Thomas smirks at him. "Rescue isn't the same thing as salvation."

Cooper wonders if this is a Melville quote.

Thomas shoos the onlookers. "Go away. Look for the helicopter!"

Reluctantly, the villages drift away. Then Thomas sits on the dirt floor in front of Cooper, who can barely keep his eyes open. Thomas is still wearing his old-fashioned headset, pulled away from his big reddened ears.

"How much do you think your boat is worth?" he asks.

Cooper feels an icepick of dread pierce his heart. He squints hard at Thomas. "Are you gonna sell my boat?"

Thomas seems to beam at the thought. "I'm just asking, man."

"Are you, like, a pirate or something? Where the fuck is this place?" It occurs to Cooper that he might never find this island again.

"This place?" Thomas smiles slyly. "Do you know how many islands are in the Marshalls?"

"More than a thousand," says Cooper. "I've done my homework."

"Good for you, my man. It's easy to get lost out here. That's what I like about it."

"I can't lose my boat. It's all I got."

"Is that self-pity I hear?"

"It's the simple truth, Thomas. I'll pay you for keeping it safe. I'll pay you whatever you want."

"So you *do* have money," says Thomas with satisfaction. "They pay you programmers well, don't they?"

"You talk like a pirate, not a do-gooder from the Peace Corps."

"The Corps was long ago, my friend. As for doing good, that's always a matter of opinion. I don't know that I did anybody good when I was encouraging the so-called natives to join the modern world."

"You came out here looking for the great white whale, didn't you?"

"Oh, you're one to cast aspersions, my little Sinbad. You've made the amateur's mistake, getting an infection like that."

"I might be a fuck-up but I'm no thief."

"Are you calling me a *thief*? I just saved your life!"

"At a cost."

"Drive into an emergency room with that leg—you don't think it's going to cost you?"

"Okay, how much?"

Thomas shrugs. "Let's wait to see if you survive."

"That's a terrible thing to say!"

"I thought you'd like the simple truth." He pats Cooper's good knee, then stands. "The world will look different to you once you're recovered. You may think of me in a better light."

Cooper ties off the wheel of his drifting mind and now stands on the foredeck, the swells rolling past like the great backs of whales, his sloop nosing through the chop, the cloudless sky as blue as hope—soon he will sight land, he tells himself. Soon.

"I'm sorry," Cooper says. "I'm unreasonable, aren't I?"

"You've got an attitude, I've noticed." Thomas upends his can of beer, so tiny in his hand, drains it, then smacks his lips.

"Is the Army really coming to rescue me?"

"You think I want a dead American on my little island?"

"So this is *your* island?"

"Yes, sir."

"Would you get serious for one second?" Cooper asks. "Just one serious second?"

The big man sighs, glances out the doorway, pats his beard absently, then seems to confess: "Sometimes I wonder how serious I truly am. I don't know what happened to me any more than I can explain what happened to my Melville collection—I used to have 28 books. Right here in my fridge. Now there are fifteen."

Cooper feels himself sinking slowly into a too-warm bath of delirium. If only he could sleep through this or wake up. He feels his head nod; the empty can of beer drops from his hand.

"You better not die on me, Coop old buddy. Come on, you're almost home."

Gasping, nearly weeping, Cooper sucks in a lungful of air, his head booming. Home? Where would that be?

But then, sure enough, he hears a familiar sound like something from home: the putter of a distant lawnmower.

"Who's cutting the grass?"

"That's your ride," Thomas says. He steps into the sunlight.

"There's no airstrip," Cooper says hoarsely. He limps out. Thankfully his damaged leg now feels numb. "No way they can get to me."

"Oh, they'll think of something."

It's a military plane. A-48? Y2K? 40.08? Cooper sees a white star on its tail. Everyone is waving now. The plane circles, then circles again in the too-blue sky. The silver-white clouds look like frosty sea horses.

Cooper takes another step expectantly but somehow misses the ground and collapses. Sea horses bob over him like carousel steeds.

Then a dog hungrily licks his face. Another sniffs with a cold nose at his injured leg.

Thomas waves them away. Kneeling next to Cooper, he says in a low voice, "Your boat's in good hands, stop looking so *injured*, man." Then he stabs at the sky with one fat finger. "There's your ride!"

Cooper sees something black blossom abruptly from the plane's tail. A parachute? Breathlessly, he watches as it drifts lazily over the island in small, agonizingly slow circles. The islanders gaze at it with reverence, as if they beheld the approach of an ancestor's spirit. With growing terror, Cooper regards his oozing leg and recalls that he could have pulled into a different lagoon and found a different island; he could have caught a different fish or let the big blue go; he could have flown out here and been safe. A wave of nausea slams him like a crushing breaker. You can't go under, he coaches himself, not yet. The figure falling from the sky—this could be anything: maybe not the stealthy emissary of Death; maybe, instead, a behemoth bird come to carry him away. Or maybe the smiling angel of God come to deliver him another chance.

TWO

Nora and her four fellow Diversity Delegates know they can't say aloud what they're thinking as the noon ferry chugs away from Echo pier on its way to Ebeye, two nautical miles north of Kawjalein: *they will smell Ebeye before they see it.* Ebeye is so gross, it's cool to go there, just so you can say you did. Garbage is always smoldering from one end or the other of this little island and, because it's just half the size of American-occupied Kwajalein but has four times the people, it's been called the Calcutta of the Pacific. It's like something from a PBS special. No place is more crowded or trashy. Old, fat, forever sweaty Mister Norman has an explanation for that, like he's got explanations for everything. He's the Advisor to their Diversity Delegates Club. Today he's arranged for them to deliver discarded computers to Ebeye High. It's 2004, a new millennium, and everybody all over the world is online except for the Marshallese!

"The thing is," Mister Norman explains, "nobody owns land on Ebeye. In fact, all of the islands, every little sandy speck of land, are owned by only a handful of families. Most of those families live on Majuro. How far is Majuro, our capital island, from here?" He pauses to hear the answer and wipes his sunburnt face with a sweat-soaked handkerchief. Until she met Mister Norman, Nora had never seen anyone use a handkerchief except to pretty up the breast pocket of a suit.

Todd Williams answers: "Approximately 300 miles due east." Rumor has it that Todd is still a virgin. Next year he'll be going to Harvard.

Norman nods his satisfaction. "Everybody who isn't a member of those land-owning families—that's about 13,000 Marshallese on Ebeye—all of those people are just renting space. You get what I'm saying? There's no motivation for the Marshallese to build nice houses or plant pretty gardens. As far as they're concerned, they're just passing through."

Nora and Todd and Stef and Tabatha nod like they get it, but they don't get it. If Nora was living here, God forbid, in some sun-blistered tin-roofed shack, she'd do something about it. She'd fix it up. She'd plant flowers.

The ferry lurches as the pilot gears down. The ferry is a decommissioned barge-like Army transport with a white tarp strung overtop to keep the sun off. Two new hydrofoil catamarans are being shipped from New Zealand soon to replace these old boats. The world is catching up to the Marshall Islands!

Ferry passengers sit on wooden benches that remind Nora of church pews. The Marshallese women and girls dress in the most colorful *muumuus*: big bright flowered prints that extend nearly to their ankles. To sit among them is to smell their coconut oil, which they use as hair dressing, perfume, and skin lotion all at once.

Mister Norman paces at the front of the boat, pausing now and then to peer ahead. Nora imagines he's rehearsing his next lecture. The way he talks, you'd think he hated Americans and thought the Marshallese were gods. He married a Marshallese woman when he was in the Peace Corps eons ago. Rumor says that his wife stands to make a lot of money if her family can win its suit against the American government for having suffered in the Eniwetak disaster, when the Americans' nuclear fall-out drifted over in 1954. Some say that's why Mister Norman works so hard to make Americans look bad.

He and his wife and their many children live on Jaluit, which isn't much better than Ebeye, Nora has heard. Nora has been to Ebeye only once since she's been dating Jeton and that was at

Christmas and she and Jeton didn't get a moment alone. Not that there's any place to go on Ebeye. It has no trees to speak of. The "town" is an uneven grid of mostly paved streets. There is shack after shack, only the smallest yards, if any at all, dirt and sand at your feet and overhead a web of electrical wires and phone lines slung from low poles. Stray dogs, cats, and chickens dart past, and stray children, so many children, and idle men, so many idle men, the air smoky from burning garbage and other fire, and Japanese motorbikes speeding by dangerously close.

"In fifty years, all of these islands will be under water," Mister Norman says, sweeping one hammy, freckled arm towards the small brown mound that is Ebeye in the salt-spray-misty distance.

"Global warming!" Stef blurts, like she's on *Jeopardy. Correction, Ms. Galen: What is Global Warming?*

"Maybe not," Todd Williams says. "If we can reduce our carbon footprint and take measures to build up these islands, we could turn it around. I'm going to work on this in college."

Mister Norman barks a laugh. His yellow teeth remind Nora of ancient ivory and time so deep she can't even imagine how far back it goes, like Mister Norman himself, who looks too old to be teaching, almost too old to be alive.

He snorts: "You do that, Mister Williams, you save us all from oblivion, would you?"

Todd grimaces and kind of shrugs as he leans against the rail and stares at Ebeye. A small funnel of black smoke drifts from one end of the island.

Stef says, uptalking in protest, "Mister Norman, last week our club, the Environmental Advocates, sold 220 carbon footprint vouchers?"

This makes Mister Norman nearly choke with laughter. He's heaving, his eyes red and tear-filled. "Oh god," he gasps. "Oh, my little hopefuls!" He coughs. He swallows. He sighs: "Oh shit, the world is too much for me!" Then, wiping at his eyes, he sucks up a big breath and says, "Sorry, kids. I know you want to help. And you are helping, aren't you. We've got these computers to deliver, don't we?"

Todd and Stef and Tabatha and Nora sort of nod in agreement but nobody knows what to think. If it's all a joke, if the world is already ruined the way Mister Norman says it is, then what's the point?

Bringing gifts to Ebeye makes Nora feel good—like she's putting herself on the line somehow. Most Americans wouldn't dare come here, even though it's only two miles away from Kwajalein. The Marshallese people, really, are very nice, even if they don't have a fraction of the cool stuff Americans have.

"We go for the wrong reasons," Mister Norman says, still wiping at his eyes, "and we do almost everything wrong, but it's better than not going or doing at all."

Mister Norman is kind of entertaining when he revs up. He's as crazy a person as Nora will ever meet.

Here's the coolest thing about the trip: Nora's parents have no idea she's on Ebeye. They can't keep up with her many co-curricular activities. She's planning to surprise Jeton, who hasn't been able to get near her since she got grounded after her parents caught them fucking on the patio last week.

God, did that freak them out!

As soon as the DDs step off the boat, Todd and Stef wheeling the computers on a freight dolly, a crowd of children swarm after them.

Mister Norman has taught the DDs how to say the official greeting:" "*Io̧kwe eok!*" Which sounds like "Yuck-way!"

"Don't you surrender a penny!" he warns—because the children are always asking for money. Even a quarter is a big deal to them.

He calls the Republic of the Marshall Islands "a nation of children" because the average age of its citizens is, like, sixteen: a fact that makes Nora giddy with fantasies about how different the world would be if teens ruled. There's nothing teens couldn't do, if only the grown-ups would get out of the way!

"Sup?" the little kids are saying. Most don't have shirts; none have shoes; and a couple of the smallest don't even have undies. Playing in puddles, dragging sticks and palm fronds behind them, chasing dogs, they look happy enough. And nobody appears hungry.

"Who looks after the children?" Nora asks.

"Their parents are working or looking for work or fishing," Mister Norman says. "There's probably a cousin or aunt nearby."

The causeway project is the biggest employer now. It will connect Ebeye to the several islands just north of it, which will create more room for all of these people. Mister Norman says that space is so precious out here in the Marshalls a California company has been trying to get the Republic to build landfill with American garbage. "If that's not the most fucked-up proposal you've ever heard, I don't know what is," he said. "But, hell, why not? We've already dumped all kinds of atomic fallout on these people, haven't we?"

He went off on that one for about an hour. Whenever he rants, Nora calls it "the Norman Invasion."

Mister Norman is leading the way, right down the middle of the street, which has been paved recently. The shacks on either side are painted as varied and brightly colored as the women's muumuus. And every fifth house seems to be a small church.

Mister Norman walks so fast, Todd and Stef can't keep up, pushing that heavy cart.

"Mister Norman, slow down," Nora calls.

He stops. Then a motorcyclist speeds by, nearly swiping him. "*Eājāj wōt!*" he shouts after it.

Nora assumes this is a curse, though it could mean anything, like "thanks a lot!"

"Sup? Got a quarter?" a little boy asks Nora.

She shrugs in response.

"Quarter?" he repeats.

Then Mister Norman shoos him away.

Suddenly the sky opens up. A pile of afternoon thunderheads has tumbled in from nowhere. Nora and her companions are drenched within a minute. Leaving the cart of computers at the curb, they run to the corrugated tin overhang of the Independent Baptist Church, which at a glance looks like another shack.

"See that?" Mister Norman says, nodding like the know-it-all he is. "That's why I had you secure the computers under a plastic tarp."

Then, like a message from God, a Toyota pickup roars down the street in the torrent and slams full into the cart, computer parts spilling and spinning like shrapnel—and making such a loud smack! that Nora, Stef, and Tabatha scream in unison.

The truck screeches to a stop, sliding several yards, the rain still gushing like whitewater.

"Serves us right," Mister Norman says in disgust, stepping into the downpour. "Serves us fucking right!"

The driver clambers out. "Very sorry," he says. He looks Indian and he's young, of course, but not a teenager. Like most Marshallese men, he's wearing khaki trousers and a T-shirt. The Marshallese love American T-shirts! This one says "AC/DC" across the front.

Then the rain stops—just like that—and the sun glides out, rays glinting from the blue-oily puddles on the asphalt, and the children are playing again, dogs barking after them, and the air is smoky again with the smell of burning garbage and maybe barbecued chicken.

The driver helps Mister Norman and the DDs pick up the wrecked computers, but many of the pieces disappear with the children, who dart in and out, grabbing what they can as if this were a game. The DDs load the junk into the back of the man's pickup, then the man drives Mister Norman and the DDs to the high school. But no one at the high school seems to know that the computers were coming. A stout middle-aged Marshallese woman nods "yes' to everything Mister Norman says but she can't tell him anything he wants to know.

It's so un-PC to say it, but all middle-aged Marshallese women look alike to Nora. They are short and stocky and have thick black and/or graying hair that's been cut to the shoulders or tied back in a knot. And they wear long flowered dresses and no make-up and still have nice smiles but every last one of them seems to have let herself go. It must be all the children they've had. You can't keep up with all those children. Nora has promised herself that she'll have only one child. Well, maybe two. Or maybe none. But she won't ever let herself go.

She and Stef and Todd and Tabatha help the driver unload the broken computers onto the sidewalk. The sun is so hot, they are almost dry from the downpour already. Nora feels a trickle of sweat skid down her spine. She'd like to be fresh for Jeton, but nothing stays fresh for long in this climate. She thought there'd be a ceremony to celebrate the computers or some gathering where she'd see him. He doesn't even know she's here! Still, it's two hours before the next ferry.

Forget trying to find his house because there are no street numbers, no directories, no maps that would show her where he lives. Forget GPS out here. It doesn't exist, not on phones, anyway. And Jeton doesn't own a cell phone.

* * * *

"You're wasting your money," Jeton tells his cousin Mike.

Mike is on the video machine, playing Space Spiders. He says, "I got money to waste."

The machine goes *Ka-blam! ka-blam! ka-blam!* as Mike muscles into it.

Jeton slugs down half the Tsing Tsoa Mike has just bought him, letting the foam burn his throat.

They are at the Lucky Star Bar and Restaurant, where Jeton

hopes Mike will buy him a lunch of shrimp lo mein. The Lucky Star is dark, like all the drinking places, with only a single plastic window up front and a few light bulbs strung over the bar, which is a painted countertop made of chipboard from the Philippines. A few young men Jeton does not know sit at a table near the window. They are laughing and seem to have money. Maybe they are from Majuro. Two old men sit at the end of the bar watching the TV, which sits on a box behind the counter. The program— something in Spanish—comes by satellite from Manila.

Jeton should be in school and Mike should be at the causeway, but, "Fuck it," Jeton said when Mike met him this morning. Mike told him that they would take the "day off," as the Americans put it.

Mike is two years older than Jeton and much lighter-skinned—*wūdmouj*—because one of his grandfathers was Japanese. Mike also has a fine black mustache that Jeton admires. And, unlike Jeton, who is short and has thick legs, Mike is tall and has an easy stride. Jeton thinks sometimes that Mike is the man he should be. But it is becoming clear to Jeton that he will not be like Mike, who has a high school diploma and has traveled as far as Japan and now drives a loader for the construction crew at the causeway.

Mike's plan is to sell electronics on Ebeye, ship them direct from China, he says, and make a fuckin' fortune!

Jeton's plan is—or was—to love Nora forever. Since their trouble with her parents last week and Nora's surprising announcement about returning to the States, Jeton has felt *jebwābwe*, like doing something crazy. Nora's parents may ask the American police to ban Jeton from returning to Kwajalein. Americans can do that to the *ri-Majeļ* because the Americans have paid the *Majeļ* Republic a lot of money to build their missiles on the island.

In two weeks Nora flies away.

Jeton met her for the first time when his high school soccer team played the American high school soccer team. Jeton was the *ri-Maje̦l* goalie. Already he had lost one tooth up front from protecting the goal. Nora said the missing tooth made his smile look "cute."

"You hungry?" he asks Mike.

Ka-blam! Mike is already at level twelve, alien spiders raining from the video sky: *ka-blam! ka-blam! ka-blam! blam!blam!blam!* So much noise! Mike's handsome eyes expertly scan the screen, his thumbs pummeling the joysticks.

"Sounds like one of us is hungry," Mike says at last.

Jeton wants Mike's money but, at the same time, he does not want to see Mike spend so much. If Mike keeps spending what he makes, he will never open his electronics shop. This is a frustrating thought because it is so American, worrying about what has not happened yet. Jeton suspects this comes from spending time with Nora.

He says, "Mike, what happened to your electronics business?"

"Man, I'm saving for it," says Mike.

"Right *now?*"

"Fuck you, Jeton. Least I got a job."

Ka-blam! Level 15. The game is over. Without glancing at Jeton, Mike feeds the machine more dollars and starts again.

Jeton looks with envy at the custom chopsticks Mike carries in a leather case from a loop at his belt. The chopsticks, carved from whale bone, he got from his Japanese grandfather before the old man died.

"Let me try," Jeton says.

Mike glances at him and smirks. "You don't got the reflexes."

Jeton sputters his indignation. "Best goalie on Ebeye—I got reflexes!"

Mike lets him have his seat. The blue-green alien spiders drift down from the yellow video sky like ash Jeton has seen raining over the Ebeye landfill. When the pretty spiders touch Jeton's fat little space ships, the ships explode.

"You got to blow them spiders up," Mike says. "*Fire*, man!"

Jeton thumbs the joysticks, jerking them as he fires with both barrels. *Ka-blam! ka-blam! ka-blam!* so loud it hurts his ears, spiders splintering into shards like glass against rock, rockets streaking red lines across the screen, more and more spiders falling, his ships exploding until Jeton pushes himself away from the machine in frustration.

"Fuck it!" he says, his face burning. He wants to slam the video screen with his fist.

"You don't have to get angry, man. It's a game."

"Fuck it. I never liked these *bwebwe* machines."

"You're like a old man, Jeton. These machines gonna make me a million dollars."

"You don't got enough to buy a machine like this."

Mike sits again at his machine, then feeds it more dollars. "Not today."

"When?" There it is, Jeton thinks. They are talking like the *ri-pālle*. Tomorrow? Next week? Next year?"

"What do you care, Jeton?"

Ka-blam! Mike starts firing. He is steady, relentless, his eyes focused. Maybe he can do what he says. Maybe Jeton needs to be like Mike. See the alien spiders and shoot, see them and shoot. Shoot shoot shoot. No letting up.

"I *don't* care," Jeton lies. "I'm gonna—"

His sudden assertion stops him because he is not sure what he is going to do or be. It seems everyone else has a plan.

"You gonna *what?*" Mike says.

"I'm gonna be goalie on the national team."

The national soccer team trains on Majuro. They fly to Manila, Tokyo, and Sidney to play other teams. The star goalie, Abbetar, wears no shoes and has lost five of his front teeth saving the ball. Who could be tougher than Abbetar?

Mike laughs. "You replace *Abbetar?*"

What is it the Americans say? "Stranger things have

happened."

"You come over to the causeway," Mike says, still firing, alien spiders splintered into purple bits. "Maybe I can get you work."

"The causeway is a mistake," Jeton says. He watches Mike's face to see what happens. "I heard all about it when I was on Kwajalein."

"What you hear?" Mike is up to level 10 already.

"It's gonna ruin the lagoon because it blocks the waves."

Ka-blam! "Nothing can ruin the lagoon," Mike says. *Ka-blam!*

Jeton finishes his beer. "It blocks the waves, man!"

"It doesn't block the waves. I work on it. I see."

"*Ibwijleplep*. Storm waves. The American engineers say so."

"They say so because they are jealous—because they aren't building it."

"We *ri-Majel* don't know how to build anything," Jeton says. "We're stupid."

"*I'm* not stupid," Mike says. "And I'm building the fucking causeway."

That's better: he wants to see Mike mad.

"Causeway's gonna ruin everything," Jeton continues. "You should quit."

The spiders are coming so fast, Mike can't stop them. Suddenly his ships disappear in a black and blue video cloud. He loses the game.

"Fuck you," Mike says, pushing himself away from the machine. "Fuck you!"

Jeton isn't sure if he is saying this to the machine or to him.

"Good reflexes," Jeton mocks.

Mike stands up slowly, wipes his hands on his blue jeans, then—without looking at Jeton—turns away and walks to the door. He has the kind of intent, closed-up look on his face that Jeton has seen on men who fight cocks.

"Your causeway ruins us!" Jeton calls after him.

As soon as Mike is gone and the door has shut out the bright sunlight again, Jeton feels terrible. Why has he treated his cousin so badly?

He hears the young men laughing from the front of the room. Maybe laughing at him. He hears the Spanish program speaking its musical language from the TV set behind the bar. And somewhere at the back of his mind he hears the video game blowing up spiders and spaceships.

When he gets outside, to the rain-puddled street, the air thick with lunch-time aromas—of *bwiin-enno*, fried leeks and sausage—he does not see Mike. Small children who should be in school are playing tag, darting from and through the narrow paths between the hunched-up houses. Like shrimp in tide pools. Several young men and a few older men are sitting in the shade of a breadfruit tree nearby, sharing cigarettes. Men and women are walking away from him, each carrying a straw or plastic bag, on their way to catch the two o'clock ferry to Kwajalein.

Jeton knows that when he sees Mike again, Mike will have forgotten that Jeton was so *kajjōjō*, hateful. That is how it is with the *ri-Majel̦*. Americans are different: they will not let you forget anything.

Jeton could *jaba*, hang-out, with the men by the tree but they are going to talk about women and Jeton does not want to talk about his.

Maybe he will go to the pier, where there are a couple of bars and restaurants. Maybe someone will offer to buy him a bowl of fried egg and rice.

He could go home, but no one is there. His mother is a maid on Kwajalein, his sister a checker at the Americans' supermarket there. His younger brother and sister are at school. Or maybe playing in the alleys. His older brother is on Majuro working with his father, who makes soap in the copra factory. They visit Ebeye every three months, bringing with them samples from the factory and smelling of coconut that seems to have gotten into their breath and become a part of their body sweat.

This is something else he never thought of until he met Nora. His smell. Nora says to him, "I love your smell. It's so *un-American.*" This seems to be a good thing, though Jeton does not know what it means. And he is afraid to ask. Where is Nora now? He wants to fuck her bad. He wants to love her hard. He wants to be with her forever.

* * * *

"These are the only places you'll find authentic Marshallese food," Mister Norman says. He's treating the DDs to lunch at one of Ebeye's" "take-outs," a plywood shack about five by four feet, with a single large open window for service. "We should try some *jukjuk* and *bwiro!*"

"What?"

"Coconut-rice balls and preserved breadfruit!"

The woman inside looks to Nora like every middle-aged Marshallese woman she's seen: heavy, her hair pulled back but messy from the humidity, her face broad and friendly and without a dab of makeup. She wears a cotton shift of a brightly flowered pattern.

Her take-out is well-provisioned, the shelves behind her displaying stacks of Huggies disposable diapers, cans of Starkist tuna, boxes of Kellogg's Frosted Flakes, piles of Snickers candy bars, and stacked tins of SPAM, the national favorite. None of it is cheap.

Mister Norman pays for the Marshallese stuff—"real food," he calls it—then passes it around.

Tabatha grimaces at the brownish paste on her pandanus leaf. "Is this gonna make us sick?"

"It's a miracle the crap you eat every day doesn't make you sick," Mister Norman says, downing a handful of raw papaya strips—which are so crunchy they sound like potato chips as he chews.

Nora pretends to enjoy the Diversity lunch but drops her serving behind her into the weeds. All she can think about is finding Jeton.

Before Gus and Jan grounded her, they let her meet Jeton one more time—at Kwajalein's Emon beach on a Saturday afternoon. She couldn't get into trouble there. Jeton showed up looking sweaty and worried, his visitor's tag clipped to the tail of his T-shirt. Nora was sitting on a picnic table in the only empty pavilion. She patted the plastic bench for him to sit beside her. Nervously, he glanced beyond the pavilion, then pecked her on the forehead. It was the usual blinding sunny afternoon, big silver-white clouds floating fast in a dreamy blue sky. Children were frolicking noisily in the swim area, marked off with orange floats.

Some teenagers were water skiing farther out, several of them sprawled on the ski deck. Though Nora knows she could do it if she tried—she's an athlete—she hasn't learned to water ski in the two years she's been living on Kwaj. Ironic, isn't it? Like living in Manhattan and never visiting the Statue of Liberty. It's something she'll joke about with her college friends, she has decided. The secret truth is, she's afraid to swim out to the ski deck. It's moored over the drop-off, where the white sand falls away hundreds of feet into the black-blue depths of the lagoon.

The drop-off! You're swimming along in the bath-warm water and you can see the squiggly white-sandy coral-studded bottom and then suddenly it's gone and the water goes cold as a deep-bottom current thrills between your legs and there's nothing below but darkness, not a single fish anymore, and it's like you're drifting all alone in deep space. A shark or *something* could snatch you in an instant and drag you down and nobody would be able to help you. Gone! That's what the drop-off is about. That's why Nora has never learned to ski.

When Nora told Jeton she got accepted to Cal State-Sacramento and would be living with her grandparents next year, Jeton fell silent and drew back. He kept turning his head and squinting at her like she'd suddenly gone invisible.

"College!" she exclaimed. "Aren't you happy for me?"

After a long silence, in which Jeton stared at the sandy concrete below his feet, he said, "You could go to college here."

"Majuro?" she answered. "That's *junior* college, Jeton. Cal State is a *real* college, the whole four years."

He wiped at his face and pushed back his pretty black hair. "When does this college start?"

"September," she said. "But I'm flying to Sacramento right after graduation."

"June?"

"Jan and Gus insist," she explained sadly.

"Because we are fucking?"

"Yeah, I guess."

"You tell them you love me?"

She sighed. In some ways Jeton is just a boy. How could she explain that there is love and then there is love? Sure, she loves him. She's never loved anybody more! But what does that mean, really? If she had to tell him the truth, she'd admit that all of this out here, as nice as it is, with the free movies and the year-round summer and all the great kids to hang with, it's like a dream. But none of it *sticks*—that's what she'd like to explain to Jeton. What really matters is life in the States, where people take notice. Most people in the States don't even know about this little piece of America in the middle of the Pacific ocean!

"Aren't you happy for me?" Nora asked.

Jeton, her lover, her sweet, good man, nodded yes. "You're the best," he said.

That nearly brought tears to her eyes. She kissed him on the mouth. She didn't care who was watching. Then she kissed him again. Then he pulled away and said, breathlessly, "I gotta go."

"I'm way grounded," she reminded him.

"They can't keep us apart," he said. Then he took on his goalie look, like he was about to meet the opposing team.

"Let me see what I can do," she said—to calm him down because she knew he might do something crazy, the way he's crazy on the soccer field. Like he doesn't care what happens to himself.

"You can come to Ebeye?" He sounded surprised.

"I can come," she promised.

And here she is.

She's not big-headed or anything but sometimes, really, she thinks she's super blessed. It's not like she's especially good or holy or anything like that. But sometimes the greatest things happen to her. Like right now: she's standing here, pretending to eat this Marshallese paste with her Diversity Delegates and Mister Norman is luging on one of his bobsled rants about nuclear fallout, how America tested H-bombs in the Marshalls forever—sixty seven bombings in all—and the fallout was horrible and the Marshallese got all fucked up and deformed and the money the Americans gave hardly covered the cost of relocating people to different islands and nobody but nobody can clean up the places that were bombed, it's gonna take, like, a million years. . . . So Mister Norman is going on the way he does—a "Norman invasion"—and then, out of nowhere, Jeton walks up to her and says, "Hi, *lijera*."

Nora nearly fucking faints!

It's a Hollywood moment that the senior class is going talk about for weeks!

Nora takes Jeton in her arms and plants a big one on his gorgeous lips. And now Jeton looks like he's about to faint because, as Mister Norman will tell you, the Marshallese don't do PDAs! No, never!

Then, as if announcing she's going down the hall for a drink of water, Nora says she and Jeton are going to take a little walk.

"That's fine," Mister Norman says. "We'll be right behind you."

* * * *

Nora and Jeton walk on the oceanside, the best place Jeton can think to take her because everywhere else is too crowded. He once told her that Ebeye is the most wonderful place on earth. He described the sweet scent of fried onions, the smoky aroma of grilled chicken, the muddy alleys, the crowds of giddy children, the bright blues, reds, yellows, and greens of painted plywood, the laundry flagging on lines behind every home, the sputter and stink of motorbikes, the chaos of radio music, the yelping of dogs. . . . But now, with her at last on his island, he is sure that she cannot appreciate these things.

There is too much garbage, he realizes—plastic Coke bottles and bright white chunks of Styrofoam from broken beer coolers and disposable diapers washed up like dead fish. This is why Americans think the Marshallese are dirty. Just beyond the garbage-strewn sand, four small children are afloat in a doorless refrigerator. Flagging their arms, they shout in triumph as shallow waves push their boat to the shore a few feet, then suck it out a few feet, back and forth. The tide is coming in, the reef exposed in high places, sun glinting from trapped water.

Carefully, Jeton says, "The best islands are to the east in the Ralik chain. Everybody says so."

"Really?" Nora says, though he can tell she is only being polite.

"There is one called Wotje. The Japanese brought dirt from Japan to make a grand garden there."

"You mean during World War II?"

"Yes, long ago." Gingerly he toes aside a disposable diaper. "It is very beautiful."

"Are you going to move there?" she asks.

"With you," he says, wanting this to sound like a promise or a proposal. But it sounds so much like a question he secretly berates himself: bôkâro!

"I told you I have to go to college, Jeton."

"Nobody is *making* you go, Nora."

"I want to!"

When he doesn't answer, she adds: "You could go too."

"I am no good in school."

"You could start with junior college—on Majuro."

It tires him to hear her talk like this, pretending that he is school-smart. "Why do you say these things you know are not possible?"

"Because I believe in you!" she says. "Because anything's possible, isn't it?"

"Anything?" He wants to laugh bitterly. Is it possible to make Nora stay?

He promises himself that he will not be a baby—*eokkwikwi*—who cries for her attention or a baka fool who believes she will do whatever he wants just because he says she should. He understands for the first time what she has meant by the expression "get real." Money is real to Nora. Plans are real to Nora. The future is real to Nora. So he will give her all of that by letting her believe that he agrees with everything she says. It is the curse of the *ri-Majel* to be so giving, so polite.

THREE

Seven degrees north of the Equator, every day is summer. That's the problem, Alison decides. Who can concentrate? Her students do little more than tolerate their time in her class. If they ever look at her with wonder when she wields a brush like a conductor's baton or tangos across the front of the room in her enthusiasm, it is only to say that she is other, as strange as the giant squids that reportedly dwell in deep waters just north of Kwajalein.

Slouched in their plastic bucket-seated school desks, they seem all but naked, bare legs crossed, flip-flops dangling from their delicate toes, everyone in shorts and halters or tight-fitting tees, the fair ones bronzed from sunning, hair highlighted, skin gleaming with perfumed lotions. They can barely keep their hands away from each other, barely disguise their mutually-consuming appetites, barely suppress their smirks as they consider all that they're into and all that their parents don't know about them.

Cosseted, cajoled, and comforted by their parents at every turn, it would never occur to these children that they'd be lucky to achieve the same level of mediocrity enjoyed by the grownups they find so pitiable.

"It's not your job to beat them down," Erik used to tell her. "They need all the encouragement they can get."

Don't we all? she thinks now.

Erik meant that life would beat the kids down soon enough.

When the lunch bell sounds, they stream around her, a white-water rush of laughter, squeals, insults, and jests. Leaning into the second-floor railing to keep herself clear, Alison hears a few check themselves when they see her standing there: Ms. Spence, the Art Teach. Then they spill by, a torrent of great hope and mild anxiety, leaving behind the confused scent of sugary perfume, citrus cologne, body odor, bubble gum and herbal shampoo.

Their patronizing, dismissive glances make her wince. And angry. Here's the searing irony of her life among school children: they pity her not because she lost her husband in a scuba diving accident *fifteen months* ago but because, at 34, she is old already. In their world view, there's nothing left for her but to raise her two boys, then get out of the way.

Now, alone on the annex balcony, Alison peers to the lagoon's sun-hammered surface and regards the noon ferry returning from Ebeye. She and Erik came to Kwajalein to *get away from it all*. Unloading their house and car payments saved them from certain ruin. They were deep into the suburban dream—double mortgaged and maxed on credit cards—and couldn't understand where they had gone wrong. Housing is free on Kwajalein and grocery prices, like everything else, are subsidized because Kwajalein is an American military base sans the military. With the exception of a few officers and intelligence types, everybody here is civilian—mostly engineers and programmers. They've got a bowling alley and two swimming pools and four baseball fields and a two free movie theaters and, yes, summer year round. The Country Club of the Pacific, they call it.

That might be an exaggeration. Kwajalein looks great in photos but, mostly, it's a frowzy beach town of whitewashed cinderblock triplexes built in the 1950s. It seems a perfect place for kids. But live here a while and you begin to have second thoughts about that too. Stan and Doug can't wander away or get kidnapped, it's true, but they could easily drown like their father. Or get stung by a lion fish. Or pick up a rusted piece of metal that turns out to be an undetonated mortar shell from World War II.

No place is safe. That's one bit of wisdom Alison's thirties have taught her.

When she gazes at the lagoon, she finds herself shaking her head in disbelief. It makes no sense. Erik is still down there, caught in the bowels of the Admiral Tokiwa, a 7-ton Japanese destroyer that sunk during World War II. The Colonel, the island's governor, has sent divers down twice to search the wreck, but so far they have found nothing. A sunken ship, she has learned, is a treacherous place, cave-black inside. The silt inside a wreck, once stirred up, obscures light like a sandstorm. That's why all wrecks are off-limits. So why did Erik leave his diving buddy to enter the Tokiwa?

Some days she can hardly contain her anger at him for this. It makes her tremble until she wishes her heart would burst, anything to silence the screaming in her head. She tries not to think of the several, miserable visits she's made to the Colonel, who is always polite but firm in his refusal to "put at risk" his divers. When the Hono divers visit for their 6-month inspection of the Meck installation, he'll send them down again, he has promised. Only the Hono divers are trained for this kind of task. Lately Alison has asked herself what she would do if one of the divers died while trying to recover her husband's body. And now, nearly a year and a half after his disappearance, she toys with the possibility that she should stop insisting that he be found.

She has become a cliché—a widowed youngish mother, her life torn with tragedy. She's drinking too much. She's forgetting dates and meetings. She's late with her class reports. And she's started an affair with the island's senior GP, Emil Timmerman, who is notorious for his affairs. Nobody knows what to do with her. But she can't stop herself.

"You can leave," her therapist told her. "Go back to Milwaukee."

"*Without my husband?*"

"They'll send him back," she said. "After they find him."

Alison shook her head no, no, no. The therapist's office, one of three tiny rooms partitioned in a long, narrow trailer, was as cold as a meat locker. Behind her tiny metal desk, she had hung a print of Van Gogh's "Old Man in Sorrow," depicting abject grief, the subject hunched over in a chair, his face buried in both hands. Did the therapist know that its subtitle is, "On the Threshold of Eternity"? Why would she display something like that?

Alison said, "They'll never find him if I don't stay to make sure they do."

The therapist seemed surprised to hear this. She said, "Oh, that's it, isn't it!"

"Is this a revelation to you, that I feel trapped? As trapped as my husband in that sunken ship?"

"No, it's no surprise, Alison."

Then why the fuck are you acting surprised? Alison stared sourly at the therapist, Eva, a woman who seemed younger than she and untouched by trouble. Eva was, she decided, no better than a tourist, a sightseer in the land of tragedy.

"May I be frank?" Eva said.

"Are you saying you haven't been frank so far?"

Eva smiled a patient smile. "You know what I mean."

Alison nodded okay, okay, sure, she knew what Eva meant.

"You've got to slow down," she said. "You want everything settled. But nothing will be settled for a long time."

"I just want him back," said Alison. "His body. *I need him back!*"

"You'll get him back," said Eva. "But it's going to take time."

"I don't have time!" Her teaching contract runs for another year.

"Greek widows are expected to mourn for five years. Five years, Alison."

"Fuck the fucking Greek widows!"

"Is that what you told her?" Emil asks later. He is on his knees, on the floor of his office, waiting for her to begin. His office—on the hospital's third floor—overlooks the moonscape of the lowtide reef. Waves pound at the reef's edge a quarter mile away.

"Yeah, I told her *fuck it, I'm done*," Alison says. "I'm a jerk, aren't I?"

"No," Emil corrects. He turns to smile up at her slyly. "I'm the jerk! Don't forget that."

Emil is 45, surprisingly pale, but tall and trim. He speed-walks to stay in shape, wearing a sunhat with baggy shorts and a tight-fitting T and gobs of sunscreen. He has a bright, bird-like face, narrow with a beakish nose. He's nothing like Erik. But that's the point.

"Say it," Emil commands.

Alison complies: "Jerk."

"Say it like you mean it."

"You're such a jerk, Emil."

Then she remembers she's not supposed to use his name. Still, he nods his satisfaction. "I shouldn't be giving you orders," he reminds her.

"Then shut up, fuckhead, and take off your clothes."

He grins this time and starts undressing. *That's more like it.*

"Faster," she says.

He has been training her, bringing her along slowly, as if she were a virgin. At first, she didn't care. She told herself she'd do anything. This isn't love. This is something else. Their scenarios have gotten more bizarre and only recently has she put a name to it. The realization that she could do this, that she could be one of these people, shook her. It's sick shit. But it makes her *feel*. And now she's so deep in, why would she, how could she, get out?

Naked, prostrate—bent forward in the yoga "pose of the child"—Emil is whimpering in anticipation. Hoarsely he says, "Be merciful, mistress!"

When she smacks his pale back with his broad leather belt, she feels a sickening thrill, like taking a sudden plunge in a roller coaster. Her head spins, she salivates, she flails again and hates herself. God, she hates every single cell of her body! Emil knows this. He says, "I'm such shit, aren't I? I'm such stinking shit, I don't know how you can stand the sight of me." It's a taunt. It sounds like the voice in her own head.

"Fuck you," she says.

"Yes!" he says.

She flails again. A sudden stripe of blood appears on his back. It startles her. She swallows a gasp and a sudden urge to weep. The belt edge must have caught him. If she asked, *All you all right?* he would mock and scold her. She's got to be stronger. Hasn't Emil told her this every day? *I'll help you get the strength you need, Alison.*

"Mercy please," he moans. It's a lie—there is no mercy.

She flails again.

"You know I deserve it," he says. "What am I?"

"You're shit, you're an asshole, I hate you—you know how I hate you!"

Then he's sobbing and her moment's hesitation makes him implore, "Show me what shit I am!"

Trembling, nearly retching, she drops the belt. Her hand hurts. She gulps for air, as if drowning. "Turn around," she commands. This voice isn't her voice, it's a stronger woman's voice, a woman who knows what she's doing.

Blubbering, Emil is on his knees, facing her, eager to do her bidding. "Anything," he begs.

She says: "You've got five minutes to make me come."

As he begins, unbuttoning her skirt, nosing into her, she stares out the window to the exposed reef. Sun glints from the half-filled tide pools. Out there you can find black sea slugs as big as cucumbers and blue-green moray eels the size of pythons and white undulous fist-sized anemones with their stinging tendrils and jelly fish no bigger than sandwich bags but so venomous that a single brush of their nearly invisible tentacles would stop your heart within an hour.

Later, stepping inside her trailer—what do we call it? she asked Erik in jest, a home? a *trailer* home?—Alison catches a whiff of the mildewed, canned air-conditioned stink that everyone on the island has grown accustomed to, a smell she always forgets after five minutes of being inside. The place is its usual wreck: a spill of mesomorphic action figures in front of the TV, which is still on, a small dirty white sock in the hallway, and, farther on, a pair of small white briefs and a T-shirt; video game joysticks on the kitchen counter, but an empty sink, thankfully, the garbage pail crammed with dirty paper plates and plastic cups—surely the sign of slovenly mothering—and more mess on the floor: a battery-operated flying saucer, a remote-controlled dump truck, a rubber ball that looks like it's been chewed.

She, Doug, and Stan live in one of the 335 mobile homes on the lagoon-side of the island, among the service sector, low-level technicians, and younger teachers. Their neighborhood is called "Silver City." Products of the nineteen sixties, the trailers are aluminum boxes that were no doubt better built than the things manufactured nowadays. They have real wood paneling and stainless steel trim. But they weren't meant to last, especially in a corrosive climate like this. Housing Maintenance is frequently coming by to re-attach panels, staple seams, reinforce floors, re-caulk windows.

The more accomplished citizens live in white-washed cinder-block triplexes or duplexes nearby or, if really well placed in the island's hierarchy, one of the new pre-fabs on the landfill near the high school. None of it looks particularly attractive. But there's the irrepressible tropical greenery that half-disguises the decay—banana plants and coconut palms and car-sized ferns left over from the Jurassic age. When they first arrived on Kwajalein, Erik said, "You should draw some of these things."

As a child, Alison loved to draw—doodling mostly, hours on a page of curlicues and flowers. "You could design fabric," her mother offered as encouragement. *Why would I want to do that?* Alison wondered. For her twelfth birthday, her parents started her with a private art teacher. On looking at Alison's portfolio, the teacher said with undisguised dismay, "These are . . . doodles." Yes, exactly. "What about the *world*?" the teacher asked. Fanciful doodles were Alison's world. She had no inclination to draw the reality around her. She was trying to create in her drawings the kind of place she couldn't find in real life, elbowed by an older sister and brother in a small brick house at the back of a Milwaukee suburb, her father an auto salesman, her mother a checker at K-Mart. It's not that Alison was unhappy, she was simply dissatisfied with the world as it was. It needed more color, more light, more surprises.

Only in college did the question of a career begin to weigh on her. Clearly she wasn't talented like some of her classmates, who painted soulful portraits and stunning landscapes. "Vision!" her art professor lectured. "You can't make work that matters without a vision." Alison's vision of swirls and angles and starbursts and filigree and latticework and curlicues and circles within circles wasn't what the professor had in mind. "Your drawings," he declared, "are as intricate as Victorian wall paper and just as useless."

"Well," her roommate concluded, "you can always teach."

Teaching suited her, she discovered, because she is good with kids and she likes the simple self-contained lesson plans that accommodate even the least motivated student: *Today we're going to paint sky—big blue watercolor swaths across 50-pound paper.* It could be frustrating, like the time Samuel Espinoza painted both of his hands red with tempura, or the day Kaitlin Overby used a fresh tampon to paint her landscape, the class tittering through the lesson until Alison discovered the prank. But mostly her relations with students were peaceful because an art teacher occupies fairly neutral ground.

After a quick shower, Alison mixes a blender of frozen strawberries and orange juice with a handful of ice cubes and a cup of rum. A "smoothie," she calls it. Some mornings she's so fatigued and frightened and hung-over, she fears she won't be able to stand long enough to steady herself against a chair, then a wall, as she paws her way to the kitchen. Her head hammered with heart-beats and flash card images of Erik smiling, Erik yawning, Erik smoothing down his early morning cowlick, she grinds her coffee while Doug and Stan watch Nickelodeon on TV, just beyond the counter that separates dining from sitting in their cramped mobile home.

Tomorrow is Doug's birthday.

"Bake me a cake, if you want," Doug said two weeks ago at dinner.

"You want more than a cake," she teased, hoping for his wince of a smile.

But Doug, her dutiful, somber elder son—ten tomorrow—gave her his usual come-off-it look. He's the son who looks nothing like his parents. Alison used to joke with Erik that Doug was the incarnation of a Puritan ancestor. The boy has never been happy. The best he can manage is a middling satisfaction. She and Erik fretted about him for several years and finally consulted a psychologist who concluded that Doug is hard-wired that way: "We can't all be Ronald McDonald, can we?"

She, Doug, and Stan were eating at the kitchen counter. She had microwaved a frozen pizza. Stan was picking off his pepperoni and stacking them in a tidy pile at the edge of his paper plate. Stan has Erik's pretty eyes, Alison's mischievous smile, and more than a fair share of confidence and coordination. Already he's a star on his grade school's soccer team. And it's clear he can't fathom his older brother's reluctance to grab life by the shoulders and give it a good shake.

Stan said, "When I turn seven in November, you can throw me a extra big party, like combining two parties."

"We're talking about Doug's birthday, not yours," said Alison.

Stan appeared wholly occupied with straightening his pepperoni slices. Alison thinks he might be an artist. "All he wants is cake, he just said."

"We're going to do more than cake," she said.

His mouth full of half-chewed pizza, Doug said, "Whatever."

"I want to make you happy!" said Alison.

"I'm happy," Doug said glumly.

This made her laugh.

She wants the boys to know that life goes on, that even without Erik they can have a reasonably good time. She isn't sure, though, that she believes this herself. Their loss of husband and father threatens to unravel the comforting simplicities they took for granted. *It's not fair*, she wants to shout at Erik, *what were you thinking?* Always, her protests make her feel guilty. Erik fucked up. But it wasn't like he ran away to start a new life.

Or was it?

Right here, in this single thought, which she has entertained countless times, she sees a chink of light, like sunshine seeping through one seam of a locked cellar door. She dare not pry or push at it because it would lead her to the most fantastic speculation: that Erik *did indeed* run off—that he faked his death so that he could start a new life in Thailand or Malaysia.

She knows this thought is nothing but a perverse, ridiculous kind of solace. If he ran off, at least he'd be alive and the boys would have a chance of seeing him again. But then she has a second thought. What if he went into that shipwreck with no intention of coming out? This thought is pure horror. It would mean that she never truly knew Erik, wouldn't it?

She can't go there. She should never go there. But she does go there too often.

She sits on her disheveled couch and drinks her lunch and cruises through the 42 satellite channels, the world disgorged from the TV screen, its numbing variety of comedy and drama spilling onto the stained rug of her cramped "family room" and its scatter of action figures and DVD video games.

Doug's request for a cake was a joke, because Alison doesn't cook, much less bake. Erik was the cook, inventive and fearless. Casseroles were his specialty. Tuna-chicken-parsley lima and black bean. Brussel sprout potato-potroast-apple parmesan. Green-pepper-ham-salsa-corn-chip-cheddar and rice. He made the kind of mess the boys might make if they were given free reign in the kitchen. But she'd rather clean up than cook because she has no patience with recipes, just as she had no patience with the strictures of art class in college. So now she and the boys eat heat-and-serve meals, none of it particularly good or healthy. But it will do for now. Everything about their life is similarly provisional, qualified by the unspoken "for now."

She hates that she has let this happen. Which is why Doug's party matters. It's got to be right.

Pounding on her trailer door startles her. Before answering, she sets the half-empty blender carafe in the sink, then surveys her chaotic surroundings, which elicits from her one long sigh. There's too much to clean up so she won't even try. When she opens the door, she is surprised to see her best friend, Gayla. Tall and full-figured, Gayla has the broad shoulders of a swimmer and the gold-brown complexion of her Jamaican grandmother, though she herself grew up in Evanston, Illinois. She is the high school vice principal.

Right, Alison remembers: *school*.

"You know what time it is?" Gayla asks.

The day's heat roars through the open door.

Alison glances down at her own unadorned wrists. She used to own a watch but can't recall what happened to it. "Lunch time," she says at last, sounding as mindless as one of her students.

"An *hour* ago," Gayla says. "I don't know why I still cover for you."

"Because you love me, Gayla." Alison attempts a smile.

"I can't love you that hard, girl. Not like this. Let's go."

"It's one of those days," Alison says. She locks the door behind her.

"Don't even start," Gayla says. She opens her bamboo-handled sunbrella, then sets the pace with a determined stride, her braids swinging.

The roadways among the trailers are sandy and half-shaded with palms. Alison has always liked them for a stroll with her boys.

"You see your therapist this week?" Gayla asks.

Alison listens to the lap and crush of waves returning on the tide. Some mornings the lagoon is as calm as a lake. She says, "I quit therapy."

"Oh, that's smart!"

"Be nice to me," Alison says.

"I'm being too nice and you know it. Keep on like this and you've got maybe one more warning before you lose your job."

"They'd fire me at this point in the semester?"

"It's been done before."

"I won't let that happen," Alison says quietly.

"Won't you?" Gayla sounds hurt, nearly in tears, which isn't like her. Wonder Woman, Alison has called her in jest. She is very much like Alison's brother, Eddie: focused, self-directed, authoritative, accomplished. Gayla is the woman Alison will never be. But Alison can make Gayla laugh. She is the yin to Gayla's yang. Their husbands worked together at the weather station.

"No, I won't let that happen," Alison says. "I've got plans."

"Plans?" Gayla turns a curious gaze to her.

"Yes!" Alison lies. "I've applied for a masters program in Art Ed."

Gayla's voice skids into falsetto: "Since when?"

"I didn't want to say anything until I was sure."

"What school?"

"Online, through the University of Wisconsin." These an-swers come unbidden, easily, and the lie brings a thrill similar to her abuse of Emil: the world's possibilities open in perversely gratifying ways. Oh, how she hates herself!

"You've been accepted into the program?" Gayla asks.

"Yes!" Alison says matter-of-factly. "I start studies at the end of the month."

"Well, that's a good thing," Gayla says cautiously. They step onto the asphalt of Pacific Drive. "You're excited, right?"

"Of course I am! " Alison lies, lies, lies. "I'm getting some focus, I'm marching into the future—progress is my middle name!"

"Smart ass."

Suddenly Alison pictures herself spanking Emil's hairy white ass.

She hears a sudden pop behind her, like a hand smacked across someone's face. When she turns for a glance, Alison sees that a gull has just dropped a slate-colored crab to the asphalt. Miraculously, the crab has survived. Dragging one damaged leg, it scurries into the shade of nearby weeds. Then the gull touches down on the asphalt, tucks its wings in, pivots its gleaming white head, but can't find its lunch. Head bobbing, it waddles to the shoulder of the road and blinks its beady eyes in confusion.

"Did you see that?" Alison asks. "Look back there."

Gayla looks. "It's a bird, Ali."

Alison is about to explain the mini-drama she's just witnessed but then decides there's too much she can't explain already.

"Want a mint?" She offers the roll to Gayla.

Gayla eyes the mints, then Alison with glum disdain. "You think that's going to cover the alcohol on your breath?"

Alison feels a trickle of sweat spill from her scalp. She smells the ocean's salt spray and the fish-stink of sun-baked coral and something else—maybe it's the smolder of her burning heart. She says, "Sorry. I know I'm fucking up."

Gayla lets her sunbrella collapse and steps into the shade of the school's portico. "So you've told me about twenty times, hon'. I'm not asking for excuses, just don't insult my intelligence."

"I'm sorry!" Alison says quickly. "You know I love you for helping me."

"Love isn't enough, Ali. I'm risking my own job. Can you

teach today or not?"

"I'm fine." Alison attempts a smile. "Really."

"Then get up there and do it. I'm not coming after you again."

"Thanks." Alison reaches for Gayla's hand but Gayla is already walking away.

Yes, Alison thinks, *that's what I deserve. I'm shit.*

When everyone on Kwajalein first learned of Erik's "disappearance," they swamped her email with condolences and crowded her kitchen with grilled chicken and potato salad and teriyaki steak and hummus and tabouli and cheese balls and three-bean salad and spinach lasagna. They approached her tentatively and spoke softly. She must have seemed as delicate to them as a kite caught in a tree. Alison was grateful for their time and attention but then, after a couple of months, when depression began to slow her down like a low-grade fever, she wondered about the growing distance between her and the rest of the world, especially those she thought were her friends. What did she have to offer anyone except her crushing tragedy? No wonder she felt so isolated, even shunned. She scared people, she realized. She was a drag.

"I've ruined it," Alison told Gayla just five months after Erik's death. "That's what it is. I've ruined it for them!"

"They just feel awkward," Gayla said.

"No," Alison said. "It's like I've smashed the windows of their tidy houses. They can hardly stand to look at me."

"It's a terrible tragedy, Ali. Nobody knows how to handle it."

"*You* know," Alison said. "You treat me like I'm still alive."

Gayla nodded her head in sympathy.

"I don't want to be the Object of Pity!"

"It will pass," Gayla said. "Give it time."

"I don't have time," Alison said. "I'm thirty-three!"

Gayla laughed. "And I'm thirty-nine. We've still got time, hon'."

But that was a year ago. Today Gayla has made clear that Ali has run out of time. She has fallen so fast and fallen so low, it stuns her even as she watches it happen day after day. If she didn't have her boys, she might kill herself. Really, she might. How's that for low?

Her classroom is 60's-era: high-gloss linoleum floors, celery green cinder block walls, and a single row of six windows nearly white from the afternoon sun. The air conditioning is always too cold, the wall clock always too slow. She has missed one class already but is nearly on time for this one. When she enters, twelve juniors regard her with mild indifference. She's the Art Teach, after all. Back in the States, a lot of schools don't even teach art any more.

Alison draws a breath. Her rum lunch is just now hitting her, the room going wobbly. She says, "Today's lesion—lesson—is a watercolor wash." She begins to sort through the brushes on her desk, stalling for time.

Red-headed, freckled-faced, adenoidal Chase Sadowski says, "We did this *last* week."

Alison looks up sharply. She surprises herself by smiling. "Aren't you willing to humor me, Chase?"

He grimaces and half shrugs. "I just don't want to be bored."

"None of us want to be *bored*!" she says. "Show of hands, please. Who wants to be bored?"

Spacey Britney Losinger raises her hand eagerly before she realizes it's a joke. The others laugh.

Alison picks up a long-handled brush, then aims it at Chase. "We're going to watercolor wash—again—because anything worth doing once is worth doing twice. Don't you think?"

"Depends if you teach it better than last week," Chase says.

This wins a few titters.

Children don't know their limits. That's why they're testing out their cruelty all the time. They have felt too little pain in their short lives. Already Alison sees mean streaks in her two boys. Doug didn't want to invite Arnold Arnold to his birthday party. "You have to invite Arnold," she told him. "He's in your class."

"He's a loser," Doug said glumly. "He's gonna suck the fun out of everything."

"You're lucky you're not the loser," Alison said. It secretly pleases her that Doug and Stan are popular. Not team-captain popular, but popular enough to avoid the persecution poor Arnold Arnold suffers. Maybe his parents thought that giving him such a name would make him a stand-out. It has only made him a target.

Arnold Arnold—known to his classmates as "The Bug"—is slump-shouldered and pencil-limbed, with a head too large for his body.

"It looks like he lives under a rock!" Stan said.

"If you don't invite him," Alison said, "there will be no party."

"Not fair!" Doug said.

"That's bullshit!" said Stan.

"Don't use that language," Alison said. "Or you won't get a party either, Stan."

"Fine, invite him," said Doug, "it'll be a sucky party anyway 'cause we don't have the *Stone Deaf Death Rangers* video."

"What's that?" she asked.

This made Stan laugh in disbelief. "You haven't heard of the Stone Deaf Death Rangers?"

"It's game they made into a movie," says Doug. "It's so popular nobody can get it."

He meant nobody out here *in the middle of the Pacific* could get that highly prized video.

With a knowing smile, Alison said, "I might be able to get it."

"No way!" the boys said in unison.

"Way," she said.

Wide-eyed, they regarded her with suspicion and wonder.

Yes, that's more like it, she thought: *Super Mom!*

Alison asked Emil to buy her the DVD while he was in Hono last week. No problem, he said. But she forgot to get it from him at lunch today. Isn't that why she went to his office in the first place?

She phoned April Arnold a week ago to invite Arnold to Doug's party. Alison doesn't particularly like April, who is as petite as a twelve-year-old, is fond of wearing pink, avoids the sun at all costs, and seems to take great pride in being a native of Atlanta, Georgia, as if she were an Old South debutante. But Alison likes her troubled son. Arnold has the quiet, watchful demeanor of a talented painter she used to know, a boy who could draw anything he saw. She suspects that Arnold is "special" in a good way like that.

April said, "You'll make sure nobody bullies him, right?"

"I hate bullying," said Alison. "I want him to have a good time."

"You know his allergies?"

"Peanuts and milk products, shellfish and cured meats, and what else?"

"All nuts," she said. "And no cheese, of course."

"I think I said no milk products."

"Some people forget that cheese is made of milk."

"I won't forget, April."

"He's a good boy, you know."

"Yes, I know. Are you going to send him?"

April's silence, pondering the risks to her odd little boy, was the kind of agony Alison wouldn't wish on any mother. At last April said, "I'll send him. He'd like a party."

So everything has been arranged. Alison ordered a double chocolate cake from Rosalia Velasquez, the best baker on the island. Tonight she'll clean up. It will feel like Christmas Eve, the boys giddy with anticipation. Tomorrow she'll get the video and the cake. By the end of the evening tomorrow, she and the boys will be exhausted and gratified, even grateful and perhaps surprised at their good fortune. So she was half right when she spoke to Gayla earlier: she is getting some focus.

"Water is the most difficult medium," she tells her class.

"Yeah, I remember," Chase says. "It's unpredictable."

"Like life!" Brittney quips.

They gather around Alison's easel to watch as she strokes a one-inch Grumbacher over the textured paper, soaking but not drenching it. To her peripheral left, she sees Chase snaking his hand into Cook Butler's shorts, though Cook affects a poker face; to her peripheral right she sees Britney gazing out the window, where the cumulus clouds are rolling by as big as white elephants. Someone is wearing too much nutmeggy cologne. At her right elbow, Dana McGinty is whistling softly what sounds like "If I only had a brain."

"See how quickly the paper absorbs?" Alison says in her sing-songy teacher's voice.

Someone—Steve Richardson?—says, "That's cool," and Alison feels a surge of satisfaction warm her face as she lets the deep blue bleed from one stroke to the next.

FOUR

When Cooper wakes, he knows he's higher than he's ever been. It's got to be an opiate of some kind because he's all but levitating. At first he thinks he's waking from a nap—he feels the bob and sway of his boat. Then a different reality starts to take shape: he's on drugs, okay; he's been injured, right; he's in a hospital, of course . . . but then things get vague again and he can't explain a distant kind of dread that tugs at him, like someone calling to him from across a canyon: *Watch out!*

He's so high, he knows the warning doesn't register the way it should. This bothers him. He knows he should get up. He really has to get up. But, damn, he's so high, he can only giggle at how crazy this is. *Get up!* Maybe not. He can't have been here, in this hospital, for more than a day. Oh, wait: he remembers the trip, the trippy trip.

Like a lightning flash, it comes to him: the Army rescued him, as that bull walrus Thomas promised. A medic parachuted down with impressive precision to assess Cooper's injury. "Oh, baby, this looks bad," the medic said, at which point Cooper, in shamed defense, tried to explain how he had carefully ministered to his wound but to no avail. The medic didn't seem to be listening. Slapping at the radio on his harness, he said, "We got to get him out of here, man."

They pulled Cooper up in a rescue harness, into the bowels of a thundering Black Hawk chopper, which had followed the HN-130 Hercules out to the island. Then they flew him straight to Kwajalein. And so—ironically—he arrived at his destination ten days earlier than he had planned. At Kwajalein's modest hospital, a young internist examined the wound, found it gangrenous, and called for an immediate amputation. An IV'd sedative was already leaking into Cooper's left arm when the doctor told him, "I'm sorry, buddy, but this is a simple thing. It's your leg or your life."

It all happened so fast, Cooper could hardly focus on the urgency of this request. Leg or life. Wasn't there another choice?

As soon as Cooper signed the waiver, the doctor suited up, the orderly radioed Hono Army Hospital for some virtual consultation, two nurses prepped Cooper, and that was that. While the GP talked to the Hono doctor, sometimes cracking a bad joke ("This time I'm a leg up on you, Chuck. . . .") Cooper felt himself swinging in the rescue harness. Everything below him— the little island, the islanders, Harold-the-mayor, the big bearded Thomas—grew smaller, as if he were a movie camera receding for the picture's closing shot, framed between his two dangling feet.

His feet. He tries to look at his feet but can't raise his head. He is alone, he realizes, in a room whose door is open to the hallway. A strap as wide as a seatbelt holds him to the bed. Two IV bags are dripping into him, one on each restrained arm. He calls for a nurse. His voice seems to rise from behind him, slurred and syrupy.

If he weren't so stoned, he would yell. But as frantic as he thinks he should be, his mind won't rise to the alarm. At last a nurse arrives. She says, "It's about time you woke up!" She goes straight to his IVs and turns them off.

"How long have I been out?"

"Three days!" Now she's unplugging his arms, pressing adhesive bandages to the holes.

"No fucking way."

"Way!"

He can't read her name tag. She is a short, thick-boned blonde, in her late twenties, with a bunny-small nose, full cheeks, and pink-framed eye glasses that look too big for her face. If she were in the States, she'd live in an apartment complex by the interstate. Maybe newly divorced with a kid and dreams of a Carnival Cruise vacation. She says her name is Inez. He asks her what drugs he is on. Morphine, she tells him. Tomorrow it will be Demerol, then a transition to Tylox.

"I'm so fucking high!" he says.

"That's how it's supposed to be," she says. "But you're all right—right?"

"I'm scared shitless," he says, "but I don't feel scared shitless except in a really far-out disconnected way."

"If you want scary," she says, "I got plenty of things to tell you."

"About my leg?" he asks.

"About the *world*," she says. "I hear you've been on a boat for, like, a year."

"No, not that long," he says.

"Maybe you don't know what's going on any more."

"I don't know that I've ever really known what's going on," he says. It's supposed to be a joke, but Nurse Inez doesn't seem to get it.

She says, "Should I tell you all the news?"

"Is it good news?" He attempts a smile and discovers, with alarm, that he can't feel his face.

"Nothing good happening these days," she says brightly. "More than 500 of our boys are dead in Iraq so far. Still nobody's found any weapons of mass destruction. The Iraqis think we're dominators, not liberators. I bet you didn't hear about the guy they *beheaded*."

"Beheaded?" Cooper pushes himself up a bit. Did he hear right?

"I've got the video at home," she says eagerly. "It's awful."

"You've got a video of a beheading?"

"I didn't take it!" she says, holding up one latex-gloved hand as if to swear an oath. "It was all over the news."

"Who beheaded who? And why?"

"It's war, Mr. Davies. That kind of thing happens in war."

"I know we're at war," he stammers, "but how in the hell—"

"It's craziness," she says. "The Arabs caught an American reporter and cut his head off because they're angry. Everybody's angry. Especially about the prison scandal. President Bush gave a speech yesterday and he mispronounced it three times. Even that made people angry."

"Mispronounced what?"

"Abu Ghraib. Is that so hard to say? Go ahead, say it after me. Ah-boo Gray-b."

"Abu Ghraib."

"That's right. You're going to be a good patient." Then she winks at him. "I've got pictures of the Abu Ghraib atrocities—all of them—which I downloaded from the internet. If you want I'll bring them in."

Has the world slipped off its axis while he was sailing across the Pacific?

"No, thank you! Maybe I should nap," he says, desperate to get away from her gleeful gloom.

"Okay, Mr. Davies." She snaps off one glove, then the other. "You want me to read your cards to you?"

"I got cards?" Suddenly he is very hungry. "Someone I know?"

"Who do you know on Kwajalein?" She says this in good humor, but it is a reality check. He can't quite grasp that he is on an island 4250 miles west of California. He's been alone on his boat for so long, he has simply assumed that now, landed at last, he would be within reach of anybody, everybody. But he's not in reach. He's out *here,* on a sand speck in the middle of the Pacific.

Nurse Inez reads him the notes, the first from his co-workers, a card whose photo shows a group of orangutans piled onto a hospital bed: "What some people won't do to get out of work!" the caption reads. "We're thinking of you, Cooper. Keeping your seat warm in the quad. See you soon. Your A-team." Then a crowd of signatures. Inez reads every name. Eight in all. The other note—from the Colonel, the island's "governor"—is handwritten on impressive letterhead, The United States seal in one corner, the Ronald Reagan Ballistic Missile Defense Test Site seal in the other.

"Dear Cooper, we are thankful that you are safe and sound," the Colonel writes. "The doctor tells me you are going to be fine. We look forward to welcoming you into our little community. I will drop around soon to visit. Until then, I am yours sincerely, Colonel 'Sandy' Sanderson."

Later, after dozing off and on, gazing at the stripes of sunlight across the room, and wondering about his boat, where the fuck is his boat?, Inez returns to help him with the bedpan. Only then, as he leans to one side while she snugs the pan into his crotch, only then does he see his stump, the bandaged nub pressing into the mattress. He nearly pukes at the sight of it. But he doesn't puke because he's convinced suddenly that it's not really him. His leg is still there. He can feel it. So this stump, with its intermittent hotwire of pain, this stump is not his. It's like a loaner. Until they return his leg.

After Inez takes away the pan, a weather-beaten orderly sidles up to the bed and says, "Hey, sailor, you ready for a ride?" Then, without asking, he hikes Cooper off the mattress and sets him into a wheel chair.

"This is Jimmy," Inez says.

All arms and legs, Jimmy looks like a sixty-year-old roofer who has seen better days, his face sunbrowned to a squint. He wears green scrubs, his stringy gray hair contained by a net. He reeks of cigarette smoke.

He says, "You've had some wild time, haven't you, pal?"

"I'm still having a wild time, aren't I?" Cooper says.

Jimmy grins and nods his head.

"I want you to see the view from the lounge," Inez says cheerily, walking ahead. "Hospital's one of the tallest places on the island. You can see the lagoon!"

Lagoon: what a romantic word! How heroically brave, hero-ically sad, heroically misunderstood Cooper felt when sailed from Half Moon Bay without Lillian and Bailey three months ago. He's not sober enough to take a measure of his regret. But he pictures himself trying, like a deckhand dropping rope into the water to measure fathoms.

"Where's my boat?" he asks.

"I'm sure your boat is in the water, where boats belong," says Inez.

Jimmy parks Cooper in front of the three windows, each as big as a beach towel. Cooper surveys the island for the first time: he sees whitewashed cinderblock duplexes and triplexes amid a clutter of palm trees and too-green greenery. The place looks run down and overgrown. Beyond the furzy green lies the turquoise expanse of too-blue water. Then he sees an old gray-metal trans-port plying away from the island.

"Where they going?" he asks.

Inez leans into the window. "That's the afternoon ferry to Ebeye."

"Ebeye?"

"Where the natives live."

When Cooper doesn't answer, she adds, "You know, the Mar-shallese?"

My leg is gone. My leg is gone. My leg is gone. My leg is gone. My leg is gone. My leg is gone. My leg is gone. My leg is gone. My leg is gone. My leg is gone. My leg is gone. My leg is gone. My leg is gone. My leg is gone. My leg is gone. My leg is gone.

But he can still feel his leg.

"There's our celeb," a young doctor greets him.

"You're the guy!" says Cooper. He means to say, *You're the guy who took my leg!*

"Yeah, I'm the guy!" the doctor says with good humor. Then he wheels Cooper away.

Inez calls, "Later, gator!"

"You're the talk of the town," the doctor says.

"There's a town?"

The doctor chuckles. "No, not at all. We have a department store that looks like a bargain barn, a snack bar attached to one side, the post office attached to the other. Then there's a kind of hardware store in a prefab building. That's your downtown. Oh, and we have a grocery store half a mile from that. We call it Surfway. Isn't that cute?"

Cooper likes speeding through the wide hallway, strangers nodding and smiling at him. Maybe he *is* a celebrity.

Celebrity fuck-up is more like it. He is so shamed by what has happened, he doesn't want to call his parents, though he knows they're waiting to hear from him. He last talked to them via Skype from Honolulu. And Lillian, would she care to know?

The doctor wheels him into a rectangle of sunlight in front of his desk. He's younger than Cooper remembers, a short athletic man with a weak chin and wavy dirty-blond hair. He pulls his desk chair around so that he can sit nearly knee to knee with Cooper. He's wearing a short-sleeved plaid shirt, wrinkled khakis, and classic Jack Purcells.

"I've visited you many times, my friend, but I'm not sure you remember."

Cooper tries a smile. "Inez says I was out for three days."

"We weren't going to let you stay down any longer than that," he says. "There's a lot to do."

"I am," Cooper begins. *Happy to be alive? Grateful that you saved me? Scared out of my fucking mind?* "I am a little confused right now."

"We have a counselor you can talk to."

"Where's my leg?" The question surprises Cooper as much as it seems to surprise the young doctor.

"Cooper—"

"I'm just curious. What do you do with a leg?"

A piece of him loose somewhere in the world—it's an

unsettling thought.

The doctor eyes him as if to search out a symptom. At last he says, "Nobody's sorrier about what happened than I am. It was the last thing any doctor would want to do."

Cooper nods his understanding. "I would have died. I know that."

The doctor nods yes. "It was a difficult procedure, but I was careful and I had help."

"You still haven't answered my question, doc."

The doctor's name, Cooper remembers, is Boxer. He wears a wedding band. Is everyone on Kwajalein married? The place must be crawling with kids.

Boxer looks disappointed or hurt, his thin lips pale, his eyes narrowed and unfocused as if he's withdrawn into himself.

The voice in Cooper's head says, *Half a leg is better than no leg. Half is better than none.*

Then he hears Boxer say, "It's gone, Cooper," so directly, so surely, that there's nothing more to say.

Gone.

Something—maybe the drugs—allows Cooper to say, "You did a great job, I'm sure."

Boxer nods a silent thank-you, then describes with increasing enthusiasm the business of rehab, which will be "slow and painful." Through it all Cooper nods dutifully, like a soldier hearing his assignment. There is so much to do, he doesn't try to keep it straight. All he knows right now is that he wants to get out of his chair. He wants to walk. And get to his boat. He's got to get to his boat.

When the orderly returns him to his room, Cooper meets his first visitor: a big-bellied, bald man who looks to be sixty and is dressed in a white T-shirt, dirty khaki trousers rolled up nearly to his calves, and rubber flip-flops—like a hip summer kid from the States, though Cooper suspects the old man has been dressing this way for decades. He has a big hound-dog face, thin legs, and the mottled complexion of a man who should but consistently fails to avoid the sun. In fact, he's blocking the sunlight at Cooper's window. It appears that he's been here some time, perhaps picking through Cooper's fruit basket, smelling the flowers, reading the cards.

He offers his small hand, which Cooper takes with some effort. "Art Norman, Cultural Liaison. If you're too tired I can come back."

Cooper regrets his own weak grip. He wonders how bad he looks.

"I'm fine." He waves away the glum orderly, then returns his gaze to the visitor. "Come back for what?"

"Your orientation. Haven't you checked your schedule?" The liaison lifts a sheet of paper from atop the EKG at the side of the bed and waves it at him as if it were wet. His close-set eyes give him a shrewd look; his downturned mouth suggests a fretter.

"I rate a personal visit from the Cultural Liaison?"

"We don't want you starting without knowing some basics about the Marshallese people."

Cooper nods agreeably. His first day out of bed and already he's getting lectures? "Why isn't a Marshallese person telling me this?"

"They don't like to talk about themselves. You will not find a more modest people. They don't wear shorts, you'll notice. Do you know what *io̧kwe eok* means?"

This sounds like Yuck-way Yuck.

"Something like 'greetings,'" Cooper says. "I read it in one of the guides."

"It means 'love to you,'" the liaison says with satisfaction. "The *ri-Majeļ*, as they call themselves, never ever want to disappoint you, so they will tell you whatever it seems you want to hear."

"I've heard," Cooper muses, "they are promiscuous."

The man winces, his mouth working as if on a jawbreaker. "Like rabbits?" he says. "Jungle bunnies maybe?"

"I didn't mean to be insulting," Cooper says quickly. "I'm just telling you what I *heard*."

"Crap like that makes my job a joy, you know that?"

Cooper raises both hands in surrender, then asks: "Am I going to work with the Marshallese?"

"You will be among them." Breathless already, the liaison gulps for air. He appears to teeter ever-so-slightly from foot to foot. As big as he is, it seems he seldom sits still. Sourly he says, "They do all of the menial labor on this island."

"Do they mind?"

"Hell, it looks like they don't mind a God damn thing. But they mind!"

Cooper nods agreeably. "I guess you mind too."

"And you don't?"

"Sweet Jesus, Mr. Norman, I just got here. Nobody's told me a thing!"

"They won't either. Do you know these islands have the high-est per capita rate of attempted suicide in the world?" The liaison's face is nearly the color of liver. "This place will fuck you up, son!"

Cooper would like to believe that the man is a jokester, hazing him for a laugh. But until the old man reveals the joke, Cooper feels an urgency to keep talking: "The Marshallese don't live on Kwajalein, right?"

The liaison nods, seeming calmer now. "They live next door, on a little pile of sand and shit called Ebeye. We ferry them in every morning so they can do our dirty work, then we ferry them back. They can't be here after sundown."

"What, it's like some kind of apartheid?"

At last the liaison smiles. And Cooper thinks of attempting a smile of his own.

"Keep talking like that," the old man says, "and you'll win me over."

"Does the Colonel know," Cooper begins but then thinks bet-ter of it. This can't be the liaison's job to alienate every newcomer.

"Fuck the Colonel." Art Norman lets one hand fly up as if

to flash the finger. "I'm two years away from retirement. They couldn't find someone to do my job if they paid twice the salary. Which would still be shit."

"Look," says Cooper warily, "I don't want to get off on the wrong foot."

The man raises his flaking, freckled brow in surprise. "Are you trying to be funny?"

"Did you think that was funny?" Cooper asks.

The old man sits wearily on the bed, lays down the paper he pulled off the EKG, then shakes his head in dismay or disgust. "I know I'm a fucker, Cooper. I'm not having a good day. And I know you've had a hard time." He sighs: "I'm sorry."

Cooper searches for something reassuring to say but can think only of sleep. His ass aches from sitting too long in the sling of the wheelchair. He elbows the arm rests to readjust his position but it doesn't help. His arms itch where the IVs were, his mouth tastes as if he's been sucking a handful of rust, and his right thigh is beginning to send him a deep, throbbing signal of distress.

When he looks up finally, he sees the liaison watching him as it seems everyone has been watching him today, to see what he'll do next.

Wiping one freckled hand over his forehead, Art says, "I'm not exactly giving you the official version, I guess you could tell."

"Fire away, Art. I want the straight dope."

A bit of sunshine glows from the liaison's face. Without preface, he begins: "Fact one: for at least 2,000 years the Marshallese have lived from hand to mouth, day to day—taking what they could from the lagoons and the plant life—on flea-speck atolls whose aggregate size would fit inside Washington, D.C., but whose ocean territory is as vast as half the continental United States."

"Okay," says Cooper dutifully. "They're tough and resourceful, these people."

"You miss the point, son. These people have no place to go.

Do you know the ocean's rising? Highest elevation out here is twenty-eight feet—and that's the old missile launch-mound at the other end of this island, courtesy of the U.S. Army. Actual average elevation is more like four feet. Before they're done, they'll all be living in public housing outside Los Angeles."

"Four feet?" Cooper asks.

"Maybe six, what difference does it make?"

"All right," says Cooper. "I'll give you eight feet and still they're screwed."

"Now you get it." Art nods his approval and Cooper finds this reassuring, as if talking with his own father, who has always possessed the right answer.

"Fact two: The Marshallese have evolved into one of the most compliant, self-effacing people in the world because how else could they have survived together on these tiny rafts of sand? Unfortunately, their amiability has made them thoroughly exploitable. Spain, then Germany, then Japan, and now the United States have all held the *ri-Majel̦* hostage in one form or another."

"You said they don't like to talk about themselves."

"That's right."

"And they don't wear shorts."

"Don't get fixated on the details, Cooper. I'm talking big picture right now."

"There's a lot to keep in mind, big picture or small," Cooper says.

"That's why I'm here."

"Then you're my Jiminy Cricket?"

"Your what?" he barks.

"You know, my conscience. Like in the Disney cartoon?"

"I need you to focus, Cooper. If you're too drugged up, just tell me and I'll come back."

"I'm fine. I can listen to this. It's fascinating."

The liaison eyes him briefly, then nods as if to confirm that Cooper is sincere. "Okay," he says. "Fact three: the Marshallese never developed a sense of time or consequence as Westerners know it, since everything out here remains relatively constant, and certainly they never developed the notion of *future*, since there was little or nothing to work toward, nothing to possess, and therefore nothing to save."

"Nothing to save?"

"For these people there is *no reason to save*, do you hear what I'm saying? There's no winter here, no reason to hunker down and wait it out. A typhoon's not going to last but a day or two before it moves on. This sense of ongoingness—"

"Infinitude?"

"Fine, infinitude—it has its effects, Cooper."

"Like the Australian aborigines who believe we live in a world unbounded by time?"

"No, not like the Australian aborigines," Art says. "There is time here, just not Western time. Not consequential time. Not *deadline* time."

"So that's why Americans think they're lazy?"

"That goes without saying."

Cooper closes his eyes and thinks of lazing in the rope hammock on Lillian's redwood deck after the sun has burned off the Montara fog finally and a warm breeze rises from the meadow across the street, carrying with it the salty scent of ocean waves and the sweet smell of rotting grass. And somewhere behind him he can hear Lillian singing an old show tune—"Good mornin'! Good mornin'!"—while she makes her chocolate chip, walnut-oatmeal cookies; and he knows Bailey is nearby too, in the down recliner, listening to old folk rock through her headphones and reading "Wuthering Heights" for the tenth time. Do they need a dog? he wonders as he swings there ever so slightly. A yellow lab? Would this complete their happiness?

FIVE

Cousin Mike drives the loader like a Boston Whaler, one hand easily on the steering wheel, the other hand idle, his arm draped over the seat. The loader is a dusty orange tractor on four man-tall tires; it grumbles loud and chugs out choking clouds of diesel fumes. Mike makes the loader's bucket rise high as he pulls away with another load of rocks. Jeton wants to drive the loader. But Jeton doesn't know how to drive.

Mike turns out smartly, then guns away, bouncing in his seat as the loader dips and climbs. *Lucky cousin!* Jeton thinks. Mike has been working here for nearly a year. All of the Filipino foremen know him and seem to respect him. Mike's hardhat sits back on his head the way the foremen wear theirs.

Jeton has no hard hat. He doesn't have work boots either. Instead he wears his church shoes, which are too tight for him. He wears them without socks, his feet sweating and blistered.

As promised, cousin Mike got him this job. His mother thinks he is still in school. So does Nora. He has used cousin Mike's cell phone to call Nora. She would not talk for long. When he said, "I've got to see you, *mōtta!*" she said, "Not now, Jeton. I'm super busy." *Mōtta:* "partner," "mate," "wife." The thought of her gone makes him queasy, like he has not eaten for days. He believes that she will change her mind. She must change her mind.

The first two mornings Jeton arrived for work, Mike tapped the big silver watch on his own wrist and said, "You get one of these, Jeton. It will make you sharp."

Wājepādik.

Mike is full of advice. Mister Loader-driver. Mister Business Man. Mister Fore Man.

Jeton is the youngest of the six-person crew. The others are nearly thirty or older. Young men do not usually get work because there are too many older men looking. The others know that Mike is Jeton's cousin but this doesn't seem to matter to them.

Only one of them—the oldest man—has a hardhat, which is cracked down the middle and too small for him. It sits like half a coconut on his head.

They pull rocks and shovel gravel from coral pits that the Filipino men explode with dynamite. The holes they make with the explosions are big enough for a small speedboat. It takes Jeton and the others all day to clear out one or two of these, tossing the stone into the loader bucket.

After five days of this work, Jeton's hands are scraped, swollen, and blistered. He gets so thirsty, he can't drink enough soda—which he buys from young boys who come around with warm cans they have probably stolen from snack shops.

Even though nobody works fast, Jeton is the slowest. On his first day, after a few hours of sorting rock, Jeton said, "This sucks." He said it several more times until one of the men mimicked a crying baby. Then they started calling Jeton "*Eokkwikwi*." Crybaby.

They work at the eastern end of Ebeye, a flat stretch of rocky white landfill, just beyond the crowd of houses. Nora calls these *pelak*. Shacks. They are not colorfully painted out this way because these are the newest.

The causeway is a wide white road stretching nearly a mile through the shallow water that washes over the reef. Jeton cannot see the next island because it is too flat but he has heard that the causeway has nearly reached it. Anyone can walk to the end of the causeway to see for himself after the day's work is done, but few do. Some have tried fishing from the causeway but the fishing is not good. Maybe because the work has muddied the waters on either side. Many of Ebeye's fishermen talk about this, making guesses. Some shake their heads doubtfully and cluck their tongues.

The Marshallese people are ruining the islands, the Americans say. It is not clear, though, what the Americans want the Marshallese to do. Go away?

While waiting for the Filipino dynamite men to set their charges, Jeton and the others sit on rocks and share a cigarette.

Elbo, the man with the hardhat, who is old enough to be Jeton's father, makes a joke as he surveys the clouds that are gathering. "Jeton, you bring soap for the shower?"

Jeton can hardly keep from nodding off, perched on a flat boulder that is almost too hot in the sun, waves and wind loud in his ears. It is *bwiltōñtōñ*, the hottest part of the day.

One of the men gets up to *raut*, piss, turning his back and then letting the wind carry his trickle past him.

Jeton has not been sleeping well. He has been thinking too much about living with Nora on Wotje, where the breadfruit is mature and the abundant coconuts go to waste and the teeming waters are untouched by fishing nets.

On the day they got in trouble—it was after his soccer game—Nora smelled sweetly of soap, her dark wavy hair still wet from the shower. Jeton smelled of the game. He had tried to wash himself at the water fountain near the field. Nora said she liked his smell.

They talked in whispers. Her parents always were upstairs, watching cable TV in bed. *Watching porn!* Nora joked. *That's why they don't come out.* So he and Nora were alone on the darkened patio, its green plastic corrugated roof burdened with flowering vines, its redwood fence obscured by miniature stands of bamboo.

Shivering at Nora's cool touch under his shirt, Jeton's nipples went hard.

Her tongue played with his. He wanted to drink her down

like milk from a coconut. He said, "I want you, babe, can you feel that?"

She smiled hungrily: "I can feel you, my man. Go down on me?"

And he was there, on his knees, tugging at her shorts, caressing her thighs.

The smell of her reminded him of sunlight on tidepools. He tongued her salty sweetness—it seemed he could never go deep enough—until she pulled him up, took hold of him, teased him and he had to bite his lower lip to keep from groaning. Then, at last, both of them collapsed onto the chaise longue and he was inside of her.

She tried to share the music she was listening to, giving him one of her earbuds, but he didn't care about the music. Even though *ri-Majel* teens listen to hip hop, the *ri-pālle* beat feels wrong, too deep and hollow. The *ri-Majel* beat is lighter—it comes from chants and church. It does not have all that bass, all those drums.

So he let the bud fall from his ear. The music seemed to transport Nora, her eyes closed, her head nodding to the pounding.

His toes braced against the chaise arm, he was pushing slowly the way she taught him, making it last.

"That's good," she coached, the noise—boom-chacka-boom—pulsing from the earbud that dangled between them. "You are the best, Jeton."

Hoarsely, he said, "Yes, babe." Make it last.

Warm rain begins in a steady pour.

"Hey, Jeton, you wish you was a kiddy again, don't you?" Elbo says.

Jeton turns to study the old man's yellowed eyes, his bushy graying mustache, his half-toothless mouth. For "kiddy" Elbo has used the word *kaerer* to suggest a spoiled child. A momma's boy.

"Yeah," Jeton says. "Anything would be better than spending time with a venereal disease like you."

The others cluck their tongues. Someone says, "*Ōkkōk!*" Ouch!

Elbo smiles to reveal his single gold tooth in a nest of four brown ones. "Jeton is a real man, eh? Like *ṇaṇ!*" Like dick stink.

A few men snicker.

The rain has created a puddle where they crouch. Jeton wipes his face to clear the water from his eyes. He glances to the reef where the dynamite men are. How much do they get paid for blowing holes in rock?

Elbo is puckering his lips at Jeton. Even from this distance, and even in the rain, the old man reeks of beer. He is a *ri-kōṃṃan kōjak.* What Americans call a "clown."

Jeton says, "Cover your ears, old man. They are going to blast again."

Elbo and the others turn to the reef where the Filipinos have laid a wire out to the blast site. One of the Filipinos holds the detonator in his hand like a cell phone. Then, without warning, the rock ignites with a head-jarring Ba-RUMPF! Suddenly gravel is raining over them and the wet air stinks of seared coral.

The Filipinos gather their things without looking at Jeton or the others, and then Mike drives them back to the end of the causeway.

"*Kūbwe!*" Elbo calls after them. Pile of shit! When he shouts this again, his too-small hardhat falls off his head and shatters against a rock. This makes the men laugh. Elbo kicks the pieces away, then he laughs too.

By lunch time, the rain has stopped and the sun is burning. The other men walk to the pier where there are restaurants. Jeton stays behind, hoping that Mike will invite him out but Mike has not returned from his last dump—and it doesn't look like he will return any time soon. So Jeton goes home.

He is surprised to find his *maṃa* there, making stir-fry on her two-burner propane stove. She is a short woman with thick arms and a small, round face, her long graying hair bound in a knot at the back of her head. She wears her green flowered work dress, one of three she owns.

"I hear you got a job." The way she says this, he knows she is angry.

"Cousin Mike helped," he says. "I need money."

"Father Joe says you did not tell him." Mister Joe is her priest.

"He is not *my* father." Jeton watches her chopping cabbage with a big knife.

She works fast—chop, chop, chop—cutting this way, then that, then flicking the pieces into her oiled pan. Her kitchen has a single faucet over a plastic basin that empties under the house, a small plastic table with two plastic stools, a counter of chipboard balanced across two stacks of cinderblock, and a single shelf above that to hold cooking oil, soy sauce, salt, flour, and pepper. The chicken-wire window next to the table opens to the neighbor's green plastic corrugated wall, two feet away.

This is Jeton's favorite room because of the savory cooking smells and the many memories he has of his mother making meals for him and his brothers and sisters.

She takes an onion from the straw bag on the floor. "Were you going to tell me, your ṃaṃa?"

"I have been busy. Look at my hands." He holds them out for her inspection. She glances up, pausing only a moment before cutting into the onion.

"This is a good thing, your bloody hands?"

"It is hard work," he says. He waves away a cloud of flies that hovers over his mother's cutting.

"School learning is hard work too," she says. "If you want a job, you can go to the soap factory on Majuro with your father and brother."

"I don't want to work in the soap factory."

"You want to work on the causeway?"

"It is good enough for now."

"When the causeway is done?"

He smiles, knowing that she can see him from the corner of

her eyes. "I can be a senator from Ebeye."

"Men in *kajjokok*! Who are you to speak for Ebeye?"

"I am Jeton DeGroen!" His name is from the days of the Germans—a hundred years ago—and his grandmother is a landowner!

His mother says, "All senators have a high school diploma."

"I will be a new kind of senator."

"*Rijajeḷokjen?*" The ignorant one?

"I will throw the biggest party on Ebeye!"

Everyone knows you have to throw big parties to get elected.

"You have no money."

"*Būbū* has money."

"Your grandmother will not waste her money to feed a little fish like you." Onions never make her cry but they are smarting Jeton's eyes. "You get your diploma," she says. Chop, chop, chop. "Then you can talk big." She shakes her head sadly and clucks her tongue.

Jeton sits at one of the stools, flicks a *juwapin*, cockroach, from the table, then rests his chin in his aching hands. His mother does not know that he has a *ri-pālle* girlfriend. If she did she would be *bwiḷok mejān*. Embarrassed.

He watches her open a can of SPAM. She dumps out the contents, then stirs it into her pan. The salty-sweet aroma makes his mouth water.

Here are Betra and Samson, shouting their greetings, home for lunch. Ten-year-old Betra wears a bright pink flowered dress, her black hair pulled back with a plastic clip. Like Samson, she is barefoot. Apparently Samson has lost his T-shirt again. He wears only his shorts.

"Yi! What happened to your shirt?" Jeton asks.

Their mother turns with a stern look. *El jab mejān ettōñ.*

"He threw it into the lagoon!" Betra says.

"I was trying to catch a eel."

"Then it sank."

"The eel or the shirt?" Jeton asks

"Both!" Samson laughs. Eight years old, he is the baby.

Samson looks like Jeton, people say, a handsome boy. But he is not as smart as Betra. She is wiry and intense, her hair too thin to be pretty, her face too narrow. Their mother hopes that Betra will go to college.

Betra tells them the new *ri-pālle* words she learned at the Catholic grade school: *crown of thorns*.

"What's a thorn?" Samson asks.

"Like this!" Jeton prods Samson all over with a plastic fork. Samson squeals with delight and tries to squirm away.

"Sit," *mama* says.

"Jesus died for our sins," Betra says, so confident, so proud of her knowledge.

"That's right." *Mama* turns a smile to her.

Maybe Betra will make up for the many disappointments *mama* has borne. Jeton is the third of her children who has not stayed in school.

"Jesus was a good man," he says, trying to please her. He releases Samson finally.

"Was he from Majuro?" Samson asks. All the important people are from Majuro, the capital island.

"That is silly," *mama* says. She spoons the stir fry into four plastic bowls.

"He was from farther away," Jeton says.

"All the way from God," Betra says.

"I have not heard of *that* island!" says Samson, laughing again.

Jeton opens two warm cans of cola, which they share. His mother eats standing up, as does Jeton. He blows on his food after every other bite to keep the flies off.

After lunch, their *mama* returns to Kwajalein on the next ferry while Jeton, at her request, walks Betra and Samson to school. Jeton knows that Father Joe will corner him with a lecture if he sees him. So Jeton determines not to be seen.

He walks Betra and Samson only as far as the Baptist grave-yard—its stunning white crosses always make him uneasy—then he waves them off. "You come too," Betra implores. "You will have fun."

Jeton smiles at her. "School is not fun for me."

"We play games in *my* class," Samson says. "That is fun!"

"They will not let me sit in your class, Samson."

"Maybe they will let you sit in my class," Betra says.

"I have already learned what they teach in your class, Betra."

"But you have not learned enough!" she almost whines.

The truth of this strikes him. How can he learn enough?

On his way back to the causeway, Jeton meets cousin Stevie and Lino. They look *poktak*, messy. Their khaki trousers are dirty with splotches of fish blood and silvery smears of fish scales.

"Come with us," Stevie says. "We're going *kuḷab*." Drinking.

Stevie is *jakmeej*, dark-skinned, and shorter than Jeton, has a good belly already, and sideburns, and always wears Rayban sun-glasses. Since dropping out of high school three years ago, he has used his boat to fish deep water. He was able to buy the boat because he got money from his grandmother's Rongelap nuclear fall-out settlement.

"I got no money," Jeton says.

Lino says, "I thought you were working the causeway."

Lino is broad-chested and a head taller than Jeton and Ste-vie. His grandfather was Hawaiian, he claims. Stevie lets Lino help him fish because Lino is good at pulling nets and gaffing.

"They haven't paid me yet," Jeton says.

"The causeway sucks," Lino says. He is wearing an orange and black baseball cap that says, "Baltimore Orioles," which must be a brand of beer, Jeton decides.

Stevie exhales a stream of smoke, then French-inhales the way the Chinese sailors taught him on Majuro. "We got money."

He pulls out a roll of twenties, then glances mischievously at Jeton over his Raybans.

"Where'd you get that?" Jeton gasps.

"We caught a marlin."

"Nobody catches *ḷōjkaan* any more."

"We did!"

"Took us four hours," Stevie says. "This morning two miles off Pikeej."

"The *ḷōjkaan* are almost died off, everyone says so. Where is this big fish?"

"We sold it, man, what do you think?" Lino says.

"Some Japanese guy. Right off the pier. He took it to Majuro."

"He's gonna put it on ice and fly it to Japan."

"He paid us cash. Hundreds."

At the Lucky Star, Stevie orders fancy Japanese bottled beer and French fries with mayonnaise and double-cheese nachos. They sit at a table near the video games and play the latest Majuro disco on the CD jukebox. One of the most popular songs right now is about *kilaba*, suicide. The singer repeats an old saying: "*Ne ri-Majel rej kilaba, rej kālọk jān ni.*" When *ri-Majel* people commit suicide, they jump off coconut trees. He is telling young people not to kill themselves. Some say the high number of suicides is a national problem.

Father Joe has taught Jeton that suicide is a "mortal sin." *Jeṛọwiwiin mej.* A very bad thing. "That's only if you believe in heaven," someone joked.

Jeton knew a boy last year who hanged himself because he felt too shamed for having slapped his mother during an argument.

"*Jān ni,*" the singer repeats. "*Jān ni.*"

Off coconut trees

Off coconut trees. . . .

After their third beer, Lino tells Jeton and Stevie about his two *kōrā*, girlfriends. One of them is fifteen years old, the other is twenty-seven. Then he shows off his love scars, purple welts from cigarette burns on his left hand—seven of them in a neat half circle. The newest one is a pus-filled blister.

This is something that Nora will not let Jeton do, burn himself when he is about to come. The burning is supposed to make you come really good. "Why should you advertise to the world your sex life?" she said. "It's childish and boastful. And it's disrespectful of your loved one." Jeton could only shrug and say that it is something that many of the young men do proudly.

Jeton sees Lino glance dismissively at Jeton's unscarred hands. But Lino says nothing.

Stevie says, "At the dock we met a *ri-pālle* who says he's wants to build up our islands."

"His company will pay us a hundred fifty million dollars," Lino adds.

"Us?"

"The Republic. *Ri-Majel.*"

"A hundred fifty million every year," Stevie says.

Jeton waves him away. "Everybody has heard of that," he says. "The Americans want to bring their rubber tires and *kwōpej*, garbage, here."

"*Landfill*," Lino says. "It will raise the islands."

"It will raise a stink," Jeton says. "Who wants to live on garbage?"

"We already live on garbage!" Stevie says. "Why not get paid for it?"

"Who was this man you met?"

"He wants to talk to landowners—like your *būbū*. He wants them to sign a paper. Then the President and the Nitijela will have to listen."

"He wants to talk to *me*?" Jeton asks. An American businessman wanting to talk to him—this would be something Nora might respect. "Did he ask for me by name?"

"I told him about you," Stevie says. "About your grandmother who owns part of Kwajalein."

"Also part of *Bok* and *Maaj*," Jeton adds eagerly.

"He says tires can make new reefs," says Lino. "Increase fishing."

"Who gets to live on the land the garbage makes?" Jeton asks.

He imagines an island of his own, something high and well protected from storm waves.

"I don't know." Stevie fingers cheese dip from the nacho plate. "I have seen pictures of landfill in the States. It looks *lukwi*, real."

"They pack it down under sand," Lino says knowingly.

"When have you seen landfill?" Jeton asks.

"The causeway is landfill," he says with a smirk.

This makes Jeton feel stupid. Quickly he says, "But it's not garbage, it's rock. I should know, I dynamite the rock."

"You dynamite the rock?" Stevie asks.

Jeton nods. "That is my job now. We lay down sticks of dynamite, then we blow them up."

Lino purses his lips at the mouth of his empty beer bottle, then blows, making a low mocking note. "How do you blow them up?"

"With a—detonator." Jeton is relieved that he remembers the name of the thing. "It is the size of a cell phone. You push a button. Then boom!"

"I want to see this," Stevie says. "Show us how you do this." He is peering at him skeptically over his Raybans.

"I am not going to work right now," Jeton says. "I am going to see this *ri-pālle*. What is his name?"

"It begins with a 'D,'" says Lino. "He is at Bella Vista."

"Can you spell his name?"

"I don't need to spell his name," says Lino. "I'm not going to see him, you are."

As Jeton leaves them, he says, "Come by tomorrow, fishermen, and I will blow up the fucking causeway—just for your pleasure."

"Yes, cousin. That will be *rippa*!" Stevie laughs, using the Japanese word for "splendid."

Lino laughs with him.

Relaxed from his three beers, Jeton laughs too.

SIX

With trembling fingers, Alison dials Gayla. She steps away from Stan and Doug into the shade of a nearby palm. When Alison arrived on Kwajalein, she vowed she would not use a cell phone. It was just too stupid an idea. The island is three miles long and a quarter mile wide. But here she is, just like everybody else, cell in hand and happy for the convenience. Stan and Doug watch her cautiously. The woozy swim of Ali's head could be remnants of her last rum buzz or it could be fear. Probably both. *This can't be happening!*

Alison got the day wrong. Doug's birthday is today, not tomorrow. It's a silly mistake, isn't it? A mistake like this could happen to anybody. It's just silly. So, the cake she ordered won't be ready until tomorrow. And she hasn't gotten the all-important *Death Rangers* video from Emil.

Gayla doesn't answer. Her absence feels like a betrayal. Gayla would have known about Doug's birthday. Gayla would have kept track. Never mind it's not Gayla's job to clean up after her. Alison glances at her cell screen: the party starts in seventy-two minutes. When she turns back to Doug and Stan, she sees that already they know she has fucked up. They are getting used to it. That's why they didn't say anything this morning. Still, they can't hide their disappointment. The sad realization weighs on them almost as heavily as their father's absence.

Alison's better self—her old self—berates her: *You've become so useless, you've practically made them into orphans! And don't start blubbering, it will only make it worse. You want to cause a scene to feed the gossip and make these boys targets at school?* Alison draws herself up, swallows her panic and self-loathing, then turns a brave smile on her boys.

Stan stares up at her skeptically. Doug's eyes are wide with fear.

Her apologetic, pained expression betrays everything, she is sure. *I am so sorry, sweethearts. I would never hurt you intentionally. Never!*

She says, "Okay, we've hit a little snag. But it's going to be fine. Here." She hands the trailer key to Doug. "You and Stan get home and clean up. I've got to pick up the rest of the things."

"What things?" Stan asks.

"The video and the cake, silly!" She tousles his hair, then peck's Doug's salty forehead. "Go on!"

When she sees them pedal off without a backward glance, she swallows a sob. She dials Emil. He answers on the fourth ring.

"It's me," she says. "That video—I need that video now."

"Ali? What's wrong?"

"My son's birthday's today and I need that video."

"Yeah, I got the video. But I've got to step out. I'll put it in an envelope on my office door. Is that okay?"

"Great, wonderful. Thanks, Emil."

"Come see me tomorrow?"

"Sure." She disconnects, then hops onto her bike, a blue mountain bike—another stupid idea. Kwajalein is as flat as an airport. Before stopping at the hospital, she speeds to the island's only bakery, not bothering to lock her bike out front. Inside, it smells of burnt sugar and warming bread. The man behind the counter looks Vietnamese. He' about thirty, smooth-faced, and wearing a T-shirt under his white smock. His hair is swept back in a pompadour, like he's a rockabilly singer.

"I've got to have a cake," she tells him.

He smiles, showing off his pretty teeth. "Sure, we can do you a cake." He pulls out a pad and pencil. "When you want it?"

"Now."

"That's funny." He glances down at his pad, ready to write.

"No, I mean it. I need it now."

He looks up and blinks once. "We close in half hour, ma'am. All we got left is donuts."

His expression has changed. She can see that he doesn't trust her because she must look crazy, as panicked as a cokehead. She hears the banging of empty racks from the kitchen. Somebody in back is singing "Volaré" with a Russian inflection.

"What kind of donuts?" she asks.

"Vanilla custard."

"I'll take them all."

"Eighteen?"

"All of them."

Five minutes later she's dropping her bike in front of the hospital, which isn't much to look at: three stories, sand-colored, it could be a small office building. Heavy bag of donuts in hand, she sprints up the stairwell to Emil's office. Her sweat-soaked shirt clings to her back. The hallways are deserted. As a girl, she liked hospitals. She thought they were exciting like airports, everybody going somewhere. Now they fill her with dread. Going to Emil's office nearly every day for the past two months has been a kind of test, though she's not sure what she's been trying to prove.

Ah, Emil has come through! She yanks at the manila envelope taped to his door and fishes out the *Stone Deaf Death Rangers* DVD. The hottest movie in the world for ten-year-olds. Yes, this will save the day and the kids won't think twice about donuts instead of cake. *Isn't your mom cool—she does it different!*

A sound behind Emil's door—a gasp?—gives her pause. He's in there, she is sure. Fucking somebody else? She can't even think about it. She could dial him now and find out. She does. Silently. Her ears burn. There it goes: his phone plays "Our Day Will Come," the old disco version. She hears it behind the door. It plays and plays. But no answer.

She has told herself that she doesn't care about love, that she's got nothing invested in Emil Timmerman. But this hurts nonetheless. She steps away. *Go on*, she tells herself, *get out of her*e.

The eleven boys from Doug's class—minus Arnold Arnold—have already arrived by the time Alison gets home. Doug and Stan have served all the colas they could find but still don't have enough. They need ice too. And there's no meal. But Alison's got a plan. "Everybody in front of the TV," she says. "We're gonna watch *Stone Deaf Death Rangers*!" She waves the jewel case over their heads.

"No way!" gasps little Todd Hansen.

"I've seen it," big-bellied Billy Baker claims.

"Liar!" Geo Smith blurts. "It's too new."

"It's on pay-per-view," Matt Osterbauer says.

Doug is watching them as if they were on a distant shore and he were drifting away on a solitary ice floe.

"I think," Alison interjects, "it's worth seeing again, even if you've seen it five times. Dudes, it's *Stone Deaf Death Rangers*!"

They clamber onto the couch and spill onto the floor. Alison hands the DVD to Doug, his cheeks flushed with satisfaction that almost brings a smile to his face, though she sees too that he's anxious about his responsibilities as host.

"Be sure to check the outtakes," Alison says. "I've heard they show some slow-motion clips, including the eye-gouge scene."

"Oh, man!"

"The eye-gouge!"

"I've seen it, it's totally gross."

"Liar!"

"Way—there's a clip online you can download."

The movie starts and they fall abruptly silent. The screen shows a blizzard of gray-black static, then a wobbly shot of a movie screen in a dark hall—someone's video of the movie. It's *Stone Deaf Death Rangers* all right. But it's a bootleg!

"It's not the real movie!" Matt Osterbauer says.

"It is the real movie," Alison says, lightheaded with disbelief. "Only it's an *underground* copy."

"Underground?"

Why the fuck did Emil get a bootleg?

"Bootleg," she says. "It's the only copy we could get."

"I can hardly hear it!"

"Turn up the volume."

Stan turns it up. The static hiss is almost as loud as the soundtrack.

"This sucks."

"Give it a chance," Alison pleads. "It's impossible to get this video, boys! You've got a cool bootleg copy!"

"It's illegal to watch!"

"It's okay," says Alison. "The legal stuff doesn't apply out here."

"This sucks."

"Who here has ever seen a bootlegged movie?" she asks. Nobody answers. "That's what I thought. This adds to the excitement, doesn't it?"

"The screen wobbles."

"It sucks!"

"Here, how about some treats?" She hands out the donuts. "These are special birthday pastries."

"They're donuts," says Billy Baker. 'Where's the cake?"

"This is something different!" she says. She dares not look at Doug. "Now, everybody settle in while I get the food."

"What kind of food?"

"The best!" she says. "I'll be back in a minute."

Panicked, her ears ringing, her cheeks burning, she slams out of the trailer without a glance to Doug or Stan. It's still light out, a good hour from sunset, which occurs at 7:00 PM every day all year round. Her scalp tingles, sweat coursing down her face. Food? Fuck! She had this *planned*. For *tomorrow*. It was going to be *great*.

She phones Rosalia.

Rosalia answers on the third ring. "*Diga?*"

"Rosalia, it's me, Alison Danvers, you know that cake I'm supposed to pick up tomorrow?"

"Hi, Alison. Yes, double chocolate velvet."

"Have you made it already?"

"No, like I told you, I make everything fresh the day of. And I can't change the order now."

"Do you have any cakes lying around?"

"I do not understand."

"I need a cake now. This very minute."

"Now? What happened to tomorrow?"

"It's complicated. Do you have a cake I can buy now?"

"I have brownies I made for my family."

"Can I buy them?"

"They are not for sale. Sorry."

"I'll give you fifty dollars."

Rosalia's sudden silence is promising.

"Please, Rosalia. This is an emergency."

"What about tomorrow's cake?"

"I'll still buy that too."

The island's only supermarket, affectionately called Surfway, looks like a holdover from the 1960s, with narrow aisles, limited stock, and two check-out lines near the automated plate-glass doors—the kind that open when you step on the rubber mat on either side. It's a sad class of store you can still find in the States if you drive to the downtrodden ends of smaller cities, where early suburbs never got brighter or better. That's where she and Erik grew up.

Surfway was Alison's first surprise as a newcomer to Kwajalein, it was so eerily familiar. Even now, she finds that walking into the store is like walking into the long disappeared A&P of her own neighborhood, where her mother would shake her head at the browning iceberg lettuce and bruised bananas and wonder aloud if the produce manager wasn't simply buying everything that no other store wanted. "They brag about their sales," she would laugh, "but what good is a cheap price if you're buying bad food?"

Still, she would shop nowhere else.

"Milwaukee has lots of stores!" young Alison would protest.

"Why should I go somewhere else?" her mother asked one afternoon.

"Because this store sucks?"

"Don't use that word."

"Sucks?"

"You're as bad as your siblings."

"Not bad enough to get out of shopping, it looks like." Alison was twelve at the time.

"You have to learn what all this means," her mother said, waving at the shelves of groceries. "How to shop for a bargain."

Everything in her mother's house was a bargain, from the generic sodas in the pantry—brands with names like Sweet-Enuf and Ever-Fresh—to the hand-me-down shoes in the closet Alison shared with Evelyn, her sister. Alison used to dream of the day she would never have to shop for bargains again, when she could spend whatever she wanted, whenever she wanted.

Now, like her mother, she finds great satisfaction in searching out bargains. And she admits to herself that she misses her Saturday nights back in the States, when she watched TV with Erik and the boys and cut out the newspaper coupons, stacks and stacks of them.

The closest thing to a coupon here is Erik's social security checks. Every time Alison deposits one at AmeriBank, she fights back her bitterness because she and Erik came here to climb out of the hole, not dig it deeper. But now, just as in Milwaukee, Alison is only getting by, with nothing in savings. Everything extra goes to paying off the debts they dragged with them from the States.

Food for a crowd of ten-year-olds? The best bet seems to

be microwaveable fried chicken and hush puppies. That should do. The checker in her lane is a Marshallese girl wearing one of the flowered dresses—like some retro 1950s thing—that all the Marshallese girls seem to favor. The plan for Kwajalein is to install more Marshallese in better jobs around the island. But it's been slow in coming. Just last year, Kwaj high school admitted two Marshallese boys from Ebeye on "scholarship." Sons of Marshallese royalty, Alison suspects. She's heard that no Marshallese are allowed to spend the night on Kwajalein.

Ever professional, Rosalia has placed the brownies in a white baker's box, secured with a red ribbon. Alison writes her a check, then absently kisses Rosalia on the cheek. "You're a life saver!"

"Don't forget tomorrow's cake," Rosalia calls after her.

Alison pedals fast. Her sweat-drenched T-shirt feels as heavy as chainmail. The sun is gone but the indigo sky is bright with big clouds. Palm fronds clatter in the breeze, the ocean-salted air fragrant with the aroma of grilling steak. They call this paradise because it's summery and always green. But paradise for Alison was autumn in Milwaukee, the trees bright with change, the air as crisp as a cold apple. What nobody will admit is that long summers wear on you just as hard as long winters.

When Alison skids to a stop in front of her trailer, hops off with her bags and box, she hears no laughter from inside. In fact, she hears nothing. *Please*, she prays, p*lease give me this one and I'll pay you back big time—anything you want!* She's about to open the door, when Matt Osterbauer walks out, nearly knocking her into the giant jade plant beside the steps.

He says, "Good night, Mrs. Danvers."

"Don't you want some fried chicken and brownies?" she asks.

"I gotta go." He doesn't even look at her.

Inside, she finds Stan and Doug sitting on the couch. Nobody else. The movie is still playing but something's wrong with it. There's no picture, only the bad sound.

"Somebody nearly caught the bootleg guy," Stan explains.

"So he's hiding the camera."

Alison bites her lower lip until she tastes the coppery tang of her own blood. "How long has he been hiding the camera?"

Stan shrugs. "A long time. We started taking bets on when he'd show the picture again. But everybody got tired and went home."

Alison tilts her head towards Doug, who won't look at her. He appears catatonic. She says, "Look what I got—fried chicken and hush puppies and fresh baked brownies!"

"I ate five donuts," Stan says.

Alison kneels to meet Doug's eyes. "Dougy?"

"I'm not hungry," he says. He looks around her to the TV's black screen.

A stake through her heart would feel less painful than Doug's dour, I-am-so-screwed expression.

Someone raps on the door. *Thank god, they've come back!* Alison swings open the door: "Welcome boys!" she nearly shouts. But there is only one boy on the steps: Arnold Arnold, wearing a long-sleeved checked shirt and Bermuda shorts—and black socks with his sandals. Why would a mother force a boy to wear socks with his sandals? He's not a bad-looking kid, really, those small ears, that firm chin. Okay, his eyes are little wide-set and his pale skin, always reeking of sunscreen, nearly glows. And it doesn't help that he's got two first names.

He says, "Am I late?"

"No, Arnold, you're right on time."

SEVEN

When Cooper learns that his operation was an AKA (above-knee amputation), he wants to make a joke out of it, something to do with an alias, but nothing clever comes to him. He worries that the drugs have dulled his mind. So he recites the numbers he has learned recently:

He's taking 5-6 Tylox a day.

He has 121 stitches.

Which the surgeon will remove in 24 days.

Today is his 5th day in the hospital's acute care unit.

He will spend then next 14-21 days learning how to walk on crutches.

The only other patient here is a 26-year-old programmer who had the misfortune to step on a stone fish that injected the sole of his left foot with 4 poisonous dorsal spines.

Kwajalein is 3.5 miles long, 1/4 mile wide.

There are 2,145 people here.

26 of them are Army, not counting the sailors on the cutter patrol crew.

There are over 13,000 Marshallese living on Ebeye, half a mile away.

Ebeye is 2 miles long, 1/5 mile wide.

Crutch work will demand 60-120% more energy than normal walking.

He will be on crutches for 30-60 days, depending on his progress.

After he receives his measurements for a prosthesis, it will take the orthotist 10-15 days to make his custom plastic leg.

"You must be pretty coordinated to sail a boat all by yourself, right?" Dr. Boxer asked hopefully.

Everywhere he's been in the hospital, people have told him that he is brave and resourceful and that he will do well in rehab. The island's paper, "The Timepiece," a desktop-produced, 10-pager that reminds him of high school, did a feature article on him this week. He finds the paper oddly fascinating because it mentions nothing about the outside world: no war in Iraq, no Abu Ghraib investigation, no 9/11 inquiry, no Chinese threat to take back Taiwan. Instead there are little columns of happy chat about doings on the island: Alexander Lark, a resident for twelve years, has just finished carving a sculpture of Smoky the Bear out of a piece of drift wood ten feet high; Marianne Stevens, a resident for two years, is pregnant with her third child; Sam Woods, a resident for eighteen years, will be retiring to Spain's Gold Coast in August. There are two pages of island sports news, about the men's, the women's, the children's, the teens' mountainball league, volleyball league, soccer league, tennis club, scuba club, swim league, and running club.

And there, as front page news, is Cooper himself, sitting in his wheelchair and smiling feebly, looking—he is stunned to realize—like a man who doesn't know where he is. A bedraggled amnesiac. Somehow the photographer got him to wave a thumb's-up at the camera.

"After battling the Pacific for nearly 4,000 miles," the article begins, "brave sailor Cooper Davies was almost to Kwajalein on January 22. Little did he know that a simple fishing accident would change his life forever. . . ."

If he weren't so stoned, the humiliation would make him gag.

Lillian, can you believe this?

Had he made it safely to Kwajalein, if he were now well established in his job, he could call her and she might listen. As it is, he's done nothing but proven her right. He wants to blame Bailey.

From the start, Bailey was a challenge for them both. She was very smart, her teachers agreed, and made good grades without studying, though it wasn't clear which direction her intelligence would take her. She expressed interest in very little beyond vintage folk rock, which she listened to constantly. Lillian was convinced that Bailey had inherited her way with plants because, as with her studies, Bailey succeeded at cultivation with very little effort. "You know why I'm so good with plants?" Bailey joked, "I don't patronize them. I don't coddle them like toy poodles."

Lillian's house contained a potted jungle that took a good two hours to water in a complicated process of staggered schedules and discerning inspections that Cooper didn't even try to comprehend. "You're going to have to learn," Bailey cautioned him one morning early in the relationship while he was waiting for Lillian to return from an errand. "I'll teach you." Trying to be a good sport, he followed Bailey around as she instructed him in the fine points of watering. "This can be your job from now on. Every time you come over, make a test. Like so." She demonstrated by poking her pinky into the soil of a large majolica jardiniere that contained a rubber tree.

Bailey had just turned fourteen, was still fond of wearing her black outfits. She wouldn't be as tall as Lillian but her face would be very much like her mother's, with a sharp nose, pale eyebrows and a baby-doll complexion. A cute kid with some attitude, Bailey would turn out all right, he decided. He was flattered that she had taken him so quickly into her confidence.

Increasingly over the years he had wondered what kind of father he'd be and here, at last, was an opportunity to make good on that prospect. He and Bailey would become best friends—and he'd be very careful about respecting her father's place. He would not get in the way.

"Now, don't tell mom you're in training," Bailey made him promise. "Because that would spoil the surprise. Then, once you've got the hang of it and she sees her plants flourishing, we'll let her know."

That was the plan. But Lillian's plants did not flourish. They started yellowing. "I don't know what's wrong," she would muse with concern. "It seems they're not draining."

When he had a moment alone with Bailey, he said, "What am I doing wrong?"

Bailey only shrugged, music drifting from her earbuds. "I think you're doing the best you can, Cooper."

"But I'm doing everything you showed me!"

"Then maybe it has nothing to do with you." And she glided off to watch TV with the sound off, one of her favorite activities.

It occurred to him, with a surge of dreamy dizziness, that he was being set up. By the time he confirmed this, it was too late.

"*You've been watering my plants*?" Lillian shouted.

"Bailey was teaching me how," he explained, "to surprise you."

"Well, *I've* been watering my plants too!"

He was about to say, *Then you should have noticed that they didn't need watering*, but he thought better of it.

Lillian called the girl into the living room, its many windows gray with morning fog. "Bailey, what the hell did you think you were doing? Take those earbuds out when I'm talking to you."

Looking thoroughly burdened, Bailey complied. "I was trying to help Cooper understand plants," she said simply. "He wanted to help."

"I thought Bailey was in charge of watering the plants," he added, his face burning with humiliation. *That little shit, he would never trust her again.*

"Is that what you told him, Bailey?"

"I showed him as best I could. I didn't expect him to fuck up. You should be more forgiving, mom."

"A third of my plants have root rot—and I've just found white flies on three. We may lose half the house!" she exclaimed.

Bailey leaned toward Cooper conspiratorially and whispered: "Half the house plants, she means," as if she and Cooper were still buddies.

This was what threw him. It wasn't as if Bailey were gloating. She was cavalier and mischievous, true, but malicious? He couldn't be sure. Yet.

His only option was to avoid Bailey as much as possible. If he wasn't at work or with Lillian, he was at the boat. When Bailey showed up at the dock one Saturday afternoon, with her smirky friend Ashley-Jo, he was more than a little nervous. Bailey *had* never visited the boat.

"Your mom's at the greenhouse," he said. He was about to put a final coat of polyurethane on the deck. Brush in hand, he moved to the gangplank to block the girls' entrance. It wouldn't be like Bailey to ask permission to board.

Bailey was in her white phase—white denims, a baggy white T-shirt, white sneakers: she looked almost like she belonged with the boat set. Recently she had cut her hair short-short, what his mother used to call the "Peter Pan" style. She was still listening to her retro folk-rock, even making a pretense of learning to play the guitar. Ashley-Jo was the drummer in her band, Eight Mile High. Which, Bailey explained, was a play on Eminem's "Eight Mile Road," as well as the Byrds' song.

Now a high school sophomore, she claimed she was going to be a landscape architect. Cooper suspected this was an attempt to flatter her parents into the illusion that she was now on the right track. It didn't matter that Bailey showed virtually no interest in landscaping or architecture.

"Can we help?" Bailey asked from the dock.

"No thanks," he answered. "Don't you have music to rehearse or something?"

Ashley-Jo said, "Our bass player's got mono."

She was a wan girl with Medusa-like hair and a perpetually puckered look because she refused to show her buck teeth. Apparently not a fan of the white phase, she was wearing low-rider jeans and a sparkling pink WhiteSnake T-shirt that would have been a tight-fit for an eight-year-old.

It was early December. Cooper had less than a month to prepare for his and Lillian's departure. Lillian said she was close to finding someone to take over the greenhouse: she didn't want to ask her ex. Her planning seemed a little last minute to Cooper. They were both preoccupied, there was so much to do and so there had been less sex—and generally less fun—in the last six months. But that was to be expected. Once they were on the water, the world would be theirs. Bailey had announced that she was going to stay home with her father.

This seemed to depress Lillian. "I'm bummed that Bailey doesn't want to go," she told him one night. He and Lillian were lying on her bed. It was late. He could hear the fog buoy moaning in the distance. He said, "We have to respect her decision, right? And it will be a good thing for her to spend time with her dad, don't you think?"

"He'll spoil her. He'll let her have anything she wants."

Cooper wanted to say, *You really think he'll spoil her anymore than you spoil her?* Instead he said, "She'll miss you terribly, you know that."

"I'm afraid she'll change."

Ch-ch-change. Her stutter betrayed how upset she was.

"It's only six months," he said.

"And half that time on the boat."

B-b-boat.

"Don't make it sound so dreadful, Lil, it'll be an adventure. Don't you want to have an adventure?"

"Not everybody wants an adventure," she said.

"That includes you?"

She shrugged and stared forlornly into the darkened window at the front of the house, which was nothing but windows. She was so beautiful, he wasn't sure he deserved her. He didn't pretend to understand the mother/daughter bond, much less presume to steal Lillian from her daughter. But the attachment was confounding, even upsetting. How could Lillian live her life fully if she surrendered so much of herself to her child's whim?

Bailey and Ashley-Jo watched Cooper for a few minutes as he opened his can of polyurethane. He was determined to ignore them.

"Mom says your little boat isn't safe," Bailey said. "That's why I wasn't invited."

"This is going to be a long, hard trip," Cooper said. "It's not like a party you can be *invited* to."

"Still, you didn't invite me."

"It's not like you wanted to go."

"How do you know if you never asked?"

"Okay, Bailey: do you want to sail halfway across the Pacific in my unsafe little boat and not see land for months on end?"

She smiled. "Sure!"

"Happy now?" he said.

"You bet," she said. "I can skip school for half a year!"

For the briefest moment, he wondered if this was another set-up. Would she raise a stink, claiming that now she should be allowed to go?

He said: "Your mother named this boat, you know."

"It's a stupid name if you ask me."

Ashley-Jo nodded in agreement. "I'd call it Skull Cap."

"Or Dirty Dog."

"Or Death Star!"

"Or Big Bling!"

"Or Hot Pocket!"

"Or Prickly Dick!"

"OR—"

"All right, girls. When you get your own boat you can name it whatever you like."

They giggled, high-fiving each other.

"What I meant," he continued, "is that your mother wouldn't sail in this boat she named herself if she didn't think it safe enough."

"Who says she's going to sail in it?" Bailey asked simply.

Now it's time to stop, he told himself. *The girl is just trying to provoke you.*

"Hasn't she been helping me with the boat," he said. "Didn't she sand these cleats herself?"

"What'd you call them?" Ashley-Jo asked with wide eyes. "Clits?"

"He's nasty, that's what he is," Bailey said with dismay. "You're nasty, Cooper."

"Go home, Bailey."

He turned his back to their giggling, then kneeled beside the polyurethane can. Where was the lid? If he'd been able to record such exchanges, if Lillian could have heard how truly awful Bailey was sometimes, would that have helped? Or would it have disappointed Lillian to see that Cooper allowed—perhaps invited—this?

"If you drown my mother, Cooper, you will go to hell," Bailey said.

Maybe this was all it came down to: a child wanting to protect her mother. That was understandable, wasn't it?

"Ashley-Jo, he's never let me sail in the boat."

A blatant lie. Early on Cooper had asked her plenty and even Lillian had tried to coax Bailey to join them on their afternoon sails. Finally, they stopped asking.

"You've had plenty of opportunities," he said. *Where is that fucking lid?*

"How about now?" she asked.

"I'm busy."

"Just take us around the harbor," she said, sounding truly interested. Perhaps spontaneity made the prospect more attractive. "It's gonna take all of thirty minutes."

She was right, it was an easy trip—like a pony ride in a dirt rink.

"Please," Ashley-Jo pleaded.

"Please, Mister Cooper!" Bailey wheedled.

Here was an opportunity to show her what she was missing—and maybe to impress her with his skill so that, once and for all, she might respect him or, at least, leave him alone.

A pony ride: what could go wrong?

They kept pleading until at last he heaved a sigh, then said, "You'll have to wear life vests."

"Sure!"

"And do everything I say."

"Aye, aye, captain!" The girls saluted.

His ears burning with pride as they gingerly stepped aboard, he handed each a PFD, showed them how to snap in, then set them in the safest seats, in the cockpit. He untied fore and aft, put on his own life vest, started the motor, then wheeled away from the dock, the girls applauding.

"I've never sailed before," Ashely-Jo said.

"It's a great sport." Cooper tried not to sound pompous. "It just takes a little practice."

It was a fair afternoon, overcast but bright, the sun a white glow at 2:00. Wind was no more than 7 knots, hardly a wave in the harbor. Sail traffic was pretty heavy, though, so he'd have to keep an eye out for the weekenders who didn't know the rules. More than a few times he'd barely scraped past some yahoo who hadn't been watching the traffic.

"You haven't really been sailing that long, have you?" Bailey asked.

"I've been on the water all my life," he said.

"But those were tiny boats," said Bailey. "Back in Baltimore harbor."

"The Chesapeake Bay," he said.

"That's, like, six feet deep, right?"

"You can't take any body of water for granted," he said.

"Look, a bird!" Bailey exclaimed, waving to the gull that lit upon the Alberg's bow. "Is that allowed?"

Cooper grinned at her childish wonder. "Why not?"

"Are we gonna see whales out here?" Ashley-Jo asked.

"We'd have to leave the harbor for that," he said. "But, sure, they're out there."

"Let's do it!" Bailey said.

"Not today."

With only the mainsail up, they were going slowly. He tacked to the starboard to steer clear of a cabin cruiser that was lolling ahead.

"C'mon!" Ashley-Jo whined. "Let's see a whale!"

"Next week we can all go out, if you'd like, and I promise we'll see a whale." This was more like it, he thought: maybe he could calm Bailey down with a few excursions before he and Lillian left. And then their absence would make the girl's heart grow fonder.

A sudden gust gave the boat a jolt and the girls yelped.

"Just the wind," he said. The canvas snapped as the Alberg plied ahead, heeling a little. The wind had picked up surprisingly fast. "This is the fun part!"

They were now in the middle harbor and he'd have to tack soon to crisscross with the traffic.

"Oops," Bailey said. "That's not good."

Abruptly he looked to her. "What?"

"That can of stuff." Was she almost smiling?

"What stuff?"

"You were using."

"The polyurethane?"

She looked puzzled. "I guess."

"What about it?" he tightened his grip on the wheel.

"It fell over and spilled."

"Spilled?"

"All over," Ashley-Jo added. "Down there." She pointed below, into the cabin behind her.

"Wasn't there a lid on it?" he asked.

"Not now," Bailey said simply.

"Oh, fuck!" he bellowed. A three-quarter-full can of polyurethane emptied into his gorgeous cabin and now polyurethane spilling and sliding every which way? Oh fuck!

He secured the wheel. "Don't move," he told the girls.

He yanked off his life vest, then jumped down into the cabin, took one step and slipped, falling flat on his back and smacking his head against a cushioned seat. His backside was suddenly slick and sticky with polyurethane. He scrambled to right himself, his head screaming with pain. He grabbed for a nearby towel and frantically began to sop up the molasses-like goop. The towel was almost immediately useless—so he tossed it into the sink. Without another towel handy, he decided to use his polo shirt, so he pulled off his half-sopping shirt, then dropped down to his hands and knees as he wiped at the mess.

Bailey screamed.

Oh, shit, now what?

He clambered up to find her at the wheel: they were headed straight for the cabin cruiser.

"What did I say about staying put?" he yelled, though he couldn't be certain whether she had steered them for the cruiser or she was trying to steer them clear of the course they had drifted to.

He leaned into the wheel. People on the cruiser—a potbellied captain and several sports-coated partiers—were shouting and waving them away, as if that were going to help.

The Alberg heeled hard. Cooper didn't have time to start the motor.

"We're gonna die!" Ashley-Jo screamed.

Then she jumped overboard.

What the fuck?

"What are you doing!" he called.

She was flailing now in their wake. "I can't swim!"

Bailey jumped in after her.

Oh, God, what has happened here? How could this go wrong so quickly?

"It's so cold!" Bailey screamed.

"I'm coming round," he shouted. "Don't panic!"

The cruiser was sounding its diesel-powered horn in distress: was it stalled?

Panicked enough for all of them, Cooper pulled up his mainsail so quickly, the line burned his hands. Then he started the motor and maneuvered back around to where the girls were flailing—a startling thirty yards away.

It took so many agonizing minutes to reach them!

"I'm coming," he called. "It's okay, girls. It's all right!"

Ashley-Jo was smacking the waves with her open hands and wailing, taking in water—half -choking, half-spewing.

Cooper cut the engine and glided alongside, tossing a life ring between the girls, which they both ignored. Then he got his dinghy oar and held it out to them, but neither would take it. Finally, he tried to edge the Alberg closer.

By this time the Coast Guard had arrived in their speedy dual-engine stern drive and, through a bullhorn, told Cooper to back away while they fished out the girls. Which they did with impressive precision. They took the girls inside, then one of the officers half-climbed, half-jumped down to Cooper's Alberg to make inquiries. The Guard had already secured the Lickety Split to its big shiny hull.

No doubt everyone in the harbor was gaping at him now.

Dressed in starched whites (Bailey must have liked that) the officer was handsome, a few years younger than Cooper, with sun-bleached brows and a strong chin that Cooper envied.

"How do you know these girls?" he asked. He held a cell phone in one hand. Was he recording this?

"One of them's my fiancée's daughter," he said, shivering now—both from being shirtless and from the adrenalin still surging through his veins. It was all he could do to keep his teeth from chattering.

"The girls claim you *picked them up* at the dock."

"What do you mean picked them up?"

"That's what they said."

"You mean they claim they don't *know me?*"

"They said you were talking explicitly about sexual body parts," he continued matter-of-factly.

"Wait, you mean *clits?*"

"You said it, sir, not me."

"I didn't say that!"

"Beg your pardon, sir, but I just *heard* you."

"You can't be serious."

"The girls say you then invited them to take a sail."

"Okay, let's slow down here a minute. If I was the awful lech they claim, why would they get in a boat with me?"

"I don't know, sir, you tell me."

"Are you suggesting I *kidnapped* them?"

"Why did they jump overboard?"

"I don't *believe* this!" He turned a full circle in frustration, his throat aching with outrage.

"Isn't it a little cool to be without a shirt, sir?"

"Can you see this shit all over my arms? Do you have any idea what these girls have just put me through? I don't fucking believe this!"

"There's no reason to use foul language, sir."

"No, really, I don't believe this."

"I heard you, sir."

"Can I take my boat in or do we have to sit here all day and play twenty questions?"

"You need to curb your anger, sir. I'm just doing my job."

"And letting a couple of giddy teenagers make fools of us all."

"All right, sir, we'll see about that."

The Coast Guard charged him $750 for the rescue.

Later, wrapped in a wool blanket and seated in front of the open stove at home, Bailey claimed that when she said Cooper "picked them up at the dock" she wasn't implying that they were strangers. "It was just a misunderstanding," she said. "Ashley-Jo and I were so . . . overwhelmed from nearly drowning—"

"You were wearing *life vests*!" Cooper wailed.

"Let her finish," Lillian said sternly. She was so angry, he knew he wouldn't be able to talk sense to her.

"We were, like, really upset and Ashley-Jo was spitting up water and the sailors were asking us all kinds of questions like we'd done something wrong but, like, *duh*, we didn't do ANYthing wrong—it's not our fault Cooper didn't know how to sail his crappy little boat!" Bailey started bawling, and Lillian drew her in, the girl's sobs muffled by her mother's embrace.

Once she had put Bailey to bed, Lillian said: "All right, let me hear your side."

"What do you mean my *side*? Is this a contest for the truth?"

She was still wearing her dirty jeans and sweatshirt from the greenhouse, her fingernails black with soil. Desperate for relief and normality again, Cooper wanted to talk about things that mattered: who had she found to babysit the greenhouse? But a conversation like that was a long way off.

As for the afternoon's fiasco, it was entirely possible that Bailey popped the lid and pushed the polyurethane into his cabin. Had he even remembered to put the lid on the can? Could the jolt of wind have knocked over that heavy can? All right, he would concede that he should have let the polyurethane spill and slide however and wherever until he got back to the dock. But he thought he'd be down there for only a few minutes. And he couldn't believe that in so short of time they could have gotten that far off course, unless Bailey herself had started fooling with the wheel. That's where he found her, after all. And then to have the girls jumping overboard. How could he be blamed for their mindlessness?

"Clearly," Lillian said, sounding disappointed, "somebody's shown poor judgment today."

"Lil, they wouldn't even grab the life ring!"

"They were scared to death, Cooper! They could have drowned!"

"They were wearing life vests in the middle of the fucking Half Moon Bay Harbor! THEY WOULD NOT HAVE DROWNED!"

She drew back and looked at him as if he were stranger who had just come to her door for a handout. "You don't have to shout."

Near tears, he explained that he had tried in every way to befriend Bailey, to give the girl every benefit of every reasonable doubt, and yet time and time again Bailey made a fool of him. And always—always—Lillian took her daughter's side.

Shaking her head sadly, Lillian said, "You don't know what it is to be a mother."

"You don't know what it is to be a step-father!" he said.

With that, he stormed out. He slept on the boat for three nights. When he phoned Lillian finally, she said they'd have to postpone the trip, things were too unsettled. *Things? What things?* He warned her that, with or without her, he'd have to leave at the end of the month. In the end, he did just that, feeling sorry for himself and hoping that Lillian would regret her decision for the rest of her days.

Inez bustles in, raises the blinds noisily, then says, "Massachusetts has made gay marriage legal!"

"That's good news, isn't it?" Cooper says.

"Oh, yeah. Me and my partner are moving to Mass when I get out of here!"

"Oh?" he says. "Good for you!"

She starts humming, strides over to his bed, then dips a thermometer into his mouth. "But I'm not out of here yet." She waits, glances at her wrist watch. "Neither are you, buddy."

He wants to tell her that he likes good news and that he wishes her well. The glass thermometer hurts under his tongue.

"A conviction has come in on the Abu Ghraib case," she says, "the first of many court-martials, it sounds like, but you and I know that nobody big is gonna get burned. The bigshots never do." She pulls out the thermometer and studies it. "When I was a girl I never thought I'd grow up to be so cynical. I just don't trust anybody any more. Isn't that tragic?"

She hands him a paper cup of pills.

He takes the cup. "Yeah, growing up can be tough." He downs the pills with a single gulp of water.

"You've become a dopehead," she says. "Kicking the habit ain't gonna be easy."

Her eyes are magnified behind the too-big lenses of her glasses. Cooper thinks of a dour-faced grouper gaping at him from behind the glass wall of an aquarium.

He smiles. "I don't hear much sympathy, nurse."

"I don't baby my patients, Mr. Davies. You'll thank me later."

The pain, when it comes, is like an intense flame that flares through his bones from the tip of his missing toes to the base of his skull. That's the damnable thing about it, the searing pain in his long-gone limb.

"Inez, you can call me Cooper."

She all but rolls her eyes at this. "One other thing we should get straight—and I don't mean that as a pun," she says. "You're not allowed to fall in love with me."

"I wouldn't think of it, Nurse Inez!"

She nods her head skeptically. "You make a joke of it now," she says, "but later, you won't be laughing."

* * * *

Fuck this. Bedridden for the past three days, and growing weaker by the hour, Art has put off going to the hospital for as long as he could. It's a humbling, infuriating defeat to submit himself finally to the American medical establishment. But what choice does he have? He has tried every form of sustenance, from tepid oatmeal to distilled water, and none of it stays inside him for longer than five minutes. His colon is a raging coil of fire; his asshole bleeds from the abuse. Ever since his visit to Ebeye, he has been shitting almost without pause. His only relief is to eat and drink nothing. And now he is dehydrated, his skin sagging from his bones, his head a Saharan sand storm of near-delirium, his stomach distended like a malnourished child's. He had to cancel his weekend flight home to Jaluit. On the phone Jinna scolded him: "Baka-fool, you want to die? Get to the hospital! Go, now!"

She could be with him on Kwajalein. She and the children. It can't happen now, not anymore, but it could have happened years ago. As a government employee, he was entitled to housing. He and Jinna could have had one of the trailers in "Silver City," with a fenced-in patio and a Weber grill and tiki lights and candy-colored Japanese lanterns. They could have sent their kids to the Kwaj school, where they would have enjoyed an excellent education with top-notch DOD-contracted teachers. He could have brought home the wonderful—and fresh, not frozen—food you can buy at the Surfway at subsidized prices: ribeye, salmon, apricots, even watermelon. (What must it cost to airfreight a pallet of watermelons from Maui?) But Art insisted they live on Jaluit, 350 miles south—a hotter, wetter, place and so frigging remote that no *ri-pālle* go there except when a freighter docks to drop supplies.

Years ago Jinna asked him, "You think life on Jaluit is better than life on Kwajelein? You think what we have on Jaluit is something pure and holy?" The moment she said it, he knew that this was precisely what he had thought. It is pure in its way—their intermittent electricity, the mouse-sized cockroaches in the cracks of their cinderblock walls, their glassless windows and rotting wooden shutters, their perpetually mildewed bathroom, their algae-flavored water from the cistern on their roof. "Living like this, we are closer to what is real," he tried to explain. But Jinna just threw up her hands and walked away to breast feed Amon in the green shade of their porch. And never again did she try to talk sense to him about the American way of life, which she and her people envy so avidly.

Amon is now 24. Art isn't sure if Amon has ever forgiven his distraction, his inability to commit fully as a family man. The boy moved to Honolulu as soon as he could and already has fathered three children by two women. Unable to support them, despite working overtime on weekends, he seems as feckless as Art, which pains Art to no end.

When Art came to the Marshalls 30 years ago as a Trust Territory teacher, there was no air conditioning, no TV, no jet service to Honolulu, no fresh milk. Frozen meat was flown in once every two weeks. And milk came frozen in cans, like lemonade. That's what Art was seeking: certain limits. Even now, when he flies to Jaluit and watches the sandbars, islets, and coral rims passing below, it all seems so tentative. In fact, islets appear and disappear frequently: a lone coconut palm on a hump of sand, a tuft of grass, and there you have it, an ecosystem, a beginning. This he finds comforting.

Before joining the Peace Corps, he had been working as a middle school social studies teacher in Winston-Salem, North Carolina, an old tobacco town that seemed frozen circa 1960. The Vietnam war had just ended. Congress was impeaching Nixon. There was plenty to talk about in his social studies class but Art couldn't muster enthusiasm for it because so much had gone wrong in so short a time. He might have been more optimistic had he been younger. But already he was 30 and that seemed old to him. When he tried to explain to his students how America was making corrections—"That's the great thing about the U.S.," he'd say, "we can admit our mistakes!"—he felt like a propagandist. Now and then a sharp seventh grader would ask, "What's to keep us from starting another Vietnam?" or "Why did it take so long to desegregate?" or "How can we be sure we get a honest president?"

Art came to Jaluit in 1980, after serving six years on the smaller atolls of Namu and Arno. Although he had quit the Corps and was fluent in Marshallese by this time, he remained a patronized outsider. The *ri-Majel* were too damned polite. Whenever he made a mistake—an inadvertent gesture of his hand offended an elder or a slip of his tongue made him say "shit" instead of "shell"—nobody would correct him. Which meant they would not let him in. Desperately he wanted to be on the inside of something that mattered. The *ri-Majel* mattered because for over two hundred years they had been exploited and passed from possessor to possessor like a concubine.

Since leaving the States, Art had grown heavy, eating too much white rice, drinking too much beer. He had grown accustomed also to the delayed checks from the Trust Territory Administration and the languid sameness of the equatorial days. His wardrobe had dwindled to a canvas bag of khaki trousers, T-shirts, and flip-flops. Even though he was *lajinono*, an unmarried man, the Marshallese women showed little interest in him because it was clear that he was going nowhere—certainly not to Majuro, much less back to the States.

Heat rash plagued him, fungus warped his toenails, and there was never enough sunscreen to keep his balding head from burning. But, Lord, it was lovely, sunrises like the smiling face of God, nights as quiet as drifting clouds, white sand beaches, icy-sheened topaz lagoons. And the children he taught were beautiful, so kind and humorous, although wholly unambitious.

Jinna herself had managed to get a two-year degree from Guam University, a remarkable accomplishment for a Marshallese woman in those days. She was all but running both the elementary and secondary schools. She was tall for a *ri-Majel* woman, nearly 5'6", and six years his junior, with a broad serious face, pursed lips that gave her a pensive air, as if she were about to impart a secret, and a curtain of black hair that she knotted in a long pony tail. She wore those diaphanous cotton skirts from India and flimsy

T-shirts that advertised major American brands like Clorox and Hanes. Art fell in love with her immediately. She was patient and honest with him. "You *allañ*, stare too hard at women," she told him when they met. "You should be more discreet."

"I'm just trying to be attentive," he said.

"You are too attentive. You should cool it."

He didn't have to try too hard with her. She had already had an American lover, a Peace Corps worker who had just left after a two-year stay in which he had accomplished nothing except to get Jinna pregnant. Art had met the man a couple of years earlier on Arno. Lars Thomas. Jinna called him a "bookish fool." She showed neither remorse nor fear about her predicament because the *ri-Majel* don't acknowledge "illegitimacy." They have no word for "bastard." Art, who wanted to be forgiving and expansive like the *ri-Majel* said, "What the hell," because he decided he couldn't live without her—and he wanted to settle in Jaluit, where he believed he could do some good. So Jinna married him.

The early 1980s were a heady time, the Marshallese had won their independence in 1979 and were about to sign the Compact of Free Association with the U.S. It wouldn't become official until 1986, but already the islands were abuzz with the possibilities. There were petitions that Art signed happily and even some protests—boatloads of Marshallese grounded themselves on the beaches of Kwajalein in 1984 to condemn the Americans' 40-year occupation—a protest Art would have joined had he not been a *ri-pālle*.

So, in the scheme of things, what was marriage to a smart, determined woman who was carrying another man's child? He and Jinna never told Amon about his biological father—the man who ran away as soon as he learned of Jinna's pregnancy. By the time the boy was ten, Art had taken the job as Cultural Liaison on Kwajalein and, in short order, became an absentee father. He kept telling himself that this—teaching the Americans to respect the Marshallese—was the best work he could do. His life's work. Work that helped pay down the huge debt Americans had incurred after they wrested these islands from the Japanese in 1945. To be fair, the islands would have been too big a temptation for any nation, especially since the islanders had long accustomed themselves to submission. So it surprised nobody when the Americans made the *ri-Majel* their menials and used them in all the worst ways, starting with nuclear bomb tests in 1946.

Art has cajoled and argued and cautioned and scolded the Americans for years and accomplished little more than to make himself a crank. Maybe that's what his job was meant to do, turn the advocate into a thoroughly dismissible irritant. Like a mosquito, the pest that so far has not managed to survive in the mid-Pacific. In the end, his job has seemed no more than his passionate and very personal distraction. He's like a homeless man raving in the streets of a cosseted suburb. Maybe that's why Amon dropped out of school when he turned eighteen, then caged a ride to Hono, where he got a job as a concrete finisher. Amon has never come back for a visit. Always Jinna and Art have had to make the long trip east to visit him.

Reap what you sow, Art tells himself. He tried to do better with Emon, then Buster, then Elani, but he admits that he has not been home enough. He has relied too much on Jinna to do the real work. She must resent him for this, though it seems she doesn't. Whenever they fly back from seeing the grandchildren in Hawaii, she weeps and weeps and Art tends to her as if she were mortally wounded, whispering endearments, handing her tissues, stroking her hand, and hating himself for having been a selfish ass.

Elani, their youngest, is now 12. He knows he should quit his thankless job and go home to Jaluit while he has a few years of fathering left to him.

"Why are you so stubborn?" Jinna has asked him again and again.

Lying on his lumpy bed, staring at the choppy sea of his

textured ceiling, his intestines burbling and quaking, he realizes with profound sadness that he has lived a good portion of his adult life at The Transit, Kwajalein's modest hotel, perched on a coral escarpment beside the airport. It has a great view of the ocean. To save money, he subsists on cold cereal and tiny local bananas and canned Thai sardines and white rice, which is always warming in the cooker on his bureau. "Why do you want to ruin yourself?" Jinna scolds. As much money as he tries to save, he can't bring himself to pick up the spare change that falls from his pockets when he takes off his pants every night. It's just too much fucking work. So he leaves it for the maid. After his visits to Jaluit, Jinna sends him back with clean clothes and a bottle of One A Day vitamins and tidy packets of food: eel jerky, rice balls, coconut jelly, baked breadfruit.

Outside, the humidity makes him gasp. You can't get used to it, not when you work in these icy AC'd buildings. Had he gotten his way 20 years ago, he and Jinna would have built a traditional hut in Jaluit, something light and airy, maybe on stilts. But Jinna wasn't about to raise her family in "a weed covered shack," as she put it. So she got a state-of-the-art cinderblock house with a tin roof, the kind of building that was never meant for this climate. Art hated it from day one. Whenever he returns home, he sleeps on a hammock outside.

He pulls his bike from the rack beside the walk. His is the kind nobody bothers stealing: a single-gear American-made piece of shit with fat tires. Government issue. Everybody on Kwaj rides a bike. Only the Colonel and a few hotshots get cars.

It takes Art several tentative steps, a few pushes, then an act of faith to heft himself onto the seat and set off, front wheel wobbling, feet kicking for the pedals. But at last he gets it, rights the bike, picks up speed, thankful that there's no strong wind this morning.

After three minutes of sluggish pedaling, he's "downtown," gliding past a strip of beige-painted concrete buildings erected in the 1950s and '60s. To his left stands the dour contiguous hulk of the department store, the snack bar, the bank, and post office. Even though the snack bar's vinyl-cushioned booths have their appeal and the fry-grill aroma of hash browns and Portuguese sausage makes his mouth water, he seldom stops there anymore. He simply can't stand to listen to the gossip. The raging chatter this week is about the Injured Man, of course. Airlifted by Army Rescue from a distant atoll where, rumor has it:

a) he was nearly eaten by a shark,

b) he was attacked by pirates and left for dead,

c) he wrecked his boat on the reef and mangled his leg crawling to shore,

d) he assaulted a teenaged girl and was nearly hacked to death by her outraged brothers

Art could help the poor sap. He could warn him of his imminent disappointment. Newcomers think this place is paradise because it's all so fucking beautiful. Pick your favorite tropical postcard and the Marshalls will beat it at every turn. The whitest sand, the bluest water, the most colorful reefs, the most spectacular sunken ships. After a few months, though, the newcomers begin to feel an irritating itch. They can't go anywhere because Kwajalein is only a quarter mile wide and 3.5 miles long and so they keep running into the same people day after day and they're jogging from one air conditioned building to the next because the humidity here—seven degrees north of the equator—is like a steam bath's and everything they wear smells mildly of mildew. By the end of their first year, they're convinced they've made a mistake because from this distance, the States look like a neverending carnival. And they're stuck out here, 4500 miles west of California. So, when their time is up (the usual Tour-Of-Duty is two years) most people can't get away fast enough.

You can't hide out here, that's the problem. Stay inside if you like, watch satellite TV and play video games in your free time, your neighbors will know all about you: when you leave the house, when you return, who you call a friend, who you avoid. It doesn't help that Kwaj phone lines are tapped by Army OPSEC: Operations Security, whose mission "is the protection of military operations and activities from intelligence indicators (our vulnerabilities) which are susceptible to hostile exploitation." Of the 2500 civilians on the island, maybe 20 are military in uniform. There are probably many more out of uniform, disguised as computer techs and administrative assistants. This is a top secret installation. You can't even get on the island unless your life has been strip- searched by OPSEC. So there's this creepy overlay of scrutiny that nobody talks about.

As Art dismounts beside the hospital's bike rack, he can't quite clear his right leg. His foot hits the bike's seat. Then together he and the bike fall backwards. Surging through his gut he feels that slow-motion fear imported from dreams where he has told himself, *This isn't really happening.* And lightning fast he's making secret trades: *I'll take a broken leg but not a broken back. Or a wrenched back but not a fractured thigh.* But he hasn't toppled a foot when the trunk of a palm tree stops him like a firm hand. It smarts enough to bring tears to his eyes, but he knows he's okay.

He lets the bike drop with a clatter, then leans back into the tree and gulps for air. He imagines himself mouthing like a mudskipper, those little fish that flip from one tide pool to the next and sometimes land on a sun-baked stretch of reef where, bug-eyed, they pucker in a panic, then flip away again. If only Art could get on an exercise schedule—take a vigorous walk every morning—he'd be more capable, he thinks. Maybe he'd even be more effective. But here's the truth he won't admit but feels to his core: he's a burn-out, just like all the burn-outs he wondered at and disdained as a younger man. His one hope is that there's enough left of him—something solid deep inside this charred crust—to fight the big battle that is coming. Soon something terrible will happen. He feels it in his bones. Nothing's getting better, especially among the young in this very young Republic, where sixty percent of the population is under the age of 20 and unemployment is stalled at 30% or worse. Marshallese lawsuits for nuclear bombing reparations have not gone well. The bombed generation is dying of leukemia and thyroid cancer at unprecedented rates. The *ri-Majel* have the highest incidence of diabetes in the world. And one of the highest rates of suicide. Knifings are common. Plenty of fist fights. Motorbike and boating mishaps. Nearly all of these are alcohol related. Thankfully, there are no guns here yet.

Americans think the Marshallese will harm only themselves, but it won't be long before they try to hurt Americans too. Which is just another way of hurting themselves. Now hopped up with 9/11 paranoia, the U.S. Army is trigger-happy and impatient and American civilians seem to have lost compassion for "native" concerns. Altogether it's a very bad mix. This is why Art stays. This is why he's on watch every day

With a shudder, he limps into the hospital, the great white whale of American medicine.

"I am dehydrated," he says to the nurse at the desk. "I think I have a parasite—some little blob backstroking through my bloodstream!"

"Oh, my," the nurse says, "that won't do." She hands him the forms to fill out.

His hand trembles as he writes. It infuriates him that this has interrupted his work. Not that anyone expects anything from him. No one calls to check. No one stops by to chat. If he didn't venture out on his own, he would be sitting alone in his air-conditioned office on the second floor of the air terminal, waiting for the one or two days a year when the Colonel asks him to host a visiting "islander."

"Can you keep anything down?" the nurse asks him.

"Not a god damned thing," he says.

"Let me put in a call. You'll probably need an IV." Her smile is like a pat on the hand. Then she's gone in a wake of honeysuckle perfume. Or is it plumeria?

EIGHT

Alison and Arnold and Stan sit on the couch, watching the bootleg video and eating Rosalia Valesquez's brownies. The last seven minutes and thirty-three seconds of *The Stone Deaf Death Rangers* reappears on the screen as the bootlegger takes his camera from his coat, apparently in the clear now. "This guy can't even hold his camera straight," Stan says.

"One of the Rangers is missing," says Arnold. "Did he get killed?"

"It was hard to keep track without the picture," says Alison. "But I don't think any of the rangers gets killed."

"That's Hollywood for you," says Stan.

"Doug, you're missing it!" Alison calls.

Doug doesn't answer. Alison takes him a brownie. He's in bed already, staring up at the bottom of his brother's bunk. Alison kneels and lays a hand across his cool forehead. "Sweetie, are you all right?"

"Sure."

"It didn't turn out so well," she says. "I'm sorry. I made a mistake—I had it all planned for tomorrow. Wait till you see your cake."

"Thanks," he says.

She watches him staring up at the fretwork of the mattress springs. "You ever going to forgive me, sweetie?"

"That DVD sucks," he says. "Everybody's gonna make fun of me."

"It's a *bootleg*," she says. "I guess it's not to everyone's taste. Arnold seems to like it."

"Arnold's a loser. And now so am I."

"*I'm* the loser, Doug. You tell them that."

Doug sighs, his eyes closed. "Mom, you need a shower."

Alison pulls back, hurt by his frankness. "You're right. It's been a long day. I'll put this here." She sets the brownie next to a pile of action figures on his bureau. Then she retreats, stifling a sob as she draws his door shut.

"Mom," Stan calls. "Arnold's ready to go home. He says he's not supposed to eat this much chocolate."

"It's a party," she says, grateful to find her voice. "He should treat himself."

"I don't think so," says Stan. "He just puked all over the rug."

"What's wrong?" Alison rushes into the TV room. Arnold is retching over the arm of the couch.

Stan stares with mild interest at Arnold. "It's the walnuts. He's allergic."

"I thought it was *peanuts*!" Alison says.

Arnold rights himself, then wipes his mouth, his face nearly gray. He says, "Sometimes walnuts too."

"There are lots in the brownies," says Stan.

"Oh my god!"

Fourteen minutes later, Alison and Arnold are at the hospital.

"What a little soldier you are!" she says, trying not to yank him by his narrow wrist into the ER, where a nurse is waiting.

Arnold peers up at her in his innocuous buglike manner: "Soldier?"

Is it her imagination or is the boy getting loose in the joints and dopey?

A "taxi," one of the island's fare-free air-conditioned mini-vans, has brought them quickly to the hospital. It happened to be passing as Alison led Arnold into Pacific Avenue to wait for the ambulance, so she flagged down the van and, without letting her voice break, told the driver the emergency.

Here comes the empty ambulance now, red strobes flashing

but no siren. She and Arnold have just stepped inside, the darkness behind them like a blanket.

"I mean brave," she explains. "You're doing so well staying calm like this."

Arnold's smile is a harbinger of hopelessness. Then he says, "Can I come over and watch the rest of the movie sometime?"

"Of course, dear."

The red strobe pulses through the ER doors and past them like a persistent knock.

The nurse, "Inez," a bland-faced woman too young to be so stout, says to Arnold: "You come with me, my man. Your mom will sign you in."

Arnold turns to Alison, his expression half-pained with embarrassment—though, it occurs to her, that it could be embarrassment for her, not himself.

She says, "I'll be right behind you, honey."

"How allergic is he?" the registration nurse asks. She could be one of Alison's students. When did the women around her start looking so young? This one's got the teen-requisite deep tan, bleached bangs, and pink lipstick.

"I've got to call his mother," Alison says.

This causes the nurse's pale eyebrows to arch in dismayed surprise. "You're *not* his mother?"

"He was at my son's birthday party."

"His mother has to sign the consent forms."

Having forgotten her phone, Alison reaches for the landline on the desk. "I dial '9' to get out?"

Less than a minute later she hears the pickup on the other end: "April?"

"Alison?"

Alison lets it out quickly, as if ripping off a stubborn adhesive bandage. "April, Arnold's okay but we're at the hospital because we think he ate some walnuts."

"Walnuts!"

"He seems fine—the nurse just took him."

April seems to swallow a sob: "Didn't I warn you about nuts?"

"Peanuts, April. That's all you said!"

"I said *nuts*, Alison. You don't *listen!*"

Alison feels her ears burning. Was she high when she spoke to April?

"Can I speak to him?" April croaks. "I have to speak with him!"

"He's back with the nurse." Alison tells herself that she has to go slower, speak more calmly, think of the most diplomatic things to say because April has understandably taken a shortcut to panic.

"Back with the nurse? Are they pumping his stomach? Is he convulsing?"

"I think he's fine, April." Calmly now, as if talking a non-swimmer into deeper water. "Can you come down here?"

"I've got Linde. It's Rod's card night."

"I'll take care of Linde. Just get yourself down here. Wait, the taxi's still here—I'll tell him to swing by. Arnold's going to be fine. He's such a good little soldier about all of this."

"A soldier?"

"You know, brave."

"He could *die*, Alison!"

With that April hangs up. Stunned by this blow to her conscience, Alison nearly staggers down the hall. She is several yards from the nurse's station—her mind crowded with images of Arnold's face, that resigned, helpless smile—when she realizes she's walking the wrong way. Finding her way back to the ER entrance, she discovers the taxi is gone. But the ambulance driver is there, smoking a cigarette beside his white van, parked now and ticking from the heat.

He's a slight man, maybe Filipino, wearing an orange-flowered Hawaiian shirt, baggy shorts, and no socks with his black Nikes. Because he has thick black hair to his shoulders, he looks either her age or twenty years older.

"I need you to pick up that boy's mother," Alison tells him.

He looks ups, exhales smoke from his nostrils, then says, "You the one called the ambulance the first time?"

"The boy could die," she says. "An allergic reaction."

"You're supposed to wait for the ambulance." He shakes his head in disapproval, his big hair swaying.

"His mother has to be here. Please."

He pulls on his cigarette. Unfiltered. "I didn't get a call."

"You want me to go inside and call you?"

Does he almost smile at this? "I'm not a taxi, ma'am."

"You want the boy to die while waiting for his mother?"

"Like you'd blame me. Aren't you the one fed him the peanut?"

Alison watches the driver flick away his cigarette butt with practiced ease.

She feels her face burning but can't decide if it's from rage or shame.

"It was a walnut," she says. Then she tells him April's address. "A mother and her baby. I'd go with you but I've got to stay with the boy."

He stares down at the asphalt, which she can smell, like hot tar and something else. Burning stone.

"I'm *supposed* to get a call," he says.

Now she tries a different tack, this time softly: "What's your name?"

He glances up again, this time turns his head to one side, and gives her a stare, as if to say, *What're you up to?*

At last he says, "Sid."

"Sid. Just do the right thing. We need your help."

He nods his assent. "So get me fired. That's what the right thing will do."

"Please hurry," she says.

"Right," he says. "The boy could die."

She watches him back out, then the strobes flash, and Sid

guns the ambulance. Maybe to show off. Maybe because he believes her urgency.

She has always wanted to be good in an emergency. In her worried thoughts, she has practiced more times than she can count, running through every what-if that might befall her own children, marking escape routes in the trailer, secretly rehearsing CPR and the Heimlich, imagining her fluid competence multi-tasking the family's way to safety: *here, hold this; you, call 911; and you, help me with his arm.* So far her boys have escaped every travail—no broken bones, no stitches, no serious burns, no allergies. How did they get so lucky?

Walking into the ER again is like walking into a freezer, so cold it seems her breath should cloud with each exhalation. The register nurse sends her upstairs.

Alison doesn't wait for the elevator.

The ambulance driver's accusation still smarts. *Aren't you the one fed him the peanut?* She has failed this emergency, failed to be vigilant, failed the good faith of this guileless boy.

But it's ludicrous to think that he could, that he would, die. Isn't it?

When she steps out of the stairwell, she doesn't know which way to turn. She's too impulsive and doesn't listen. Instead she rushes on, eager to get to the place or the person that will make sense of the trouble. When the Colonel phoned to tell her about Erik's "disappearance," she could hardly tolerate the excruciating care he was taking as she stood there in her cramped kitchen and listened to his too-calm voice tell her that "your husband ventured unattended into the Yokiwa, at about 50 feet. Those wrecks are off-limits, as you know, and very dangerous. His scuba club stayed an extra three hours scouting for him around the wreck. Of course no one would go inside—they couldn't afford to lose another one. . . ."

She wanted to interrupt him and say, *Stop. Just stop. Say what you have to say. He's missing? He's gone? Is that what you're saying?*

"...the club stayed until their tanks were empty," the Colonel was telling her. "Then they had to come home without him."

They had to come home without him.

"What does that mean exactly?" she said. "You mean he's still out there? Alone? What is he supposed to do out there alone? How could they just leave him behind? You don't leave *anybody* behind!"

"Alison, it was obvious that he went inside the Yokiwa and did not come out again. I am so sorry."

"Wait."

"I'm sending Gus, his partner, over with the club president right now to sit with you and explain this again. They're on their way."

"Wait," she said. "He went inside the wreck, you said. Nobody goes inside. Why would he go inside?" If she could just backtrack a bit, get the facts in order, then they might figure this out—and realize that Erik didn't disappear inside that old ship, that instead he just got lost, and that he returned to the site to find that everyone had gone. And now he's swimming in circles waiting for a pick up. Is that so unlikely?

The sense of it is like finding the hidden quirk in a puzzle picture, she wanted to explain.

"Sometimes amateur divers don't think straight," the Colonel was saying. "Sometimes they take unnecessary risks. It doesn't take much to make a fatal mistake down there."

"Wait," she said. "*Where was Gus?* Divers never leave their partners. Where was Gus?"

"Gus is coming over to explain, Alison. He was with Erik. But Erik slipped away when Gus's back was turned."

"That's not like Erik. Erik doesn't just slip away." What she was saying, she realizes now, is that Erik wouldn't leave her like that. He wouldn't die so foolishly, so easily.

"I am suspending the club's license because they weren't supposed to be that close to the wreck."

"Why didn't he take Gus with him if he sneaked off?"

"Your guess is as good as mine, Alison. We're all so puzzled and upset by this."

"Why are we sitting here guessing!" she snapped. "Why aren't we out there picking him up!"

"Because he is gone, Alison. He drowned in the Yokiwa."

As those words tumbled into her head, she heard someone at the door. When she opened it, the phone still gripped in the other hand, she saw Gus and, behind him, Janet, his wife, and then, behind them, Netro Sorenson, the Trigger Fish Scuba Club president.

Gus burst into tears when she looked at him. He was barefoot, still wearing his swim trunks, a nylon windbreaker over his T-shirt. He needed a shave and his full face looked chubbier now that he'd been weeping.

Alison was grateful for his unchecked emotions because it allowed her some calm. It allowed her to pretend that everyone had gotten it wrong and that she would have to unravel this mystery by talking sense and carefully questioning each and every one of them the way she would have interrogated a group of troublesome seventh-graders.

"Gus, sit down," she said. "Does anybody want a soda?" She nodded to the fridge. "I'm talking to the Colonel now." She returned to the phone.

"Is that them?" the Colonel asked.

"They're here," she said. "Let me talk with them and I'll get right back to you." It was simple. Like getting between two boys when they fight.

She turned to her visitors. They were standing awkwardly in her small living room. "Watch for the toys," she cautioned. With her foot, she pushed away two action figures, a few CD cases, and a pair of joysticks. "Sit down."

They did as she instructed.

Janet and Netro were watching her cautiously. Gus was still

sobbing, shaking his head in disbelief.

"Gus, dear," Alison said. "Gus."

He looked up finally, tried to blink away his tears, wiped at one eye with the heel of his left hand, then leaned into Janet, who stroked his knee and stared at Alison with a look of embarrassment. She is the Manager at the island's bank and someone Alison had never thought much of one way or the other: a tough-looking woman with bright red hair and the implacable expression of middle-age boredom. Gus is one of the island's trainers. He works at the rec center, where he appears to be growing fat.

Netro, sitting next to Janet, had found time to change into his Bermudas and a polo shirt, Alison noticed. She knew almost nothing about him. He appeared to be one of those tall, cool Scandinavian types, even though he was from La Jolla, California. He managed the island's marina, which he ran like a police state, she had heard. Now, in the midst of this sudden confusion, she didn't trust him. He was staring at her like a gull on a pier post.

"Just start from the beginning," she instructed Gus. "When did you last see Erik?"

Gus ran through it haltingly, pausing to catch his breath in mid-sentence again and again, then gulping air as he began to hiccup. He and Erik had been diving partners from the beginning, he said, over eight months now. They had learned to communicate well, even in dark water. And they had made a pact never to stray more than one body-length from each other. "We knew how to be," he swallowed, "careful together."

Alison was surprised at how touching this was, to hear Gus talk of her husband as he might have talked of a loved-one. Erik *is* a good partner, she told herself. He's the one who cooks with reckless joy and he's the one who insists on dancing here and now when a good music video comes on the tube, never mind what the boys say, and he's the one who can get Stan and Doug to quiet down finally when they're ready to strangle one another, he's the one. . . .

"We were at the ship—it wasn't Netro's fault," Gus was saying. "He couldn't stop us—we were just poking around, near the doors at the stern, on the upper deck." Gus rubbed his left eye, sucked in some air, something seemed to catch in his throat, but then it let him go and he continued: "We hadn't decided anything, we hadn't made any signals to do anything. We aren't stupid. We were just poking around. But then—"

Here it is, Alison was thinking. This is the cipher that she will decode.

"Then I got distracted. There's this conning tower or what looks like a conning tower, overgrown now, hard to see what all was on it. I drifted to it. I think I drifted up a good ways." Here Gus paused gravely, staring beyond her to his memory. "When I turned around Erik was gone."

"How far away was he, Gus?"

"He'd been maybe three yards. But then from where I turned around it seemed farther. Maybe ten yards. Still not that far. But I couldn't see him. I couldn't see him anywhere in my field."

"Could he have fallen inside?" Alison asked. Only now did it occur to her what this would mean. She had been so focused first on finding him, as if that would guarantee his safety. But now to find him meant something else.

"There were no signs of that, none at all," Gus said.

"We scoured the site," Netro said. "Top to bottom and back again."

Alison wouldn't look at him because Netro wasn't the one who had lost Erik—he wasn't the last one to have seen him.

"We looked until every tank was empty," Gus said, his voice wavering. "We saw an open door. But we couldn't go in."

"How open?"

"Open enough," said Gus. "You don't know what it's like inside one of those things."

"And you do?" she asked.

"We have training films," Netro said. "Top notch divers have filmed these interiors.'"

"You can't see anything inside," Gus said. "Nothing! You get disoriented in minutes, and those ships—" his voice stalled "—they're mazes, black silty mazes...." Finally, like a surge of revulsion, grief spilled out of him again and he was bawling.

But wait, Alison wanted to say, Erik could have been a math teacher, Erik is good at mazes. Nobody has better spatial acuity. One glance and he knows the size of a window, a shoe, a glove. Erik's not the one to get lost.

Not Erik.

"What can we do for you?" Netro asked.

She looked at him finally and there she saw it in his dark gull eyes, a confirmation of the fact she had not accepted yet: Erik was gone. Erik was not coming back. Erik was dead.

This realization came upon her so quickly, she was breathless—the kind of thrilling horror she might have felt had she jumped off a cliff. Half rising from the couch, Netro seemed ready to help her. But then Alison found her breath in gasps. She was hyperventilating. The word "wait" seemed to strobe in her mind like a flashing ambulance light. Why couldn't she stop this from happening? This isn't right, she was telling herself. This isn't fair. For a moment she was transported to the night, 27 years ago, when she stepped out of bed in her bare feet and someone—her brother, she discovered later—grabbed her ankle from *underneath* the bed. And she thought at that moment that she had been cheated: everything the grown-ups had said was wrong. There really were goblins under the bed. There really were unseen terrors to fear. And now, as she was about to be dragged under and devoured, she was outraged. Liars, all of them! That's what grownups were.

It was that kind of outrage she felt now: Liars, fools! Gus, Netro, the Colonel. How could they have gotten this so wrong?

She couldn't shake the image of Erik alone in dark water, in that maze. And now she was with him, pawing the walls, panic rising in her throat. But he couldn't see her. It was his suffering that made her hysterical finally. She couldn't bear to imagine how he must have died even as she imagined it again and again.

That night, they got her some valium; the children slept with her in the bed she had shared for 12 years with Erik; and Gayla sat up watching her.

Tonight feels very much like that night. A drink would help. Two or three drinks. But she can't fuck up again. She knows this. Really, she does.

* * * *

"You've got that look," says Inez. "You need to take a pee before lights out?"

"A pee," Cooper says. "Yes, I do need a pee, now that you mention it."

"Let's get you a pan."

"You don't have to do this yourself, do you?" he asks.

"I can get Jimmy to help."

A few minutes later, Jimmy saunters in: "Hey, boss, it's that time, is it?"

"I guess," Cooper answers, hating the defeat in his voice. He can't remember when he last took a shit. What's going to happen when it's time for that?

Jimmy expertly helps unfold him from his pants, then snugs the pan between his thighs, careful not to touch his bandages. "Go for it, boss."

"Easy for you to say, Jimmy."

"Hey, we'll all have somebody holding our dick before it's over, man. Ain't no big deal."

"Thanks." Cooper tries to concentrate. He's got to pee badly but his jumbled thoughts block the urge. He pictures that blowhard Lars living on his looted boat, then Bailey slumped in the shade of Lillian's porch, listening to vintage folk rock through her earbuds and reading a novel that confirms how thoroughly misunderstood she is, then Lillian potting plants on her back deck, the sun making her orange hair look fiery, her mind occupied with the easily managed crises of horticulture. When Lillian thinks of Cooper, as she must on occasion, he is hardly different than a weather report from a distant city: easily pictured and easily dismissed. Maybe he's being unfair. He'll have to call her—she'd want to know what happened. His parents too. So much to do.

At last Cooper looks up at Jimmy and offers an apologetic shrug.

Jimmy smiles tolerantly. He says, "We got time, boss. Lots of time."

Later, Skyping through his laptop, he phones his parents. It will be afternoon in Baltimore—and yesterday, on the other side of the International Dateline. His mother will be reading the Sun with her third cup of French roast, heavy on the half-and-half; and his father will be tending his antique roses in the backyard, Bo, their tired basset hound, sleeping under the lilac bush nearby.

Making the connection takes a while, the computer chirping.

His mother recognizes his voice in an instant. "Oh, thank God," she blurts. "You made it. You don't know what we've been through, waiting here, knowing you were out there alone. Your father went out and bought four new rose bushes even though he's got nowhere to put them. He's pruned the plants down to nothing, he's so worried." Then she shouts, "RO-OY!"

Cooper hears Bo bark his basset's deep bay, as if to say, "What? What is it?"

His parents live in a well-tended Baltimore suburb. Theirs is a three-bedroom ranch with a paneled family room that features a large stone fireplace. Until he was seventeen, Cooper was responsible for mowing the half-acre yard and weeding the flower beds. Then Teddy, thirteen, took over.

"Are you there?" his father says several times. "You there?"

"Yeah, I'm here, Dad." He pictures his father in gardening

clothes: the faded canvas hat, cotton gloves, blue jeans patched at the knees, a Terps sweatshirt (no matter what the weather), and Vietnam-era Army boots, polished to a high shine. "I'm on Kwajalein."

"You son of a bitch, you know how worried we were?"

"We agreed I couldn't contact you until I arrived."

"No, that was your idea. Damn, I can't believe you made it."

"You mean you imagined me dead?"

His father laughs, sounding relieved and eager. "No, nothing like that."

"No, he didn't," his mother adds, just behind him.

"It's been a long time, I'm sorry."

"One hundred eighty-three days," his father says. "Every day I'd light a candle."

"It must be hot out there," his mother says. "How do you stay cool?"

"This is totally American, Mom. We've got air conditioning and ice and satellite TV."

"But you're in the middle of the ocean," his father says. "I've circled it on the map."

"It's like an old beach town here. Very . . . *quaint*." Cooper realizes that he's gripping the bed rail.

He's got an ocean view, when he bothers to look. He wants to be grateful, so he won't say that it looks bottled or boxed. But how can any view compare with the open ocean, the mountainous swells he troughed through, the foamy crests his Lickety Split needled?

"Quaint?" his father is asking. "What do you mean by *quaint*?"

"Do you like your job?" his mother asks.

"I haven't started working yet."

"Wait, Ruby, what did you say?"

"I said—"

"No, Ruby, not you. Cooper—Cooper, they're giving you time off already?"

"I'm in the hospital."

"The hospital?" his mother echoes.

"Did you catch a bug?" his father asks warily.

"He said *hospital*, Roy. He's hurt himself. What happened, baby? You nearly died from that hard travel, worked yourself down to nothing, lost your food—oh, God! But you're okay?"

"Mom, Dad, I am alive."

This silences them as abruptly as the sound of shattering glass. Maybe because they hear the fear in his tremulous voice.

"I had an accident," he continues, fighting self-pity the way he once fought a 50-knot wind. The pull of it makes him want to surrender, collapse into himself and weep with shame at what a pathetic, burdensome fuck-up he's become.

"He's alive," Roy reminds Ruby.

"How hurt are you, Cooper-baby?"

"I got hurt pretty badly in a fishing accident."

Cooper knows that no matter how many fishing mishaps his father and mother imagine—a hook in the hand, a ruptured disc from hard reeling, a broken tibia from slipping on the deck— they will never imagine the accident that befell him.

"How bad?"

"I got a cut that got infected," he says carefully, each word threatening to crumble like a chalky shell he grips too tightly. "My leg got gangrene. They had to cut it—they had to amputate it."

Through the window he sees a star on the horizon, or is it Venus? He concentrates on his breathing to keep from hyperventilating as he pictures himself running as a knock-kneed ten-year-old to catch the morning school bus, as a third-place one-miler on the junior high track team, as a two-goal-per-game forward on the high school's struggling soccer team. . . . *That* Cooper is gone, has run away, a thousand leggy memories long out of sight.

"What?" his parents are saying

"Cut it—they *cut* it?"

"How did they cut it?"

"Amputation," he says again. "My leg is gone."

"Gone!"

"Why would they do—"

"I would have died. They had to take it off."

"But you're talking to us plain as day," his father says. "You're right *there*."

"I'm alive, that's correct."

"Your leg is gone!"

This rouses Bo, who starts barking, as if he's caught the scent of a possum.

"You've got grounds for a *lawsuit*!"

"Mom, it was *my* fault." He feels himself gain a perverse strength suddenly, returned to his old place between confounded parents, attempting to make sense of the world for them. "I mean, it was an accident. It was nobody's fault."

"I don't believe it," his mother says, the same thing she'll say of a television commercial that sounds too good to be true.

"You come home right away, Cooper, we'll take care of you."

"Dad, I'm not helpless. I'm taking care of it."

"You've got one leg?"

"I've got one leg. My left leg. They took the right."

When they don't respond, he says, "Well, I've got one left— that's something, isn't it?"

His father starts bawling.

"Roy?"

"Dad, I'm going to be all right. Mom, tell him I'm going to be all right."

"Are you? I just don't understand it. First you leave Lillian and then you sail across the ocean like a crazy man and then you lose your leg. It isn't right, Cooper."

It sounds like his father is nearly choking with grief.

Cooper hears Bo whimpering now, beside his father—maybe in the old man's lap—working himself from barks to a howl.

"Dad, please. I can't stand this."

His mother says, "It just isn't right, Cooper."

"No, it's left," Cooper snaps. "That's all that's left is my left. There is no right any more, Mom." He draws a breath. Through the receiver he hears keening but can't be sure if it is his father or the dog. "Dad, stop, *please.*"

His mother says: "Cooper-baby, you can't just call us up and expect we will take this calmly. What do you think we're made of?"

He hears his father try for a breath but he manages only a stuttering hiccup.

"I shouldn't have told you."

"Why don't you come home," his father manages finally. "You . . . can have . . . your old . . . room."

Not if he were dying of AIDs would he return to that shaded mausoleum of a house.

Now his mother says, "Come home, Cooper-baby."

"I have *work* to do."

"Come home," his father begs.

"Will you stop saying that? Do you have any idea what this is like?"

"Don't yell at your Daddy—he's *upset.*"

He hears his father blow his nose. Then Bo lets go a hound-dog bay as if at the bedside of his dead master.

"I know you're upset too," his mother hurries on, "we're all upset, this is so tragic."

"I'm going to be all right," Cooper says.

"It's all turned so dark, Cooper. So dark."

"We can . . . support you . . . till you get on your feet," his father says. "I didn't mean it that way—you know what I mean."

"Dad, will you quiet the dog?"

"He *knows,* Cooper. Bo senses your pain."

"Roy, Cooper's still in the hospital. Cooper how long will it be before they let you go?"

"I've got months of rehab. I'll start work maybe next month. As you can imagine, it's a terrible inconvenience for my employer. But they're behind me all the way."

"You think about coming home, will you do that for us?" his mother says gently, as if reminding him of his manners.

"Sure," he says, "I'll think about it."

"Bo wants to say hello, Cooper."

Cooper hears the dog snuffling at the receiver.

"Dad, please."

"He's nothing but love, Cooper."

"Cooper, I can't say goodbye." Now his mother starts to whimper.

"I'll call soon," he says.

"Son," his father begins but can't continue.

"I'll call soon. Dad, Mom, I love you. I'll call soon." Then, with one jab of a finger, he disconnects. He's breathless, heaving.

Then someone raps on the door and peers in. She looks as frightened as he feels. A woman about his age, pale and thin, a sleepwalker maybe, her eyes deep-set, her thin lips chapped from worry, her shoulder-length brown hair too dry and windblown. He wonders what she has been through, which of her loved-ones is in the hospital.

"Sorry!" she says. "I'm lost!" Then she withdraws quickly, shutting the door again.

He wishes she stayed. He wanted to ask her, "How bad? How bad can it be?"

NINE

"If you die now, I will not forgive you," Jinna tells Art in his dream. She is wearing a flimsy cotton madras skirt and a baggy T-shirt that disguises her three-month pregnancy. This is the young Jinna he met thirty years ago. The most educated woman in the southern Marshalls. Principal of the Jaluit high school. Quietly confident, beautiful in her equanimity, her thick black hair splayed messily over her shoulders, her bare legs bruised from shepherding so many children.

"I'm not going to die," Art says, raising himself on one elbow. "Look at me. I'm too fucking angry to die."

"Where do you think you're going?" the nurse asks him.

Awake now, and startled by this interruption, Art regards her with profound disappointment. This is the noisy nurse who's taking care of Cooper, what's-her-name, little Miss Sunshine. Inez.

Easing himself back onto the hospital bed, he exhales wearily. His head is a concrete cell crowded with rowdy inmates. He sees that someone is passed out on the neighboring bed—behind a three-paneled gauzy screen. Sunlight is a blinding glare on the window. "I'm not going to let you kill me," he says.

"Your temperature was 102 last night," she says. "Dr. Boxer says we've got your little parasite. Isn't that good news?"

He tries sitting up again. The world see-saws in slow motion. "Where're my clothes?" He paws at the sheets. He hears the nurse sigh. A tidy youngish woman with big spectacles and a patronizing smile, she will not age well, he decides.

"Mr. Norman, we can't let you go just yet."

"You can't or you won't?" He's wearing a backless green gown.

He can't remember if he's been here one night or three.

She offers him a smile, like something cellophaned and frozen. Then she raises her right hand and he almost flinches, as if he expected her to do what?

You're a stupid man, he tells himself, her warm dry hand against his forehead, her too-competent eyes studying the side of his hot face. At last she announces, "You don't have a fever now."

"How long have I been here?"

"You checked in day before yesterday. Do you want to go to the bathroom?"

"Are you going to carry me?"

"No, but I'll hold your bed pan." Though she says this without a smile, he wants to believe she has a sense of humor.

"I'd rather let my bladder burst," he says.

"Okay," she says. "How about some rice pudding?"

"I'd rather have steak and eggs."

"That would be a feat, considering your condition," she says. "Until last night you were wearing a diaper."

Suddenly Art recalls the warm washcloth wipes at his backside, the reek of his liquid shit, the cauldron of his burbling fever.

He shakes his head in wonderment. "I've been here two days and you haven't managed to kill me?"

"One or two of us wanted to."

Ah, there it is: humor. But she doesn't break a smile.

"Well, you had your chance," he says. "I'm checking out."

"The doctor would advise against it."

"The operative word is *advise*."

"I'll have to get the doctor, Mr. Norman."

"You do what you have to do."

She bustles down the hall.

Art finds his clothes and, with shaky hands, dresses himself, not bothering with buttons.

A cloudless day, fever gone, his stomach grumbling—and no eels worming out of his asshole—he should be happy. He sits on the edge of his bed and catches his breath. Damn it all. His arms are bruised with IV welts. It's like he's been kidnapped, drugged, abused.

"Wake up if you want to live," he calls to his neighbor.

Ten minutes later Art finds Cooper Davies. The Injured Man.

"You!" Cooper says, sitting up in his bed. Art is touched that he has brought a grin to the patient's face. "Am I due for another lecture already?"

Art regards him with fatherly dismay. "What are you waiting for, Cooper? Why are you just sitting there?"

"I'm waiting for WiFi, man." Cooper taps his laptop. "It's as slow as dial-up."

"Comes via satellite, Cooper. Army won't let us use their fiber optics."

Cooper turns his head comically and regards Art for a quiet moment. He says, "No offense, Mister Liaison, but you look like hell."

"I've had a bug."

"He's been in the hospital," Inez says, stepping in behind him. "Now he's trying to leave."

Art gets out of her way and decides he likes her, this busy gnomish bee of medicine. "That's right," he says, watching her bustle. "I'm breaking out today."

"Did you see my article in the paper?" Cooper asks brightly.

"You serious?" Art says. Then seeing that Cooper is: "No, haven't seen it. I'm sure it was deliriously generous and well written."

"He's a celebrity," says Inez. She's flogging the air with a thermometer.

"As for your orientation," says Art, "You might as well wait for the regular session at the end of the month. The Colonel himself always offers a little speech."

"A stirring speech?"

"I appreciate your attempt at sarcasm, Cooper."

Art is about to pat Cooper's knee but realizes he's on the stump side. "The Colonel's a decent enough fellow, all things considered. He's military, that's his problem."

"What's wrong with the military?" Cooper asks. Inez inserts the thermometer into his mouth.

"What's—?" Art sputters. "Are you pulling my leg? No offense."

"Aught alout nashnal scurtee?"

Inez translates: "What about, you know, national security and all that?"

Art sees an opportunity. "All right," he says. "Nurse Inez, would you humor me by answering a few hypothetical questions?"

"I know all about you, Mister Norman. Your reputation precedes you."

"Oh, that's nice," he says. "It probably exceeds me too."

She pulls the thermometer from Cooper's mouth. Cooper says, "I wouldn't get him started, Inez."

"Too late!' says Art. "Now, nurse: the medical standards you abide by are not idiosyncratic, are they? You can't do whatever you please, can you?"

The young woman takes the thermometer, drops it into a nearby red, plastic bin—labeled with a biohazard warning—then turns to him. There is the Hippocratic oath. There are procedures we've all been trained to observe."

"By 'we all' you mean all medical practitioners in the developed world?"

"Yes, Mister Norman. If you break your leg in Zaire or Argentina or America, you can be confident that a doctor or nurse will know how to set it."

"Excellent. And a standard procedure for a leg break would be—sorry again, Coop, it seems to be our theme, doesn't it?"

"Don't worry about me," he says. "I'm drugged big time."

Art smiles: "The standard procedure for handling a broken bone, Nurse Inez, how is that arrived at?"

"Mister Norman, why don't you just say what you're dying to say?"

"Because I'm a teacher. Can you just nurse me through this a little?"

"All right," she says with an agreeable nod, her arms folded over her breasts. "We arrive at these procedures because the medical community has tested these and found them to be the safest, most useful means of handling this injury."

"The medical community would be. . . ?"

"Doctors, nurses, researchers."

"Yes, from all nations?"

"Obviously."

"And if one nation decided that when its doctors came upon a broken leg, its doctors would—forgive me, Cooper—amputate instead of set the break, what do you think the reaction would be from the larger medical community?"

"Your example is ridiculous, Mister Norman."

"Call me Art—we'll both feel better." He offers another smile. "Other nations would think what of this idiosyncrasy in the treatment of broken bones?"

"Well, duh! They would condemn the practice as irresponsible."

"Yes, precisely. And yet the practice would be effective in its way, wouldn't it? It would remedy the break."

Cooper interrupts: "At what cost, Art?"

"Do no harm," Inez reminds him. "Your hypothetical doctor—"

"A nation of hypothetical doctors," says Art.

"Your nation of doctors is doing more harm than good because their patients are now recovering from traumatic surgery instead of fractured bones."

"How long might a bone take to heal? Months? Certainly no shorter a time than an amputation would take."

"But your patient can't walk or get around!" says Cooper.

Art turns to him, laying a hand on his shoulder. "Cooper, am I disturbing you?"

"You're being perverse, Art."

"Okay, I'll stop. But you see my point, don't you, that one nation cannot dictate an idiosyncratic practice for all nations. And yet that's what the United States has done. We don't mend bones, we cut them—everywhere we go."

"That's your opinion," Inez says, "and you're certainly entitled to voice it."

"Correction, it's not only my opinion, it is the opinion of the world. Our government and its eager lackeys, i.e., the military, never pause to wonder why the world so resents us."

"Well, we are pretty damned rich," Cooper says.

"But that's a facile answer, son. There are other rich countries—our standard of living is not the highest. Our infant mortality is not the lowest. Our—"

"Okay, Mister Norman, I'm officially bored," Inez says. "And I do have work to do."

"You're bored. Really? I would have thought that an intelligent person like you would want to engage in an exchange of ideas."

Cooper says, "Argument, Art. You're argumentative."

"Argument is debate, Cooper. Why are Americans so afraid of debate and dissension? Ours is a country built on dissent and yet nowadays you'd think Americans were in some repressive cult where they're afraid to voice even the smallest criticism. Heaven forbid that I'd say anything critical of nine/eleven."

"Thousands died, how could you?" says Inez. She gathers a handful of trash from Cooper's side table, readying to leave.

"See there?" he says. "That's exactly what I'm talking about—that defensive, indignant reaction. You don't even know what I was going to say about nine/eleven."

"You want a debate?" says Cooper. This has brought color to his cheeks.

Art smiles. "Go, man, go."

"America is the *only* country that's had the guts to face down bullies and bandits all over the world. We're the only country that has taken a risk to maintain world peace."

"Then how do you explain the fact that in the last twenty years we have bombed eleven nations without any declaration of war? That's hardly peaceable."

"Now who's being facile?" Cooper says. "Peace doesn't always come easily."

"You mean peace doesn't always come peaceably? You mean sometimes we need to make war in order to make peace?"

"More or less."

"So there's peace now in the Middle East? There's peace now in Iran? There's peace now in—"

"It takes time, Art."

"Yes, there we agree. Peace takes time. But guns don't make peace. They kill, they frighten, they quell for a while, but they don't make peace. They create new resentments, they reinvigorate enemies, they invite more killing."

"What about World War II?" Cooper asks.

Art sees Inez watching with interest. He loves having an audience.

"Ah, the Great War," he says. "I'm not saying that war is unavoidable. We behaved well in that case, in part because we didn't start the fighting. Ultimately our involvement was unavoidable, as I say. But the war itself wasn't necessary."

"I don't see how you can say that," says Cooper. "Sometimes we can't avoid a fight. Chamberlain tried for peace before the war. He did everything he could to placate Hitler and still he failed."

"Good for you, Cooper. You remember England's sad old Chamberlain. Let's remember too the deals the Good Guys made during and after the war. We're sitting on one of those deals right now."

"The Trust Territories," Inez says.

"A term cooked up to disguise a land grab."

"But the Marshallese have their independence now," says Cooper.

"That's a matter of opinion. Their so-called liberation from the Japanese hasn't brought them health or prosperity, much less true liberty."

"Don't forget the Chinese and the Russians are still spying on us," Cooper says. "We've got photos of their spy ships sneaking around in these waters."

Art laughs. "Well, yeah, why wouldn't they spy on us? We're smack dab in the middle of the Pacific, on land that doesn't belong to us, and we're testing intercontinental ballistic missiles. Shit, wouldn't you want to know what's going on if you were the Chinese or the Russians or whoever else is fortunate enough to have the means to find out?"

Inez says, "What were you going to say about nine-eleven?"

Art nods to her as if to say, *Thank you.* "I agree with everyone else that it was a horror. I grieve for the lost. I commiserate with the survivors. But why do we remain so amazed at the tragedy when, instead, we should be amazed that we escaped it for so long? We bomb nations all over the world—El Salvador, Afghanistan, Grenada—we invade their lands, we ransack their homes, we maim, shoot, and blow up their civilians, and yet we wonder why anyone would try to do the same to us: *How dare they!* we think."

"We're the assholes of the world, is that it?" Cooper says.

Inez is shaking her head in disagreement.

"Don't get me wrong," Art says. "My aim isn't to make Americans hate themselves. I just want them to wake up and behave better."

"Then why aren't you back in the States teaching the gospel according to Art Norman?" Cooper asks.

"Because I'm a coward who believes life in America will drown me. So I make my stand here, where I think I might be heard." He smiles from Cooper to Inez. "But keep talking to me, and I may make you feel guilty yet."

"I have nothing to feel guilty for," says Inez.

"Lucky you," says Art. "One of the gifts of growing older is that we see with increasingly clarity how much we should regret."

"So I speak for ignorant youth?" she says.

"That's for you to find out," he says.

"Smug bastard," Cooper says with a laugh.

"Thank you for indulging me," he says. "Both of you."

* * * *

Art wheels Cooper past the ER desk, through two automatic doors, and suddenly they're outside, in the oppressively humid eighty-degree afternoon.

Dizzy, gulping air, Cooper hears the crunch of breakers just beyond the building, and palm fronds clattering in the breeze; he smells car exhaust, he hears gulls complaining.

"Here, Coop, look at this: we get free taxi service on the island."

"It looks like a shuttle, not a taxi."

Art waves for the driver to assist them. Cooper dumbly watches himself—in the chair—hefted into the air-conditioned shuttle, then secured behind the driver, Art sitting next to him. "Anything you want," Art says breathlessly, "the island's yours—you just watch. People'll be killing themselves to do for you, you make everyone feel so fucking guilty."

"Where are you taking me?"

"You like soccer?"

"I really need a nap."

"Sleep when you're dead, Cooper. I want you to see these boys playing soccer."

The shuttle glides out of the hospital drive, turns right, and there it is: oceanside, the rocky shore, the greenish-brown reef like a quarter-mile of moonscape, then the breakers chewing at the reef's farthest edge, where the water drops hundreds of feet, then a thousand. It fills Cooper with mild panic and a sudden thrill, as if he were a long-trapped miner released to the open air at last.

The first month Cooper moved to California, Brad, his design supervisor, took Cooper to a boat show in San Jose. It was thoroughly predictable—the phallic glossy power boats, the grinning suntanned girls in bikinis, the giveaways by cigarette and soft drink companies—until they came to the vintage sailboats. It wasn't hulls that excited Cooper, not the racy sweep of their lines, not the majestic rise of their masts, not the promise of their speed or power, it was instead their interiors, those tidy cabins, those warm woods and tight spaces, the sense of containment and the promise of transport to another world.

In the cabin of a rehabbed Alberg 35, Cooper sat at the dining table, inhaled the lemony scent of oiled teak, and admired the laptop-sized gas range, the long-grained arc of the rosewood ceiling, the warm glow of the caged sconces on either side of him. "You could live in something like this," he mused.

Brad grinned at him mischievously.

"What?" Cooper protested. "Did I say something funny?"

"You've been bitten," Brad said. "You're already in deep water."

Cooper opened the closet nearest him. The economy of space, everything put to use, he found. . . charming. A world in your pocket, he was thinking. You could go anywhere.

That's what he wanted, he realized: to go somewhere on his own power. He didn't try to over-think it but he suspected it had something to do with a fundamental discontent with his sedentary go-nowhere life. He didn't want to seem ungrateful or unreasonable. After all, he was doing well, getting good work. But it just wasn't enough. Maybe if he had family or raised horses or something. Sitting at the helm of a blue water sail boat he understood, for the first time, what the religious meant by "hearing the call."

"You're looking east," Art says, nodding to the water, "back to the States."

"Oh, joy."

Art laughs.

They pass, to the left, a swimming pool crowded with kids; to the right a big concrete building at the corner of a broad street— and Cooper can see straight across the island to the other side. Kwajalein looks like a 1950s cinderblock beach town gone to seed. Plenty of palms, lots of grass, everybody riding bicycles, buildings that look like dormitories, then baseball backstops and diamonds and a huge expanse of green space with a drive-in theater screen at one end, but no parking lot, of course, because nobody here owns a car.

"That's called the Richardson," Art explains. "We sit on blankets and watch free movies on the big screen."

The shuttle pulls to the grassy shoulder behind a line of tall palms at the edge of a well-manicured soccer field, where about thirty adults and just as many children and teens are gathered, the game about to start. It's a sunny afternoon, huge silver-white clouds drifting like dirigibles in the distance.

When Art and the driver lift Cooper, chair and all, from the shuttle, Cooper sees for the first time the spectacle he has become. Everyone at the soccer field stares at him, mouths open in surprise: *There he is!*

"Oh, God!" he groans.

"Steady," Art coaches. "It's gonna take a while."

Too aware of the collective concern swirling around him, Cooper feels obliged to set everyone at ease somehow. It's humiliating to be the object of everyone's conspicuous worry.

"They're all so fucking *sorry*," Art whispers in disgust, hunched over the back of Cooper's chair. "Let's go down here." He wheels Cooper bumpily along the grassy sideline, everyone nodding a greeting, throwing their pitiful smiles at him. Cooper simply wants to fade away. He fights to keep from shutting his eyes, grief like a hot coal stuck in his throat.

Art backs him into the shade of a palm. Cooper hears the

ref's whistle, the start of the game, and he wonders how long before his drugs wear off and he experiences all of this in real time.

"Take a look," Art says. "Notice the Marshallese boys don't wear shoes."

Cooper sees that one soccer team is Marshallese, the other American. High school boys. "Didn't you say the Marshallese don't live on Kwajalein?"

"Good boy, you were listening." Art pats his shoulder. "They came over on the afternoon ferry. Our playing fields are a novelty for them, all this grass. Might as well be running on marshmallows as far as they're concerned. They scare the shit out of the American boys. Watch the goalie."

The Marshallese goalie looks about 17, thick tousled hair, with a downy black mustache, and wide brown eyes. He wears a white T-shirt that says, "PRIMO," and khaki shorts. No shoes. He stands at the center of the goal casually, as if waiting for a friend.

Across the field, a handful of Marshallese spectators call to their team and cluck their tongues at missteps.

"You know, if they don't catch the eight o'clock ferry back to Ebeye," Art says, "they'll be arrested."

"I suppose it'd be nice if the Marshallese could stay," Cooper muses, "but Kwajalein is a top-security missile research facility, after all. Not just anybody can be here."

Art emits what sounds like a growl: "That's fine, Cooper. So the Marshallese are good enough to clean our toilets and mop our floors but heaven forbid we let them live among us?"

"I'm sure it's a little more complicated than you're making it sound."

"Are you trying to provoke me, son?"

Despite himself, Cooper almost smiles, grateful for the distraction: "The last thing I'd like to do today is provoke you, Art."

The American boys, in green and white shorts with matching socks and jerseys, are racing the ball downfield, their cheerleaders pom-pomming encouragement: *Let's-go! Yo, go Spartans: let's-go!*

The Marshallese defenders, barefoot every one, are very fast. What the Americans lack in speed, they make up for with organization, each passing the ball to a teammate just before he's about to lose it to the defenders. Methodically they work their way downfield. And still the Marshallese goalie stands casually and watches.

Despite his half-drugged state, Cooper feels his pulse quicken: the reckless way they sprint, the Marshallese boys play as if something larger were at stake.

Their defenders converge, trapping two Americans with the ball. Suddenly, in a surprising move, one of the Americans chips the ball over the defenders' heads to another American who races in for a slam-dunk kick. The goalie's block—a wildman's leap — happens so fast, it takes Cooper a moment to understand why the ball has ricocheted and is now soaring in a high arc towards the American's goal. And there, like ghosts, the Marshallese forwards appear, quietly settling the ball, speeding a pass across the back field, charging for the goal, and boom: they score!

Shaking his head in self-loathing, the American goalie retrieves the ball.

"Hit him like lightning," Art gloats.

The Marshallese goalie, again standing casually, is wiping his bloody mouth with the back of one hand.

As the Marshallese strikers return to mid-field for the start of the next round, they chatter enthusiastically in their language but otherwise make no show of their triumph.

Cooper clears his throat. "Didn't you say the Marshallese were the friendliest, sweetest people in the Pacific?"

"They also used to be some of the fiercest warriors," Art says. "For hundreds of years Western explorers avoided these islands for fear of the natives, who would kill outsiders without any provocation."

"Holy shit."

"It's never just one way, Coop. You're old enough to understand that. Give these people the opportunity to express themselves *truly* and this is what you get. They're all bottled up. That's why when they get drunk, they beat each other—or you and me if we get in the way."

Cooper looks again at the goalie, who stands with arms crossed, waiting. He'd give anything to be that boy right now.

* * * *

Jeton likes the taste of his own blood. Slow in wiping it away, he thinks how, later, his saving the game will be worth a few beers but nothing more. He hopes Nora will get a chance to lick his injured lip. But there is no guarantee that he can sneak away or that they can find a private place. She looks very happy, even though her team is losing. He and Nora have agreed that during these games they must pretend not to know one another. So he sees her glance his way occasionally but that is all. Sometimes when her eyes graze him he shivers.

The coach was not going to let Jeton play because he has been absent for seven days from school. But nobody is a better goalie than Jeton.

Nora is not the best cheerleader but she is the captain of the cheer squad. Right now the other girls are lifting her from the grass where she has done a split. Gripping Nora's long naked legs, they raise her in this pose. And Nora wags her pom-poms—*bwebwe* plastic muffs—and shouts, "Spartans rule!" A silly thing to shout after the *ri-Majel* team has just scored. But that is Nora's job, to shout silly things and to ignore the fact that Jeton is her man.

Several times she has told Jeton that he is so good at soccer he could win a scholarship to a college in the States—if he had better grades. Every time she has said this, he has felt blame. Americans are fond of saying a high school diploma guarantees a good job. But there are no jobs! Unemployment in his nation has been 30% for years and years. If there is work, it goes to the young men who are connected by family—the royals and their relatives. Jeton's only connection is *būbū*, his grandmother, who has offered to set him up as a taxi driver on Majuro. Jeton does not want to be a taxi driver on Majuro. He wants to live with Nora on an outer island. They would harvest coconut for copra to make some money and breadfruit for food. Fishing would be good. They would raise their children in a peaceful place. This is his answer, his future. This is why he can hardly concentrate on the game.

* * * *

Nora loves this more than almost anything, raised high by her squad, her voice a piercing arrow of enthusiasm, the adults eyeing her with envy and approval because she's so limber (Look at that split!) and young and pretty—not drop-dead gorgeous, not overly made-up, not Hollywood in any way, just fresh and clear-com-plected, with dark brows that don't need plucking and lips full enough so that no one will ever say, *You should think about collagen.*

The adults and her squad and her team and the coaches love her because she is sincerely determined never to let a bad play, or a losing game, dampen her spirits. She will shout hope until her throat is hoarse and she all but collapses from the effort because deep down she believes that she can transport her steely will into the souls of everyone around her. After one rainy game last year, she was laid up a week from over-exertion. Then she was voted Best School Spirit for the year book.

Not that any of that matters in the end. She knows she is in transition, which is why she isn't taking any of this too seriously. The serious stuff comes later, when she's in college and deciding on a career. So she can make a few mistakes. She can fuck around even. The thought of this now—as her squad raises her high in a split, shouting for their team—gives her a thrill right down the middle to her hottest spot, because Jeton is watching. In fact, it seems he's watching her more than the game. Which makes her worry for him, even as it thrills her.

When she got caught fucking recently, it could have been worse. She had just let Jeton go after their time on the patio. He had to catch the ferry back to Ebeye. She walked inside, into the kitchen. Gus and Janet were standing there, gaping at her as if she had just walked away from a car wreck.

Nora's underwear was wet from sex. She wanted to change into her pj's and listen to her latest downloads. She didn't imagine her parents had peered through the back door window and seen her doing it with Jeton. *Watched* her—yuck!

They aren't bad as far as parents go. They've pretty much given Nora everything she's wanted—except a cool name: "Nora" belonged to a beloved great aunt she never met. As a child she wanted Kaitlin or Ashley, then she thought Stefanie would do. Britney was big for a while but now it's so yesterday, though still better than Nora. Her number-one choice these days would be something offbeat and ethnic. Managua maybe. Or Tripoli.

"What's up?" she asked them.

Janet was shaking her head so sadly, Nora wondered if this was about her going away to college. Was Janet about to weep over her baby-girl's imminent departure?

Janet is the VP of the island's AmeriBank branch, a job that brought them to Kwajalein. A compact woman with short-cropped, brightly-dyed red hair and a too-pointy chin, she can make her thin lips look so disapproving—*Most people you meet, Nora, are incompetent and just trying to get by, she is fond of saying.* Honestly, sometimes she scares Nora.

Gus—a sun-tanned athletic trainer who's a few pounds overweight and well past his prime—has always been the softer touch. Most of Nora's good looks come from him. Standing just behind Jan, he was barefoot and wearing his racing-striped jogging suit. He looked . . . well, he looked about to cry. This convinced Nora that they wanted to hug her and make her promise never to forget them.

"Did you use a condom?" Janet asked.

Nora blinked. "Beg your pardon?"

"A condom—are you practicing safe sex." Janet crossed her arms, which signaled she was ready for a knock-down drag-out.

Nora felt her mouth drop open in surprise. Janet can be ruthless in an argument.

"What are you saying?" Nora asked, knowing it was too obvious she was stalling.

"You know what we're saying," said Gus. Sometimes his pout nearly breaks her heart. He's her big Teddy Bear.

Nora sighed. "I'm on the pill, if you must know."

"Do you know if that boy has other sexual partners?" Janet asked.

"You know that boy's name—you've met him." Now it was Nora's turn to cross her arms over her chest. *All right, bring it on,* as the President said recently. She was old enough to handle this.

Softly Gus coaxed her: "But *do you know,* lamb?"

"He was a virgin when we met." She tried not to sound boastful.

"And you weren't?" said Janet.

Oh, you'd better watch it, old lady, you'd better cool your jets.

"I'm seventeen," Nora said flatly. "What's your point?"

"Our point is that you are in no position to get pregnant or get AIDs, for that matter—"

"I'm not—"

"Let me finish: you are still a *dependent.* Do you understand that concept?"

"Jan, don't get sarcastic," Gus whispered.

"Unless you want to live on your own, pay your own bills, pay your tuition, and make your way all by your seventeen-year-old self, you are obliged to listen to us."

The tuition part got Nora's attention. Damn it to hell! as Gus says whenever he fucks up.

Jan was steaming, those thin lips pressed into nothing. Let her cool. . . .

"Honey," Gus began, holding his open hands apart as if to describe a measurement, "you'll have your entire life to, you know, enjoy relationships. It doesn't have to be now, not when so much is at stake."

Okay, all right, she had to swallow this like something rotten she'd already half chewed: the Boomer dose of hypocrisy. Like Jan and Gus didn't smoke their doo-bees every day and fuck like rabbits when they were her age? Like they were safe about *anything*? Just because they've survived, they think they have the right now—in their dotage—to tell her what she can and can't do? So she's supposed to save sex until, what, she's *married*? How do old people lose all sense of reality? It's like they enter the Zone of Forgetting.

"All right," she sighed. "What do you want?"

"This is not a negotiation," Ms. Bank VP said. "So long as you take our money and live under our protection, you will do as we say."

"And what are you saying?" Nora asked.

Gus tried to warn her off with his worried look: *Don't get sassy, lamb!*

But too late.

Janet announced, without a hint of gloating: "You are grounded until you graduate. The day after graduation, you are on a plane to Sacramento, to stay with your grandparents—where you will work all summer."

"At the Friendly Smile?" she asked.

"Yes, the Friendly Smile. And you will do everything Gram and Gramps tell you to do."

Oh, this was too much! The Friendly Smile is Gram and Gramp's franchise restaurant. Everything at the restaurant comes from a foil or plastic packet that you microwave or boil. Everything except the lettuce. Even the tomato slices come packaged. And don't try calling this cooking. Gram and Gramps call it "preparation," assembling all the pieces of a meal according to the franchise handbook, which offers step-by-step instructions for everything, even how to revive ruined French toast (inject it with a specially designed egg-whip). You can bet Gram and Gramps are looking forward to Nora's visit. They're gonna make a slave of her!

* * * *

"He said you made him watch some awful video," says April on the phone.

Alison can hear April's baby bawling in the background.

"I'm sorry Arnold didn't enjoy himself."

"He said he was the *only* guest—is that true?"

"The other boys left early."

"Why?"

"It's complicated, April. They left—so we tried to have a party with Arnold. He seemed to enjoy the brownies."

"He's still sick!"

Can you shut that baby up?

"Sorry, April."

There's a long pause, the baby wailing. Alison imagines April placidly watching her infant squirm and complain. Sometimes there's no reason to explain a baby's distress.

"Alison, you've got to stop drinking."

"What?"

"Everybody says so."

Alison feels the sudden scald of humiliation: "Whoa, April—you have no right to say that to me!"

The baby bawls and bawls. It sounds like the alarm in Alison's head. *Everybody says so!*

"I entrusted my son to your care and you think I have no right to question your judgment?"

I invite your little bug-eyed geek against my son's wishes and then treat him to fifty dollar brownies and you have the gall to complain?

"I only called to see how the boy was doing, April. Shame on you for being so rude!"

"I'm just expressing concern, Alison."

"Really?"

"I'd hope that if I were in similar trouble, you'd do the same for me."

Alison nearly grits her teeth to say this evenly: "April, I want you to listen really closely to what I have to say to you on this subject."

"Yes, Alison?"

As hard as she can, Alison throws her cell phone against the wall across the room.

For several minutes she stands there, listening to her heart pounding in her head. *Does everybody on the fucking island know what I'm doing?*

After she retrieves the phone, she finds it is still on and still working. She dials Emil.

"You're using your cell," he says. "I thought you hated that thing."

"Life is full of compromises, Emil. What are you doing for lunch?"

"Fucking you, I hope. Could we assume our roles now?"

"Not yet. Let's talk a little business."

"I didn't know you and I conducted business."

"Tell me about that video you bought me in Hono."

"What's there to tell? You wanted it, I got it."

"Where'd you get it?"

"Was something wrong with it?"

"It was *bootlegged*, Emil. It was horrible."

"I went to three stores, Ali—they were sold out. Then I saw a guy selling it on the street. That was the best I could do."

"It ruined my son's birthday."

After a moment's hesitation he says, "I should be punished

for that. You know what an ass I am. Say it, Alison."

"Did you *hear* what I said?"

"Do you *hate* me?"

She sighs and glances out the window. Another day in Paradise, everybody jokes, because the weather is almost always perfect here on the Equator. The boys have gone ahead of her to the soccer field for Stan's game. She doesn't want to be late.

"Emil, you were in your office when I came by yesterday. Why didn't you answer?"

"If I didn't answer, I wasn't in."

"Your cell phone rang—I dialed it."

"I left my cell in my office. It happens."

"Were you in there with somebody?"

"Are you *jealous*?" It sounds like he's grinning.

"I just want you to tell me the truth."

"But I'm a *liar*, Alison. I'm a *lying sack of shit*. You know that. Don't you hate me? Don't you want to *hurt me* for being a lying sack of shit?"

"I'm really not in the mood for this, Emil."

"I can get you in the mood."

"I've got to go."

"See you at lunch?"

She disconnects, then dials Gayla.

"Morning, Ali. Where are you on this lovely Saturday?"

"Sitting in my messy kitchen, drinking coffee." *With a couple shots of rum.* "The boys have gone to the field for the game."

"How'd Doug's birthday go yesterday?"

"So you remembered?"

"Why wouldn't I?"

"Well, I *forgot*. And I ordered the cake for the wrong day."

"Oh my god, Ali, what happened?"

"I fucked up. I've ruined Doug's rep."

"But you had the party all set up—you told me last week!"

"Rub it in. I could have used your help."

"Topher and I had a date. Sorry, hon'."

"I get the feeling you wanted this to happen."

"Why would you say something like that?"

"Because I'm a fuck-up and maybe if I fuck up enough, you think I'll get my act together."

"But you *are* getting your act together, aren't you? You've applied to get your masters, right?"

Gayla's credulity feels like a taunt. Maybe she sees through the lies and is just playing Ali. Alison sighs. She says, "You know I'm having an affair with Emil Timmerman, right?"

"Everybody knows that, Ali."

"Shit, Gayla, it's that bad?"

"Well, some people are inclined to make excuses for you. But, yeah, it's pretty bad."

Alison sips her spiked coffee and, for the first time in ten years, feels like having a cigarette. She says, "I AM going to get my act together."

"Didn't I just say that? "

"You know, his wife fools around too."

"I'm not asking for explanations, Ali. You're the one who brought it up."

Alison takes another sip and winces at its bite. She says, "April Arnold told me to stop drinking this morning."

"*Are* you drinking this morning?"

"Don't be cute, Gay."

"I'm a Vice Principal. I don't do cute."

"Where does April get off judging me like that?"

"April is a drip."

"A sober drip, apparently."

"You can be a sober drip too, Ali."

"Great. Then I've got a goal." Allison would be happy doing nothing today but talking on the phone. "I really could have used your help last night."

"So I gather. What are you going to do with your cake?"

"Give it to you. It's the least I can do for all the trouble I've caused you."

"The trouble's behind us, isn't that what I hear you saying?"

"That's what I'm saying."

"I can't tell you how happy I am to hear this, Ali."

"Yeah," says Alison, squinting into the morning sun. "I'm happy too."

TEN

On the ferry ride back to Ebeye, when the boat is a quarter mile from the lagoon's rim of reef and Kwajalein is half a mile behind them, a collection of distant white lights winking from the black horizon, Jeton jumps overboard when no one is watching. He knows to push away quickly, to avoid the tow of the boat's churning propellers. A strong swimmer, a pair of borrowed running shoes tied around his neck, he backstrokes over the boat's wake. It's hard work because the tide is going out. Soon the boat is far away and Jeton is alone in the dark water. If he were on the oceanside, he would be shark bait. But here on the lagoon side, he knows there are few sharks. Still, he has to be careful.

He can hear the water slapping exposed rock on the reef a hundred yards ahead. And at last he can see the pale expanse of sand below him—and large darting fish. Above, clouds chase each other like racing ships through the whorl of stars. The moon has yet to rise. As soon as he can stand, bullied by small waves, Jeton slips on the shoes. The reef at low tide will allow him to walk back to Kwajalein. But he has to walk fast, watch for Security Patrol, and get across before the Security boat motors by with its sun-bright spot. He has to walk careful too, watch that he doesn't slip and cut himself on the coral, which is sharp like fish knives. Salt water will ruin the leather Nikes he borrowed from cousin Mike. But fuck it.

It takes a long time, this careful walking in dark water.

As he sloshes through tide pools, slipping every other step, cursing the reef, he almost wishes a rogue wave would reach over from oceanside and pull him into the depths—then Nora would be sorry, drowned Jeton washed up on Emon beach, where Nora takes her morning swim.

When they met at a soccer game that first time, Nora said, "You're damned reckless, you know that?" She was flirting, he knew right away. He offered her a cigarette and she said, "Are you crazy?"

"Yes," he said.

That's all it took. Boom! like that.

In two days she flies to the States. Four thousand two hundred miles east. What is four thousand miles to Jeton? He has flown to Guam twice. One thousand three hundred miles. That was far enough.

After the game this afternoon, when his team walked over to shake hands with her team (they beat the *ri-pālle* 7 to 2), he got close enough to her to whisper, "I'm gonna die if I don't see you, *jera*."

Then he heard her sigh the kind of sigh he hears Betra, his younger sister, make when she looks at the mail-order Nordstrom catalogue from the States, at all those things she knows she cannot have. Nora didn't have time to answer him. And then she was gone, swept away with the other cheerleaders and the *ri-pālle* boys.

"I know, it's hard," Nora said at their last meeting.

"I own a fourth of Kwajalein!" he said, desperate for justification.

"You mean your grandmother does," Nora corrected.

"Same thing!" he said.

Jeton's grandmother gets a check every few months for leasing her part of Kwajalein to the Americans. It has been enough to buy her a condo on Guam, a new Nissan Altima LX every other year, a pork farm in Manila, but not enough to give to her huge family, every one of them with an empty hand held out. Still, she offered to buy Jeton a used Sentra and set him up in the taxi business on Majuro. Jeton pictures himself driving Majuro's long, flat two-lane road all day, every day—*ial an irooj*, the King's Road, it is called. The only road. Four or five quarters per ride. Majuro island is one mile wide and 34 miles long and 300 miles from here. They have a couple of discos and a copra plant and fifteen churches.

Fuck that.

In his mind, he hears Nora say his name, over and over. Nobody has said his name like that, like it was a valuable secret. He can smell the strawberry shampoo of her hair, the flowery scent of her body lotion—she sunburns easily. She gave him everything.

She used to say, "You're the one, Jeton, you're the only one."

He knows that in her *ettōṇak*, her awake dreams, she is already on that plane, already back in the States, going to college, dating other boys and thinking of a "major" and a life Jeton can't begin to understand.

"I will write," she promised.

"Yes," he said. "Long emails."

Now: something stutters and skips past his feet. A shrimp scuttering to safety.

Americans like to come out here with flashlights to hunt for shells at low tide. Some aren't careful and the high tide catches them, sweeps them out to deep water and they are never found. All of this is a mystery to them, the water, the reef, the life the *ri-Majeḷ* used to know. The *ri-Majeḷ* were great navigators, great canoe builders. They knew how to read the waves and they made secret charts with sticks and cowrie shells that enabled them to travel anywhere they pleased. No one knows how to do that any more, except at the Allele Museum on Majuro, where two old men work year-round hacking out ceremonial *tipñōls*, sailing canoes, for tourists to see.

Jeton once took Nora to Pikeej in his uncle's speed boat. Pikeej is uninhabited, an overgrown coconut plantation with many hidden ruins from the World War Two, Japanese bunkers and huge oil tanks rusted orange. "Oh, God, Jeton, this is so cool,"

Nora said as they combed through the jungle. Jeton had a machete, wasps bobbed over their heads, the air was sweet with the scent of *kōṇo* blossoms. They found a grassy mound that could have been a grave site or a buried ammo dump. There they slipped off their clothes and looked at each other in the filtered light. Then they kissed and kissed until their lips were raw and there was nothing left to do but exhaust each another way.

Why isn't this good enough?

Jeton comes ashore at last, wet up to the knees. As he walks, his borrowed Nikes sound like soggy mops against a tile floor.

Nora lives in one of the new pre-fabs at this end of the island. They all look alike and, for a moment, Jeton panics, hidden in the shadow of someone's central air. He doesn't know if he can remember the right duplex.

If they catch him what can they do?

Last night, while drinking, one of the older men said to him: "Loving American *likatu* is no big deal. Everyone has a story of loving American girls."

This is what he fears, that he is not special, that there is nothing in him that will make him different from anybody else. Doesn't matter if his grandmother owns one fourth of Kwajalein. Doesn't matter if he would've been a prince in another life. What is he now, right now?

Here comes the Security pickup with its big light. Lucky thing there are no dogs on Kwajalein, all that barking. Jeton scrambles farther into the shadows just as Security shoots its light where he was crouched. Truck slows to a stop, engine grumbling, light snaking through the dark stubbled yard between the pre-fabs, back porches, bamboo fence, gas grills, locked-up bicycles. Jeton pants, sucking air through his mouth, balled up behind a low fence. Shameful to be caught this way, like a shrimp curled under a rock.

Then the light is gone suddenly, and the truck rumbles on.

Jeton stands up, pushes the hair from his eyes, smooths it

back. He can smell his sweat, which he tried to hide with some borrowed English Leather cologne.

He finds the right duplex—Nora's mother put up a family name plate over the door bell, their name burnt into a slab of wood. Jeton leaves his Nikes by the back door, smells the warm-fishy odor rising from them. The door is unlocked. Nora explained that this is why Americans love Kwajalein—it is like a small town, she said, you can leave your door unlocked at night. Jeton smiles at this.

It is so cold inside Nora's house, Jeton shivers. Her cat, Simon, greets him, curling around his leg. A blue light gleams from the kitchen counter like a buoy in the distance. The house smells of chocolate cookies and ginger spice. Even in the dark it all looks familiar. He could live here, though he wouldn't clutter it up with all these little things, baskets and glass and books.

Carpet is thick as grass. Two minutes and Jeton is up the stairs. The door is closed to the room of Nora's parents. Nora says, old as they are, they still have sex. This makes Jeton smirk. It is something he would never say about his own mother and father.

He hesitates outside Nora's room, fingers pressed hard against her closed door. He does not want to scare her. If she wakes as he walks in, she might scream.

Slowly he eases the door open. Simon squeaks a birdlike meow behind him. He closes the door in the cat's face. Then the room envelopes him in Nora's baby-powdery, girlish-sweet smell. Tears burn at the corners of his eyes. Nora! The posters of pretty-faced rock stars on the wall, the crowd of stuffed animal toys on the bureau, and on the neat desk top the conch shell that Jeton gave her for Christmas. She uses it as a paperweight.

Her narrow bed, neatly made.

Her big suitcase on wheels stands next to it.

Jeton sits, nearly falls, into her desk chair and stares at her empty bed.

Gone!

* * * *

The difference between Kwajalein and Ebeye starts with the streets, Jeton decides. Here, they are wide and paved and bright with electric light. The houses are neat, they all look alike, the yards are clear of motorbikes, scrap wood, trash, and chickens, and everything everywhere is green.

Jeton prefers Ebeye. Or Majuro. The haphazard houses and the sandy streets that curl and twist like vines and the animals that run freely and the children playing everywhere you turn and the cooking smells and the women singing and the laundry flagging from the lines over the dirt yards—it all feels good. The Americans' place seems empty and haunted like Japanese war ruins on Jaluit.

Here it is, Britney's house. Plastic Chinese lanterns of many colors glow from the bamboo'd patio. Jeton hears several girls talking, laughing. Sleepover. He has guessed right. Far from the patio fence, Jeton crouches at the trunk of a palm tree and listens. He can't make out what they are saying. Maybe talking about hot boys. Maybe talking about college. Who can tell with girls? When there is a lull in the chatter, Jeton whistles. It is his special whistle, sounds like hissing and bird squeak at the same time. Everyone in his family does this whistle. Nora has teased him about it. "You think I'll answer *that*, like a dog or something?"

He whistles again. Now the girls whisper severely to one another. A wasp's nest. Then he hears his name, like a curse on their lips. *Jeton, it's Jeton.*

And he knows that he has made a mistake. He should run, he should leave Nora alone, he should give her space, something Americans are always talking about. He is making trouble. But he can't go, he won't go. Not now. He will take his punishment, whatever it is, like the day he reefed his uncle's boat, like the time he insulted his grandfather by patting him on the head like a child, like the night he got drunk and rode his brother's bicycle off the pier.

The patio door opens, a paw of yellow light leaps into the yard, and Nora—unmistakable silhouette—walks towards him. The pink of a nearby street lamp lights her face. It is the face of a smart woman. *Mālōtlōt.* The kind of woman who could live happily on an outlying atoll. Who would not cringe from cleaning fish. Who would not complain when the rains came.

She is popular, she has said, because she is not pretty like those models in the Nordstrom catalogue who scare Jeton because they look so *mej.* Dead. "Who could love them?" he asked her. "Why do Americans think these creatures are *jouj?*" Questions like these delight Nora: he can make her smile. This is how it should be always.

Tonight she wears a sparkly tank-top and white shorts and her white Birkenstocks. Tall, long legs, head up like she was walking at graduation. A woman who would sail with him through Toon Milu pass, north to Rongelap or Bikar or far-away Bokak.

What can he say to make her smile now?

He remains crouched, out of respect. He wants a cigarette, something to do with his hands.

"Jeton, what are you doing?"

His listens for love in her voice, a voice so much lower than any *ri-Majeḷ* woman or girl he knows. Americans talk deep in the throat with flat words.

"I die when I don't see you, Nora."

"How did you get here?"

"Walked."

"Across the reef?" She widens her lovely eyes. "Are you crazy?"

"Yes."

"Jeton." Sighing, she kneels near him. But then she has nothing to say.

Her freckles, he can see them now: a thousand islands he wants to inhabit.

He says, "I don't want you to go." The words hurt like fish

bone in his throat, make his eyes sting. As he swipes at his tears, he sees the other girls peering from behind the patio door.

Nora says, "What would I do here?" This sounds like a complaint.

He shrugs. "We could have fun."

He wants more than fun. He is sure she knows this.

She sighs again. Is she so tired? "We have been over this several times."

"You and me could do it, *lijera*, we could live on a island, just like we dreamed. You'd like it."

"It wasn't *my* dream," she says. Then, quickly she adds: "I'm seventeen, Jeton, what do I know about living on an atoll?"

It wasn't my dream. He tries to ignore this. Maybe all she needs is convincing.

"You could learn," he says. "You *love* it here, you said so."

"I'm *seventeen*!"

He says nothing, only stares at her, waiting. Then he does what the *ri-Majel* do best. He smiles.

"Why does this make you smile?" she asks.

"Seventeen, Nora. You can do anything."

"And that's what I want to do—anything and everything. Things I can't do if I'm stuck on a tiny island out here in the middle of nowhere."

"Nowhere?" There is no equivalent for *nowhere* in his language. *Ejjelok* maybe: nothing.

"I didn't mean it like that," she says quickly. She touches one finger to the top of his hand.

But she does not take his hand. He feels himself sinking, like a man wallowing in wet sand. Nowhere. What is nowhere?

He sees regret in her face, that sorry look he has seen after his mother loses a day's wages at cousin Amsa's weekly cock fight. *Gone*, her look says, *it's gone.*

Jeton weighs the American words of loss: *nothing, none, not, no.*

At last his *pālen* lays her hand lightly over his, brings him back abruptly, but he can hardly see her for the tide rising again in his eyes.

She says, "Jeton, don't you have any plans?"

"College, Nora? I'm no good at school."

"Maybe start with junior college."

"In the States? You don't want your *ri-Majel* boy in the States with you."

"I didn't say we'd be together, Jeton. I'm talking about your future, not about us."

"You are my future."

"I am your girlfriend, that's all. And day after tomorrow I'm going to fly away. That's a fact you have to accept."

"I don't want you to forget me," he says.

"Why would I forget you? How could I?" She lowers her head to meet his eyes.

Sitting in the half dark, palm tops clattering above them in the breeze, the girls spying on them from the patio, Security Patrol prowling somewhere nearby—Jeton understands that he wants more from Nora than she can give him. If only he could describe his feelings, he might change her mind. But there are not enough words and they are not the right kind of words.

"You will have other boyfriends," he says.

"And you won't ever have another girlfriend? You want to mummify me or something? I've got my life, you've got yours. Maybe you'll find your way to the States and we'll see each other. Maybe I'll decide I'd rather be here and I'll come back. Who can say? Anything can happen, just like you and I happened. "

He wishes she would take his hand, kiss it the way she used to, lay her face against his neck.

"You are right," he says. "I am just a boy, I don't know what I am doing."

She smiles at him. This is what he wants, that softening, that kindness. But he is lying to her. He believes that she is making a terrible mistake, that she will be in her big, cluttered American house years from now and she will look out at her big empty yard with its too-green grass and she will think of the life she could have had here with Jeton. But he knows that he cannot stop her. He knows that, as with certain lovely fish, he has to stay clear or risk great harm.

She says, almost in a whisper, "I'm not sorry for what we had, are you?"

"No, I am not sorry," he says. She will haunt him, he knows. He will see her always in his head: Nora running, Nora laughing, Nora waving to a friend, Nora's long fingers combing through his hair, Nora kissing him on the nose.

"Are you going to be all right?" she asks.

"I'm cool." Saying what the American boys always say.

"You're not going to do something crazy?"

"I will hang out till morning, then take the ferry back, OK?"

"Why don't you sleep on Brit's patio—we'll go inside." She offers him her kindest smile. "Please?"

It is impolite to deny an offer of hospitality. And he wants to make her happy. And he would like to be near her. Maybe in the morning she will change her mind. He knows this is a slim chance but it is more than he had a few minutes ago.

She does not kiss him when she says goodnight from the back door of Brit's house. He is sitting on the patio hammock, which swings slightly beneath him. The patio smells like candy sweetness. Girls. Jeton nods his goodnight to Nora, watches her close the door and disappear into the darkness beyond the kitchen. She feels sorry for him. That is not good. She will return in the morning to find him curled on the hammock like a stray dog. And he will smell of tonight's hard walking. And she will be eager to get home because she is excited about her trip. She is going places. 4,250 miles. And he is going to Ebeye. He is not going to college. He is not going to the States.

He does not lie down; there is no sleep in him. He leaves

the patio, the girlish sweetness still in his lungs. Sadness makes his heart feel like it is a piece of water-soaked wood. Sodden and sluggish. He stands in the street and stares up at the duplex, at the light in Brit's window. He imagines the girls will whisper all night long. They will give Nora advice, tell her how to dump Jeton in the morning.

He doesn't know how long he stands out here. A long time.

Then he hears a truck approaching. Security Patrol. But Jeton does not think fast enough to run. And suddenly it looks like morning, so much light around him.

He turns to the light. Truck light.

"Don't move, son."

It is the big-bellied black American officer named Ulysses. With a grunt of effort he steps out of the pickup. He reminds Jeton of his third uncle on his father's side. Except this man has no sideburns. The officer squints through the smoke of his cigarette, which he keeps at his mouth. He has his right hand on the gun at his wide leather belt. His other hand holds a big flashlight. Truck's spot makes Jeton squint hard.

"You got I.D.?" the officer asks. He stands to one side of the truck. Garble stutters through the little black radio attached to his shirt pocket. It looks like the weight of the man should pull him over.

Jeton slides his Velcro wallet out of his back pocket. Slowly. Everybody knows you have to move slow in front of Security.

The officer takes the wallet, flips it to the I.D. "Jeton DeGroen," he says. Flashlight on the I.D. "I heard about you. Your grandma owns half the island."

"A fourth."

The officer smiles, shakes his head like he knows something Jeton doesn't. "She gets a lot of money for that land. And I bet you see some of it."

Jeton wants to tell him that the land means nothing, it has always been here, it will stay here until the ocean decides to swallow it. He remembers what the teachers told him about how these atolls began. Coral attached itself to volcanoes and kept growing as the volcanoes sank. After a long time, the volcanoes were gone, sunken deep under water. But the coral remained, a circle of coral where the volcano used to be. That's what he feels inside him now, Nora gone but a hard crust left behind.

He says, "She has offered to buy me a used Toyota so I can have a taxi business on Majuro."

"There you go."

"Taxi's not my style."

"Neither is obeying the law apparently." The officer flicks away his cigarette, turns his head to the radio at his shoulder and says, "Got a code 40. Bringing him in, ten-four." Then he says to Jeton: "What's your excuse for breaking curfew, little man?"

"I don't need excuse."

"You better think one up."

In another life Jeton DeGroen would be a prince!

When Jeton doesn't answer, the officer says, "Man, in the States we'd send you to a work farm." He lights another cigarette with a silver Zippo lighter, like all the Security have, and doesn't seem in a hurry to go. Maybe because Jeton is so relaxed. Late night like this makes some people want to stand around and talk. Always somebody talking late on Ebeye—Jeton hears them every night, two or three people off here and there, smoking and talking.

"Got a smoke?" Jeton asks.

"Take the pack, little man." The officer tosses the cigarettes to him.

Like a fish flying from a wave, Jeton leaps forward—not for the cigarette pack but for the officer's big waist. Tackle him, he tells himself. Tackle him, then run away. It's not a plan exactly, it just happens. Boom! It reminds him of soccer, of diving for a shot that saves the game, his reflexes so quick, his jump so surprising, that it makes the American girls on the sidelines cheer, even though they are not supposed to cheer for the *Ri-Majel*, and then one of them, he notices, the tall, pretty one, flashes him her smile and Jeton knows he shouldn't give a second look, he knows that American girls are trouble, everyone says so, he really should leave them alone. Do not smile back! he cautions himself. But she is tall and freckled and beautiful, Miss America, and he is the center of her attention now—he remembers this so clearly, the cheering in his ears as loud as waves crashing over him. Of course he smiled back. Boom!

PART II

ELEVEN

The Alberg 35 is a remarkable boat, especially sturdy because it was constructed in the 1960s before builders knew the full capacity of fiberglass—which means they overbuilt the hulls. Its full keel makes it very stable, especially when skidding down a wave. Its swan-tail stern, its low free-board, and stepped-coach roof give it a classic look, like something from the 1920s. There's not a lot of head room, even the fans of the Alberg will tell you, but the cabin's well laid out, with a fairly spacious V-berth in the forward. Like most production boats, all of the Albergs are numbered. Cooper's was number 282, built in 1967 at the Whitby yard in Ontario, Canada. It's a number that comes to him now in odd ways, when he reads tide charts, when he works through algorithms in his practice programs, when he glances at his bedside digital alarm in the early morning. Even when he's dialing Lillian's number, "282" is right there in the middle.

He did some custom work on his Alberg, reinforcing the mast with two arches of 4-inch-wide aluminum at the step beam because, over the years, the beam had shrunk. He also increased the water hold three-fold, installed an enzymatic treatment system for his head, a larger tank for diesel, and put in a breaker panel after switching the electrical system from 6 to 12 volts. One thing he didn't do was ground the mast for lightning strikes. That's a judgment call because a grounded mast, of course, has more conductivity. He feared lightning strikes more than rogue waves.

All of this he finds consistently, thoroughly fascinating. But nobody wants to hear it. He's a bore when he tries to describe, say, the nuance of water, how a dark spot in the distance might be a coral head or a cloud shadow or a frightful anomalous chasm. Approach it at your peril! And how about this: in the open sea, some parts of the ocean are totally devoid of GPS signals. Those signals, even in the best of circumstances, are often abused and deformed by solar flares and other electromagnetic act-ups. Sometimes you have to rely on an old fashioned compass—pretty much the kind John Paul Jones used. Or Blackbeard the Pirate. And how about the garbage? Miles of garbage caught in currents and carried in ocean-wide gyres that look like the leavings of an obliterated armada. Fascinating and appalling. And porpoises racing his boat, so many porpoises he can't count them, bulleting through the whitecaps, their speed seeming to propel him, their gleeful company like a hero's welcome.

What he won't tell anybody is the nightmare that now plagues him. Actually, it's a dreamy reenactment of a mistake he made before he reached Hawaii. The kind of mistake that happens to a lot of sailors. He fell overboard for no good reason. The Lickety Split sort of hiccupped and the next thing he knew he was in the water. The stupid thing is that he wasn't tethered to his lifeline. He wasn't wearing his Personal Flotation Device either. Incredibly careless. And stupid stupid stupid. Stupid also was the luck that allowed him to grab the knotted line he was dragging from the stern. The autopilot was on and the Lickety Split was clipping along at about 5 knots. Grabbing that line, he felt the boat tug him forward. A tiger by the tail. They say that most drowned sailors are found with their flies down because they've been bumped from the stern while taking a piss. And none of them smart enough to have secured their life-lines. Like Cooper.

Sputtering, gasping, slapping through the foam, Cooper was splayed in the water like shark bait. Had he not grabbed that rope, the boat would have plowed on until it was a speck in the distance and then gone.

By the time Cooper kicked his way to the rail, having yanked himself from one knot to the next, he was nearly hoarse from howls of effort and heaves for air. With one final pull, his feet flat against the gunnels, he reeled himself up, then fell like a landed fish upon the deck. And the Lickety Split sailed on, up and down on the swells, the spray raining over him while the clouds stretched their white fingers far above.

When he relives this in his recurring dream, there is no suggestion of triumph or relief. Instead, he wakes with a gasp, his phantom leg throbbing. In the back of his head, he hears distant wailing like a sailor's widow cursing the sea. He understands that the grief is his own for the obvious loss he struggles to accept. With Sarah's help via Skype, he talks through optimistic scenarios, imagining himself jogging on his prosthetic leg (due in six weeks). He vows to try even harder at PT. He pictures himself with extraordinary muscles, a newfound energy, and an unflagging determination that will win him friends and admirers. But fear dogs him. He is convinced that the recurring nightmare is not about his past but his future, as though he were destined to make a more terrible mistake than the one he's already made.

As he swings on the fulcrum of his aluminum crutches, he is startled at how quickly he loses his breath, how his heart churns in his chest like a chipmunk in a paper bag. Gasping, he hangs forward, his underarms burning, his weight stopped on his trembling left leg. He imagines that he looks like one of those dust-colored gulls he sees at every turn—big birds watching for a handout or an opportunity.

"Coop, give us five more," Gus, his trainer, says.

Five more steps, he means.

Already Cooper's back is dripping sweat, his T-shirt clinging. Since his release from the hospital, he sweats cat piss. All those drugs. He can't eat much and has lost a lot of weight. No joke! Pale, sunken-eyed, ill-shaven, he looks like a man undergoing a different kind of rehab.

Gus, by contrast, is bronzed and meaty, though he hardly looks athletic. He's of medium height, with stout legs, and a puffy face. But he's relentless about the work, loves to be outdoors, and claims to jog 5 miles a day.

Every morning he brings Cooper here, to the "Recreation Center," a large pre-fab facility with an ocean view. It looks like any other health club, right down to the TVs hanging over the treadmills and stationary bikes. From the inside of a place like the Rec Center, you'd never know you weren't in America. It makes Cooper think of the episode from the campy "Prisoner" series, where the bad guys build a duplicate of London in order to fool their captive, John Drake, into thinking he is home again.

Gus has Cooper working in the matted area, where children practice tumbling and jujitsu. He works out three times a day, with an hour's rest between each session and a two-hour lunch. This is the last of his sessions today and he is exhausted, though he has promised himself that he won't complain.

Cooper has decided also that he won't be self-conscious about the spectacle he has become. *Let them stare, every one of them*, he tells himself, *it will only do me good*.

He looks up at Gus who is beckoning him like an eager father. Gus has unruly black hair that would better suit an Asian pop star. His droopy face almost gives him the look of a friendly dog—a basset hound, perhaps. Like Bo, his father's pet.

Cooper has fallen only once, mindful to lunge to his left in order to protect his outsized, thoroughly swaddled stump. He's pretty good at stabbing the floor with his crutches, shifting from one rubber tip to the other until his vertigo subsides. What's throwing him off—and he dare not mention it—is the leg that pretends to be there. Though long gone, his right still weighs him down, attempting to flex as he walks, attempting to help him balance, attempting to do the work that it can't possibly do. Because it's gone. The first couple of days, it was creepy. Now it's just a bizarre nuisance. He and Sarah have Skyped about it plenty. And he's downloaded all kinds of literature about it. But why do the reading? There's no cure for the phantom leg, no psychological purge that might make it disappear in mind as it has disappeared in actuality. The ghost is simply something he'll have to live with. Maybe for the rest of his life. *So, see? I didn't really lose my leg after all!* Such feeble jokes are the best he can do for now.

DataCell offered to send Cooper to Hono for six weeks of the intensive PT but Cooper sensed that it would be a mistake to absent himself from his new community for so long. By toughing it out here, he can save DataCell a lot of money, win himself some points with his supervisors, and make some connections on the island. Cooper never considered himself so calculating but, since the Benefit Specialist's visit a week ago, he has become very cautious. His every other thought now, it seems, is about survival: keeping his job, securing his future. Whatever it takes to keep from returning as damaged goods to his parents' modest rancher in Baltimore.

"You're doing great," Gus says, five stiff steps away, his bushy eyebrows raised expectantly, his hands open, fingers wriggling encouragement.

Cooper leans into the rubber crutch pads and tries not to wince, letting his left leg swing forward. It's not so hard, really. His arms quiver, though, and his palms smart as if from a recent fall.

He thought that the exercise he got on the boat would have kept him in shape—he was always running fore and aft, raising a sail, tying off a line, cranking a windlass, wrestling with the wheel. But this business of recovery is something wholly different, like learning to climb the granite face of a mountain. It is devastatingly humbling and he fights hard to keep self-pity at bay. And he worries about the medications. Inez warned him about the pills. He has too many pills and he takes them too readily.

Cooper makes his landing, sticks it, then wavers. How his body trembles!

"Don't get tricky," Gus coaches. "If you swing out like that on both crutches, you're going to fall for sure. Use your right crutch the way you would use a leg." He nods a smile, which Cooper refuses to acknowledge.

Behind him, a girl in a pink body stocking—younger than Bailey, maybe eight—is practicing cartwheels and handstands on the mat. Cooper tries not to watch with envy in the mirrored wall to his right. He hears the whirring of the bicycles and the shucking of the treadmills from the room next door. Straight ahead, behind Gus, is the salt-hazed picture window that looks to the oceanside, where now and then the wave-crash rises above the shoreline rocks. Very bright out there.

Nurse Inez told him that Kwajalein is like a modest resort town that time forgot.

"You may never want to leave," she said.

He wasn't sure if she meant this seriously. She and an orderly visit him in his trailer every few days to make sure he is doing all right. That he got a trailer is unusual. DataCell made special arrangements for him because he insisted he would be coming as a family. Otherwise, he would have been in one of the bachelor dorms just off of 7th, the island's main street. As it is, he's got one of the old trailers in "Silver City," on the island's lagoon side. His isn't nearly as nice as most, because it's transient housing, but it's a lot of room for one man on this island.

Cooper hops forward to reposition himself the right way. Time, he thinks, it takes so much time to do something so simple. The GP has prescribed him an antidepressant because Cooper has expressed anxiety over the smallest things. He can't stop thinking about his boat. And he'll talk about the Lickety Split anywhere any time. Maybe this is why the Colonel has postponed his reception for Cooper. The truth is, and maybe everybody knows this now: Cooper just isn't ready.

His phantom leg feels as solid as either crutch. It's right there, man, eager to help. How can he deny what it so convincingly insists? So Cooper, with a sudden wild thrill, lets it have its way: he lets the leg take that next step. Because it's right there!

He falls face-forward. Like someone has pulled the rug out from under him. A dirty trick. He swallows a yelp of fear, feels one crutch bonk him on the back of his head, sees the other pitch forward, Cooper's hands free but not in time to break his fall. He slams first his left knee, cushioned by the floor pad, thankfully, and he thinks he's done, okay, that wasn't so bad, but then he's abruptly off balance because there is no right knee to stop him. He falls hard on his stitched-up stump. Like someone jabbing him with a flaming torch. A hot line of pain relays through his bones, up his spinal column, then hits home, oddly, in the left side of his face. He howls.

Gus is there but not in time. Now Cooper lies curled on his side, groaning. He fights back tears of rage. With the help of an attendant, Gus gets him into his wheelchair, one of those institutional clunkers with fat wheels and plastic sling seats. Through the pulsing pain, Cooper thanks them both, wishing he could close his eyes and disappear. The little girl, now in the company of several other little girls, gapes at him from a few yards away. He hears their hungry whispers. By night fall, this tidbit of gossip will be all over the island.

As Gus wheels him outside, where the heat nearly makes him breathless. Cooper examines the bandages of his stump. Oh, yeah, the blood is coming, soaking through like fresh meat in white butcher's paper. The bone feels like it's smoldering. He won't get the 118 stitches removed for another 20 days. Now maybe longer. If he weren't still on pain killers, he would have passed out.

Gus and the taxi driver lift him, still in his chair, into the back of the van. It seems that half the island is gawking at him from the glassed double doors of the Rec Center as the taxi drives off. In the far back, perched in his chair, Cooper feels ready to weep. Wimp!

Gus sits nearby. Quietly he says, "You looked like you wanted to test that leg you lost, Cooper. That's natural. That's part of the process."

They take Ocean Road. Ocean Road hugs the shore and will take you to the far west end of the island, past the airfield, which takes up most of the island, then past the "country club" and the pathetic 9-hole golf course, right to the base of Mt. Olympus, a now defunct missile silo embedded in 28-foot mound of sand and dirt—the highest point in all of the Marshall Islands. Cooper's gotten the official tour of every site visible from the seat of a van. It's all thoroughly unimpressive.

*　*　*　*

Lib is a tiny island, two and a quarter miles wide, just 35 miles south of Kwajalein. It contains a small village of Marshallese who farm and fish. There is no dock. If you come to Lib, you must launch a dinghy so that you can beach it in the sand. Lib has generous beaches on all sides. Nobody has reason to visit Lib, despite its beauty. The small brackish lake in the middle of the island hosts no fish. Jeton believes this island would have been ideal for him and Nora.

After his arrest on Kwajalein, this is where they sent Jeton. No Marshallese has ever been sent away in this fashion. The Marshallese do not believe in imprisonment. In the past, families controlled their troublemakers. Nowadays, this is not so easy and there is a modest jail on Majuro, a cinderblock building surrounded by a chainlink fence. Mostly it holds drunks overnight.

Jeton really angered the Americans. That's why he is on Lib. As soon as he tackled the Security officer, another Security truck arrived. Two big men got out and held Jeton while the tackled officer, who was very angry, beat Jeton until he could beat him no more. That officer then went to the hospital for a pulled muscle. Nobody asked him about his battered knuckles. The next day, Jeton could see only a sliver of light through his swollen eyes. His nose was broken, as were two ribs. He was missing three teeth, his lips split. His left ear was the size of a clamshell. Security charged Jeton with resisting arrest.

Then a fat American showed up at noon and started yelling at the officers.

"Are you fucking crazy?" he said. "Look at this boy!"

The man's name is Mister Norman. He sat with Jeton in the cell and asked questions in Marshallese: "Are you all right? Can you tell me what happened?"

Jeton could only shrug. It didn't matter what had happened. He had lost Nora. Later, Mister Norman brought a doctor who bandaged Jeton, then gave him a shot and a bottle of pills. All the while Mister Norman was taking pictures with his phone. At one point, Jeton gave him the finger. Americans hate the finger. But Mister Norman only gave Jeton the finger back.

Before he left that afternoon, he said to Jeton, "They're going to pay for this, do you understand?"

Jeton nodded yes but he wasn't sure because "pay" to Americans has many meanings. Early the next morning, one of the Security officers woke Jeton up, handcuffed him, then led him to a room down the hall. He put a cardboard cup of coffee in his hands and said, "We expect you to be a good boy today." The room had no windows. It smelled of bad air conditioning. There was a long table at one end of the room and several folding chairs. Jeton wondered if they would beat him again. It did not seem likely.

But then the officers who had beaten him strode into the room, followed by another officer with a fancy cap and then a man wearing a black robe. Mister Black Robe was tall and thin, with a balding head and a long *ri-pālle* nose. He introduced himself as a "magistrate" and said, "We can settle this matter now and you won't go to prison if you waive your rights to an attorney. Do you agree?"

"I can go home?" Jeton asked. The coffee cup he held was very hot.

"If you agree, you will go home as soon as possible," Black Robe said. "And you will not go to prison."

Jeton had heard of "prison." He knew it was a dangerous place but he wondered where it would be. In the States?

"Understand," Black Robe said, "you have violated the rules of the Compact and in effect have forfeited your rights."

The man with the fancy cap said, "Do you agree, Jeton?"

Jeton nodded his head. "I agree."

"Fine," said Black Robe. He sat behind the table. "Let us begin."

They reviewed the "facts," then asked Jeton to agree or disagree with these facts. *Did you, Jeton DeGroen, jump off the ferry last night? Did you swim to Kwajalein? Did you know this was a violation of the curfew? Also a violation of regulation 324 about Kwajalein security? Did you attack Officer Ulysses?*

When they were done, Black Robe brought his hand down flat on the table and said, "Your actions, Jeton DeGroen, were most egregious and harmful. You put yourself and others at risk. You willfully broke the law on several counts. If it were within my power, I would send you to prison for a long time. However, as I must operate within the mandate of the Compact, I hearby ban you for life from Kwajalein and sentence you to six months community service on Lib Island. This sentence will be under review by your governors on Ebeye. That is all."

Then two officers took Jeton to the pier, where a big motorboat was waiting. The boat's captain was a Marshallese Jeton had not seen before. He was probably from Majuro. Jeton wondered how much they were paying this man to take Jeton away. It all happened so fast and he was so groggy from his injuries, Jeton did not have time to think through the events. He assumed that Mister Norman had abandoned him. Everybody knows you cannot trust the Americans. They say many things and make many promises but in the end they do only what they please.

So, three hours later, Jeton was dropped on the beach of Lib

Island with a bag of items they had given him: a tube of lip balm, a spray can of deodorant, a toothbrush and tube of toothpaste, a comb, a bar of soap wrapped in paper, two T-shirts, a pair of shorts, a pair of *zori*, and a roll of toilet paper. As he watched the dinghy return to the big motorboat, he shaded his eyes with his hands and began to bawl. Only now was his isolation, his punishment, becoming clear.

When he found the Lib village, he was brought to the elder, a small silver- haired Marshallese who said kindly, "Nobody told us you were coming. Do you have family here?"

Jeton shook his head no. He felt like a five-year-old before this serious, soft-spoken old man. An old woman brought Jeton a warm can of Coke and Jeton understood this was precious for them because who ever visits Lib to bring them soft drinks? *Kommool!* he said.

Then he explained that he had been sent to do "community service," whatever the Libians needed from him: he would work for them until somebody came to fetch him back to Ebeye.

"What did you do wrong?" the old man asked.

"I hit an American policeman," Jeton said.

The old man nodded his head solemnly. "And he hit you in return."

"Yes."

"Let me think of what you can do for us," the old man said.

"*Kommool,*" Jeton said again.

That was two weeks ago. His face is nearly healed. Nora is far, far away. It is not clear to Jeton if anybody knows where he is. He worries about his *mama*. At night, as he lies on his pallet outside the old man's hut, Jeton thinks about how he has shamed his family. He wonders if they will ever want to see him again. Then he thinks of the Americans and how they made jokes as they beat him. Jeton would like to make them pay for that. But how might they pay? This is such an American way of thinking, and so hateful, it makes Jeton burn and ache and keeps his eyes wide open for hours, the sky's star-spray wheeling over him like a far-away storm of sea shells.

The village elder has put Jeton to work harvesting coconuts. This is hard work because it demands that Jeton split the husks over sharp stakes. He must be careful not to slip; otherwise, he could impale one of his hands.

He eats his meals with the old man and his family. There are few children here and no teenagers. The youngest man is 30. The village of plywood and tin huts seems like an outpost for the dying, as if this were the edge of the world and nothing were left anywhere else.

When Jeton stands on the beach and peers across the water, he understands how small he is in the world. It is a new feeling. It is the feeling of growing older, of knowing that other people can harm you easily and then walk away. This thought turns in his head relentlessly as he works in the shade of a palm, slamming husks against a stake, over and over all day long.

* * * *

Working at Kwajalein's only retail store is like being pilloried: she's naked and on display to the mocking world. Not that Alison has any grounds for complaint. After losing her teaching job, it was a miracle she could get any work on the island. Here in sporting goods, she sees too many people she knows. Always they look at her with a mixture of fear and pity, as if worried that she will ask too much of them. She hangs onto her composure with a grim determination that makes her temples throb and her hands tremble. It is a cruel irony that the most popular merchandise she sells is scuba diving gear.

Gayla was in tears when she delivered the news. "Sweety, you need help and I can't do it. We've got to let you go. You'll get two weeks' severance." Alison did not press her, did not beg or whine or wail, for she had seen it coming from a long way off and was almost relieved that, at last, she had hit bottom. Now she knew where she was, at least. The hard part wasn't accepting her failure, it was finding a way to explain it to Doug and Stan.

That week she went cold turkey. The boys thought she was simply out sick. She vomited every morning, screamed into her pillow as terrorist bombs exploded in her head hour after hour, could hardly stand for the trembling that racked her body, got bronchitis and went on antibiotics, tried valiantly to eat good food and drink lots of water. Then on her ninth day the world leveled out as though her life raft had, at last, drifted out of the storm and into a beam of sunlight. She was deeply grateful for the sudden calm but not certain she could trust it. Tentatively, she tested her bounds, cleaning up the chaos of her modest home, then sending out resumes. Already the Colonel's adjutant had sent her a separation notice informing her that, without employment, she would have to return to the States within the month.

She made a mac and cheese and broccoli casserole, then sat the boys down. For the first time in recent memory, the TV was off. Doug and Stan regarded her with suspicion. She said, "You've probably heard by now that I'm no longer teaching at the school."

Doug nodded yes. Stan narrowed his eyes at her. He said, "I hit Tamara Suleski in the nose because she called you a dope-head."

Alison winced at hearing this. "Why haven't I gotten a note about this?"

"I threw the note away," he said. "They put me in detention."

"Are you a dopehead?" Doug asked.

"No, I'm an alcoholic," she said. "That's not quite the same thing."

"Are you going to die because of alcohol?" Stan asked.

"No," she said. "The alcohol is gone. I'm going to get better."

"You sure?" Doug said.

"I'm sure." She explained how alcoholism works and why some people are more prone to it than others and how alcoholics need help and should always be on guard for things that may make them want to drink again.

"Alcohol is why you got us that sucky DVD?" Stan asked.

"Yes. I'm sorry."

"And why you were going out with that doctor?"

Alison felt the heat of shame rush to her cheeks. *What have the boys heard?* "That's over," she said. "I will not see him again."

"He's a creepy looking guy," said Stan.

"Well, we don't shun people on the basis of their looks," she said.

"Not even Arnold Arnold?" said Doug.

"Especially not Arnold Arnold."

Alison has heard that April is now "seeing" Emil Timmerman! She pities poor April and has wondered if she should say something. But what is there to say? Would Alison have listened to anybody when she was on the way down with Emil?

This afternoon, Erik's former diving partner, Gus Collingswood, comes into the store to ask about spear guns. He wears his usual track suit, his thick sun-bleached hair disheveled from pedaling his bike in the wind. His crooked smile is abjectly apologetic.

"No problem," Alison says. "I've done some research on these. You know everyone's getting away from the pneumatics, right?"

She's pointing to seven spearguns hanging on the wall. Erik never swam with one.

"What's wrong with the pneumatics?" Gus asks.

"It's hard to load the powerful ones," she says, not sure if he's patronizing her. "And there's some problems with aim because you can't see the spear inside the barrel."

Selling is like teaching: read the material, then deliver it with authority and, Bingo, you're good to go! She doesn't get a commission but the store manager tracks sales closely in every department.

"You saying I should go with the old-fashioned band style?" Gus asks. His hand tremble as he gestures to guns on the wall.

His too-moist eyes show gratitude and relief.

He wants this. And Alison wants this.

"That's right, Gus. They've got the power, which you can regulate by adding or subtracting bands. You can see precisely where your spear is headed. They're easy to load. And there's virtually no maintenance."

""Wow," he says. "That's impressive, Alison."

She hands him an expensive model with a teak stock. "You won't be disappointed."

Gus takes the gun, tests its bands' strength, its level, its grip. As Alison watches, she monitors the beating of her heart and tries to ignore the clutter of disturbing images in her head: the night Gus arrived with the news, his unrestrained grief, the seeming absurdity of the situation, her husband lost in the silt-black depths of the Tokiwa. It's a kind of PTSD. "You are entitled to your feelings," her counselor told her, "but you have to able to choose when to deal with them and especially when to show them."

As she rings him up, Gus says, "I've been helping Cooper Davies with his physical therapy, did you know?"

"I think everybody knows that, Gus. He's improving rapidly?"

"Yeah. The thing driving him is his boat. He's crazy desperate to get back his boat."

"What happened to his boat?"

"Somebody stole it," he says. "On an outer island."

"Can he still sail?"

"Not so long ago it seemed there was so many things the handicapped weren't able to do. Or weren't allowed to do. But now, who's to say?"

"Are we still allowed to say *handicapped?*"

He smiles and shrugs. "*Differently abled?* Whatever, Cooper Davies could be a sailor again, I think."

"But first he's got to find his boat." She wraps the gun in a large plastic bag, then hands it over.

"He's asked Art Norman to help him."

"The Cultural Liaison—that big old guy?"

"He says Norman knows all the atolls and islands."

"That's a lot of atolls and islands."

"Yeah, well, whatever floats your boat, as they say."

She chuckles, though not convincingly. "That's a pun, Gus!"

"Thanks much, Alison." He says this as if they have made peace finally. "You're looking great, by the way."

Wearing a cotton short-sleeved blouse and sky-blue slacks with black sandals, her hair cut short, her face slightly sun-touched, she's not sure if "great" is the right word, but she is sure she looks better than she has in a long time.

* * * *

Manning's white pickup is parked in front of the Colonel's house when Art arrives—panting—on his bicycle. It's a blustery day, a strong wind charging off the oceanside reef. It rained this morning, the typical short torrent, puddles gleaming now on the asphalt. It will rain again this evening. And then it will rain and rain more for the next several months because this is the rainy season. Art waits until he's regained his breath. The colonel's house is the best on the island, which isn't saying much: a flat-roofed, white-washed rancher with a plate glass picture window on the street side and a broad terrace on the back with a splendid view of the ocean.

The Colonel—Sandy Sanderson—answers the door. He's tall and lean and has the confident swagger of a golf pro. Art sees him running 5K every morning past the Transit. Dressed in khakis, the Colonel smiles a smile that's not really a smile when he says, "Morning, Art." It occurs to Art that the Colonel might look on him more kindly if Art were fit and trim too. Art attempts to offer a firm shake when the Colonel takes his hand. But Art knows that his own hand is too small and soft for the likes of the Colonel, and he hates that he feels so self-conscious, so inferior, in the company of such men.

Manning doesn't get up from the bamboo couch when Art and the Colonel enter the living room. The room's white-cushioned furniture and spare mid-century elegance remind Art of a doctor's waiting room. Through the sliding glass doors that lead to the patio, where old pandanus trees shade the coral pavers, Art hears waves slamming the nearby shore. High tide.

Manning, a forty-something ex-cop from Fort Lauderdale, captains the civilian Security force the Army hired to look after Kwajalein's citizens. He has the ice-blue eyes of a Malamute, a bushy black mustache, and bronzed skin. His jaw gleams from a close shave. If the Colonel threw a stick, Manning would sprint after it and bring it back eagerly in his teeth. Art resents the bulge of biceps through the man's navy-blue short-sleeved shirt but takes some satisfaction in the spill of belly over his fat black belt, which creaks when he reaches over to take Art's hand.

Manning flashes his whitened teeth and Art nods in return.

Manning says, "You should wear a hat, Art. That sun isn't good for your skin."

Art sits in the nearest armchair so that the three men are triangulated around the glass-topped coffee table. He says, "If I had a hat as pretty as yours, Manning, I'd wear one."

"Let's get down to business," says the Colonel. "Art, you've filed a complaint on behalf of Jeton DeGroen but I can't entertain something like that without better protocol."

"There hasn't been ANY protocol—that's my complaint!" says Art. *Steady, old man. Pace yourself.* "Manning and his crew railroaded the boy and now nobody knows where he is. Where is he, Manning?"

"We remanded the case to the Ebeye governors," says Manning. Art can smell the man's spice cologne and something else: baby powder? "It's in their hands. It's their call."

"You tried the boy without counsel or representation!"

"He's eighteen," says Manning. "Not a boy. And he waived

his rights to counsel. We have witnesses."

Art turns to the Colonel. "This is a scandal. And I'm telling you as an expert in these matters, if you don't rectify it fast we're going to have an international incident."

Manning frowns dismissively. "What's that supposed to mean, Art?"

"It means bad press for you and the Colonel in every news outlet around the world. This is precisely the kind of story the muckrakers and flaks want." *That's right, speak their language, make it look like you're protecting their interests.* "I've got the photos of the boy's injuries—"

"He resisted arrest."

"Really? That's why he was beaten to a pulp by three men?"

"Art, I want those photos," says the Colonel. "We can't have those loose in the world."

"I want Jeton DeGroen," says Art. "Where is he?"

"One step at a time," says the Colonel. "Where are the photos now?"

"On my computer," Art lies. Actually, they are in his phone and nowhere else. All the Colonel has to do is extend his hand and say, "Hand over your phone, Art." But he doesn't because Art is nipping at their heels with a catastrophe-in-the-making. Art can see that both men are calculating the costs.

"Jeton DeGroen trespassed, broke the law on Army property—"

"His grandmother owns part of this island, maybe the plot this house is sitting on," says Art. "Kwajalein is leased property. Believe me, you don't want to get into a shouting match with the Marshallese about who has what rights on land that has been in their hands for two millennia."

"Art's right," says the Colonel. "This is tricky."

Ah, there. Manning stares at Art as though he were about to smile. That's the kind of kid Manning was, a muscled bully with big hair and an impudent smile. The more trouble he made, the broader the smile. No apologies. Boys like that terrorized Art.

"The law's on our side," says Manning. "We've got witnesses—"

"Fuck your witnesses," says Art. "It comes down to bullying and manipulation of the facts. Everybody's going to think so."

"I'll ask you to keep it civil," says the Colonel. "We're all in this together."

This is a reminder Art doesn't want to hear. But it is the truth: Art is a government employee and, chances are, when the scandal hits, he'll get skinned with everybody else.

"We did due diligence," Manning says. "The report went from our desk to the desk of Ebeye's magistrate."

"What were they supposed to do with such a report after the fact?" Art says. "They can't even get running water but three days a week on Ebeye. You think anybody over there has the time or resources to unravel American red tape for one boy on a cramped island that has six thousand boys?"

"We did what we had to do." Manning speaks without affect. Neither anger nor indignation. It's his Official voice.

"You did wrong and you know it!" says Art. "Now there's shit to shovel. Let's get the boy back and make this right."

"The boy's on Lib," says the Colonel. "No harm done."

"Lib? Jesus! He has no family on Lib. That's harm enough. What did you expect him to do on Lib?"

"Community service," says Manning.

"An American concept," says Art in disgust, "which somehow they're supposed to replicate on remote Lib—just because you say so?"

"All right," says the Colonel. "Enough! Joe, let's get DeGroen back. Art, I want those photos today. Then contact the Ebeye people and see if we can make this go away."

"He broke the law," says Manning.

Art sputters. "And you broke his nose and his ribs and then, without consultation or mediation, you sent him to a remote island where he knows nobody. Congratulations, Manning, that's never been done. A new low in American arrogance."

The Colonel touches one finger to Art's sunburned arm. "Art, you've got to cool your jets. I know you're upset. We're all upset. But what's done is done. Let's clean this up and move on."

"Yes, sir." Manning is nodding his good cop nod. Then he turns to Art. "You need a ride back? Come on, you can put your bike in the bed of my truck."

"That's the spirit," says Colonel. "No hard feelings."

Manning smiles the smile of a man who knows he will always win. He extends his big gym-callused hand to Art. Reluctantly, Art shakes, refusing to betray his pain when Manning's nut-cracker grip crushes his hand.

Outside, after the Colonel waves them off and closes the door, Manning says, "Really, you need a hat, Art. I don't like the look of those scabs on your forehead. I've been here four years and never got a burn." He raises his bronzed arms. "SPF 40, Art. You can't take the sun for granted."

With a low grunt, Art pulls up his rusty bike, then wheels it across the tough carpet of grass. "Thanks for the advice, Manning. You're an inspiration."

"You don't want a ride?" Manning opens the door of his pick-up. Black block letters on each door say, SECURITY. "A bad wind today."

"I'll suffer through it," says Art. "I expect an email from you about the boy's retrieval."

"I'm not here to get in anybody's way, Art. I'm just doing my job, following the letter of the law."

Art waits until Manning has driven off before launching himself onto his bike, then wobbling precariously into a nasty headwind.

TWELVE

Allison is still getting faculty/staff emails from the school. Principal Callahan has called for a special assembly at noon because there was a second beheading in Iraq and two of last year's seniors were just blown to pieces by an IED. "The Heroes of '04," Callahan calls them. Alison can't imagine what the principal is going to do or say at the assembly. He can't make the children pray together. And he's lousy at speeches. Maybe he'll get Yolanda Peterson, the librarian, to sing something soulful. And the kids will be in tears, as if they aren't traumatized enough.

When summer break starts in two weeks, Stan and Doug will be taking classes in Tai Kwan Do, swimming, drawing and painting, soccer, t-ball, and Marshall Island culture. And still it won't be enough to keep them busy. Alison can't get any time off from work to look after them and worries that they'll learn to live apart from her. Dutifully, she goes to counseling once a week. Whenever Doug and Stan ask her a hard question—"Do you still want to drink sometimes?"—she answers as honestly as she can. She's holding nothing back, she wants them to know.

But she doesn't know how to explain the war to them.

"Sometimes we fight because that's the way to make the world safe," she says.

"What did Iraq do to us?" Doug asks. They are eating in their dining area. New rule: no TV during dinner. Tonight's fare, a culinary feat for Alison, is a cheese and spinach casserole made with cream of mushroom soup and topped with fried onion rings. Something her mother still makes.

"Did the Iraqers burn the American flag?" asks Stan, who has learned that this could get one arrested—or sent off the island.

"They were developing nasty weapons," Alison says. "Which they were going to use to hurt a lot of people."

"Everybody has nasty weapons," says Doug. "Mister Norman, the cultural expert, told us about America dropping nuclear bombs on islands right here."

"What islands?" Stan asks eagerly. "Where?"

"Bikini and Eniwetak," Doug says smugly. "Right here in the Marshall Islands."

"Nuclear bombs?" Stan asks. "The ones with the mushrooms?"

"Right here," Doug repeats, relishing the curious respect Stan is showing him. "Many times. And the fallout was everywhere. And people got sick."

"That was a long time ago," Alison says, trying to quell their excitement. "And it was a mistake."

She has heard about this—and about that island, Runit, where all the nuclear waste has been dumped under a cap of concrete, off-limits now for 250,000 years.

"A mistake that happened over and over?" Doug asks suspiciously.

"You've got to be stupid to keep mistaking over and over," Stan says.

"Well, America has done a lot of stupid things," she says.

"I thought we were the greatest country in the world," Doug says.

"We are!" Alison says. "Of course we are. But sometimes we make mistakes."

"Then the war in Iraq is a good thing?" asks Doug.

Stan narrows his eyes skeptically. "We're making a mistake. That's what people say."

"The president and his advisors think this is the right thing to do, so we're doing it," Alison says.

"Do you think it's the right thing to do?" Doug asks.

Alison thinks of Erik and her fear, thirteen years earlier, of the Gulf War. How different would their lives have been had he gone? Now, it seems, Erik's drowning will always be tied up in Alison's mind with the miscalculated Iraq war, which was supposedly finished—"mission accomplished"—by the time Erik entered the long-sunk Japanese battle cruiser.

Yes, she wants to tell her boys, *the war in Iraq is a terrible mistake. Just as coming here to Kwajalein was a mistake.*

So why not leave? her parents keep asking her. Even Erik's parents. Everyone wants to see the boys growing up. "You've got nothing to prove," her brother Eddie told her just last week on the phone. It was Eddie who convinced Alison to stay with Erik years ago.

Alison was seventeen and Erik eighteen when, to their mutual surprise, they started dating. Erik was as familiar to her as the neighborhood they both shared and, at first, he seemed no more exciting. But he blossomed in his senior year, filling out, growing another couple of inches, and looking decidedly grown-up with his mustache. She liked how he talked about the fall of Rome or the rise of the middle class the way other boys talked about video games. And he seemed fearless about the prospect of the draft and the Gulf War, which had just started. "It's living history," he joked. "Why wouldn't I want to be a part of that?"

"Because it's about killing," she said.

"I'll be a medic," he said. "Not everybody carries a gun."

That night she knew she wanted him. Not because he was foolish enough to welcome war but because he so clearly knew that he would survive whatever would become of him. Like her, he had applied to the University of Wisconsin-Milwaukee, a big urban school for the kids who couldn't afford Madison.

During one of their recreational drives that summer—she borrowed her father's Delta 88—she found a dirt road and pulled into a stand of trees. There, hastily, dripping sweat in the closed up car, they wrestled their way to each other's skin. When he came, she wasn't sure whether or not she came too, so much was going through her—the satisfaction of feeling his release, the bass-drum booming of her heart in her head, and the simple thrill of having made this happen.

She had lost her virginity at sixteen to Billy Nichols, who had won third place for the butterfly in the state swim meet that year: he had flattered her into his parents' bed. Then she dated Terry Schuler for six months but, just when she thought they were going to be forever, he went Goth on her. As she entered her senior year of high school, she felt idle and out-of-it. Then Erik was around, casual and easy-to-please, asking nothing of her but clearly interested. He lived a block away. She had been ignoring him for years, and now it seemed there was something more to know. It was like finding a secret garden (one of her favorite books) in a back yard she had passed every day without a second glance.

When they started college in the fall, however, Erik got to live in the dorms, while she commuted. It ruined him. His grades plummeted, he partied with suite-mates from Illinois, and then he started dating a girl from Des Moines. By the end of the year he was on academic probation and his father wouldn't pay any more for dorm life.

Alison spent the better part of her sophomore year ignoring Erik. She made the Dean's list. She started her art major. She felt centered. Her sister and brother had preceded her at UWM, Elise having dropped out to get married before she graduated. Eddie was a senior in Alison's sophomore year and, for the first time since they were small, Eddie started acting like a friend, taking Alison to lunch once a week at the Chili Bowl on Oakland Ave.

"You should give Erik another chance," Eddie advised one day.

"Asshole," Alison said. She had ordered the Meat Lover's Delight, which was chili with sirloin strips under a mound of finely shredded cheddar.

"Didn't you tell me last year that you loved him?"

"Past tense." The Chili Bowl had booths to one side and a counter with stools on the other, with hand-written specials on a big board over the grill. The place had been there as long as Alison could remember and had always represented to her the East Side, where the nice houses and bookstores are and the college kids congregate. She and Eddie were sitting in a booth.

"Don't lock yourself down, Ali. You're too young for that."

Eddie was a handsome, more confident version of her, she thought: her brother was wearing his hair short that year, almost a crew cut, something their father had worn at the same age, except in this case it was flattering, showing off Eddie's rosy skin and amber, almond-shaped eyes. He had taken to wearing baggy khaki trousers and scuffed penny loafers, with white socks, and vintage well-pressed white shirts that he had found in thrift stores and wore untucked. He had this whole retro-50's look going that seemed completely unsuited to the boy Alison had grown up with but now wholly fitting for the man Eddie had become. Soon Eddie would have his degree in Pharmacy and would probably move out-of-state—he already had job offers as far away as Florida. What Eddie didn't have, and didn't seem to need, was a girlfriend. Alison figured it was just a matter of time before he came out.

Alison tried her chili—it was still too hot. The windows behind Eddie were steamed foggy. It was March, the streets still icy, and mounds of dirty snow at every street corner. As always, the Bowl was noisy from the lunch-time crowd, mostly college students.

Alison said, "I don't *need* this, Eddie. Men are such babies, they don't know what they want. I thought Erik was better than that."

Eddie nodded his head in sympathy. He had ordered a bowl of the Veggie Bliss, though Alison couldn't recall if Eddie had declared himself a vegetarian.

"Ali, he's just now becoming a man—and . . . ." Eddie tried a spoonful of his chili.

"And?" Alison realized that she wanted an answer, something that would allow her to make exceptions to the plans she had fixed so firmly in her mind.

"And *nobody is better than that*," Eddie declared. "You or I or anybody will be lucky to find someone who will forgive—or tolerate—our faults."

"You're saying my standards are too high?"

"I'm saying that your standards are unrealistic, yes. There will come a day when you will make a mistake greater than Erik's and he will make one far greater than *this*." Eddie gave her that I-love-you-but-don't-be-stupid look that he had developed so well over the years. Alison felt both grateful and embarrassed because she was, she realized, still too young for all she wanted.

Gently Eddie said, "If every mistake marks an end, then how will we get on in life? Will it be nothing but a string of dreamy beginnings?"

This is the first time since Erik's drowning that Alison has recalled what her brother advised so long ago, though she and Eddie have talked plenty on the phone. Maybe now, as then, Eddie is watching and waiting for the right time to offer more advice. So much of Alison's life this past year has been advice from all sides. Her parents insist she return to Milwaukee, where her sister Elise lives with her husband and three kids: "Stan and Doug need to grow up with their cousins," he mother says. Every argument sounds reasonable.

But nothing has been reasonable in her life on this little island. Even now she finds herself doing stupid things, like stealing away on Doug's bike after dinner so that she can idle in front of Emil Timmerman's house. Emil lives in one side of a spacious duplex that has a screened back porch and a large side yard. There are only a handful of duplexes—maybe 20 total. The triplexes, which are much more numerous, have cramped fenced-in back yards that are hardly more than patios. Still, these residences are something to envy because they look solid and established in comparison to the sprawling trailer park that fills a two-block-wide band of the lagoon side, from the pier east to the swimming area.

As she stands in the middle of Lagoon Road in a gentle rain and studies Timmerman's house, Alison imagines she might look like someone who has paused to check her phone or recollect something forgotten. A light snaps on in Timmerman's living room. She sees someone walking to a rattan chair—Emil's wife, though at this distance she can't see any detail. She's older than Alison and more accomplished: a pilot for the commuter flight to Roi-Namur. The woman sits to read a book. No cable TV for her. Is she reading a mystery or thriller or something literary like Jane Austen? And where is the good doctor at 7:30? Working late with his newest patient?

Alison tells herself that she has no intention of doing anything as stupid as the many things she's already done. Still, she stands in the street, now soaked, and spies on a woman she thinks she should pity. Alison would like to believe that she herself has rebounded gloriously out of pity's reach, that everyone now regards her with renewed respect, even admiration. That's why she has told nobody, not even Gayla, that she is nose-diving into debt and bankruptcy because her job at the department store does not pay her enough. She's drawing on savings, her insurance money, to meet her bills. How stupid is that? And still she waits for the Army to dredge up Erik's body when she should, she knows, be taking care of business and getting on with life.

* * * *

The time difference is still hard to work out. California is eight hours *and a day* behind—it feels totally backwards wrong, though Cooper can do the math. It will be mid-day in Montara. Lillian will either be at the greenhouse or on an errand, maybe stuck in traffic on Highway One, which is too narrow for the crowds that have moved to the coast. It's probably foggy because, during the summer months, the inland heat draws the ocean mist, which hugs the coastal hills for most the day. You can drive over the hills to the heat and sunshine on the bayside—it'll take 30 minutes—but Cooper always preferred the cooler coast and its fickle weather. So why is he out here where it's always sweltering in the eighties at noon and no lower than 75 at midnight? That's the kind of question Lillian will ask. Cooper has no ready answer. Multiple choice:

I thought it'd be an adventure.

I wanted a change.

I thought you'd be with me.

I don't know what I'm doing, really.

If he wheels his chair to the window in his "living room," he can see a piece of the too-blue lagoon. Jimmy, the orderly, comes by every other day to check on him. Gus comes by thrice a day to take him to PT. He's still taking heavy doses of opiates, which explains why he hasn't decided to kill himself out of despair. It's not his absent leg that haunts him, though that *is* an issue, it's his abysmal loneliness. In his boat, at least, he was going *somewhere.* There was always the horizon and the promise of a destination. Here, in this decrepit mobile home, its air-conditioner reeking of mildew and its kitchen overrun by cockroaches the size of mice, he might as well be in a submarine.

"You are what I call type triple-A," Lillian told him. "A man in search of a project."

"Is that a bad thing?" he asked.

"Not at all." She smiled. "As long as you don't make *me* a project."

He suspected that she liked to see him busy because she kept busy herself. Bailey was one of her projects and she spent a great deal of time driving the girl from one activity to another. It is likely that Lillian was relieved to see Cooper go. Until he arrived, she was well settled in her tidy A-frame overlooking a Montara meadow. Despite all the good that came from their loving each other, it was a messy arrangement. There were a lot of things they hadn't worked through yet—and not just big stuff, like shared finances, but small stuff too, like where Cooper's collection of vinyl record albums would go, a collection he started in college and didn't even listen to any more but couldn't bring himself to dump. Which was why Cooper still kept his apartment in Palo Alto.

"Can't you just digitize all that and put it on an Mp3 player?" she asked.

"I know you're joking," he said.

"No, really, don't you want to lighten your load?"

"Look who's talking," he teased. "You must own a hundred vintage flower pots and vases, each with a plant in it."

"One hundred thirty three, to be exact," she said.

"Talk about weight!"

"But they're plants!" she said.

"But my albums are vinyl!" he said. Then he described the beauty of album design, how the esthetic of album covers grew directly from the esthetic of book design, an art that's been lost since the advent of the CD. "An album collection is both a library of music and of art!"

She shook her head in mock dismay. "The next thing I know you'll be asking me to move so that you can accommodate your album collection."

This stopped him short. He had assumed that they would have to move. He said, "My stuff will not fit in your house, Lil."

"Then put it on your sailboat!" she joked.

He's had too much time to think of these differences, and yet the more he's thought of them, the more he convinced himself that they could be worked out. He's made a career out of working through problems. His success as a programmer, his ability to input hours of code without error, one methodical batch file after the other, grows from a long-familiar compulsion to see the job through. That's why he was able to prepare the Lickety Split and sail all this way—almost perfectly. And that's why he can't let

Lillian go this easily.

His phone call brings him to Lillian's answering machine. It's one of those terse, male-voiced, canned responses favored by single women and the elderly: "No one can take your call at the moment. Please leave your name and number after the tone."

When Cooper was with Lillian, she used her own voice and, at his insistence, included him in the message: "This is Lillian, Bailey, and Cooper. . . ."

Now, to hear the generic answer gives him a pang of remorse. He has been erased.

"Lillian, it's me, Cooper. I've arrived on Kwajalein." He pauses, wondering how much to explain, how much time the machine will give him. "I've had an accident but I'm all right. I start—"

"Cooper?"

She didn't used to screen her calls.

"Lillian, I just wanted to let you know I made it."

"God, it's been a long time!"

He hears the waver in her voice that signals anxious excitement—like the time he heard her talking to her mother about her father's recovery from cancer.

"Yes," he says, "it seems very long."

"Were you scared? You must have been scared a lot."

How lovely her stutter sounds when she says sc-sc-scared.

She was scared. He hears that now. She was scared for him. And quickly, like a rogue wave, his recollected fear and loneliness tumble over him. He tells her about the early morning—one of the many mornings he could not sleep—when he was at the wheel, cutting through small swells, and he saw the back of a whale nearby, black and gleaming as it broke through the foam. So he steered over to it. Within ten minutes he was there, beside the beast. And the whale did not move. It was injured, he decided. Or dead. Then, with horror, he realized that he had come upon a barely-submerged freight container, thirty feet long. A nudge from a wave could have smashed the huge thing into his fiberglass hull, like a brick shoved into a wine glass.

He wants to describe to her the desolation he felt at that moment, how he realized that he was as inconsequential as flotsam, that he could sink in a second and never be found. But instead he gets chatty, as if recounting an adventure: "You better believe I got away from that container fast!"

"Oh, God, Cooper."

"I was scared for days after that," he continues, so pleased to be talking easily, so happy to know that she cares to listen. "And I never went near anything again, no matter how intriguing it looked."

"I dreamed of you sinking." She swallows a sob. "I listened to marine radio reports. A few times I went down to the marina to see if anyone would know anything."

He pictures her on the dock, in one of her billowy cotton smocks and baggy pants, the wind making her orange hair rise as she peers into the distance like a sailor's wife of old. In his imagination he tries to focus on her face, the delicate crow's feet as she squints, the flush of her freckled cheeks, her pale unlipsticked lips, her long fingers shading her green eyes.

She missed him. She *watched* for him. She waited.

"I couldn't have called you even if I'd tried," he explained. "Satellite connection was spotty at best."

"Your parents must have gone mad."

This stops him finally because he hears the censure he deserves. She might as well have said, *How could you do this to the people you love?*

His first impulse is to defend himself, but instead he begins an apology because there's so much he knows he can't make right at this point: "I didn't know, Lillian. I didn't know how long the trip would be—I mean, of course, I knew but I didn't *really* know."

"What didn't you know? You had it as well researched as one of your programs."

"I didn't know what I was feeling. I didn't know how it would make others feel, like my parents. Like you."

"You left so quickly, it seemed like you were running away."

"I left on schedule," he says carefully.

"You didn't have to leave at all."

"On the boat, you mean."

"Yes, I mean the boat. You were obsessed with that boat."

"I didn't know it bothered you that much."

"It bothered me."

"Why am I hearing this only now?"

"There was no talking to you before. Maybe you've gotten it out of your system."

He's been dreaming of the Lickety Split, of the bob and dip, the spray in his face, the wind hard against him. He has requested the Army tell him where he was picked up but the Army isn't inclined to reveal any information about its operations—and Cooper's rescue was an operation. (No pun!) So he has asked Art to help him locate the remote atoll and Art has agreed, though he hasn't seen the old man this week.

"Out of my system," Cooper repeats, testing the words.

"Is it?" Lillian asks.

How can he explain what the Lickety Split means to him now that it has carried him so far so faithfully? Is it a shallow attachment to feel grateful? Is it foolish to feel awe when he steps onto its nodding deck and considers the many ways it has defied destruction as it has plowed into a forty-foot trough, nosed over a steepled crest, tipped sideways till its mast skimmed the whitecaps, then righted itself and kept on?

"My god, Lillian, you have no idea!" he croaked.

"I know it was hard, Cooper. I understand."

"Do you?"

"I've been going crazy waiting for this call. My nails are bitten to the quick."

"You've always bitten your nails, Lil."

"Not to bloody stumps," she says.

Then he remembers his leg. It amazes him that he can coast

for a few minutes at a time without thinking of it. But always it returns, an importuning companion, jerking, itching, aching. It hasn't forgotten him.

"I've had an accident," he says.

"An accident, that's right, you mentioned it as you started your message. What happened to your boat?"

Hap-hap-happened?

"I wish it were only my boat."

"But it can't be that bad—you made it."

"Yeah, I made it." He explains his story as matter-of-factly as he can, grateful for having had plenty of practice. When he gets to the leg, he speaks of it as if it were a friend who, because of drug abuse, say, or reckless driving, met an untimely and most regrettable demise. And now, after having buried this friend and mourned his loss, Cooper is ready to move on—slowly, more cautiously, but ready nonetheless.

"I don't believe this," Lillian says. She sounds angry.

"Unfortunately, I don't have the luxury of disbelieving."

"It's not fair, Cooper!"

"Who's to say what's fair? It's not like I bought a guaranteed reservation for safety. It just happened."

"Had I been there it might *not* have happened," she exclaimed.

"So you're going to blame yourself?"

"Don't you want to blame me?"

"It never occurred to me that I should blame you," he lies.

"Cooper, you *can't* be all right."

"Because I'm not blaming you?"

"Because you're all alone in a new place and now you're. . . ."

"Handicapped? It's all right to say it."

"It's just not fucking fair! What are we going to do?"

"Right now I'm going to learn how to walk," he says. "I'm already on crutches, then they're going to give me a prosthetic leg."

"Oh god! What do you expect *me* to do?"

He hears her loneliness and desperation and only now begins

to appreciate what she's been through. Why did it never occur to him that he didn't have to *sail* to Kwajalein? He could have worked things out with Lillian. They could have flown to Kwaj. Had he run away?

He says, "I'm kind of taking it one day at a time, Lil."

"Are you on drugs?"

"Of course."

"That explains a lot," she says.

"I guess."

"Is the phone connection always this bad—what's that noise?"

"I don't hear a noise," he says.

"You don't hear a clicking?"

"I don't hear a clicking. It might be OPSEC."

"OPSEC?"

"Operational Security. They're allowed to listen in on any call."

"And do what?"

"Take notes, I guess. I don't know. This is a top security installation, Lil."

"I don't want somebody listening to the things I have to say to you!"

"That can't be helped."

"I'm an American, Cooper!"

"So am I!"

"Hey, OPSEC spooks, get off the fucking line!"

"There's no need to talk like that, Lil."

"We're being spied upon. That doesn't bother you?"

"It's my job, Lil. You know all about that."

"Better be careful what you say, Cooper. They don't know what I KNOW."

"Stop it. This is no time for jokes."

"Who's joking?" She sounds drunk. "I probably know all kinds of secrets you've told me."

"I've told you nothing. Now, please, stop."

"You talk in your sleep. Do THEY know that?"

"Lil, really, this is unfair."

"All right, all right. I'm just joking, OPSEC spooks. Put your pencils down. It's just a ha-ha-ha joke. Okay?"

"Real convincing, Lil. Why are you being a jerk?"

"Because I'm pissed as hell that you left me and got yourself hurt." Suddenly she's bawling.

This makes Cooper bawl too. She stops for a moment, then he catches up with her and stops too, then she starts again and he follows, back and forth for a long time, it seems. "Look," he says at last. "This is a good start for you and me. We can deal with this, can't we?"

"Promise me you won't get bitter, Cooper."

"I'm not bitter. I've got goals. I'm going to learn to walk again!"

And find his boat. He's going to fucking find his boat.

Lillian blows her nose. He imagines her wiping her eyes with the heel of her hand, mascara smearing. "Is anybody helping you?"

"I've got lots of help. Everybody's being really nice."

"Shall I send Bailey your love? You know she was devastated when you left."

"She hates me, Lil."

"No, you're wrong, she loves you dearly."

He sighs. "Sure, send her my love."

"God!" she chokes.

"We'll talk soon," he says.

"I want to see you happy, Cooper."

"I'm going to be happy," he says. "I'm going to be fine."

It takes five more minutes of good-bye before she hangs up. Then Cooper sits for the longest time, staring at the worn linoleum floor through the spoked wheels of his chair and thinking, if he's chairbound the next time he sees Lillian, he'll wish himself dead.

THIRTEEN

Jeton's cousin Stevie motors all the way from Ebeye to pick up Jeton, who has promised to repay the money his father, three uncles, and brother put together for Stevie's fuel and time. It took the shortwave radio operator on Lib a week to get through to a radio operator on Majuro, where Jeton's father and brother live, and then another week for them to make arrangements on Ebeye, where cousin Stevie lives.

Jeton has watched for Stevie every day for two weeks, scouting the horizon from Lib's northern beach. When the boat arrives finally, it cannot dock. Jeton has to swim out to it. A hard swim because the water is rough. Cousin Stevie and his first mate Lino help him into the *Irooj*. Panting and soaked, Jeton looks up and is surprised to see so many people on the boat: women wearing their finest *muumuus*, men wearing their Sunday shirts, many children carrying straw bags and canvas totes of food for a *kam̧ōl̗o*. "We wanted to party on Lib," Stevie says, "but then we forgot there's no dock!" A "party" for the *ri-Majel̗* is what the Americans call a "picnic." The *ri-Majel̗* love nothing more than a picnic.

"We will *kam̧ōl̗o* on Ebeye!" Jeton says, wishing he had money to make a party for everybody he knows, he is so grateful to be going home.

The bright blue *Irooj* moves slowly, low in the water like an old man bathing—like Jeton's great uncle Adolphus. It is a big old boat, the kind Americans call "cabin cruiser," with a big cranky diesel engine below and a large hold for deep-water fish. Stevie's name for the boat, Irooj, means "king" or "chief"—American-English words that come close to the *kajin Ṃajel* word but don't really *bọur* the meaning.

A Republic flag flutters from a small rod on the wheelhouse roof. The Republic flag is dark blue with a bright sun on the left side, then, at an angle from left lower corner to right upper corner, an orange streak and a white streak that expands like the tail of a comet.

Waves spill over the sides as the chop kicks at the *Irooj*. Sput-sput-sput, the old blue *Irooj* says, spewing its black clouds of exhaust. Then waves wash down the deck and over the stern. It is not far to Ebeye but maybe Stevie should not have let so many people come. Jeton worries about the rain because the low-riding boat cannot take much water.

He sits up front, on the boat's nose, with the children. The children are sharing a small mackerel, *mōlmōl* that got washed onto the deck. They eat it raw, passing it around, nibbling at it like candy. The Americans would find this disgusting, Jeton decides. When the fish comes to him, he shrugs away the offer, though he knows this is rude.

The children talk about Abbetar, the goalie for the national soccer team. He has committed suicide—hanging himself in a Majuro hotel room—because his girlfriend was unfaithful. Who would have thought that a tough man like Abbetar could be so soft?

The women have started singing a *ri-pālle* church song. They sing because they are happy to be on the water, away from crowded Ebeye, and on their way to a *kaṃōḷo* maybe on one of the uninhabited islands nearby. The *kaṃōḷo* is the kind of visit the *ri-Ṃajeḷ* have made for hundreds and hundreds of years: *ri-Ṃajeḷ* from one atoll kept peace with *ri-Ṃajeḷ* from another atoll by coming together to share their harvest. It was *booj toonṃur*. "The bond that unites."

The church song Jeton remembers from grade school: "Jesus

loves the little chillll-dren, all the children of the world!" It doesn't sound the same as when the Americans sing it. The *ri-Majel* chant it. Sounds like a prayer, Jeton thinks. No, what's the word? Incantation. Like a spell. Nora taught him many words like that.

When the afternoon rain begins in earnest, Jeton picks his way through the children, who sit or squat here and there, many of them blocking the window of the wheelhouse. Then he steps through the cluster of men who are leaning at the rail on either side and smoking. The women are congregated at the back: "All the children of the world!" they sing. These are older women. The young women are left behind to work. Those who are lucky enough to get work.

Shaking off the wet, Jeton steps into the wheelhouse, where his cousin is piloting. "Can you take me to Kwajalein?" Jeton asks.

Stevie is smoking, staring at the window ahead of him. It doesn't look like he can see past the crowd outside. He wears his Raybans, even though there is no sun.

"No," Stevie says. "It is *bwinimjaad*." He jokes, using the old word for "forbidden."

Jeton laughs. "You have a boat. You can go anywhere."

"Not Kwajalein." Stevie exhales a stream of smoke in the fancy French way. "They banned your ass, Jeton."

"You know that for sure?" says Jeton.

"Everybody knows that for sure. Besides, your *lijera* is long gone."

"Everybody knows that too?"

"Sure, everybody knows that. You are famous fuck-up now, Jeton."

When he recalls that school is out already, Jeton realizes that he has failed his senior year. Everybody must know this too.

The rain has finished, the clouds breaking up. The sun begins to burn through again. Soon puddles will be steaming from the deck.

Jeton stares out the window, wondering what Nora thinks

of him now. He imagines himself taking Abbetar's place. Jeton will be a famous *ri-Ṃajeḷ* soccer player who visits the States for a tournament! Nora would come to watch him and she would cry to see how he dives without fear for the ball.

"Here," Stevie says. "You steer."

Stevie shows him how to cut into the waves with the big boat so that it is a smoother ride. It is very different in a smaller boat. The Irooj plies the water easily.

Jeton is grateful for this. Maybe he can work for Stevie. Maybe he can help catch a *lōjkaan* that a rich Japanese will buy.

Lino appears at the wheelhouse door and says with a grin, "Jeton is a sailor now?"

"Fuck you," Jeton says.

Lino says fishing might be good, so he has brought out the big pole. Stevie and Lino go to the stern to fish. From the windows, children watch Jeton steering. This makes Jeton concentrate on the horizon and think how a sailor must think, of the hours and the days that mark a course over the sun-bright water.

He has nothing to show for his stay at Lib. No gifts for his ṃaṃa, no goodies for his friends. The *ri-Ṃajeḷ* never come home empty handed. Unless you are a fuck-up like Jeton. On Ebeye he will spend his days hanging out with the other useless boys and old men. Had Nora stayed, they'd be on their way to Wotje in this very boat.

He would have had a plan.

He would have had a life.

The green rind of Kwajalein surprises him when he sees it in the distance. Immediately he knows what it is and it strikes him that he must act now or never again complain about Nora leaving and how badly the Americans lie.

In his dreams, Jeton has seen himself pilot Stevie's bright blue boat right up Emon Beach, where the *ri-pālle* "sun-bathe." He has seen himself step off like the prince he might have been a hundred years ago. And no one questions his right to be there.

With the wave of one arm, he says, "All of this, from here to there, belongs to my family. So you will have to leave." And they do, quietly, respectfully. Then Jeton sets up his own house in the midst of the cleared land—a house so big it holds all of his brothers, sisters, cousins, uncles and aunts. The biggest room goes to his *būbū*, of course. She is proud of him for having done what all *ri-Majeḷ* should have done years ago. The Americans are allowed to stay, he decides, but only on landfill that they themselves have built with garbage and old rubber tires. And they must pay for this. Throughout the Republic, the *ri-Majeḷ* once again have all of the best land, all of the reclaimed coconut plantations and *ri-pālle* housing, all of best springs and reefs. And the Americans live in the worst parts, where there are no trees and nothing is green and the fishing is poor. But they pay more for this than they have ever paid for "leased" *ri-Majeḷ* land.

Closing the door of the wheelhouse—then locking it—Jeton steps to the controls, pulls the choke out a little, nudges back a bit on the throttle, then feels the engines grumble in protest, coughing chug-a-chug.

He coaxes the Irooj forward. He has only one scare before he sets his course: a white ridge of coral leaps up from the dark blue near the drop-off and the Irooj's hull just misses snagging it before Jeton steers away, relieved that he does this well.

It is no more than a mile—a straight shot—from here to the white sands of Kwajalein's Emon Beach. If he pushes the Irooj at full throttle, he could be there in five minutes, ten at most. He prays that no swimmers get in his way.

Stevie comes to the window of the wheelhouse door. "Hey, man, what's up?" He is tapping the glass.

"I got it," Jeton says.

Stevie has taken off his Raybans. He holds a hand over his eyes to shield it from the sun-glare on the windows. He presses his forehead to the glass. "Jeton?"

Jeton tries to make the Irooj run faster but the boat, he

realizes, holds too many people. Everybody is talking loudly now, watching Kwajalein growing larger, the children pointing.

"Let me in, Jeton."

"We're going to protest," Jeton tells him.

"What are we going to protest?" Stevie asks, blinking.

Since living with the Americans, the *ri-Majel* have come to a new understanding of jumae, "protest."

"We are going to protest against the Americans."

"Why the Americans?"

"Because they fuck us up."

"You joking?"

"Hey, man, where you going?" Lino asks, appearing behind Stevie at the window.

Stevie says: "He's going to fuck up the Americans."

"Who said?"

Stevie slaps the window of the wheelhouse door. "No joking, man, what are you *doing*, Jeton?"

Lino says, "Turn around, Jeton."

"Too late to turn around," Jeton says. His blood jumps in his veins like fish flying over a wave.

He's only five boat-lengths away from the buoys that mark Kwajalein's swimming area.

And here comes the Army cutter, plowing towards them at top speed. Why didn't Jeton see it before? It's three times bigger than the Irooj and sits high in the water, with long-barreled guns on the upper decks.

"Fuck," Stevie shouts, "turn around, man!"

"Too late to turn around," Jeton says.

The cutter is circling now, a big gray steel shark. Its turbine engines make the air shudder and moan.

A loud American voice—flat and low-pitched—sputters from the ship: "You are trespassing. Turn around now. You are trespassing on the USAKA security zone."

USAKA: United States Army Kwajalein Atoll.

"They gonna shoot us?" Lino asks.

Stevie kicks open the door, shoves Jeton aside, then cuts the engine.

"Keep going," Jeton tells him. "They won't hurt us."

Jeton steps out of the wheelhouse and waves at the cutter as if he were waving to family from the pier. "*Iọkwe!*" he shouts. *Goodbye!*

Uniformed U.S. Army sailors wearing orange vests and green steel helmets stare at them from the railings; they carry rifles but do not aim them.

"Don't shoot!" Lino calls, holding his hands high in the air. The other passengers do the same, everybody fluttering their hands.

The big waves rolling from the cutter make the Irooj bob and dip, foamy water washing over the sides.

"If you do not turn around you will be arrested," the American voice is saying. The U.S. Army sailors are pointing fingers and shaking their heads sadly like they are watching a school of dolphins stranded on a beach.

Then the cutter passes so closely—roaring—Jeton could almost slap its steel side.

"Shit, cousin, they're crazy!" Stevie says.

The Irooj bobs and bounces roughly because it is at a standstill.

"Turn on the engine," Jeton calls.

Lino says, "We're sinking, man," as calmly as saying, Your shoe's untied.

He is right, the boat is too low in the water and the chop is too high. The Irooj noses into a big wave, then lurches as if hit head-on.

"No way! Stevie shouts. He tries to start it up again, but the Irooj only coughs. "No way!"

· "Fuckers!" Jeton shouts.

"We gotta turn around!" Stevie says. He wipes water from his face. He looks sick-pale. He's still holding onto the wheel but the Irooj's engine has stopped.

Jeton helps him with the wheel. He hears himself gasping with effort. But it's futile. The Irooj is too crowded, the chop's too high, and now the cutter's wake is swamping them. Children are dropping off the bow. The men and women have crowded to one side, waving for rescue.

The loud American voice says: "You are trespassing. Turn around now. You are trespassing on the USAKA security zone."

Stevie is muttering a prayer: "Jesussonofgodandpurevirigin-mothermary

pleasehelpthissinneranddeliverhimuntothegraceofgodal-mightyforchristsakeoh

pleaseohfuckplease!"

His ears ringing with confusion, Jeton admits to himself what he has long known: he is a stupid boy, inclined to do stupid things—for reasons that never make sense afterwards. He hates himself for his own limits. He hates himself especially for what he is doing now, ruining everything for everybody.

Stevie says, "We're sinking, man," as calmly as saying, The sun is high.

The Irooj goes down so fast, Jeton is up to his knees in water before he jumps. As the boat dips, then disappears, it draws him into a roaring vortex of white bubbles. It seems the Irooj will suck him to the bottom. Pushing through the whirling white, his eyes open to the stinging water, Jeton can see the bottom, no more than twenty feet below, the white sand and bright coral shimmer-ing. Then he sees children all around him, some swimming, some sinking like sacks of rice, their eyes open, bubbles pouring from their nostrils, their mouths wide with wonder. And Jeton knows he must collect them. He must collect them all.

When he surfaces, a child under each arm, he is among a crowd: the women reaching for one another, their dresses floating like jelly fish around them, the men dog-paddling and calling instructions to the children, the children squealing and swimming every which way, like a bucket of overturned shrimp. So much water and foam!

White life preservers rain over them, hitting the water like the slap of open hands. The cutter has stopped, the salt-fishy air tainted with acrid diesel fumes. The Army men are calling down to them and lowering yellow rubber rafts.

Jeton dives again to search for children. Final, slow-motion bubbles erupt from the Irooj's rusty hall as Jeton pushes. *What Marshallese child does not know how to swim?* he wonders. And yet, here he finds one passively sinking and then another. He grabs them by their T-shirts and yanks them to the surface. Army men in rubber rafts are lifting children from the water as fast as Jeton can fetch them. Such a mess!

And then it's done. All children have been collected, many swimmers drawn into lifeboats. His heart flailing like a fish in a jar, Jeton floats on the surface to recover, gulping for air, a great dome of sun-stunned silver clouds wheeling overhead. He hears, yards behind him, the effusive chatter of Marshallese men and women thanking God, thanking the Army, thanking Luck, thanking each other. An American is calling to him: "Swim this way, young man."

Angry at himself, and angry at the U.S. Army too, Jeton will not swim to their arms. He is surprised to discover that several children—the older boys—are with him. Good swimmers, they are treading water. They seem to smile a greeting as he regards each. They watch him expectantly as if he were the leader. Do they expect something of him?

"Who's gonna pay for my boat?" Stevie is shouting. He slaps away the preserver nearest him. "Who?"

"We will get you a new boat," Jeton promises. "Come!" He swims towards shore.

"Where you going, baka idiot!" Stevie won't follow.

The Irooj, now at the sandy bottom, is still streaming big

bubbles from its hold as Jeton pushes through the many preservers, then swims to the beach, followed by the several children. The cutter can't follow because the water is too shallow here—they have entered the *ri-pālle* swimming area.

A few *ri-pālle* are watching from the beach, their hands shading their eyes.

Panting, Jeton staggers ashore with the children—he is surrounded by the children from the Irooj. Six, seven, eight of them, they seem more curious than scared. Dripping water, their eyes wide with wonder, most have never been to Kwajalein, this strange *ri-pālle* place.

"Americans nearly killed us!" Jeton shouts. Then to the children, he says: "America is unfair. Americans don't care!"

After saying this a few times, the children pick up the chant. It's like a game: *America unfair! America don't care!*

* * * *

Dear Cooper: Mom said you nearly died from your accident. I told her I never had anything against you! I especially dont have anything against handicap people!!! The world's alot nicer to handicap people than it use to be! They use to be called cripples. Ha ha. Mom says if you come back I'll have to be extra nice. I told her thats no problem. Ashley Jo isn't my friend any more. I asked Mom if you two are getting married. She wont say. Is it a secret? Its been foggy here. Pretty soon I'm getting my learners permit. Write if you want!

Bailey

* * * *

"We've cleaned up your room, Cooper!"

"Why, Dad?"

"For your homecoming, silly!"

"We'll have a party," his mother says on the extension.

"Mom, Dad, I'm not coming home."

"You've got to come home, Cooper. Nobody's going to care for you out there on that island."

"I'm getting care. I've learned to use crutches. Tomorrow I start my job!"

"How can you work on crutches?"

"It's not like I'm doing construction, Mom."

"You want to say hi to Bo?" Bo's chain collar clatters against the phone. Cooper can hear the old dog panting. "Bo, it's our Cooper! Yes, COOP-PER!"

Bo lets loose his Basset bay. It's so loud Cooper jerks away from the receiver. "Jesus, Dad, give me some warning!"

"Cooper, he's waiting."

Cooper sighs. "Hello, Bo."

"*Louder,* Cooper!"

"HELLO, BO!"

Bo barks. And barks. And barks.

"Okay, thanks," says Cooper. "That's very sweet."

"Just showing you what you're missing," his father says.

"Mom, Dad, I appreciate your concern. Really. But let me work it out."

"What is there to work out?"

"I've got to get my boat back!"

"Oh, Cooper honey, your boat is gone," his mother says. "You can't let it become a substitute for everything you've lost. You see that, don't you?"

"Ruby, he doesn't want to hear that." Then: "Cooper, file your claim with the insurance company. We'll get a nice powerboat and go fishing on the bay. Won't that be great?"

"You hate fishing, Dad. Besides, I think I know where my Alberg is. I've just got to get out there."

"And do what? How do you expect to get it back?"

"I'll sail it back."

"You can't sail, Cooper—you can't even walk!"

"All I need is somebody to pull the lines—you know, man the sails. A crew of one, maybe two. It's not rocket science."

"Is that some kind of joke because you're working with rockets?" his father asks.

"Missiles are not rockets exactly," says Cooper. "And it's not science the way you're thinking of it, it's engineering."

"Cooper, Lillian agrees you should come home and stay with us."

This shuts Cooper up. Since when has Lillian been talking with his parents? "I didn't know you were talking to Lillian."

"Why wouldn't we talk to her? She's as worried as we are."

"You're making plans for me, you and Lillian?"

"We're trying to get organized," his mother says. "Lillian is so very nice. I wish you'd listen to her. Men have a hard time listening and you've been a little preoccupied, you have to admit."

"You understand that I'm under contract for a year, that I can't break that contract?"

"You could break it easily enough," his father says. "These are extraordinary circumstances."

"Yes, they are," says Cooper. "That's why I'm staying."

"You're not going to upset us with your stubbornness," his mother says. "We've decided that. We're going to love you all the harder until you come to your senses."

"You want Teddy to visit you out there?"

"No, I don't need to see Teddy right now."

"Your brother loves you."

"And I love my brother but listen, folks, I've got a job. I'm under some pressure, you understand? I've got to make this work out."

"All right, all right," his father says. "You hear that, Ruby, he's under pressure. That's what we suspected, Cooper. You're working with those top secret types and building rockets. It's a long way from designing games, we understand. But know this: we're here for you."

"I'm touched," he says. "I mean it. You two are the greatest."

"Hear that, Ruby, he says we're great. We are great, aren't we, hon?"

His mother blubbers, "We're holding onto our hearts, Cooper. We're praying for you"

"All right, Ruby, he's got to go. Cooper, here's Bo to say goodbye!"

The dog is howling when Cooper hangs up.

* * * *

Alison hoped to have found Erik by Father's Day. It was the one thing she was certain would happen. In spite of all her harangues and her petitions to the Colonel, she feels guilty for not getting this done: Father's Day mocks her, shames her.

While other boys are buddying up with their dads, Stan and Doug will be following an elaborate treasure map Alison has painted so that they can find a) a basket of candy bars (Hershey's variety pack), b) the Stone Deaf Death Rangers video game, version III (Cave of the Glowing Teeth!), c) a CD of Angel D, the latest teeny-bop hip-hop sensation, and, in a gesture of optimism, d) a five-volume DVD set of "Mister Science's Mad World of Really Awfully Neat Factoids!", an encyclopedia in disguise, which maybe the boys will use.

After a breakfast of Coco Puffs and powdered donuts, they pedal west with Gayla and her husband, Topher. It's an overcast, blustery day, heavy rains predicted later. Their first stop is Sands Beach, which was called "Bachelors' Beach" in the days when the singles and marrieds were segregated.

Today, for the first time Alison can remember, Gayla has dressed sloppily—at least for Gayla: she's wearing a baggy yellow blouse and baggy white pants that make her look heavy.

"You ever hear the old-timers talk about what used to happen on this beach?" Gayla asks.

"Screwing around is nothing new." Alison pedals hard for

three revolutions, then lets her bike coast. "Glad to know I'm in good company."

"You've got to feel better now that your monthly's back, even if it is the mother bitch of all periods."

Alison swings off her bike and scooters to the pavilion, where Topher and the boys have parked already. They've let Topher hold the map while they scramble into the bushes for the treasure Gayla and Alison hid earlier this morning.

Secretly Alison made all kinds of promises to herself and God if only her period would return. When her period did come finally, in the middle of the night, she was so occupied with cleaning up the trailer and so weary from worry, she didn't recall her promises. The next day, with school ending and the boys to look after, her month-long scare seemed little more than self-indulgent panic. These are strange days, she tells herself. Anything could happen.

"Yeah," Alison says at last. "I'm trying not to hate myself for being so stupid."

"The good doc will get his eventually."

"I doubt it," Alison says, sitting next to her on the picnic table. "Guys like that never do."

"I'd be pushing pins into his voodoo doll every night."

"I'm not going to waste my energy thinking about him one way or the other," she says.

They stare after Topher and the boys, a sight that makes Alison ache. Topher is a quiet and gawky and very sweet. He'd make a good father.

At last Alison says what she's been wanting to say to her friend for weeks: "I've got to go back, Gayla. I can't pretend any more."

"Hold on, honey, what are you saying? Have the stateside people—your well-meaning family—ganged up on you and broken your resolve?"

"They've been working on me plenty. But, no, they haven't been unreasonable or unthinking. My decision comes down to money: I can't get a job here that meets my bills. I'm going broke fast."

"Oh, no!" Gayla turns away as if scalded. "This is my fault!" She stifles a sob, then looks at Alison with a tear-streaked face.

Startled, Alison has never seen her friend so emotional. "Gayla, it's all right. I deserved to lose my job. You know that!"

"I don't want you to leave!"

Alison takes her hand. "You'll visit me in the States. This is hardly the end."

Gayla wipes her eyes hastily so that the boys don't see her like this. She's shaking her head doubtfully. "The minute you hit Stateside, hon', you'll feel the pull. Things will change for you. It'll be hard for us to stay in touch."

"Since when have you been a pessimist?" Alison jokes.

"All right, honey. Running away doesn't have to be a tragedy as long as you know why you're running. And where."

"My brother is going to help. I'm not above accepting help at this point."

Gayla nods in agreement. She's staring after Topher and the boys as they dig in a sand dune, the wind blowing up gusts of powdery sand. Alison can see her friend fighting back the tears. She squeezes Gayla's hand and says, "You know, Topher would make a great father."

"Funny you would say that."

"Oh?"

"I was going to tell you today, hon', but then your news kind of knocked the wind out of me."

"Tell me you're what? You're pregnant?"

Gayla's now-beaming face announces the fact.

They squeal so loudly, clapping and hugging each other, that Doug steps from the bushes and shouts, "What's the matter? Mom?"

Alison waves for him to continue. "We're excited about the treasure," she says. "Did you find it?"

"Stan's hogging all the clues!"

"You're close—keep looking." She turns back to Gayla. "So, this was planned?"

"Not really. Yes, sort of. I don't know. I just went off the pill to see what would happen."

"Fabulous, Gayla." With one arm, Alison pulls her friend closer. "I'm sorry to miss the birth. I'm so sorry. But we will catch up. We will see each other!"

"You're sweet, hon'. Yes, we'll catch up."

"I can't wait for that grand day! Take videos. You can post them online. We'll talk on the phone, we'll email all the time. I'll share with you all my best tips. And I'll miss you madly, my dear Gayla, but we won't lose touch!"

It's a promise Alison makes earnestly and fervently. But she realizes with rising sadness that it is a promise she will very likely break. If there's one thing she has learned since moving here, it's that a wish can cheer you, give you a boost, even move you from one point to the next, but in the end it's a delicate thing, like a moth beating at a window pane. Is this pessimism? She doesn't want to lose hope! But perhaps this is what comes of growing older: you must accommodate yourself to a revised understanding of the world and admit that wanting something, even wanting something until every bone in your body aches, will not change your life.

FOURTEEN

Manning says, "We pay them 32 million dollars a year for these few stretches of sand and this is what we get for our money?"

"Will you shut up?" says Art. He has borrowed an onlooker's binoculars. He sees several boys swimming to shore, having eluded the grasp of the Army crew.

Manning signals to four nearby policemen.

"No, you don't," says Art. "You keep away from these boys."

"Arrest the interlopers and be done with it," says Manning.

Art turns to him. "Two words, captain: international incident. So back off."

As the six boys rise from the water and stride up the beach, the onlookers—women and children from the surrounding neighborhood—applaud. This hardly makes sense but seems to be an expression of sympathy. With remarkable composure, the boys sit in the sand to catch their collective breath. When Art recognizes the oldest—Jeton DeGroen, the missing boy banned to Lib—he growls: "Shit, Manning, you reap what you sow. Do you hear me?"

"What?" Manning frowns and shakes his head in puzzlement. "You're such a drama queen, Art."

Art hands him the binoculars. "Take a look, big man."

Wearily, Manning takes the binoculars. "Oh, god damn!" He focuses to get a second look.

"You were supposed to pick him up, Manning."

"We had it scheduled. Goes to show you what we're dealing with. I knew that guy was trouble."

"He's not trouble," says Art. "You made him into trouble! He's here now only because of what your men did to him. Don't you see that?"

Manning tries to hand the binoculars back but Art won't take them. Manning says, "This guy might be a terrorist."

"You can't be serious—you can't be anywhere near serious, Manning. This is a lovesick boy who's acting out because his *ri-pālle* girlfriend returned to the States. If you try to make anything more of it, you will humiliate yourself and probably lose your job."

"I'm afraid you just don't get it, Art." Manning motions again to his men.

Art snaps: "Keep your flying monkeys off that beach until I've had my talk with the interlopers, as you call them. That's protocol and you know it."

Manning motions for his men to stop. "I'll give you ten minutes, Mister Liaison."

"Give me thirty," says Art, then he steps into the sun, which has just broken through the clouds. As he approaches, the boys squint at him. Sun-browned skinny boys with curly hair. He hears a few mutter, "*Belle*," which sounds like "bell-ee": *foreigner. Whitey*.

The boys sit close, almost in a huddle. Art crouches in the sand at a respectful distance, then introduces himself in Marshallese. Jeton, the apparent leader, insists on speaking English. He says, "You owe us a boat."

Art says, "I don't owe you anything, young man."

"The Army sank our boat—you saw it. Everybody saw!"

The boys nod in agreement.

True, the Army cutter was reckless.

"What do you want?" Art asks. "Besides a boat. Why did you come here?"

"We came here," Jeton says, "because America is unfair."

The kid is right and Art feels for him, but Art knows better than to stir this kind of trouble. The Army is too edgy and Kwaj

Security is itching for action.

"Did you pilot that boat into these waters?" Art asks.

Jeton glances back as if to verify that they are talking about the same thing. Art sees that the boy is losing will, stalling. Standing out is one thing the Marshallese do not seek. And shame for them is the worst of fates.

"It is my cousin Stevie's boat," he says.

"It was, you mean. It's gone now. Is that what you wanted?"

Jeton's expression betrays his growing confusion and pain: "What I wanted?"

"Yes, it seems you want a lot."

Jeton draws himself up, looking defiant. "My *būbū* owns one fourth of this island!"

"Correction," says Art. "Your *būbū* owns *one-fourteenth* of this island and her family has been handsomely paid for its lease."

When Jeton offers no come-back, Art says it again: "What do you *want*?"

The old fat *ri-pālle* is rude and bold and Jeton knows that he is no match for him. This talk of want and wanting is shamefully American, not at all the kind of talk that fits the man Jeton hoped to be. Americans are always grabbing and getting and buying—it's all "wanting" for them. They want these islands for their missiles. They want the *ri-Majeḷ* to clean their houses, move their rocks, weed their flowers. They want air-conditioned houses full of clothing and toys and appliances. They want big steaks on their grills and bowls of ice cream swimming in fudge sauce and baked potatoes filled with shredded orange cheese. They want super deluxe extra fancy grade-A number one U.S. certified Everything.

Is that what Jeton wants?

When Nora rode on top of him, coaching him to go slow, she would say, *You're my man, Jeton. Nobody's better. Nobody will ever be better than you.* She made him whimper, it went so slow. Sometimes they wept together afterwards, a happy-funny-oh-my-god! kind of crying. He wants that back. That would be enough.

"Art, you gotta listen to this," Manning calls. He's waving a walky talky.

With effort, Art turns. It's so frigging muggy, his T-shirt is soaked with sweat, his forehead burning. "Can it wait?"

"No."

Art gets to his feet, groaning. He feels light-headed. Did any of this bullshit have to happen? In the shade of the picnic pavilion, Manning hands him the walky talky.

With a grimace, Art takes it, then depresses the red button: "Yeah," says Art into the crackling mouthpiece.

"This is Captain Jenks from the cutter, over."

Art says, "Great job swamping that Marshallese boat, Jenks. Over."

"Who the hell are you? Over."

"You know who the hell I am. Over."

Some of the onlookers have given the boys cans of soda and bags of chips. In the distance, the cutter remains idle, nodding gently with the waves. On deck, the bright clothing of the new passengers is clearly visible.

Captain Jenks says, "We're missing the pilot. Over."

"The pilot is here, on shore. Jeton DeGroen. Over."

"They're telling me the pilot went down with the boat. Over."

"No fucking way!" Art says.

"Watch your language. Over."

Art sees it now, a rowboat beside the cutter, a diver dropping over the edge for a look-see.

"You mean drowned? Over."

"Looks that way. Over."

`"No confirmation? Over."

For a minute, then two, then three, there is no answer. Art waits, sweat tickling his scalp. If somebody drowned, this is going to be a nightmare. Unlike the Marshallese, who will grieve hard—the Americans are going to want to point blame. *Why are we such assholes?* He, the hopeful white knight come to save the dark folk from their fucked-up life, has spent his life answering this question.

The walky talky crackles abruptly, then the captain says, "Bringing the body up now. The boy's name is Lino Kamaka. Over."

"Oh, hell!" Art hands the walky talky back to Manning as if it were burning his hands. "Damn it all!"

Manning shrugs. "Sorry, Art."

As Art approaches the boys again, he tells himself that he is going to save this foolish boy who has caused so much harm—he will not lose this one to suicide—but, as he sits again in the hot sand, a sudden sadness clutches at his throat, a grief that seems to cradle his children and every child he has known. Then he coughs and coughs until Jeton hands him a cold soda and Art, tears in his eyes, says "*Eṃṃon!*" in gratitude and downs the too-sweet drink.

Jeton says, "*Iọkwe*," which could mean "love to you" or "you're welcome" or "okay."

"Americans sank our boat," Jeton says, as if to reclaim his confidence. "We weren't doing anything and they sank our boat!"

"America unfair!" one of the children blurts. Jeton shushes him.

"The American boat told you to turn back," the old *ri-pālle* says. He looks very tired, his voice hardly louder than a whisper. "But you did not turn back."

"We did nothing wrong," Jeton says. Why does he feel so uneasy?

"Then what is it you have to say?" the *ri-pālle* asks. "You are going to speak for the *Ri-Ṃajeḷ*?"

Defiantly Jeton proclaims, "If Americans was not here, I would be a prince on Kwajalein! yes, I will speak for the *Ri-Ṃajeḷ*!"

"Really?" the *ri-pālle* says. "Are you an *irooj*?"

The question makes Jeton's face hot. He cannot lie about this.

"Many women own land, is that correct?" the old *ri-pālle* continues like a school teacher. Whenever an American starts talking like this, it ends in a trick.

Jeton sees his young companions nodding their agreement. Yes, many women own land.

"Your *būbū* is an alap, Jeton—she owns some land, is that correct?"

"My *būbū*," says Jeton, thinking of *būbū*'s Nissan Altima LX, her condo on Guam, her pork farm in Manila, her house on Majuro. "She owns land."

"She does not belong to a royal family, does she? *Alaps* are not royalty, are they?"

"No," Jeton says. "She does not belong to a royal family."

"That means you are not *irooj*," the old man concludes, determined to shame him. "You could never be a prince because you do not belong to a chief's family. Your *būbū* owns some land. That is all. Many *būbū* own land. Isn't that right?"

Jeton nods in agreement. He feels his stomach tumble like he'd been caught by a big wave.

"So let us be clear about what just happened," the old *ri-pālle* says. "You got confused steering your boat, isn't that so?"

Jeton looks at the old man's red face for a moment to confirm that, yes, the old man is giving him a way out. But already the event is confused in Jeton's mind. He was steering the boat, yes. But he had not shut off the engine. And he had not tried to harm the Army ship. *He has not harmed anyone!*

Defiant again, Jeton says, "We came to see the Colonel. Your *irooj*."

His companions titter at this because Americans don't believe in things like chiefs, kings, princes.

Jeton continues: "He treats us like shit."

More titters.

"The Colonel will not see you," says the old man. "This is not how things are done."

"Fuck that, how things are done," Jeton snaps. "We got hepatitis on Ebeye and highest diabetes in the world and the most crowded place and babies everywhere—the Colonel does nothing about that!"

The children mutter their agreement, understanding Jeton's anger, if nothing else.

"Are you speaking for all Marshallese people? Are you *authorized*?" The *ri-pālle* says this word in *kajin Ṃajeḷ: komaroñ.*

Jeton sifts the shell-white sand through his fingers. Knowing that he cannot disguise his lie, he says, "All *Ri-Ṃajeḷ* are authorized."

The old man finishes his cola, then wipes his sweaty scalp with a white handkerchief. Finally, shaking his head sadly, he says, again in *kajin Ṃajeḷ* so that there can be no mistaking: "They have just informed me that your friend Lino is dead—he drowned."

It is, Jeton realizes, the *ri-pālle*'s last resort. And it works.

The children started bawling. Then Jeton.

The *ri-pālle* lets them go on a while, then he asks again: "So you were confused and you didn't know where your boat was going?"

"Yes," Jeton says. "I was . . . confused."

"And you lost control of the boat?"

"Yes," says Jeton. "I lost . . . control."

"You had no intention of doing any damage?"

"No," says Jeton, "I had . . . no intention."

Jeton cannot put into words how *pok*—confused—he feels. It seems he has no place to go and nothing worth doing. So he can only sit here and weep like an *eokkwikwi*, a spoiled baby. It scares him because he does not know what happened to Jeton DeGroen, the star goalie who was afraid of no one.

He pictures himself in the water again, fetching children from the bubbling vortex, the bright blues and greens of the lagoon reflecting sunlight and playing it against the white sand below. Diving deep, he catches child after child and then, his lungs nearly bursting, swims them to the surface. The slap of water sounds like applause to his ears. Yes! He is saving lives—a hero, a Jona, a fool who can't see that just twenty feet beneath him his cousin's friend, Lino, is piloting the Irooj to heaven.

* * * *

Cooper's visitor is Terry Thatcher: "No relation to the long-retired Mrs.," he says. "I'm your keeper, Cooper."

Cooper wonders if this guy is his immediate supervisor or the lab's lowest man on the pole. He looks no more than thirty and wears baggy nylon shorts, a mostly wrinkled pink polo shirt, and canvas sneakers without socks. With his black wavy hair and dark complexion, he could be Indian or Latino or even Marshallese.

"My keeper?" Cooper asks.

"Your answer man." Terry steps inside, pulling the door shut. Heat seems to roil off of him. "You must rate to get your own trailer." He seems to survey the place, which makes Cooper wish it were cleaner and tidier.

"I appreciate your taking the time," Cooper says. "You flew in from Roi-Namur?"

"It's only forty minutes north, Cooper. Not a big deal."

"I've read the material," Cooper says. He pegs back with his crutches.

"Great." Terry pulls out a note pad and yellow pencil. "Let's sit."

"Do I need to take notes?"

Terry smiles: "Nothing as dramatic as that. We're just going to review the philosophical parameters." He seats himself in Cooper's wheelchair. "You mind?"

"Not at all. It's probably the most comfortable seat in the house."

Cooper eases himself onto the couch. He secretly prays for a well behaved phantom leg: no bolts of shocking pain, no twinges of irritation, no maddening itches.

Terry leans forward: "You probably have a lot of questions about our coordination with the Army."

Cooper wants to confess that he's just not ready for radar re-entry physics—that, really, all he wants to do is find his boat and get back on his feet, never mind that just last week he assured the benefits coordinator of DataCell that he is ready and eager to do his job.

Sarah, from her houseboat thousands of miles away, has told him that his confusion is a natural reaction to his circumstances and she assures him that he is not an imposter, that DataCell knew what it was doing when it hired him. "No," he said, "they're deceiving themselves, their heads turned by fringe technology. Trying to think out of the box, they're tickled that they've hired a gamer. It sounds sexy to them. But it's a mistake!"

"I can see you don't know where to begin," Terry says.

Cooper tries to speak but manages only to say, "Well."

"As you'll recall from the interviews, we are most interested in the algorithms you developed for the Stone Deaf Death Rangers game."

"Part III," Cooper says. "The fallout episode."

"Yeah, where the shooter tries to knock out incoming missiles. That's cool stuff."

"Thanks."

Terry taps his open notepad with his pencil. "Had you come here thirty years ago, you'd've been working on one thing and one thing only—tracking test missile shots. Period."

"With the radar on Roi."

Terry nods yes, of course. "We now use our facilities to work all angles, doing near earth and deep space surveillance, helping everyone from NASA to NORAD. Did you know we performed 43,000 space trackings last year and 250 other space operations?"

"That's a lot of tracking." Cooper feels like a brown-noser.

"No matter how far afield any of our assignments may seem, it all comes home when we start talking about missile defense." Terry wags his pencil thoughtfully. "That's who butters our bread, the Missile Defense Agency."

"I understand our focus is on mid-course and terminal phase interception." Cooper is simply reciting his orientation material, blathering to win this man's approval.

"That's right. We're not going to worry about the first phase, boost interception."

"It's the toughest," says Cooper, continuing his recitation, "because it involves laser technology. Only a three to five minute window, I understand."

"Yeah, tough stuff. Eventually we'll interface with the THAADS—"

"Terminal High Altitude Area Defense Systems," Cooper chirps.

Terry smiles tolerantly. "You don't have to prove to me that you've read your stuff, man. Relax."

Cooper nods okay, hoping his face doesn't show his embarrassment.

"By the time you're done," Terry says, "you'll know so many acronyms nobody outside Tradex will be able to understand you."

Cooper realizes that he would like that, to be on the inside.

"You read how our eleven island radar sites here in USAKA give us outstanding triangulation," Terry continues. "Man, we can catch this shit coming, going, upside-down, and sideways." He grins proudly.

Cooper wonders how much radar science he'll have to learn—or how much he's capable of learning. And how fast?

"I guess I don't have to tell you, Cooper, that the missiles haven't changed all that much in the last thirty years."

Actually, Cooper doesn't know this. After he nods knowingly, Terry continues: "So you know that they're potentially smarter today, but not much faster. Smarts count more than speed, everybody figured that out long ago. Now—" Terry begins to draw on his pad. "The one thing most people got wrong after the Soviet system collapsed is the assumption that we don't have to worry about their ICBMs any more." He has drawn a neat, childlike illustration of a hammer and sickle, one handle laid crosswise over the other.

"But the Soviets can—" Cooper begins.

"Who?" Terry draws a bold line through the hammer and sickle.

"Okay, the *Russians* can still develop their missiles."

"Wrong, Cooper. Think again."

"All right," Cooper says. "They can still *fire* their missiles, as can the Chinese."

"Now you're getting somewhere." Terry flips the page, then begins another drawing. "It's enemy missile *deployment,* not development, that we've got to worry about. Nobody's got the money for development any more."

"Except us," says Cooper.

"Which is why we're doing it. Anybody can fire a missile. Nobody—but us—can *shoot one down.* So, when the tenderhearts start whining at you about your bloody work with missile defense, you tell them that." Terry has drawn a rocket flying at an angle. On the nose cone, he has drawn a frowning cartoon face. The enemy missile, no doubt.

Actually no one's given Cooper grief about his imminent work with missiles. Everybody wants to thwart nuclear war and the terrorist threat, right?

"If we consider terrorist potential," Terry continues, "then without question we'll be looking at conventional weaponry. That's good news because it means all the study we've done on missiles for the past forty years will be useful, you see? We'll be looking at old Soviet and Chinese missiles that terrorists have gotten their grubby little hands on. And chances *are,* there won't be but one or two, let's say even three, fired at any one time. That's provided that *any* of those clowns could get the technology together to fire the things in the first place. Or the *second place.* First, they've got to get the missiles, don't they?"

Cooper waves one hand to make him stop. "Okay, what you're

saying is that for all intents and purposes, it's impossible for terrorists to manage these weapons. I mean, how are they possibly going to build a missile silo or launch pad without being detected by our satellites?"

Terry points the pencil at him. "That's right."

"Then why are we bothering with all this development—the goal of laser interception especially, if terrorism is our primary worry these days?"

Terry looks at him with disbelief. "Are you trying to put yourself out of business, pal?"

"I'm just saying—"

"I hear you." He waves the pencil as if to dismiss him. "But don't even go down that path, man. As long as there's *no guarantee* that the current stock of warheads in the hands of the current crew of no-goodniks *can be trusted*, we've got an ICBM scenario. It's as simple as *that*."

"But it's so Cold War."

"But it's still the world we live in, Cooper. Remember we signed the ABM Treaty with the Soviets in 1972. Can you tell me where the Soviets are right now?"

"Okay, we just covered that. There are no Soviets any more so there is no treaty."

"Bingo, babe. Let's just do the best we can with the technology we have. If terrorists start popping them our way, we'll be ready. If not," he shrugs, "we'll still be ready."

"For the off-chance that some North Korean psycho will fire one at us?" says Cooper.

"Stranger things *have* happened, haven't they?"

Only in the movies, Cooper thinks. "If we're only concerned with conventional, and probably old, weapons," he says, unable to let this go, "we could give up the high-end stuff, couldn't we?"

"We work towards THAADS because we can, man. Expense can't be an issue—because everything's expensive. Each test shot costs us a hundred mill, you know."

"I didn't know."

Now Terry draws another smaller missile arrowed at the mean-faced missile. The little one has a smiling nose cone. "Cooper, I can see your vision's clouded by the old SDI stigma." Terry flips to a clean page and starts drawing what look like little bursts of light. "Okay, the Star Wars Defense initiative is dreamy. We can all agree on that. But, think about it: so was the idea of going to the moon or flight itself. Laser technology's getting better every year. Imagine, if we can perfect THAADS and destroy foreign launches at the earliest phase, before their boosters separate. It would paralyze the world's ability to wage ballistic missile warfare!" He smiles the teacher's knowing smile. "Isn't that worth the money?"

Cooper nods agreeably. He wants to be a good student but he can't help thinking that this investment—these billions and billions of dollars on deterrents for something that hasn't happened yet and may never happen and even if it does happen it will be on the most miniscule and inaccurate scale—this is like spending billions to perfect a new kind of fly paper.

When Cooper doesn't speak up, Terry says, "I see I've given you plenty to ponder—that's my job."

"As my keeper?" Coopers phantom leg bucks like a dog startled from a nap. He grips the idle crutches to steady himself.

"If you don't know the context," says Terry, "you can't do the work the right way."

"You mean with the right frame of mind."

Another buck, then a bite of pain. Cooper stifles a gasp.

Terry is smiling. "You're one of us now—the Roi rats—we operate as a team: each programmer like one synapse in a single mind."

"That sounds scary," Cooper jokes.

"It should sound scary to the terrorists and the diehard commies. We hope!" Terry closes his notepad decisively. "Any questions?"

"Where are you from?" he asks.

"Oh, yeah," Terry chuckles. "I *forgot that question*. I could see you squinting hard to figure me out." He pockets his pad.

"Sorry, Terry. I hope you don't think I'm being rude. But—"

"No, problem, Cooper, I'm hip to the novelty of finding a Marshallese programmer out here."

"So you *are* Marshallese?"

"Yeah, but I've cheated a little." He leans back and begins wheeling to and fro slightly, his hands on the wheel-guides. "My parents moved to Phoenix sixteen years ago—the Compact gives us citizenship status more or less, you know. So I grew up American. Got my degrees at M.I.T., the whole bit."

"That's extraordinary!"

"So they tell me." He grins immodestly. "I'm a kind of on the outside, you could say."

"And you're okay with that?"

"You mean do I regret not living on the reservation?"

"Is that what you think of the Republic?"

"It's not my scene, that's for sure. America is where it's at."

"And your family?"

"Most of them are Stateside now. Compton, La Jolla, San Fernando Valley. If you ask me, it's just a matter of time before every kid from the Marshalls ends up in the States. These islands are getting swallowed up."

"You say that so calmly, Terry!"

Terry's smile could be taken as resignation. Or indifference. "Like missile defense," he says, "moving on doesn't have to be a bad thing, does it, Cooper?"

Two days later, Cooper manages the airplane gangway by himself, using the arm of a flight attendant for leverage as he hops up the seven steps. They settle him into seat number one, at the bulkhead, where there's plenty of leg room. Any irony here? he wants to ask, stretching out—and feeling his old friend, the phantom limb, aching right down to the ghost of his toes.

He distracts himself by watching the others come aboard, all of them smiling their warmest welcomes, patting him on the arm, winking, saying things like *You made it, congratulations!* A few are wearing well-pressed Bermudas with black knee socks and leather shoes.

It's the geek express to Roi-Namur, man, what did you expect?

The plane is a Beech 1900-D, a twin-prop commuter that's as noisy as a cement mixer. Everyone wears ear plugs or headphones, he notices.

At an altitude of only a couple thousand feet, the flight takes thirty or forty minutes, small islands passing quickly below them: sand, palms, too-blue water, white reefs, one after the other, here and gone, here and gone.

"Look for sharks," the older man across the aisle tells him. He's one of the black socks. "They'll appear to be tadpoles from this height."

When Cooper gazes down, he feels dizzy for the first time ever in a plane. He swallows a mouthful of air, then glances to the bright bulby cumulus above.

"I'm keeping a log," his neighbor continues. "I've counted twenty-seven black tips, ten lemons, four grays, one hammer-head, and six tigers. Tigers are the ones to watch for. They'll eat you in a minute!"

You've got to make an effort, Cooper tells himself. *These are your co-workers.* "Are you a scuba diver?" he asks, nearly shouting across the narrow aisle.

The man laughs. "No way, José!"

The other passengers are reading books, fiddling with their lap tops, or nodding off. Fourteen in all.

In his phone conversation with Lillian too early this morning, she told him he needed a better plan.

"You've got to include me in some of this," she said. "We need shared goals."

"Some of this I simply can't share, Lil'."

"I know you're in pain, Cooper. That's why you're pushing me away. Do you have another girlfriend?"

"That's unfair."

"I'm entitled to an honest answer."

"You know, talk like this isn't helping our relationship."

After a stubborn pause, she said, almost like a challenge: "Do you know where I am right now?"

"Are you going to make me guess?"

"I decided to take a little vacation and it'd been years since I'd been east and I've never seen Baltimore. It's really nice. It's not 'The Wire'!"

"You're not serious!"

"I was *invited*, Cooper."

In—in-in-vited.

"This can't be for real," he said.

"Your parents are the sweetest people. Here, your mom wants to say hello."

"Cooper?" he heard his mother say, as if he were ten again and she were rousting him from oversleeping.

By this time he was sitting up in bed and flailing for the light switch: "Mom, what are you doing inviting Lillian to your house?"

"She's delightful. A cute girl. That Bailey's smart too."

"I can't believe you've allowed this to happen!"

"You settle down," she whispered harshly. "I'm allowed to do what I see fit. And right now I see fit to get all the support and comfort I can muster, 'cause, Lord knows, you're not helping me and your father through this terrible ordeal."

"Do you realize that in just a few hours I'm supposed to start my first day of work?" he said.

"You can get a job any old place, Cooper. But you've got only one family. And, if you're smart, only one fiancée—who's sitting right here waiting for you to come home and make sense of your life."

At this point Cooper seriously considered slamming down the receiver. But the dramatic gesture would have made him feel good only for the moment and then he'd pay for it in the long term—maybe for years to come. So he gripped the receiver until his fingers ached and said, "Mom, the phone's breaking up on this end; it looks like we're going to lose our connection. You know I love you and I'll call you soon and tell you all about my job."

"Cooper, stop this nonsense—I don't hear anything breaking up."

"There's plenty of breaking up on this end," he said, relishing the irony. "Tell Lillian that I'll email her."

"You just said you'd call."

"I'll do both."

"Wait. You talk again to Lillian."

"Love you, Mom." Then he hung up.

After that, it took him an alarmingly long time to catch his breath.

Roi-Namur comprises two mitt-shaped islands that the Japanese land-filled together before World War II. There are significant Japanese military ruins remaining, Cooper has read. Of particular note is their crumbling commanders' bunker, which miraculously survived the American pummeling. There are other bunkers too and a few gun emplacements. As on other battlefield islands, there is a mass grave for the Japanese dead, marked by a concrete plaque.

The moment Cooper steps onto the tarmac after his careful climb down—everyone waiting patiently behind him—he is met by Terry, who's got a golf cart to drive him over to Tradex, the "Tracking and Discrimination Experiment." The rest of the passengers climb onto bicycles, which apparently everyone keeps at the concrete airfield.

Although Cooper saw the Altair radar on his approach to the island—and it did look big—he is unprepared for its spectacular size up close. It's easily as large as a professional baseball diamond.

A white skeletal scoop that rises ominously 150 feet from the jungle, it looks like something from an early James Bond movie.

When it swivels slowly his way, Cooper gets a creepy chill.

Terry is dressed a little neater than when they last met, now in a crisp blue polo shirt and khaki Bermudas, with clean canvas tennis shoes.

"My man, you made it," he says. "How do you like this door-to-door service?"

"I'm flattered," Cooper says, snugging his crutches between the golf cart seats.

Terry takes off abruptly, the cart whining as he stamps the accelerator to the floor. The hot wind feels pretty good.

When Terry stops abruptly at Tradex Road, Cooper has to hang on, snatching at his crutches to keep them from spilling out of the back.

"Could you read that out loud, please?" Terry points to the large roadside sign in front of them.

"*Entering potential RF hazard area. Stay on the road and do not loiter.*"

"These are posted in all the hot spots," Terry says. "If for some reason you're out here when we turn the Big Boy on, you'll hear the buzzers and see the lights." He points to both on nearby striped poles. "Here." He hands Cooper a weighty plastic ID tag the size of a wallet. "This is your Lincoln Labs' film badge. The Safety Office will collect it each month to measure how many rads you've taken in. We're all about safety here."

A few others from the plane pedal past. Some nod a greeting.

Cooper dutifully pins the tag to his shirt. He reviews what he knows of the radar: the Altair (Advance Research Project Agency Long-Range Tracking and Instrumentation Radar) can track as far away as 22,000 miles. Most of the radar have broad-band and narrow-band capabilities. Target resolution for the L-band is a close 30 feet or so. S-band gets even closer.

"What happens when the Big Boy's on?" he asks.

The Big Boy, he has read, does the hard work, tracking dispersed targets. That's what you want during missile attacks.

"If you're out here, you stay clear," Terry tells him. He points to another roadside sign farther on that says, *Warning, RF radiation hazard. Do not proceed beyond this point.* "It spits major rads a full city block, man."

Then Terry takes off so quickly Cooper has to brace himself against whiplash.

"Is this thing souped up?" he jokes.

"I did a little tinkering, yeah," Terry says proudly. "You get bored, you know. It can't all be golf and snorkeling, though I have perfected my drive out here."

To be a good sport, Cooper asks, "How have you perfected your drive?"

"I order a gross of balls from China every month. Then, with my Chi-Chi Rodriguez vintage one wood, I rocket those babies into the ocean. Pow, one after the other!"

"Every month or so?"

"It's got to be regulation balls, otherwise you're wasting your time. I can drive, oh, maybe two hundred yards."

"Sweet Jesus, that's far!"

"Island life gives you focus, if you let it." He nods as if to ponder this. "Here we are."

"Not much to look at," says Cooper. Except for the huge radar on the roof—about a third the size of Altair—the Tradex facility could pass as a u-store-it warehouse.

"Nothing is 'much to look at' out here except the scenery," says Terry.

They pass through two ID-sensitive security doors, then Terry nods a greeting to the guard who checks their IDs again.

"Aren't you cold in that outfit?" Cooper asks. "What is it, 60 in here?"

"Got to keep the hardware happy," he says. "As you know, we're working with major mainframes. One of the best systems in the *world,* my man."

When he was accepted for this assignment, Cooper pictured the "lab" as an airy, high-ceilinged room with skylights overhead, work-stations on the periphery, and a command network at the center—dominated by a transparent two-sided flat screen Mercator projection of the world, mapped out in heavy grids. Like something from a James Bond movie. Until now he hasn't been able to shake that silly vision.

As he suspected, the lab looks as mundane as an insurance office, the men and women working in padded cubicles. Sure, the screens are oversized and everyone's networked to the mainframe and there are some interesting missile photos on the walls, thanks to high-altitude reconnaissance. But, otherwise, it's a workplace, nothing more.

Though Terry tours him through the building and shows him his cubicle, with its wide-screen monitor, Cooper doesn't get to talk to anybody except in passing because everyone's analyzing last night's missile intercept, which failed.

"You can understand why we're a little crabby today," Terry whispers.

"Am I keeping you from your work?"

"Not a big deal, Cooper. Right now, you're my assignment. So let's get a sandwich."

They drive across the island, past the air strip, then through the golf course to pick up a couple of sandwiches from the "Cafe Roi." Then Terry motors to the ruins of the Japanese Command Bunker. Made wholly of concrete, now black and scabrous with age, the bunker sits on a concrete plinth whose stairs are also crumbling. Its rusted iron-plated window shutters and doors are the color of dried blood. Cooper can see, in the upturned cornice at the roof's edge and the spacious doorways and windows, the Japanese design. The place looks like a small temple.

"I want you to get the full effect on the first day," Terry says.

The ruins are posted with small wooden signs that say: "This structure unsafe. Do not enter."

Cooper isn't sure what effect he's supposed to get "fully." The ruins look innocuous enough. The island itself, on this side, has the look of a country club in backwater Florida, expanses of tough lawn interrupted by clusters of palms: plenty of open space and no one around.

"I guess they're just going to let these ruins rot away," Cooper observes, crutching into the grassy shade of old coconut palms.

"What else would you do?"

"I don't know," he muses. "It's remarkable they have survived."

"And you want to save them, don't you, just because they have survived." He hands Cooper a plastic-wrapped ham and cheese sandwich. "Americans are a nation of pack rats, eager to save anything and everything that's not in their way. I've started a collection of bottles I've found along the shore. And a collection of shells, of course. And a collection of drift wood."

"I imagine your fellow Marshallese think that's odd."

"To them I'm odd all the way around." He bites into his sandwich. "I'm used to it. Not that I see many of the *ri-Majel* up this way, except in the housekeeping and clean-up crews."

Cooper wonders if any part of Terry feels sadness at this.

At a loss himself, Cooper says, "Roi seems a nice place. Very pretty."

"I'd rather be in Phoenix, man."

"Or Boston?"

"Too cold. I was born for warmth." Terry talks as he chews. "Some things you can't escape." He's staring pensively at Cooper's crutches—or the leg that isn't there. "You know, I bet you could learn to snorkel with only one leg."

"Snorkeling hadn't occurred to me," says Cooper with a polite smile. "It'll be a while before I'll have time to give it a try."

"Well, think about it," he says. "Sit down. Relax."

It is very difficult to sit down when leaning on two crutches, Cooper is about to explain. But he has practiced. It's getting up afterwards that's impossible. Still, with great effort, he eases himself down, then unwraps his sandwich. It's the kind you could get anywhere in the States: two thin iridescent pink ham slices, yellow mustard, too much mayonnaise, and a yellow square of cheese on very soft white bread.

Cooper takes a bite. The sandwich is bland but good enough. He hears Terry humming as he eats, the man staring into the distance, where the ocean bites at the shore. Maybe Terry drives his ball out that way.

"You don't mind losing all those golf balls, obviously," Cooper says.

"Not at all," Terry says. "Plenty more where they come from. And it's all for a good cause."

Cooper thinks of peasant factory workers in China punching out golf balls, five thousand a day. What is that work compared to his own? Is his work—despite its many acronyms—any more useful? He suspects that it is not. In fact, it may be less than useful, like selling parachutes to people in high rise buildings in the expectation of another 9/11. Do you really think that, when and if they hit your building, you're going to have time to dig out your chute, strap it on, brace yourself at the window (assuming your window opens) then bail yourself into the city traffic fifty stories below?

There will always be crazies, there will always be bombs. Everybody knows that much. What nobody knows is how to live with that uncertainty. The work at USAKA must make some people feel more certain, especially at the Pentagon, he imagines. Never mind that the fruits of this labor have been decades in coming. In the meantime, year after year, the engineers, technicians, and programmers like himself burn billions of America's dollars on their computer screens and in their finely drawn schemata. In many ways, it's no more or less than alchemy, Cooper decides, everybody looking for the formula to make gold.

It's easy to understand, then, the joy of Terry's hobby, smacking balls high and long, then watching them drop one after the other into the whitecaps. There's something comforting in such waste, he realizes, something as contained and simple as a yawn.

FIFTEEN

Jeton hopes that when he dies he gets a funeral like Lino's. The mourners stand one after the other on the sandy paths between the rows of whitewashed crosses in the Baptist graveyard, everyone dressed for church. Jeton too, with his short-sleeved white shirt, his clip-on necktie, his too-short Sunday trousers, and his leather shoes, which are scuffed and scraped from working on the causeway. Stevie and Mike are here and friends from the Consolidated High team, where Lino had been a center on the soccer team a few years ago. Jeton's mama is here but not his little brother and sister. Two rows away he sees Father Joe, mama's priest, who wants to talk with him. There are so many people, they spill into the sandy road, which a high storm tide washes over every few minutes. Those in the wet road have taken off their shoes, holding them in their hands like offerings.

Now, with both arms raised over his head as if reaching for God, the minister stands beside the grave, where Lino's particle-board coffin has been laid. He talks happily about Lino as a baby, as a strong boy, as a fisherman. Lino's mother and father cry-smile as the minister reminds them that Lino is in heaven. Jeton sees many heads nodding yes, yes, heaven! Then the All-Glory Baptist choir, dressed in their ruby-red gowns, sings "Bringing in the Sheaves!" and Jeton pretends to sing too, though he cannot remember the words. Then he loses his place in the song because he is trying to remember what "sheaves" are.

Nobody has blamed Jeton for what happened. And Jeton knows that nobody will ever say anything about it, even Stevie who is sick over the loss of his boat, the Irooj. It was a bad day, everyone says, an unlucky day, a day that Jeton has already started dreaming of—except in his dream he turns into a giant turtle and carries Lino to shore.

He fears that soon Lino will come to him in his dreams. Water will run from his nostrils and ears, like water from an empty shell. He will be as pale as fish belly. He will say, "Jeton, we're sinking, man!" Jeton tells himself that when this happens he will not be rude to Lino's ghost. He will say: *Yes, Lino, we are sinking. I am sorry.*

Jeton's mother does not ask what happened. She is happy that Jeton is home and alive. "Are you going back to work on the causeway?" she has asked. He has not answered because Mike has not offered any work. Mike buys Jeton beers and lets Jeton watch him play *Space Spiders!* and sometimes Mike jokes with him about *likatu*. But that is all. Jeton feels that he is a ghost in Mike's life now. Stevie spends all of his time at the marina, doing odd jobs and begging other pilots to make him a first mate. He does not go drinking any more.

The Americans have banned Jeton from Kwajalein for life. If he returns they will throw him into an American prison forever. John Amatu, the Ebeye sheriff, brought by a large sheet of paper to show Jeton that it is official. Pointing with one thick, dirty fingernail, he jabbed at the words "persona non grata," which is the label the Americans have given Jeton. It means they never want to see him again.

Now, Jeton as he wanders Ebeye, looking for something to do, he gets advice from everyone: Leave the Americans alone. The Americans pay the Republic a lot of money. The Americans are crazy. The Americans will kill you if you bother them again.

He accepts all of the gentle scolding and chiding, hoping that everyone will see that he is not a stubborn *bwebwe*, not a *jona* who ruins everything.

* * * *

From the *Majuro Times:*

Biggest Meteorite in the World?

Majuro, RMI: Marvin Thomas, Ph.D., has carried to Majuro what may be the largest meteorite in the world. Dr. Thomas and his colleagues discovered the astral stone two months ago after a surprising early morning meteor shower in Maloelap Atoll, 150 miles northeast of Majuro. Australia's Bureau of Meteorology confirmed the unusual fallout, which yielded some striking satellite photos. Dr. Thomas will display the meteorite on Majuro until scientists from Australia and Japan arrive to inspect the remarkable rock, which is said to weigh half a ton. "I am proud to bring this wonderful discovery to the world," said Dr. Thomas. "I am in negotiations with several museums who are interested in obtaining it."

Accompanying photo: Dr. Thomas smiling at the camera, one hand on the meteorite.

* * * *

Majuro from the air looks like a green streamer unfurled across the sand.

"You know Robert Louis Stevenson visited Majuro," Art says. "He called it the Pearl of the Pacific."

"Why would Robert Louis Stevenson visit Majuro?" Cooper asks.

Art rolls his bloodshot eyes: "That's a stupid question."

The plane feels more like a bus, the passengers are so . . . casual, everyone dressed for a backyard barbecue, it seems, barefoot children roaming the aisle, over-full straw bags spilling from nearly every seat. Cooper and Art are the only "bell-ees."

"I've never felt so alien," Cooper says.

"You mean you've never felt like a *minority*," Art says. "Wait till we land."

Feeling a surge of gratitude—which almost feels like affection—Cooper regards the older man, his jowly unshaven face, his peeling pate, his small cynical eyes. "I really appreciate your helping me get my boat back."

Art glances out the window as the plane banks. "It's your dime. And it gives me an excuse to see some relatives."

"Your wife must miss you being gone all the time."

"The *Ri-Majeḷ* are used to separation. Of the 60,000 souls in this nation, one third are elsewhere. It's globalization of the worst sort. A diaspora."

"They're looking for jobs?"

"Had we done it right, there would have been jobs here—aqua-culture, tourism, coconut. But we never do it right, do we, Cooper?"

"Why not, Art?

"I like you, Cooper. You pitch me softballs."

"I'm just curious."

"You're asking about human nature. No easy answers there. Unlike most Pacific nations, the RMI gets plenty of money and American assistance. It's not about money. If it were, every kid in the States would be graduating from high school, right? And sixth graders in America would know how to read at the sixth grade level. The reason it doesn't happen is deep-structure shit, Cooper. It's how we've organized our culture."

"How have the Marshallese organized theirs?"

"It's been dismantled—that's the problem—blown to a million pieces, as scattered as the islands themselves. These people have been colonized for two hundred years. They had it all, Cooper, and now there's nearly nothing left. They were the best navigators in the Pacific. The best! They could set out in dugout canoes with their families and few worldly belongings, and sail. It was crazy shit. Just sail into the open ocean. Thousands of miles. And they'd find land because they could read the sky, the flight of birds, even the waves. You've seen the stick charts they sell at the tourist shop?"

"That spindly thing no bigger than a placemat and made of reeds and cowrie shells? Somebody put one in my gift basket."

"They made stick charts of the ocean—250,000 square miles of water in this nation alone. Charts that could take them anywhere. They were the best, Cooper. Fishermen of unparalleled skill. And the bravest mother fuckers. They'd do whatever they had to do. They'd fight like demons, love like angels." He shakes his head sadly.

"They were good at tattoos, I've read."

"Yeah, very cool tattoos. Head to toe. The early Spanish explorers called the 'Los Pintados,' the Painted Ones. Missionaries washed that away. It took them a while but, by the 1950s, nobody was doing tattoos. Fuck the fucking missionaries and their fucking good intentions!"

"So how do the Marshallese get it back?"

"How does anybody? Westerners cluck their tongues and shake their heads at the plight of Africa and the horror of African genocide. Monstrous shit, everybody agrees. But what's the mystery? Africa has long been eviscerated by colonization. There's no center of gravity, Cooper."

"Okay, so everybody—and everything—drifts. You make it sound hopeless!"

"There will always be hope, Cooper, because hope is fundamental to human nature. Hope brought you across the Pacific, didn't it? It keeps you thinking you can pull it off, doesn't it?"

Cooper feels his face warm with embarrassment. Has Art been reading his mind? Is he that transparent? "Pull what off, Art?"

"All the shit you're trying to pull off—getting normal without your leg. Trying to be the same person you used to be."

"I know it won't be the same," Cooper says carefully.

"Sure, you do, son. And you're gonna try till your heart breaks. I can see that."

"I don't need your pity."

"And you're not going to get it!" Art grins as if to encourage him. "I don't even pity the Marshallese, who deserve some pity. They've made plenty of their own mistakes. "

"You could have worked for their government." Cooper wants to sting Art and make him wince. Just a little. "They could have used your help."

"They don't want my help," he says. "I'm a *ri-pālle* ."

"That sounds like a cop-out, Art."

"Maybe it is. But the answer is complicated. A little country like this can't generate an intelligentsia large enough to promote, much less sustain, its ambitions. So it's always farming out the best and hardest work to foreigners. So nothing sticks, nothing stays home. And it pisses the Marshallese off. They end up shunning the people who could help them and resenting their own best and brightest who are thoroughly distracted and running after the American dream."

"What are you calling the American dream?"

"Cars, flat screen TVs, cell phones, stereos, alcohol, resort vacations—consumer shit, Cooper. Numbing, mind-rotting piles of it."

"Americans are to blame for that?"

"Oh, no, you can't be that simplistic, Coop. Americans are just bauble-dazed peasants. They're doing what most anybody would do after stumbling into Ali Baba's cave. Forty years ago, before I left for the Corps, the most popular show in the States was 'The Beverly Hillbillies.' That's us. We're eating supper around the pool table, thinking it's a fancy dining room. And we're hemorrhaging money to live like that. It's tragically hilarious."

Cooper lets out a slow whistle. He says, "You're the man who knows too much, Art. I don't know how you can live with all that in your head. "

"Tell you the truth, I don't know either."

With a bump and a scrape and a wind-roar of de-acceleration, they have landed. Everyone on the plane waits until the stewards half-carry Cooper down the steps to the tarmac. Then, to his excruciating embarrassment, the passengers walk behind Cooper, observing his agonizingly slow crutch-pace because to pass him would be rude, apparently.

"Just shoot me and put me out of my misery," he mutters.

Art chuckles. "Everyone's being so sweet, Coop. You should learn to be more gracious."

A low tent-like structure made of large timber and open on all sides, the terminal looks like a national park pavilion.

Art's relatives—sister-in-law Ada, brother-in-law Billy, aunt-in-law Rosemary, three teenaged boys, two teenaged girls, and five smaller children—greet them in the terminal as soon as he and Cooper pass the indifferent customs officer. It looks as though the relatives are wearing their best flowered shirts and muumuus, having skipped work and school for this occasion. Ada, Billy, and Aunt Rosemary take Art's arm for an affectionate squeeze. The small children attach themselves to his legs. Everyone is chattering, grinning, nodding. Art has brought gifts of American candy, cigarettes, and the ubiquitous SPAM, which he passes around, looking like a tropically dissolute Santa. He wears his seedy shorts, his dirty "Endorsed by No One" T-shirt, his battered flip-flops.

Smiling painfully, Cooper hangs back, leaning into his crutches, already his back soaked with sweat. The younger children gape at him as if he were a ghost. The older children won't look at him at all.

He nods politely when Art introduces him, then the women present him with a lei of powerfully scented white flowers and a crown of tiny purple flowers. "It's tradition," Art says. "We might have borrowed it from the Hawaiians." Cooper says, "*Kommool*"—thanks—over and over. Everyone nods and smiles until Cooper doesn't know what to do, so he says *Koṃṃool* again, which starts another round of nods and smiles. Then they make their way to the vans, which are the smallest vans Cooper has ever seen: Korean micro-vans. Cooper gets the front seat of the first one, Art wheezily helping him while the others look on with concern. It must be rude to touch a stranger. This does not apply to children, apparently, because their hands are all over him, a couple of tykes tugging him in as clambers onto his seat.

"Yuck-way," Cooper keeps saying. This makes the children giggle.

He lets them play with his crown of flowers, which they pass around.

Eventually all fourteen passengers are oystered into the two micro-vans. The main road is the only road. The island is mostly that narrow. Cooper can see the water on both sides. Lagoon to the left, ocean to the right.

The teen drivers take the 30-mile drive ever-so-slowly, probably for fear of breaking an axel or hitting children, who are everywhere, it seems, darting in and out of the road. Art and the grown-ups talk in Marshallese, while two children paw at Cooper, stroking his shoulder, touching his ear lobes, curling his hair. This makes him think that, despite his experience with Bailey, maybe he could be good with children.

The houses are *not* thatched huts. Cooper was expecting thatched huts. Stupid *ri-pālle*! Mostly it's brightly painted cinder block, with rusted tin roofs. But there are also some handsome stucco buildings. Dirt yards. Rusting Asian-made cars. Everything is rusting. Bright flags of laundry on lines. Palm trees and so much ocean. Where are the crowds and third-world squalor? Cooper starts scolding himself for his prejudices but then the landscape changes. This must be the town coming up: Majuro. Few trees here. Plywood huts and hovels packed onto dirt lots. Pigs and dogs and chickens running as freely as the shirtless, sometimes naked, children. The single-story, cinderblock businesses, the rusted vehicles, the aroma of grilling meat mixed with the stink of car exhaust—the traffic backed up now at the speed bumps in front of the fire station—the sandy, dusty paths in lieu of sidewalks, the litter, the islanders idling in the shade, every man with a cigarette, the soul-crushing sweat-wringing heat: the town seems an outpost at the edge of the world.

They drive on and it gets more crowded still. Art has called this a nation of children and Cooper sees why. Children are playing in rain puddles, dashing through dirt alleys, chasing dogs, kicking a half-deflated soccer ball, watching teenagers playing volleyball in someone's tiny dirt yard. Does this island never end? Ocean on both sides, waves crashing against rock, the humid air as odorous as a tide pool. Why weren't these islands washed away a thousand years ago? It all seems so incredibly fragile, a crowd of shacks on a spine of coral like barnacles on the back of a floating log.

"You okay, Cooper?"

Cooper forces a smile and half turns to the back seat. "I see gravestones in many of these yards, like a few steps from the front door—what's with that?"

"The *Ri-Majel* like to be close to their relatives."

They pull into the shade of big trees, behind a small cinderblock house: they are facing the bright blue-green lagoon. A small house is next door. Otherwise, there is no crowd on this half acre plot. It's a large plot of land for Majuro.

"It belongs to my wife," Art says. "Women own the land. Don't ask me why. It's just the way it is."

Cooper leans into his crutches, savors the shade. He says, "That makes you an *alap*, doesn't it?"

"Oh, good for you!" Art slaps him on the back. "You've been reading up. Here's my wife's sister!"

She's broad-hipped woman with a single streak of grey down the center of her black wavy hair, which is slicked back with coconut oil and knotted behind her neck. She smiles graciously and says: "*Iọkwe*, Mister Cooper." She does not shake his hand or move to touch him in any way.

Apparently she speaks little English. Cooper expected she'd be more Westernized. She wears the traditional flowered sack dress. And no shoes.

He thanks her for the hospitality: "*Kọṃṃool* tata!"

This makes her laugh politely.

Art shows him the "guest house"—a thatched hut he had an old hut-maker construct recently. "Pandanus leaves mostly," Art explains. "He's teaching me how to do it. I'm going to turn the entire compound into something you would've seen eighty years ago."

The hut is lovely and very small, about seven feet square with a nine-foot ceiling, open at the eaves for light and air, and a door-way and window, both with leafy flaps for privacy.

A giant tree, with a black-barked trunk six-feet in diameter, canopies Cooper's hut and a thirty-foot expanse of white sand that meets the lagoon. The steady lap and whoosh of wave-wash makes Cooper sleepy. A nap would be nice but there's too much going on—he has to see everything. And his boat. He's convinced that Thomas has brought the Lickety Split to Majuro.

Art stays in a plywood shack about ten yards away, nearer the water. Cooper imagined the old man might live modestly, but a plywood shack with a corrugated plastic roof? "This is an outdoor culture," Art explains. "If you're living right, you're spending most of your time outside. If you need a toilet, you'll have to go to my sister-in-law's house. At night just pee on the lagoon side of the big tree."

"Thanks. Are we going to have time to track down my boat today?"

"Not today, my friend. We're obliged to be sociable. That means a party. Everything here revolves around entertainment and eating. You're the guest of honor. You up for that?"

"I'm flattered."

"Sure, you are."

Near a picnic table beside his shack, Art builds a fire with coconut husks. He's got five boys gathering them. His sister-in-law sits in the sand by the water, scraping meat from freshly cracked coconuts into a big plastic bowl. Cooper sits in a sling chair nearby. Art has given him a beer. Two small boys sit in the sand below him, stealing glances at his stump, now covered with what looks like a stocking cap. A few more kids are hovering nearer the tree. Art explained to them that Cooper did not lose his leg to a shark. "They'd find you curious even without your injury," he says. "Marshallese children don't have much interaction with the *ri–pālle*."

"Is there something I can do?" Cooper asks.

"You'd insult us if you tried," says Art. "Americans have a difficult time being gracious guests. They don't know how to sit and receive. They think they have to offer some kind of exchange in the form of work."

"We're polite, we *ri–pālle*."

"Actually, *ri–pālle* are presumptuous. They don't know how to follow others."

"I'll follow you, Art. Just lead the way."

"That's my boy." He's got the fire smoking. "These have to burn down to coals. That will take a while."

After his third beer, Cooper falls asleep in his chair, his head nods waking him abruptly every few minutes. At one point a dog licking his hand wakes him. He hears the Marshallese murmuring, dogs barking in the distance, the waves lapping, a motor boat buzzing far away, children frolicking in the shallows, Art laughing with his relatives. He smells the sweet husk smoke and the grainy steam from a boiling pot of rice. It occurs to him that the difference between him and Art is that Art lives for the time he is not working. Cooper lives for work. And Cooper has been proud to say as much.

When he opens his eyes finally, it is late in the day and he has to pee. With some effort, he pushes himself from the chair. One of the smaller boys attempts to help by yanking on one arm. "*Koṃṃool!*" Cooper says groggily.

He finds Art near the water, wooden mallet in hand, pounding on a handful of bright green leaves against a cutting board. "You like octopus?" Art asks.

"I've never had octopus, Art."

"You're going to have some tonight. But it's got to be tenderized. That's what I'm doing with these kirin leaves." He shoves aside some leaves to reveal the shiny, gray-brown mottled tangle of freshly-caught octopus.

"Holy shit, Art, it looks like that thing was alive a few minutes ago!"

"You're gonna love octopus—with coconut milk and lime!"

* * * *

In the morning, over a cup of strong tea, Art hands Cooper a bowl of rice sprinkled with fish flakes. "When in Rome," he says.

"Why not sausage?" Cooper nods to the pig pen.

"Pork is very dear. Not even you rate pork, my friend."

They wait an hour for Art's nephew to arrive with a borrowed vehicle. It's a rusted mini-van without sideview mirrors or wipers. Its plastic upholstery has been shredded from overuse. Art gets in to drive, making his nephew sit in the back. Cooper, riding shotgun, fingers for the air-conditioner and Art laughs. "Where do you think you are?"

The radio gets one station. It plays "island music," which seems a hybrid of American country and disco, sung in Marshallese. "Hear that?" Art nods to the dashboard. *°Ñe Ri-Majel rej kilaba, rej kālọk jān ni.* "It's a song about suicide: *°Ñe Ri-Majel rej kilaba, rej kālọk jān ni.* When *ri-Majel* commit suicide, they jump off coconut trees. It's supposed to be funny but it's not."

"I've read about the high rate of suicide in the Marshalls."

"Among the young men here," Art says somberly, "it is the

highest in the world."

"Good god!"

"That's the Republic's future." Art nods to his nephew in the back, a mild-mannered boy of sixteen who's wearing an "Orlando, Florida!" T-shirt, baggy surfer shorts, and flip flops. He holds a cell phone to his ear. He smiles when he sees Cooper staring at him. "A high school drop-out with a six-month-old son by another sixteen year old. It wouldn't take much for him to hit the wall. The only thing—the ONLY thing—that keeps a kid like that from hanging himself is the extended family. *Būbū* takes care of the baby. The girl works as a maid at one of the hotels. And this one mostly hangs around, looking for work or a meal, like the rest of the teenagers. Speaks pretty good English, though."

"If someone just opened a business here," Cooper muses. "All these young people eager to work."

"Unemployment is as high here as it was during our great Depression in America, my friend. And globally these are flush times!"

"There's got to be a way!" Cooper says.

"You need training and infrastructure. Getting goods on and off the island is a major undertaking and very expensive. We can't compete with Vietnam or Malaysia or even Indonesia for manufacture."

"What about these discount stores we pass? They seem to be doing well."

"That's probably the best bet for a business because everything comes from China. China's close by and still cheap. But that won't last."

"So what do you suggest?"

"I don't!" He turns into the asphalt lot of a bowling alley.

Cooper pulls up his crutches. "I had no idea there'd be a bowling alley on Majuro!"

"You see the sign?" Art points.

It's a plastic table-sized placard mounted on a dolly. In black block letters it says, "METEOR HERE!" and, just below, "*iju rabōḷḷọk!*"

The whitewashed cinderblock building looks like it's been here for thirty years. "This isn't just a bowling alley," Art says. "It's a bar. The favorite hang-out of one of the chiefs, as a matter of fact. "

Just inside the smudged glass doors, Cooper finds Harold-the-mayor sitting at a small table. He's wearing a polo shirt, wrinkled khakis, and a T. Rowe Price ball cap. He grins, showing off his silver tooth, but doesn't seem to recognize Cooper.

"Five bucks!" he says pleasantly.

Cooper turns to Art. "Isn't that a lot of money?"

"Not for you," Art says. "Not to see the ninth wonder of the world!"

"It is a wonder!" Harold-the-mayor assures them. "Biggest meteorite ever!"

"I thought it was one of the biggest," Cooper says.

Harold-the-mayor turns his head in puzzlement. "Have we met?"

"I'm the geologist! I mean the guy who isn't the geologist."

"Oh, you! Sure. Your leg got worse, eh?" He offers a sympathetic glance at Cooper's crutches. Then, brightly, he adds: "For you—three bucks!"

Cooper sighs. "Are we using American currency?"

"There is no other in the Republic," says Art. "Three for me too?"

"Okay, why not!" Harold takes the money. "You're lucky you come early. Beat the crowds. It has been a sensation!"

"What becomes of this money you're collecting?" Cooper asks.

"Dr. Thomas is handling the finances!" It sounds almost like a boast. "We're going to build a world-class resort on our island. And all boats will rise!" He makes a rising gesture with both hands.

Art mutters: "Ten to one, Thomas and the money disappear."

"What about the meteorite?" Cooper mutters in return.

"If he could steal it, he would. But, I guarantee you the government is going to confiscate it."

"Oh, that'd be rich."

"Just to be sure, I'm going to phone the Minister of the Interior and suggest that this thing's a national treasure. It's not like the Republic allows anyone to lop off a piece of an island and sell that, right? So why should it allow this *ri-pālle* to abscond with a rare geological artifact?"

Cooper chuckles: "You are evil, Art."

"Lars Thomas is a scallywag!"

The meteorite looks larger that Cooper remembers. Orange and oblong, it sits on a rectangle of dirty carpet inside a cordon of sailor's rope. About ten or twelve men are standing at the cordon, staring at the rock. Nobody's bowling, but several men have beers in their hands. Most are smoking.

Somebody stretches one hand for a touch.

"Easy does it, fellas. That's precious shit."

Looking no different than two months ago, a Tsing Toa in one hand, a fistful of corn chips in the other, Thomas recognizes Cooper immediately.

"Look at you!" he bellows. "You made it!" Grinning, the big man headlocks Cooper with the crook of one beefy arm.

Cooper tries to keep his balance. "You mean I survived?" he croaks.

"Damn straight you survived." He releases Cooper, then inhales his handful of chips. "I called in the rescue, didn't I? Those motherfuckers came, didn't they? You're alive, aren't you?"

Is Thomas fishing for gratitude? But he's right. He did save Cooper. Why hasn't it occurred to Cooper to be thankful for the help he got on that one-in-a-million island? Suddenly feeling guilty and self-conscious, he glances down at his phantom leg. It twitches.

He says, "As you see, I had a little trouble."

"But you're doing fine, Cooper! You're out in the world, with one leg to spare! I'm proud of you!"

Cooper forces a smile. "Do you know my friend, Art Norman?"

Thomas gapes. "Art Norman? Son of a bitch! I wouldn't've recognized you!" He turns to Cooper. "He was thinner back in the day." Then he reaches for Art: "Give me a hug, big guy!"

Art looks like he's going to comply. But then, drawing near, he head-butts Thomas. Stunned by the blow, Thomas falls back, his nose spurting blood.

Cooper fulcrums forward to get between Art and the now-fallen Thomas, who's cupping his nose with both hands. A puddle of beer pools around him.

The other men watch with mild interest. "*Ri-pālle* fight!" one of them says gleefully.

"No," says Cooper. "No reebelly fight! It's a just misunderstanding, isn't that right, Art?"

Art rubs the pain from his forehead, then smiles with satisfaction. "I've waited years to do that."

"What's *wrong* with you?" Thomas asks, still on the floor. He dabs at his nose with the tail of his t-shirt, then examines the blood. "So much for the Peace *Corps*!"

"Your son is *twenty-two* years old," Art says, "and you never once, not once, asked about him!"

"He's not my son, he's your son—I let him go!" Thomas talks through his cupped, bloodied hand. He's still sitting on the floor, his shorts wet from spilled beer. "It was winner take all," he says. "That's the rule, man. I'm no cry baby."

Art shakes his head in disgust. "The boy had his suspicions but what could we say?"

"You could've told him I was dead." Thomas gets unsteadily to his feet. Cooper steps closer as if to protect him. Someone hands Cooper a beer. Cooper hands it to Thomas. Thomas downs a swallow, then smacks his lips. He says, "Well, then, how is my/

your son?"

"He's in Hono working construction. Not exactly an intellectual like you, Thomas, but a good kid."

"Okay, all right, then the world runs well, doesn't it? And the recovery of our mutual friend here gives us reason to celebrate. Give these men some beer!"

Three beers later, they are eating lo mein at the snack bar—Thomas's treat—and Thomas is telling them about his *plans* to open an eco-friendly lodge on Maloelap that will attract conservation-minded tourists worldwide. "I know it sounds like a reach," he says, "but the plan could work with the right leverage. This is the center of the world, right here. Everything that's gonna happen is happening here now—global warming, garbage drifts, population explosion, pandemic diabetes. We are the eye of the storm!"

"You got that right," says Art.

The two men are talking like old chums!

Thomas continues: "The garbage we see here comes from all over the world. It's gonna bury the Marshalls if the ocean doesn't swallow them up first."

Cooper shakes his head in confusion. "Why would tourists want to come here for garbage and global warming?"

"Because they want what's real, Cooper. They're tired of the theme parks and the fantasyland shopping malls. That fairy tale shit doesn't wash in the post 9-11 new millennium. They want raw, close-to-the-bone experience!"

Art is nodding thoughtfully. "You might have something, Thomas."

Cooper glances to him to see if he's joking. He looks serious.

"I don't believe this," Cooper says. "Nobody's going to fly five or seven thousand miles to look at garbage!"

"Not just any garbage," Thomas says. "The world's garbage."

"If you advertised this as the essential eco-conscious adventure," Art muses, "you could sell rescue packages—volunteers could clean up the garbage on the islands—it's hip deep in some places—and they could volunteer for shifts in the diabetes clinics and help tutor the children in English."

"Brilliant, Art!" Thomas raises his half-empty beer bottle as if to toast.

"Tell me more!"

"The Republic could be encouraged to promote this, especially if the government got a cut. We could turn the Marshalls into a survival lab. I think the world would pay attention."

"Fuck me blind, yes, a SURVIVAL LAB!" Thomas bellows. "Art, you've got to be my partner!" Then Thomas raises one big finger to Cooper's nose as if to push it like a button: "You wait long enough, Cooper, and find yourself in the right place at the right historical moment, you just might make yourself useful. You in?"

"In what?" Cooper sputters. "We're just bullshitting. And Art is just having fun. Tell him, Art."

"No," Art says, "I'm serious, Cooper. This is our chance. Sell the meteorite and invest the funds in this venture. But forget Maloelap. It's got to be Majuro."

"Done—Majuro it is!" Thomas extends his big hand to Art's. They shake.

"I don't fucking believe this!" Cooper says. He finishes his beer. He is surprised to see a crowd—three-people deep—around the meteorite. There must be a hundred people here.

Thomas turns his bleary eyes to Cooper. "You in, Coop?"

"I still have no idea what you're talking about."

"Cooper has only one thing on his mind, Thomas."

"Oh, of course!" Thomas smacks his own forehead. "Your boat!"

"Yes!" Cooper says eagerly. "My boat!"

"Here." Thomas digs into his pockets. "Oops!" He grins sheepishly. "I don't know what happened to the key. But the Lickety Split's moored at the Uliga marina. You can't miss it, my man."

SIXTEEN

The Uliga dock yard is a dusty lot snugged up to a concrete launch ramp. A short wooden pier extends from one side. The yard holds a few damaged fiberglass cruisers. The bait shack sells beer. Like everywhere else on Majuro, there are men idling in the shade, smoking cigarettes.

Among the several sailboats moored in the shallows twenty yards out, the Lickety Split looks distinctive because it sits low and broad in the water, its cabin hunkered, its rigging spare. It's clearly an old boat. Watching it, Cooper holds his breath as if spying a long-lost loved-one from a distance. Nothing looks changed. But he knows the boat is in bad repair because of its long passage from the States. And now it's been sitting idle for a couple of months. The hull crusty-green with barnacles, it has lost a knot of speed, at least. The sails are down but sloppily draped over the beam. Cooper recalls the dreadful squalor of Thomas's hut.

"Let's get out there," says Cooper.

"You don't want to go to the authorities?" Art asks.

Cooper leans forward on his crutches, then turns a skeptical smile to his companion. "You're joking, right?"

Art raises his bushy brows. "I'm just saying, you could get the thing wrapped up and shipped to Kwajalein, right?"

"I've got to see it and assess the damage."

"It can't be too damaged." Art peers across the water, squinting into the reflected light, the sun low on the clouded horizon. "They sailed it all the way from Maloelap."

"Let's go." Cooper swings forward.

They can't find Cooper's dinghy. So, one of the Marshallese men who was sitting in the shade of the marina store paddles them out in a rowboat. Cooper hands him a twenty dollar bill. The man says, "*Kommool*," then stands and grabs a stanchion near the cockpit to steady the rowboat. Cooper gets up ever-so-carefully, tosses his crutches ondeck, then, replicating the exercises he's been doing for weeks in PT, chins himself up and over, bellying across the bright fiberglass deck like a seal.

Art has a harder time. The rower has to help him, pushing hard on Art's backside, then Art kicks. The rower ducks Art's errant foot and his boat jerks away.

"*Iọkwe*," he calls, then picks up his oars and rows back the way he came.

"*Iọkwe*," Art gasps, still on his belly. "*Kommool tata!*"

Cooper drops himself into the cockpit, then slides into the cabin, which Thomas failed to lock. Cooper pictures himself as a child on monkey bars. Getting around now is like that: it's all about gripping and pulling and sliding and swinging. He's too excited to consider the rising pain in his stump. To one side of the cabin ladder, he sits in the well-worn teak chair and he switches on the systems: half a tank of diesel remaining, clean water down to a quarter tank, black water—sewage—is full, battery bank for utilities reads "12-volts," which means it'd be dead in two days. In other words, Thomas-the-slob wasn't watching anything. Still, it's amazing that it's all here, whole and waiting for Cooper to take charge.

"How's it look?" Art asks from up top.

"Come down here and help me."

Cooper has Art do a full inventory. Food's gone, except for a box of saltines and two pounds of rice. Portable radio/CD player is gone. Cooper's clothes are gone, except for two dirty T-shirts. All of the cookware is gone, except for a big pot. Two of three tool boxes gone. Binoculars gone. Telescope gone. Blankets and sleeping gear gone. Both fire extinguishers gone. Fishing gear gone except for a lightweight rod with a spinner and 20 pound line. His library—27 books—gone.

But major equipment is still in place: radar, VHF radio, GPS, gyrocompass, barometer, depth finder.

And, in the secret compartment behind one of the settee panels: a key to the ignition, a pair of waterproof binoculars, a sheathed survival knife, and a 45. Ruger pistol with two clips of ammo.

"What the fuck?" Art rears back when Cooper pulls out the Ruger.

"Emergency measures," says Cooper. "In case I got blown off course and found myself in a dangerous situation."

"Nothing good comes of a gun, Cooper, no matter what the situation."

"Not to worry, Art. It's unloaded." He opens one of the bench seats. "Here, put this on."

"No thanks. If we sink after you blow a hole in the hull with that pistol, I think I'll be able to swim to shore."

"Humor me," says Cooper. He makes sure the charts are in the navigation cabinet. No charts! Thomas probably used them for toilet paper. Damn! But this won't stop Cooper. It's all or nothing now.

If he called the marina for refueling, Art might panic. So they'll have to make do with half a tank of diesel. With the larger tank he put in, that's not such a big deal. It's only 300 miles to Kwajalein.

"Let's go up top and see how bad it is." Cooper slips on his life vest and nods to Art, who reluctantly slips on his but doesn't fasten it because his belly won't allow him. Cooper turns to grab the ladder and is dismayed to discover that climbing up seems nearly impossible. "Don't help," he says to Art. "Let me figure it out."

It takes a few minutes. If Cooper muscles up, leans back, using his weight as a counterbalance, then hops his knee to the next rung, he can do it, oh so fucking slowly.

On deck at last and winded, he positions himself in the cockpit, checks the lazarette at the stern and finds the inflatable life raft inside the compartment, packed down to the size of a suitcase and ready for ripcord inflation.

Cooper says, "The worst thing here is chafe."

Art nods like he understands, then says, "Chafe?"

"The lines are frayed at all the blocks and cleats. Won't take much to break them. Everything chafes on a boat. Just too much motion, too much friction." Cooper reaches over and adjusts Art's PFD so that it's fastened snug. "Do me a favor, Art. Snap these clips from your vest to that jackline."

"Jackline?"

"Right there. Just snap onto that black line. Good, man. Now walk to the bow and crank up the anchor with the windlass. We've got to check that anchor."

Art regards Cooper with the narrowed eyes of a man reading an eye chart. "You want me to walk all the way up there and pull up the anchor?"

"That's it. I'll nudge the boat forward a bit so the anchor disengages."

"Then we'll be drifting, Cooper."

Cooper smiles with fatherly patience. "We can always drop the anchor again."

Art gives a grudging nod. Then, like a tentative tightrope walker, he steps forward gingerly.

"That's it, Art. No rush."

But there is a rush. Any moment, Lars and his men might return, expecting a place to sleep. Cooper's not about to entertain those pirates. *Nobody's getting this boat again. Nobody!*

Cooper inserts the key into the ignition. The engine grumbles to life. Art glances back at him with suspicion and fear.

"You're almost there," Cooper calls. "The windless is on the port side. See it? That big chrome crank?"

Art kneels at the windlass, then begins to turn the handle. Cooper nudges the boat forward. A small jolt—the anchor bucking from its coral catch—kicks Art's hand from the crank. "Yikes!" he says.

"You're got it, Art. Crank some more."

Within minutes, they're free and the dripping anchor is hooked on deck. "Now what?" Art calls.

Cooper stands on his leg and leans into the wheel, incredulous that he's upright and in control, motoring the Lickety Split out of the marina. In a light rain, the sunset is a greenish gash on the horizon. The lagoon is lake-calm. Cooper is at the bottom of Majuro's green horseshoe. He estimates it will take less than an hour to get to the top, where it opens to the ocean.

"Hey, Cooper, what's going on?" Art is breathless by the time he reaches the cockpit. He wipes his face with one hand. "Where you going?"

"We're going home, Art."

Art winces as if bitten by a fly. "Kwajalein?"

"It's just a bit over 300 miles. Not a big deal. Take us three days."

"No way, Cooper! That's the craziest thing I ever heard. If you don't turn around right now, I'm jumping overboard!"

"You don't like sailing?" Cooper teases.

"Sailing makes me sick."

"Me too but give it a chance and you'll love it, Art."

"You're grinning like this is a game! Do you even know where you are? Do you understand how dangerous these waters are, how many coral heads and barrier reefs and spurs these islands have?"

"Art, think of the sailors centuries back who had no GPS, no radar, no bearings but their instincts. It doesn't matter that we don't have any charts. We've got enough navigational aids and electronics to get us there."

"We don't have CHARTS?"

"Kwajalein is lit up like Las Vegas. It's got one of the biggest electronic footprints in the world—there's no way we can miss it."

"Cooper, listen to me. I've got children. Seriously, Cooper. You can't kidnap me like this."

"Art, I take this very seriously. And I won't let anything happen to you. This is a short jaunt."

"You've got one leg—one leg, man! And I don't know anything, ANYTHING, about sailing."

"Look, we'll anchor at the northern end of the atoll and wait till morning. We're both exhausted from the events of the day. Tomorrow, we'll be thinking more clearly, don't you think?"

"All right. Tomorrow. I'm hungry. Is there anything to eat?"

"Saltines. We'll have to do some fishing."

"We don't have bait. How can we fish without bait?"

"We'll figure something out."

"Will we, Cooper?"

Angry, Art goes below deck. After pawing around for five minutes, he finds a light. Though the dark woody interior of this old boat has its charm, he hates boats. They are deathtraps. Below deck, he feels entombed. The boat creaks and rattles and knocks, the engine sputtering. Water running against the sides sounds like sawing. If he were a younger man, he might swim ashore. The thought of being trapped on a boat in deep water terrifies him. He finds the bag of saltines, eats all but a handful as he sits on a bunk and stews. He underestimated Cooper, who seemed so helpless and demure when in the hospital. What's that novel by Jack London about a tyrannical captain? *The Sea Wolf*. Art makes a pillow out of his life vest, then settles in, hoping for a brighter day tomorrow.

When Cooper cuts the motor, he can hear the pass ahead, the noisy crush of water where the lagoon meets the ocean. He moors well away from the shore but not so far that he'd be in the shipping lane. Majuro gets some big boat traffic. He flicks on the stern and bow lights. He sits in the cockpit and surveys the portside darkness. Scattered lights in the distance mark Majuro's long curve. Through the drizzle Cooper hears thunder grumble. He counts: one one-thousand, two two-thousand . . . until he gets to five. Tomorrow he'll have to get a fix on his position, check the weather, dead reckon a course. No charts will make it a challenge. He wouldn't do it if it weren't mostly open water. Is he banking too much on luck? Does he have any left? Bone-deep pain rises from his stump. He pulls a ziplock bag of pills out of his pocket, takes one, then eases back. He's so jacked up with adrenaline, he'll never get to sleep.

A rude thump against the hull wakes him. It's still dark, nowhere near morning. He wipes the rain from his face, shakes it from his arms, remembers where he is and is surprised he fell asleep. He hears hushed voices on the starboard side. Fuck. With one crutch, he hikes himself up, then peers over. Three men in a boat. Dark bulky men, little more than silhouettes. Pirates.

Cooper pulls out his pistol, flicks off the safety, aims high towards the pass, then fires. The Ruger's crack sounds less than threatening but it's unmistakably gunfire.

"Whoa, brudder, easy now," one of the men calls from the small boat.

"Get away," Cooper says.

"Hey, we brought you some vodka, brudda. Thought you might wanna party."

The smaller craft has drifted back a bit. Cooper can make them out better now in the dull reflection of boat light: three men standing in a small outboard. You don't paddle out to a strange vessel unannounced if all you want to do is party.

The men wear shorts and T-shirts, nothing else. They might be drunk. One of them holds a length of something. Maybe a machete.

Pirates usually are out to strip a boat. Hit and run. They seldom kill the passengers, though it's hard to say because statistics are spotty. Of the 1,000 lives lost at sea every year, how many are sailors whose boats have been scuttled by pirates? In deep water nobody can hear you scream . . . .

"Get away now!" Cooper calls. He aims the Ruger at the men, clutching his crutch with his right hand. He suspects the men are sizing him up, calculating his resolve and his ability to balance. Cooper can feel his heart pulsing at the tip of his trigger finger. He's never owned a gun before this voyage. And he's never practiced shooting. He couldn't hit the side of a barn on a clear windless day.

"Cooper, what are you doing?" It's Art, behind him.

"Visitors," says Cooper. "I caught them trying to board."

Art calls to them in Marshallese. They answer. Art asks a question. They answer again. Then Art says something that makes them exhale in disbelief. Or fear.

"Hey, we go now," one of them says. "Easy, brudda, we go now, okay?"

One of them starts the motor and quickly they putter away, swallowed by the dark. All the while Cooper aims the Ruger at them. Art lays a gentle hand on Cooper's arm and eases him down.

"We're good now, Cooper. They're gone."

"Fuckers wanted to steal my boat." His eyes burn with tears. "Nobody's gonna get my boat!"

Art takes the pistol from him. "They were curious, maybe drunk. They weren't pirates, Cooper."

"Gangsters, then, thieves—whatever."

"We don't need this anymore." Art tosses the pistol into the lagoon.

"Art! That gun cost five hundred bucks!"

"You'll kill somebody with that thing. We're almost home, right? Let's get some sleep, son."

"What did you say to them?"

"I told them that you were crazy and that I was taking you to a hospital and that I couldn't prevent you from shooting them if they stayed any longer."

"They seemed to believe you."

Art pats him on the back. "Oh, yeah, Cooper, they believed me."

* * * *

Like most old buildings on Ebeye, the Head Start is made of plywood and scrap. The bright pink paint, inside and out, is new, however, and the corrugated tin roof leaks only during a hard rain. Best of all, there's a concrete floor. One of Jeton's many chores is to sweep the floor with bleach and water at the day's end. Niki, his boss, has been teaching him "holistic education," which is a fancy way of saying that you make a game of instruction: you have the children sing their numbers and dance in circles and spell simple American words like "cat" and "road."

Jeton assists Anjua, a teacher-in-training. She's in charge of 50 children every morning, another 50 every afternoon. This morning they will try to teach numbers, Anjua tells him.

Anjua is 16, short, and already heavy in the hips like the older women. She reminds Jeton of American girls because she seems too proud for a *Ri-Majel*, her gaze too direct. Somewhere she has learned to braid her hair like the Americans. But, like the older *Ri-Majel*, she does not wear shorts and her cotton dress falls always below her knees. Definitely not cool.

"We will count to tens," she says.

"Ten," Jeton corrects.

He has offered her a seat—their only chair—at the room's rickety table but she would not take it. So now he sits.

"Ten, yes," she repeats. Why does she never smile? "One-two-three-four-five-six-seben-eight-nines-ten."

Jeton wishes she spoke better American like Niki, who lived for five years in California. It has been one month since Jeton's *aploñloñ*, his trouble, as the adults call it. He is still a "persona non grata" on Kwajalein. He will never go back. When his *būbū* heard of his trouble, she said it was time he came to Majuro. He would live with her, she said, and work in the soap factory with his father and brother. She said nothing about buying him a taxi. It seems this is no longer an option. He has come to realize that he is just one of many family members expecting help from *Būbū*. This may explain why *Būbū* is often away, inspecting her pig farm in Manila or staying in her condo on Guam.

He got work at Head Start—volunteer only, not paid—because he asked for help from Father Joe and Sister Bette.

"You're back!" Father Joe said, grinning when he saw Jeton at the screened door of King's Crown Elementary, a concrete two-story compound built around a sandy yard. Its sky blue paint was peeling and chipping badly, none of its windows were glassed. Shirtless children were playing in puddles nearby, sitting, sliding, and stamping in the water. Other children were running through the school's courtyard. Still others were climbing the tattered chainlink fence that gated the yard.

"Hey, get off there!" Father Joe called in American. "Now!"

"Is that you, Jeton?" Sister Bette was an old woman who wore blue jeans and T-shirt with sandals. She handed Jeton a cigarette from her pack. She was already smoking.

"*Iọkwe.*"

"How about some tomato soup?" Father Joe asked.

"Hai," said Jeton. "I like soup." American soup is sweet and salty, reminding Jeton of coconut milk stew.

Jeton sat at their plywood table while Father Joe stirred a pot on his small stove, which looked like the stove his mother used, except newer.

Sitting across from him, Sister Bette pinched a flake of tobacco from her tongue, then said, "We saw you at Lino's funeral. We were very sad for his family."

"Yes," said Jeton. His fingers trembled as he lit his cigarette with his silver Zippo. He had been dreaming of Lino every night. Sometimes Lino was a coconut crab he was trying to catch. Coconut crabs have such powerful claws they can snap a broomstick: boom! like that. Other times Lino walked on water like Jesus and he would find Jeton sitting in a little rowboat in the middle of the lagoon. He would say, "What's up, Jeton?" Only he didn't look like Jesus, he looked like Lino.

As a coconut crab, Lino was angry and snapping. As Jesus, Lino was calm and careless. In both dreams, Jeton felt horrible because he knew he had done something wrong. He knew the coconut crab should not be loose, scurrying through the dried palm fronds where it can hurt somebody. He knew that Lino should not be outside the boat walking on water. "Get in here," he told him. Lino just smiled. Then he would say, "No way. We're sinking, man."

That's when Jeton would wake up.

After two weeks of these dreams, he came to see Father Joe and Sister Bette. They used to teach him in Sunday school.

Father Joe poured him a mug of soup. "Jeton, do you want to finish high school?"

Jeton knew for sure he didn't want to go to Majuro and work in the soap factory. His mother had stopped asking about school, but he sensed that she was praying about it. "You would have to study on your own," Sister Bette said. "Then you would take a test, called the GED. Are you prepared to do that?"

"Yes," he said. No more "maybe's" about school, he promised himself.

As he sipped his soup, pausing now and then to draw on his cigarette, Father Joe said, "I was talking to Niki Labuk the other day about her Head Start program. She says she's looking for an apprentice teacher—a teacher in training."

Jeton looked up at the old man, who seemed unnaturally tall, as if he had stretched to be closer to God. "I am too ignorant to be a teacher," Jeton said.

"Teacher in training," Sister Bette corrected. "You would be with the youngest children."

"What do I have to teach?" he asked. Even as he said this,

he wondered at the possibility, thinking of the teachers he had known. Most of them were ministers of one sort or another. Jeton does not want to be a minister. He knows nothing about God.

"It will be simple lessons," Sister Bette was explaining, "but difficult work. Do you think you can handle difficult work?"

Though Sister Bette was smiling, this sounded harsh to Jeton, like she was scolding him. He wanted to tell her about how hard the work was in the rock hole when he was helping on the causeway.

"I am not afraid of hard work," he told her.

So Jeton went to Head Start. In the late afternoons and at night, he studies his lessons so that he can earn his high school diploma. Sister Bette checks his studies by asking hard questions. He has time for nothing else. It is taking a long time.

"We count like this," Anjua is saying to him. She steps away from the table and begins a dance: movement flows gracefully through her, from her shoulders to her hips, her arms waving like deep-water coral, her two black braids swinging.

Majel, girls know how to dance! Jeton thinks proudly.

Anjua leans forward, takes a step, claps her hands once, then again. "One, two, buckle my shoe. Three, four—"

"Wait a minute," Jeton interrupts.

Anjua stops abruptly, looks at him in puzzlement. She has large brown eyes and full cheeks that would be much darker if she spent time outdoors. "You don't want to dance?"

"Our *ajiri* don't have shoes, *jatū*. They won't know what a buckle is."

He calls her *jatū* "my little sister," so she won't feel insulted.

Still, she looks injured. "We need song!" she says.

"We can make one up."

"Not you!" This is a joke: everybody knows that Jeton cannot sing. His voice veers and dives, unable to hold a melody.

He smiles at her and waits for her smile in return, but she only gazes at him as if she were waiting to see through sandy water. This is why she has no boyfriend, he decides.

At last he says, "Let's get some rocks and shells. The children can count those."

Outside the sky is mixed up from the morning rain, big blue-black clouds huddled high. Shirtless, shoeless children are playing in the puddles, chasing each other with sticks, digging in the dirt with shells, tossing plastic scrap they have retrieved from the abundant garbage near the water. The Head Start program can accommodate only 250 children a year. The rest go unattended, like these.

Jeton sweeps one hand in a wide arc. "Highest birthrate in the world!" he calls.

Anjua looks at him skeptically. "You sure one of these isn't yours?"

He laughs. "You are funny, Anjua."

Children are frolicking in the garbage-cluttered shallows, where waves make the plastic bottles and Styrofoam bits and plastic bags and food wrappers bob and dive.

"Look at this," Jeton says. "What will become of us, *jatū*?"

"Stop calling me '*jatū*,' please. It is condescension."

"Condescension?" Jeton searches for the meaning.

"You look down on me."

He shrugs, tries to smile. "You are short."

"You are not funny, Jeton DeGroen, you are arrogant. You think because you have a big family name you are *irooj*."

No, not any more. The big man, Art Norman, made clear to Jeton that he is not an *Irooj*. "I am not arrogant."

"Everybody say so." She stoops to collect a broken fan shell.

Everybody? It angers Jeton that he wants to win this girl's approval. Who is she?

"Everybody loves me," he says boldly.

"See there?" She holds up her shell as if it were evidence. "That is arrogant."

"Why wouldn't everyone love me?" He squints at her through

the morning glare. "As soon as I get money I will run for senator."
He knows this is not true. He knows that nobody would vote for
him even if he had *Būbū*'s money. Still, he can't stop himself from
boasting.

"That remains to be seen," Anjua says.

This is their boss's favorite expression. Niki believes nothing
until she sees it—not the promise of funding, not the offer of
supplies, not the imminent arrival of a new teacher.

Now it is Jeton's turn to stoop for a shell but he does so only
to hide the heat in his face. Anger is of no use with someone
stubborn like Anjua. The girl's confidence stings him: she sounds
like she knows things he does not.

He picks up half an abalone shell, too big for the children's
hands. He says, "You wouldn't vote for me?"

"I'm too young to vote." She picks up a small silvery rock that
turns out to be a scrap of foil. She shakes off the sand and keeps
it anyway.

"I want to help our *ri-Majel*,," he says. "You know we have
the highest diabetes rate in the world?" Such things he has heard
mostly from Americans.

"You propose to do what?"

"What?"

"Your plan, Jeton DeGroen. What is your plan?"

"To help—I want to help!"

"How?" she sounds exasperated. And she will not look at him
now, pretending to be absorbed by her hunt for shells.

"I will find a way!" he says.

"Not good enough," she says. "Any little boy," she waves a
hand at the children behind them, "any little boy has the same
desire. Big wishes, big promises!"

"You think I am a little boy?"

"You talk like one."

He is 18, but she is right, he does not feel grown up. And he
has no answers for the problems he sees on Ebeye—problems he

might not have noticed had he not spent so much time on Kwajalein with Nora.

When they return, they find their classroom crowded already with children. Anjua dutifully circles the room and checks each name on the attendance roster while Jeton attempts to get all of them to sit on the floor. These are the poorest children; a few show up in nothing more than dirty underwear. They are 5, 6 and 7 years old, some of them hyperactive, some of them lethargic, all of them distracted, most of them giggling. Fortunately, there is nothing in the room for them to break, except the table, which has been broken many times.

"Look at the table!" Jeton tells them. He points eagerly to the front of the room. "It will turn into a shark!"

This makes the children laugh, and for a moment many of them sit and watch. But he and Anjua never have their full attention. *That's the way it is*, Niki has told them. *That's the way it will be always.*

"Today we are going to learn to count," Jeton announces in *kajin Ṃajeḷ*: "Juon, ruo, jilu, emân...."

Many of them—at least half—don't know how to count in *kajin Ṃajeḷ*. They look puzzled, blinking at Jeton and giggling.

"*Bōnbōn*," Anjua repeats, wriggling her fingers at the children. Many wriggle theirs in response. It seems children are born for games and nothing more.

Anjua and Jeton arrange the children in ten groups of five. This takes nearly an hour, because the children won't stay in their groups, interlopers running to and fro. So much shouting. So much laughing. Each group takes possession of a rock or a shell. Then Jeton assigns a number to each group. Round and round they go, repeating the numbers, each time the children clucking their tongues or shouting as one of its members holds up the rock or the shell.

Then something goes terribly wrong: the children think that the numbers are the names. This rock is named "one," and this shell is called "two," and that shell is "three." When Anjua tries to clarify, counting in a different direction, the children are confused. And they try to correct her: "No, no, this rock is called one, this shell two, you see?"

Her face takes on that peering-through-sandy-water look, then she heaves a sigh and starts over. Jeton tries to help by repeating her lesson, counting off his fingers. Does she realize that they are not being "holistic" enough? he wonders.

When it's time for a snack, one of the helpers, a twelve-year-old girl, brings in a bucket of orange Kool-aide with a single plastic cup and a large plastic bag of loose saltine crackers, which Anjua and Jeton distribute to the grasping hands. So many little hands clamoring for the treats, Jeton is reminded of anemones roiling in a tidepool.

"How many crackers do I have?" he asks them. He waves three overhead.

"Those are crackers!" the children are shouting.

"How many?" Anjua repeats.

"Crackers!"

"I hold how many crackers. One, two, three, four?"

"One."

"Two."

"Three."

"That's it," Jeton shouts, pointing to a frail girl with frightened eyes. "Three crackers."

"Three!" the others shout. They are reaching and grabbing and pulling and laughing. "Three!"

Anjua tries it now with two crackers. "How many?"

"Four."

"Ten."

"Two."

And so it goes until it is time for the children to leave. Some simply wander off. Some are met by older siblings. Some linger outside, playing in the sandy dirt.

With a bleach-saturated rag, Anjua cleans up after a boy who has had an "accident," *pijek*.

"Time to go," Jeton reminds the lingerers. "*Iọkwe, Iọkwe!*"

They run to him, hang on his arms, laugh when he pushes them off lightly. An hour later, the children are gone finally and Jeton is sitting outside on a cinderblock eating his sandwich of white bread and SPAM, pausing now and then to swipe at the flies. Anjua sits nearby, in the shade of the building.

"You can have this seat," he calls to her.

"No thank you," she says, practicing her American. When she takes a sip from her can of her Coca Cola, Jeton thinks of diabetes. Too much sugar in the *Ri-Majạl* diet, doctors say.

All the things his people must do to better themselves! Where should they start?

Maybe this is why Anjua does not smile. Already she is overwhelmed by the diabetes and the TB and the children and the flies. As if all that were not bad enough, the ocean is rising.

"Global warming," Jeton says to her.

"I know about global warming," she says. She is eating a bag of Cheese Doodles with her Coke.

"The ocean will swallow us like a grouper," he says.

"I am not afraid," she says.

"Land fill can make us rise above the ocean," he says knowingly.

"Land fill is garbage," she says.

"Recycled garbage," he says. "That is a good thing. The *Majal* should learn to recycle." He has been reading about this with Sister Bette.

"Then you teach them, Jeton DeGroen."

"Maybe I will," he says.

When they return to the class for the afternoon session, Anjua starts sweeping. The room needs more light, Jeton decides. The two unscreened windows face east. Outside, dogs are barking nearby and a motor runs like a chainsaw. The air stinks of diesel exhaust.

"The world does not think about the *ri-Majal̩*," Jeton says sadly.

Anjua stops her sweeping and looks up at him thoughtfully. "Then we will make them think."

"I did that. I went to Kwajalein," he says. "I made a protest! But no one cared."

She shakes her head in disagreement. "Somebody cared. Somebody sent you here, to Head Start."

"Here we do nothing but babysit," he says in disgust.

"Maybe for now that is the most important thing."

"Maybe for you, *kōrā*, not for me."

"Okay," she says. "When you are senator you stop the sun from shining, okay?"

"I am not going to be a senator," he says.

"That is the first smart thing I hear you say."

He regards her closely. "Why don't you ever smile?"

"You do enough smiling for both of us."

"Because I am arrogant?"

"You are scared too. We *ri-Majal̩* smile when scared, everybody know that."

The motor outside stalls, sputters, starts again. Jeton smells machine oil.

"I am not scared."

"You are scared of the rising ocean, you are scared of how small you are—you will drown. And you are scared of me."

"You?"

"Because I have my diploma and you do not."

Jeton assumed that she was a drop-out. Like him.

"You have your diploma? You *graduated*?"

She carries a handful of dust and cracker crumbs to the open doorway, then flings them into the sandy yard.

"I will go to Guam University next year." She says this as simply as saying, I will go to the store for bread.

"You are only 16!"

"That scares you, right?"

Yes, he admits to himself, it does scare him, because he doesn't know when he will earn his diploma. And Anjua will go to Guam, where there is a city and a university, and she will learn so much she could become principal of the high school, if she wanted, not a lowly teacher's assistant. The thought of this makes him feel as useless as the garbage high tide brings every day.

"Will you come back to help us?" he asks.

"Of course I come back. Ebeye is my home."

"Maybe you will want to go to the States, to California, and buy a car and drive to shopping malls."

"Why would I want to do that?"

"Guam will change you," he says. It fills him with sadness to think of more *ri-Majal* leaving for the United States. Maybe they will desert their islands long before the ocean rises. Jeton pictures himself sitting on a deserted Ebeye with only the ghost of Lino for company.

"I will come back!" Anjua says. It seems her face has softened.

Jeton nods okay. Then, carefully, he says, "I think I could become a teacher."

"You *could*," she says.

"It will be a lot of work," he says—to let her know that he is serious.

"Yes," she says. "And you will not make much money."

"You mean I will not be able to buy a Hummer?" he jokes.

"No," she says with a seriousness that makes clear she does not know what a Hummer is.

"A Hummer is the most expensive American car," he explains. "And it is very big."

She nods as if to say, I see. Then she says, "I have not heard of Hummer, I have only heard of humdinger."

"Humdinger," he muses. "Is that a bird?"

"It is American expression I learned in school," she says. "It mean big, like big mistake."

"I know about big mistakes," he says, surprised at how wise and tired he sounds.

This, at last, makes Anjua smile—he sees the small upturn of her lips. And he takes this as a signal of accord and acceptance. But he can't be sure because now she turns to the children who are pouring in, children shouting and laughing, so many children, all the wildness and hope of the *ri-Majaḷ*—they jostle her, flow around her, pull her forward, this small girl with the future tight in her hands; and Jeton watches enviously because, like them, he feels the strong tide tug of her hope.

SEVENTEEN

It has taken a week to pack everything and now, on the eve of their return to the States, their trailer is crowded with cardboard boxes, their luggage stacked by the door. The furniture, which belongs to the government, remains in place, however, so it's an odd feeling to know they're moving out when their home still looks lived in and livable. It has rained hard all afternoon. And it is still raining hard. So hard, they have to shout to be heard. At first the boys were amused by this, but now, Alison can see, they are frightened, as if the thunderstorm would tear off the roof and wash them away.

"Okay," she says in a funny-loud voice, "here's what we'll do. We'll make peanut butter and jelly sandwiches with marshmallows—a big pile of them—then we'll camp out in front of the laptop with all the pillows we can find and we'll watch a DVD."

The boys like this plan but won't fetch any of the provisions without her.

So, quickly they rummage through the fridge for the food they need—everything else will have to be tossed in the morning—then they bring the sandwich fixings to the coffee table, where Alison has set up the laptop.

They discover that they have left only three DVDs unpacked: a copy of "Spiderman" that's so scratchy with skips they can't watch it, a copy of "Barbie As the Princess and the Pauper," which neither Stan nor Doug will watch—and nobody can explain why it's in their possession—and then that bootleg copy of "Stone Deaf Death Rangers," which they haven't watched since Doug's disastrous birthday party.

Stan says, "Let's see the bootleg—we can describe all the scenes that aren't shown!"

They have now seen the real DVD countless times and have the thing memorized.

Doug inserts the disc. The bootlegger's camera shows a shaky movie screen, then the opening scene abruptly starts at midpoint. Stan giggles. Doug says, "He missed, like, five minutes of it already. What a slacker!"

"He has shaky hands," says Stan. "I bet he's a drug addict. Did you have shaky hands, mom?"

"I wasn't exactly a drug addict," she says. "No, I didn't have shaky hands."

"She's an *alcoholic*," says Doug.

"Alcohol is a drug," says Stan.

"That's right," says Alison, fighting to keep her voice steady. "Alcohol is a drug."

"Turn it up," says Doug.

Rain on the roof sounds as loud as hail.

The screen has gone black already. "That wasn't even five minutes into the movie," says Alison. "I can't believe this guy could even sell his recording."

"I can't believe you bought it!" says Stan. He's nearly shouting.

"I thought you were going to describe everything we're missing," Alison shouts.

"Forget it!" says Stan.

"Yeah, forget it," says Doug.

Alison turns off the DVD. Stan nestles into her side, whimpering. Then, on her other side, Doug starts, quietly sobbing. Her arms around each, they lean into her as she kisses the salty, sea-fresh forehead of one, then the other.

"It's been hard, hasn't it?" she says. "Really hard."

Doug nods yes, staring glassy-eyed at the laptop's empty screen.

Alison glances to the ceiling and wonders that it holds up.

How many years of tropical storms have these old aluminum containers withstood?

"We're all gonna drown," says Stan.

"No, we're very safe," says Alison

"If we drown," Doug begins but then stops himself. Absently, he wipes his runny nose against her shirt sleeve.

"If what?" Alison asks. She feels her heart deflate. "You're not thinking about dad, are you?"

Stan surfaces. His nose is running too, but Alison has nothing to offer except her other shirt sleeve. "He left us," he says.

"Not on purpose," Alison says evenly. "He is gone, you are right."

Stan shakes his head sternly. "He didn't have to do that."

"No, he didn't, but sometimes we don't know what's best for us and then—"

"We drown?" Doug says.

"Yes, sometimes it's as bad as that. We drown. But you and I and Stan are not going to drown today."

"How about tomorrow?" Stan asks.

That's better, she thinks. *Give us some of that vinegar, Stan.*

"No, probably not even tomorrow," she says, smiling. "Dad was a great guy. We love him very much and we miss him very much, don't we?"

This brings them both to tears again—her babies in her arms, it's all she can do to keep from sobbing herself. But she's got to talk through this.

"We will remember dad every day and every year," she says. "We will take from his memory all of the good things he gave us. You remember how he used to turn up the stereo and sing AC-DC?"

"That was horrible," Stan says.

"Remember how he used to make what he called his Madman Casseroles?" she continues. "What was the worst one?"

Doug looks up, blinking. "Peanut, basil, and tuna," he says.

"That nearly killed me."

Alison laughs, her vision going watery at last. Stay with it, she tells herself. "And. . . what . . . about the oregano, garlic sweet potato?"

"He was crazy!" Stan says, with a tearful laugh.

"Maybe once a year we should make a Madman Casserole in his honor," she says.

"Let's make one tomorrow," Doug says. He seems to brighten at the thought.

"We can't tomorrow," she says. "We're leaving, remember?"

"We'll make it so bad, we won't be able to touch it," says Stan.

"We'll make it so bad, he would be proud of us," Doug says.

"But tonight we have peanut butter and jelly with marshmallows," says Alison. She opens the jar of peanut butter, Doug tears open the bag of marshmallows, and Stan digs his fingers into the grape jelly.

"Use a knife," she tells him.

"I don't have a knife, I have a spoon."

"Leave some for the rest of us," Doug says, "or you're not getting any marshmallows."

"I'd rather have jelly than marshmallows anyway," Stan says.

"Liar," Doug says.

* * * *

Art's growling stomach wakes him early. Or he thinks it's early. Last night's hard rain was like a lullaby as he slept in the cradle of his berth. When he gets on deck, desperate to pee, he sees that it's raining still but not so hard. Cooper is sitting behind the wheel, a fishing rod angled over the stern. He wears a yellow plastic poncho and a big floppy rain hat. He says, "I caught you a couple of fish, though I don't know what those are." He nods to a couple of one-foot jacks on the cockpit deck.

"How can you fish without bait?" Art asks. Then, stunned, he hears the snap of the sail and sees that the boat is plying open water. No land in sight. "What the fuck, Cooper?"

"I use little strips of leather I cut from an equipment bag. Works pretty well." He's setting another hook. "Let's hope I don't snag something big with this tiny rod."

"Where are we?"

"We're about 20 nautical miles northwest of Majuro, headed 8.7 degrees north, 167.7 degrees east. That's Kwajalein. From what I can see on the map, there should be nothing in our way— it's a straight shot. We're getting pretty good sail from the main."

"There is no such thing as a straight shot in these waters, man! How can you even operate this shit all by yourself?"

"It's just takes a windlass and a single line to raise and tack the mainsail, Art. I've got the upper body strength for it, though I'll need you to help me with a few things."

"Who's steering the fucking boat?"

"That's Iris, the autopilot. Well, not really a pilot. She's just mindlessly following the course I've set."

"People don't steer their boats any more?"

"Not really. It's a waste of time and energy. Iris does a better job than I, as long as nothing goes wrong."

"Right!" Art bellows. "What could go wrong out here in the middle of the Pacific fucking ocean?"

"Art, you seem really overwrought. We're on our way, I've got my boat back, you've got dreams of making Majuro an Eco-tourist destination—everything is right with the world!"

"You're high, Cooper. That's the only explanation for what's happening right now." Art listens to the wind ruffing in the sail, the boat noisy with the slap and spit of water. Then suddenly he realize that he's soaked to the skin from the rain—and he has just peed his pants. "Oh, fucking-A!"

"Can you do something with those fish, Art?"

Art peers ahead into the rainy-gray distance. The waves are low rounders. Maybe the rain is keeping them down. Glancing into the water, Art sees deep into the clear blue. He knows that what looks like 20 feet is actually 200 feet, the water out here is so pure.

"You sure you know where we are?"

"I all but grew up on the water, Art. We're good!"

"Then what's that out there—are those white caps?"

"Oh, shit."

"Oh, shit, what?"

"Those are breakers on a coral mass, probably."

They're less than a hundred yards straight ahead. "Can we steer clear of them?"

"We'd better. Art, where's your PFD?"

"My what?"

"Your life vest. Put it on."

"There's no time, don't you need my help?"

"PUT IT ON!"

Art clambers below deck, finds his vest, falls into it, tries to buckle it with his trembling hands. He hears Cooper cursing above him, slamming something, pulling something else, cursing some more. Back on deck, Art says, "What do I do?"

Cooper's at the wheel, where he's rigged some strapping to the stanchions to keep himself stable. The mast has turned sharply. "Tie in to the jackline," he barks.

"The jackline?"

"The *jackline!*"

Art remembers the jackline. He ties in. He's gasping.

"Now crawl to the bow, Art. On hands and knees. I need your eyes up front."

Trembling, groaning, Art crawls forward. Spray sheers off the bow, rocketing at him. Wind roars in his ears. The boat heels hard to starboard and he slides with it, clawing for a cleat, then a stanchion, then a block. A wave washes over him, a warm soaking that suddenly goes cold. Art gulps for air. Clutching the anchor's windlass at last, he shouts: "Now what?"

"Watch the water," Cooper shouts, "Point to breakers. Show

me where they are!"

"There!" Art points portside. "There! There!" It seems they
are surrounded. A wave smacks the boat's prow, the boat rises
like a rearing horse, then heels hard again. Art hangs on, howling. Then—through the gloriously clear water—Art sees them to
his left: monstrous mushroom-headed blue-green coral heads as
big as whales, blossoming from the ocean's bottom. "THERE!"
He hears a sharp crack as one nips the boat's bottom. OH MY
GOD! They are sailing through two giant nodes of coral: Scylla
and Charybdis, water boiling on each side. Art pictures the boat
broken on the gorgeous stony growths and himself floating in
slow motion down, down into the beautiful night-blue deep,
bubbles flooding from his open mouth. And then, circling him,
he pictures Cooper grinning a madman's grin, happily sinking to
his doom.

But the boat doesn't break and Art doesn't fall overboard.
They keep on, the Lickety Split heeling hard and plying through
the foamy breach of coral-roiled water. Art vomits, then vomits
again. Heaving hysterically, he lies there for a long time until he's
calmer. Only then does he realize that they are clear of the hazard.

When he looks back to the cockpit finally, he sees Cooper
flashing the thumbs-up. "That was close, wasn't it?" Then Cooper's laughing. Mad man!

Later, below deck, Cooper makes Art some tea. Art has yet
to control his trembling. Cooper says, "I'm sorry, Art. I know you
didn't ask for this. But we're in it together, so let's make the best
of it."

"You nearly killed me."

"No, not at all. You were tied in and I was in control of the
boat."

"It didn't feel like you were in control. Why aren't you up
there right now on watch?"

"Let's talk about that," he says.

"This tea tastes awful."

"The water's gone bad," says Cooper. "That's why sailors used to drink nothing but rum and hard cider. Those don't go bad. We'll have to boil it."

"I thought you did boil it."

"That makes it potable," says Cooper. "Not tasty. Look, Art, there's a cyclone moving through the southern Marshalls. I just got the report this morning."

"A cyclone?"

"We won't see the full impact."

"A *cyclone*!"

"We have to set up our storm sails. I'll need your help with that. Two jibs, that's all. Then I'll set the storm anchor off the stern."

"You said you wouldn't let anything happen to me!"

"I'll do everything I can to bring you home safely, Art."

Cooper says this so seriously, so earnestly, Art realizes that they are in serious trouble and that he may never see Jinna and the children again. How can this be?

* * * *

Since learning that Anjua got a scholarship to Guam University for next year, Jeton has felt irritated with himself. It is the kind of irritation he might feel after throwing back a really good fish he has spent 30 minutes pulling to the pier. What the fish is exactly—his education? his career? his reputation?—he isn't sure. He knows only that he must do things differently; he must stop being a fuck-up. So why is he here at the bar with his cousins?

Ka-blam! Mike is playing his favorite video game. *Ka-blam! ka-blam! ka-blam! blam!blam!blam!* If there were women here, they'd be crowded around Mike.

Jeton sits next to Stevie at the bar. Stevie is not talking. He stares at the strings of white lights that hang over the bottles behind the bar. Jeton imagines that, in his mind, Stevie pilots the Irooj into deep water. Then he thinks he hears Stevie say, "I wanna die, man. I just wanna die." Then Jeton thinks of the famous soccer player Abbetar, who hanged himself with a telephone cord because his Filipina girlfriend dumped him. If Stevie had lost a girlfriend, then Jeton would know what to say. Jeton would show his love scar, the dime-sized purple welt on his left hand—something he secretly gave to himself so that he would fit in with the other young men. "See this?" he would say. "That cigarette didn't burn me half as much as my *pālen* did."

Jeton taps Mike's shoulder, enough distraction to make Mike miss one shot, then another. "Shit," he says.

"We got to go," Jeton tells him.

Mike shrugs him off. "Let me finish my round."

Jeton taps him again. This time Mike glances over his shoulder and sees how Stevie is—like a *timoṇ*, a ghost. So Mike leaves the screen even though two girls walk in and there's plenty more game to play. "Where we going?" he asks.

Jeton pulls Stevie by the shirt tail and says, "Let's go look at *wa*." The boats.

Rain is falling hard, the streets swamped. A typhoon is coming, some say. But so far it's just typical wet season. Work on the causeway has stopped because water is backing up just like the Americans said it would. The Americans are jealous of every *ri-Ṃajaḷ* success.

Children are playing in the streets, even though it's dark. They stand up to their knees in puddles, splashing at each other. Some call after Jeton and Stevie and Mike for quarters. Two quarters buy a Coke; one will get you a Chinese candy bar.

Rain cascades from the tarpaper roofs, sheets of it flashing blue over every other window as the water reflects the glow of TV screens inside. Even the one-room *pelak* have electricity: lines draped from windows to the nearest electric pole, where a tangle of splices and connections sometime spark and sputter in the rain.

Jeton and his cousins are soaked shortly, but the water is

warm. At the lagoon, they stand under the green plastic awning of the Sacred Shepherd Baptist Church. Boats in the lagoon bob and roll, the water growing rougher by the hour. The lagoon has risen by a foot, the water smacking at the underside of the pier, spray geysering through the slats. Ebeye has three piers but the boats are moored wherever there's room in the shallows.

"Which one do you want?" Mike jokes.

The spot of pier light undulates over the rolling waves like a mantaray. The rain is a gray glimmering sheet.

"That one." Stevie points to the nearly new boat that belongs to Hideo Kabua, who bought it from a Japanese restaurateur on Majuro. The boat sits in the water like a giant banana, 30 feet of shiny white fiberglass. Its engine, in the rear, is as big as a washing machine.

"You can't do anything with a boat like that," Jeton says.

He speaks loudly over the rain.

Mike lights three Winstons at once, then hands out the extras. Mike squints like a movie star as he pulls on his cigarette and Jeton wonders if he practices in front of a mirror.

Stevie says, "A boat like that, man, it speeds."

"No good for fishing," Mike says.

"Can't carry many people either," Jeton adds. Just two days ago Jeton was down here asking if anyone needed a pilot or a captain. If he could get Stevie a job doing what Stevie knows best, doing what Stevie loves, then Stevie would be all right. Nobody in Stevie's family has the money to salvage the sunken Irooj. It would probably break apart anyway if someone tried to pull it up.

"You can go anywhere in a boat like that," Stevie says dreamily.

"Hideo." Jeton says the name derisively, as if to suggest that Hideo has done nothing to earn or deserve his good fortune.

Mike gives him a skeptical look, one brow raised, as if to say, You joking?

Hideo is one of the king's sons.

"Fuck Hideo," Jeton says.

"Life isn't *jimwe*, eh?" says Mike.

"I can make it go without a key," Stevie says. "Hotwire!"

"You can't borrow Hideo's boat," Jeton says. "That's trouble."

"Fuck it." Stevie holds his cigarette in the Chinese manner, pinched between his thumb and forefinger. When he takes a drag, he kisses the filter.

"A bad night for a ride," Mike says.

"It's not a problem for a big *wa* like that," says Stevie. He's staring intently at the marina.

Jeton's stomach feels a sting of dread. He imagines Stevie stealing Hideo's fancy boat, then speeding over to Kwajalein, where the Army cutter would intercept him: but Stevie could outrun them with Hideo's engine. Then what? Stevie plows into the Kwajalein marina like a suicide bomber?

"Let's go play some video," Mike says.

"I need a boat," Stevie says.

Suddenly they're talking in Marshallese.

"Some day you'll get a boat," Jeton assures him.

"Let's go play," Mike says.

"I'm never gonna get a boat," Stevie says.

Jeton sees that Stevie is weeping, though at first it is hard to tell because of the rain and the bad light.

Mike lights fresh cigarettes with his big Zippo, then hands them out.

The pause gives Jeton a moment to consider how Cousin Stevie might kill himself tonight. "Cousin, look at me," Jeton says. "I am the biggest fool on Ebeye." To say this makes his face burn with shame. "I am not a sailor like you or a fisherman like cousin Ramos or an entrepreneur like Mike—I am . . . ." He shrugs. He doesn't know what he is or what he should be. And now, to see Mike and Stevie staring at him in puzzlement because, like Jeton, they have been taught to save face always, Jeton feels his own doubts choke him. He takes a nervous pull at his cigarette, then sputters and coughs on the smoke.

Mike smiles kindly and pats Jeton on the shoulder. "You see, Stevie? You could be like Jeton but you are not. That is lucky."

Stevie nods in agreement, rapidly wiping away his tears. "I do not want to be like Jeton."

"Nobody wants to be like Jeton," Mike says. With this, he winks at Jeton, who feels betrayed though he pretends to enjoy the joke.

"Let's go," Jeton says in American. Then he leads the way back through the pooling streets and pouring rain so that Mike and Stevie cannot see his own tears.

At the Lucky Star, Stevie wins three games in a row and Jeton quickly gets drunk on the beers Mike buys. He never intends to get drunk but, when others are buying, this often happens. He is on his last Tsing Tsoa when Mike leaves with a pretty Majuro girl who is his next door neighbor's visiting cousin.

Jeton takes Stevie to his house. They are slopping through ankle-deep water in the street. The rain gushes from the black above.

"I gotta keep my eye on you, Stevie, and keep you outta trouble!"

"Ha!" says Stevie. "You are funny, cousin. Who gets into more trouble than Jeton DeGroen?"

* * * *

Cooper boils a pot of water, then pours in rice, then drops in the two fish and covers the pot. He really doesn't have time for cooking—already the waves are getting high, the Lickety Split starting to rollercoaster up and down, the propane stove rocking in its gimbals as he steadies the pot. But he and Art are going to need the calories. Never mind that they'll be puking by the time their rough ride is done. That's guaranteed.

While Cooper tends the pot, he has Art gather the emergency supplies—the knife, the reel and packed-down rod, the binocs, a gallon jug of bad water, the EPIRB (Emergency Position

Indicating Radio Beacon), a space blanket, and a twenty-foot coil of rope. Normally, there'd be dehydrated food packs, energy bars, flares, a flare gun, a first aid kit, foul weather gear, and more. But Thomas and his minions took all of that. Art stuffs the gear into a battered backpack. Evacuation will be tricky because high winds might blow the life raft from their grasp as it inflates. Even if they manage to hang onto the raft, it's going to be a feat for a cripple and a fat man to clamber inside the thing and get it adrift without swamping.

All of this Cooper finds exhilarating. The mounting problems set his mind spinning like a gyroscope, assessing one contingency after the other, the variables arrayed in a way that brings to mind incoming missiles brightly lit on a radar screen and his single chance to separate out the dummies and target the one that holds the payload.

Over their meal of rice and boiled fish, Cooper explains foul weather procedure. They'll set up a jib on the forestay and another on the backstay. These are small triangular sails that will keep the Lickety Split steady in a strong wind. Then Cooper will play out the storm anchor.

"How can we anchor here?" Art asks. He nervously nibbles on the fish, which he holds like a cob of corn.

"The storm anchor is nine nylon buckets strung out on a sixty-foot line. It sinks below the stern and acts like a giant finger held to our tail to keep us steady. If all goes well, it will prevent us from pitch-poling."

"Pitch-poling? I don't like the sound of that."

"It's when a wave kicks us end over end. Some sailors have survived pitch-poling but barely. We'll set Iris to steer. Then we'll hole up here."

"Down here?"

"It's all we can do. I'll go up every hour to check on the rigging."

"What about those movies that show the sailor gamefully

clutching the wheel as he heads into the storm?"

"That's a last resort scenario. If the waves get too big, you steer manually to avoid washovers. If the boat takes too many boarding waves, the gear gets swamped and water drowns the engine. Then you're dead."

"Dead?"

"Dead in the water. Time to abandon ship."

Cooper studies Art's reaction. The old man looks understandably shaken but there's something more. Cooper worried that Art would be reduced to a cowering helpless heap of hysteria. Instead, Art seems almost fatalistic, as if to say, "All right, let's get on with it." Maybe because of his age and the many disappointments he has borne, Art knows not to beg or wail.

It takes them two hours to set up the storm jibs. Tied to the jackline, Cooper snakes out to the forestay jib tack to inspect wear on the line. The line is almost gone and he has to replace it. This takes another hour as Art hugs his left leg to give Cooper purchase and Cooper fights with the wind, the free end of the sail snapping and stuttering as he tries to catch the clew. He ignores the roaring pain in his stump. The wind now whistles eerily through the rigging. Sailors of old mistook this for the banshee calls of sirens luring sailors to a treacherous shore.

The wind is shifting and may soon be at their backs, which will propel them dangerously. It's a Force 8 blow so far and might top out at 40 MPH, if they're lucky. It's so noisy on deck, they don't bother shouting. The waves are now foamy, cresting at fifteen feet and arching high over the Lickety Split's stern as if to bury her but then, remarkably—thanks to the boat's good design— the waves slide under and the Lickety Split plies on, her nose up. Huddled at the stern, Art feeds Cooper the storm anchor as Cooper plays out the rope, dropping one nylon bin after the other into the churning deep. Each drop feels like a prayer.

Below deck at last, Cooper and Art strip off their sopping clothes, then wring them out in the galley sink. The cabin creaks and moans, loose items banging inside the lockers. The floor seesaws in long dips and rises. The water-rush against the hull sounds like white-water rapids.

"Holy fuck, what a mess," Art says. He sits naked on the galley bench. "People call this recreation?"

Cooper sits naked at the navigation desk. "Drink some water, Art. You won't be able to tell you're dehydrated until it's too late."

"Your water tastes like puke. I could use a whisky."

"When we're back, I'll buy you a bottle." Cooper flicks on the radio. A male Marshallese voice speaks through the static. "What's he saying?"

"Storm," says Art. "Danger. Don't go out."

"Anything else?"

"There's gonna be a bake sale at the Baptist church on Wednesday."

Cooper turns to him: "Really?"

Art barks a laugh. "Man, I wish I had a bridge to sell you."

"You're the one to talk, you and Thomas dreaming about setting up eco-tourism on Majuro. You weren't serious about that scheme, were you?"

Art shrugs. "What would we have to lose?"

"Besides your shirt and your reputation? You don't think the world would take exception to your making a mockery of this little island nation?"

"Well, I admit, it'd have to be spun just right."

If Art notices that Cooper's stump is bleeding, he doesn't let on. And maybe that's just as well. "Art, let's get our clothes back on."

"Does that matter?"

"It's some protection. And keep that PFD snug."

"I think I'm gonna be sick."

"Here." Cooper hands him a plastic bucket. The sight of it makes Art's face turn from ashen white to bluish gray. He vomits abruptly into the bucket, wipes his mouth with the back of his trembling hand, vomits again, comes up for breath, shakes his head in dismay, then vomits one more time.

Cooper holds out a stainless steel cup of water. "You okay? Drink up. And eat some more rice, if you can."

"Funny, Cooper."

Cooper won't go up until Art, still naked, has put on his PFD. Art complies, then says, "Go on, Sinbad. See if you can save us."

The noise on deck is a macabre symphony of whistling lines, howling wind, snapping sails, crashing water. Clambering into the cockpit, Cooper slams shuts the cabin door, which seals like a hatch, then clips himself onto the jackline. He squints into the spray and surveys the rigging. As if on cue, the forestay turn-buckle breaks loose, making the jib whip wildly back and forth. If the seas were calmer, Cooper could fix it maybe, but now the only option is to take down the jib sheet and make the most of the rear jib. Drawing a deep breath, Cooper worms forward on his belly. It's slow, painful going, his stump burning. When the Lickety Split rises high on a crest, he braces himself for the slam-down, gripping whatever he can grab.

Two years ago, when the old boat was new to him, he replaced all of the worn hardware. But now he sees the chrome cleats and stay-ends and . . . everything is rusted. Wearied from hard use and extreme corrosion, the Lickety Split simply isn't seaworthy. She's a strong horse run too hard and now she's susceptible to a fatal fall. Lying below the jib, Cooper reaches for the snapping sail, but then the jib foot—an aluminum rod—smacks him in the mouth and he sees stars. He collapses facedown on the deck, his mouth filled with the salty warmth of his blood.

He's lying at the tip of the bow: a few feet more and he could be the boat's figurehead. He turns over to watch the wildly whipping jib, he waits, then grabs the loose turnbuckle and pulls himself to the sail. After many minutes of gasping work, hugging the line as one wave, then two, slam him, he gets the jib down.

Clutching the small sail, he makes his way back to the cockpit, where he discovers that the yang, which stabilizes the boom, has split apart and now the boom is swinging wildly to and fro. The wind has ripped through the rear jib sail, which flutters like a scarf. Soon it will be in tatters. The storm is tearing the Lickety Split to pieces, bit by bit.

Cooper wraps the boom with the mainsail line on one side and then the jib line on the other and ties it taut. But the wind is so violent, the tie won't hold for long. Without sail, the Lickety Split is at the mercy of the waves. Cooper slaps off the autopilot, then switches on the engine. As the wind propels a steep wave into the stern, the boat rockets down a crest, a forty-five degree fall, the engine whining as the propeller leaves the water. Cooper steers hard to engage the rudder, then the boat slams into the trough, wallows before the propeller catches, and then, finally, the boat chugs forward, nosing ineffectually into the next crest, waves spilling over the bow. Then it's up again, the next wave like the upturned palm of a giant hand lifting the Lickety Split with head-surging speed. Then down: Cooper rudders the boat so that it's snug against the wave wall. When it hits the trough, he steers away from the next swell. If the bow were to stab the swell coming out of the trough, it would stick nose-first, its back end heaving up and over.

So much of hanging on, of getting through, is a matter of headwork, he knows. Not losing faith. The storm could go on for hours. Days even. He can't allow himself to think that far ahead, can't even acknowledge his growing weariness, the cramp in his left leg, the flames in his other, the stabs in his back as he leans into the wheel for balance. It's like long distance running, looking only at the path just ahead of your burning feet. There's no reason to peer to the horizon. You may never get there.

Cooper isn't sure how long he holds onto the runaway Lickety Split. What he does know is this: sometimes, no matter what you do, even if everything you're doing is right, you still get clipped. Call it rotten luck. As he might apprehend a flash of lightening,

Cooper sees the broaching wave rolling over his beam on the portside. When it crushes the boat, he throws himself into the wheel and hangs on for dear life. The wave rolls the boat over, he is under water for one second, two seconds, three seconds, then the boat rights itself, water seething from every nook, cranny, and well.

Cooper vomits, then howls his relief. Then he sees what he most feared: the mast is down and the engine is dead. It's textbook endgame.

EIGHTEEN

When Jeton awakes, it is still dark. He hears dogs barking Dogs are always barking on Ebeye. But somehow this sounds different, persistent like a warning. Next door a baby is crying: a faint but distinct complaint beyond the racket of rain. Lying on his cot in the closet-sized pantry behind his mother's kitchen, Jeton stares at the ceiling and thinks it remarkable that the roof does not leak.

Wind makes the plastic over the rusted screens on either side of him billow and snap. He tries listening for his mother's snore. Betra and Samson often complain of it because they share her room. Jimkin, his middle brother, sleeps at his girlfirend's house His father and oldest brother are working on Majuro. His older sister sleeps at a cousin's house. Some nights Jeton finds himself taking this inventory, as if to answer the question, Where am I?

Rain pummels the roof; the dogs bark; the baby cries.

Then he remembers Stevie, who was sharing his cot.

Jeton sits up, swings his feet off, then yelps at the cold that seems to bite his legs. No, not cold exactly: wet. He stands abruptly—he's up to his calves in water.

They say that one day all of Micronesia will be under water— maybe before Jeton is an old man. Even though teachers have explained this, how the ice at the top and bottom of the world is melting, it makes no sense to Jeton. How much ice can there be?

Now, sloshing through his mother's swamped house, he decides that Ebeye is not sinking. There has to be some other explanation.

The house is not much larger than Stevie's lost boat, the Irooj: kitchen with a small table, a 2-burner propane stove, and a refrigerator the size of an ice chest; one room for the TV and two bamboo chairs; then his mother's room, with its two cots and a rosewood chest she is still paying for. He finds her lying on her back, her mouth open. She wears a cotton slip that looks like a housedress. Her snores are as loud as gull chatter. Betra and Samson are awake in the bed they share, watching the rising water with fascination.

Betra lies on her stomach and dangles an arm over the bedside, tracing her fingers across the water's surface. Samson is pushing everything he can find into the water to see if it floats: pages from a calendar, a paper napkin, a paper cup, a pencil, the lid from his mother's face cream, a plastic bottle, a plastic bottle cap.

Though it is night, it is as bright as a full moon because of the street light next to their house.

"Samson wants to be a *jela*," Betra says. The noise of rain on the roof makes it hard to hear her. She is smiling.

"Do you see?" Samson waves his hands over the things he has set afloat.

"Did you try to wake *mama*-?" Jeton asks.

Betra raises her brows in question.

"The water," says Jeton, "doesn't that worry you?"

"It is unusual," Betra says finally.

"It's *bwebwe*!" says Jeton.

Samson has waded over to his mother's cot and is pushing at her shoulder. "Look, *mama*—!"

"*Enana*," she says, one hand pawing the air in protest.

Betra puts her few things into a purple plastic backpack while Jeton takes down his mother's dress from the nail next to the doorway.

When Jeton's mother sits up, blinking, she says, "*Jete awa kiiō?*"

This makes Betra laugh. "It's nana time," she says.

Jeton's mother rubs at her puffy eyes, then fixes her three children with a suspicious gaze.

"It's the tide," Jeton says.

Samson makes a playful splash. "See?"

She stares in disbelief at the water that surrounds them. "Mother Mary!"

When they open the front door, a surge of water floods in, swamping Samson, who flounders and kicks. Jeton fishes him out by the collar of his T-shirt: "Stand up, little brother!"

Samson rights himself uneasily, spitting water. "Where's my hat?"

"What hat?"

"Why is the water so high?" their mother asks. "What has happened?"

"My Yankee baseball hat," Samson says. "It's gone!"

"We got no time to find your hat," Betra says.

"I can't swim," their mother says. "None of us knows how to swim except you, Jeton."

Jeton pictures himself swimming with the three of them on his back. "I will get you another hat," he tells Samson.

"A Yankee hat," Samson says.

"A Yankee hat," Jeton repeats, thinking now of the promise he made to Stevie. The Marshallese are notorious for making promises they never keep—Jeton has heard the Americans say this. But the Americans don't understand that when the Marshallese are making promises, they are simply trying to be polite: a promise can make people happy for the moment, the way Jeton has made Samson happy right now That is the good of promises.

Jeton hikes Samson onto his back, then the family moves into the crowded street, where the water is waist-high. Neighbors are shouting for their loved-ones, small children on the backs of larger children. Betra has trouble keeping up. *Mama* pulls her along by one arm Three dogs paddle past frantically, their heads barely above water, their eyes rolled back nearly to the whites.

It is just a matter of time before the sharks come, Jeton thinks.

The rain pounds steadily, the drops as big as quarters.

Jeton hears the sputter of a motorboat, then sees it wallow through the intersection ahead: it is already too crowded and will probably capsize as others grab for it.

If this were only rising water, people could stay afloat; it would not be so difficult. But the water is growing rougher, surging as the high waves tumble in.

Ahead in the crowd Jeton sees cousin Mike, two aunts and an uncle. When Jeton catches up, Mike says, "Where's Stevie?"

"He was drunk like me," Jeton says, as if this answered the question

"You're still drunk," Mike says dismissively. "Follow me."

Samson starts singing, "Jeton's drunk, Jeton's drunk."

Jeton feels more scared than drunk. In the intermittent glow of street lights and windows, the rain looks green. Within minutes, he loses Mike in the crowd. It's hard to tell the panicked talking from the downpouring tumult.

His mother close behind and Betra between them, Jeton stops in front of the Good Day Variety store and lets the crowd press past. Betra is up to her neck in water.

"Here," Jeton says. "Climb to the roof." He lifts Samson to the top of a soda machine and instructs him to reach the low roof nearby. Betra follows. Agile and eager, the children move quickly, then wave down, grinning from their perch. Next, Jeton's mother tries but she's too heavy and doesn't have the strength to pull herself up. Jeton offers her the stirrup of his intertwined hands. He strains to hoist her—he feels his elbows pop from the weight, his shoulders burning—but then she buckles and falls back, slamming him into the store's grilled window.

Jeton tastes the salty bite of his bloody tongue. "Damn!" he says in English, shaking his head to clear away the stars.

His mother rises from the water, sputtering. In the red glow of the soda machine, she gapes at him with a wide-eyed m*ejān kaamijak* face—like those masks the Americans wear at Halloween.

If she drowns, he realizes, this is what she will look like when she returns to haunt him.

He shouts instructions into her ear and, trembling, she nods her understanding. "Okay?" he asks.

"Okay," she answers.

Then he's down on all fours, holding his breath in the deepening water, as she steps onto his back. Now, slowly, he rises, keeping his back straight, wanting to scream at the pain, his lungs kicking for air like a landed snapper. He prays to no god in particular, prays that his mother finds the strength, that her capable hands find a hold, that she pulls up, up, up.

When he breaks the surface finally, nearly sobbing, he can't tell any longer where the weight is. But then he sees that his *mama* above him, kneeling precariously on top of the soda machine.

"Stay there, don't move," he says.

Behind him he hears a crack, like a tree splitting in half, and he knows it's a transformer blowing, a common sound on Ebeye. Two more cracks follow. Then the lights are gone—boom! like that—and a communal wail rises from the darkened island.

Jeton makes a basketballer's leap for the roof lip: he grabs hold but pulls away only tarpaper. Then a passerby gives him a hoist up and Jeton scrambles onto the lower roof. When he turns around to offer a hand to his helper, he sees only more passing crowd.

Quickly he pulls his mother up, then they clamber onto the higher roof of Good Day Variety, a cinderblock building that should be able to withstand the storm waves. About 50 others are up here too, families with their chickens and goats, the children running too near the roof's edge. Jeton wonders if the roof will hold. Buildings on Ebeye are poorly made, everybody knows. Jeton cautions Betra, Samson, and his mother to sit toward the edge, facing the lagoon.

From this height, he sees streams of flashlight rising and crossing like poles of yellow bamboo on other rooftops. Below, on higher ground, several stalled cars and pickups send wavering blue-green beams into the rising water. And beyond, where the waves are tumbling in from the ocean, he sees the luminescence of foam in thin jagged lines.

More lights approach from the lagoon: lanterns on the boats. Now bigger boats are able to motor through some of the streets. There's the Blue Lady a block away, looking eerily lovely, its strings of white lights glimmering from its mast. Some people swim for the boat. Jeton hears much shouting. There will never be enough boats for all of Ebeye's 13,000 people.

Suddenly an orange light drizzles from overhead: a single flare rocketing a smoky arc toward Kwajalein, just two miles south. Another follows. Then another.

"Fireworks!" Samson exclaims.

Several of the children are pointing with glee.

"There," Jeton says. He wipes rain from his eyes. "Isn't that Hideo's boat?" It's a big white apparition in the near distance.

"Hideo doesn't care about us," his mother says.

Peering through the downpour is like peering through a swirl of sandy water: the many lights shift and bleed in the haze and the shapes swell then shrink instantly.

"Stevie said he was going to borrow Hideo's boat."

"Hideo would not be happy about that," his mother says.

"Maybe Hideo's on Majuro."

"Stevie knows better."

"Wave. Let him see where we are." Jeton flails both arms.

Ah, there it is, Hideo's big white boat—now the size of a bread loaf. But it does not come nearer, though people aboard are waving. They are illuminated by the white lights under the boat's canopy. Jeton cups his hands over his eyes. Who are they?

"Is it Stevie?" Betra asks. She waves too.

Jeton cups his hands, then shouts, though he knows his voice won't carry in the rain.

"Why are they waving?" Jeton's mother asks. She sounds tired. "They are not coming here."

"Is it Stevie?"

"I'm cold," Samson says. "Let's go someplace else."

"We're waiting for cousin Stevie," Jeton tells him. "He's coming with a boat."

"Not that boat?" Betra asks.

Already the big white boat is lost in the rain. At first, it seemed there were many boats plying nearer and now it seems there are none.

Jeton fingers the rain from his ears, then wipes at his face with both hands. "No, not that boat. Let's wait and see."

"I could've brought my umbrella," his mother says.

Then Betra chirps, "I won't have to wash for a month!"

Jeton turns to smile at her, smoothing the soaked hair from her face. He wonders if his older brother and sister got on a boat. And cousin Mike and Anjua, the smart girl who won a scholarship. And Stevie. If Stevie was too drunk, if he didn't watch where he was going. . . .

Someone flashes a light into the street and Jeton sees so many things afloat: buckets, pans, corrugated plastic, cans, clothes, plastic bags, a plastic tricycle, a drowned cat.

The water is now halfway to where they stand. Maybe they will be safe here, though they are closer to the oceanside than Jeton would like. Right now, the waves coursing over Ebeye and channeling through the streets seem manageable because there is so much to break their currents: walls, trucks, cars, houses. But soon, who knows?

Jeton tells himself there is nothing to do but watch and wait. Maybe Stevie will come. Maybe the rain will stop. Maybe the Americans will arrive with their big boats and save them all.

Samson whimpers, huddled into his mother's stomach. Betra

shields her head with her backpack. The others on the roof are hunkered down in small groups, even the chickens and the goats. How did things get so bad so quickly? Jeton imagines that had he been a better man, had he graduated from high school and gotten a job on the causeway, maybe he and his family wouldn't be here tonight, stranded on top of Good Day Variety.

Though he knows there is no *wun*, no logic, to this thinking, he feels the blame nonetheless—because he has no more aim in life than the many things floating on the tide.

He pictures below him, in the store, all of the new things— beauty aids and stove pots, carpet sweepers and inner tubes, vol- ley balls and rubber boots—rising with the water Then he re- members the raft on the wall. He could fetch that.

Thirty minutes later, as he climbs into the store, he is sur- prised by the rats—they seem to be everywhere. From his perch on the broken window high up, he sweeps Betra's penlight across the second-story floor of Good Day Variety—a boiling carpet of gray rolls away from him, leathery tails whipping this way and that. Then he aims the light higher: as big as kittens, the rats bolt and scamper from shelf to shelf. Even over the dull thunder of rain, Jeton hears their fat-bodied thumps and thuds as they tumble down the stairs. He steps to the floor, then quickly finds a bucket of wooden spoons. He heaves the bucket down the stairs, hears the spoons clattering, followed by several heavy splashes that spoons would not make. Then he follows. He's barefoot and soaked—it feels odd to be out of the rain: his ears ring, his scalp tingles. Good Day Variety is like an underwater cave, black and ominous.

Jeton finds water halfway down the wooden steps. Shivering, he wades in, then, penlight in his mouth, he dives. Soft things bump his head: plastic plates, half submerged canisters, plastic balls, rats. The water is yellow-brown in the weak light. When he surfaces—gasping, nearly spitting out the penlight, which he snatches from mid-air—he finds himself treading water and there it is above him, hanging from the ceiling: the big yellow raft. It has been there as long as he can remember. Twelve feet long.

Gently, tentatively, he touches down, first one foot then the other, and he finds himself only chest-deep. His teeth are chattering. Why is he afraid of the rats? At least there are no stone fish, no sharks, no moray eyes.

When he hears small sloshings in the darkness to either side of him, he slaps the water once, twice, three times. The feeble beam of Betra's penlight falters like a blink. Jeton feels his heart echo the warning with a blink of its own: he has little time. Ignoring the silver glow of small eyes and the clumsy scramble on the shelves above him, he finds the step ladder nearby. He wades over and pulls it to him. Two steps and he's under the raft. One more step to be sure. Suddenly he feels himself slipping across a slick surface.

He curses himself for taking that last step. He hits the water face-first, as hard as a bad dive, his sinuses stinging. Then all is as black as the blackest dream. He surfaces quickly, coughing, wiping at his eyes. The penlight is gone. Frantic, he combs through the water with both hands. Black, black, black.

For a moment, he is petrified. It's as if he has come to the end of a short and miserable journey and now, the rising tide behind him, he realizes he is lost, there is no getting back.

But this is silly, he tells himself. He can get back. Of course he can get back.

Can he get the raft?

He hears the taunts: *Jeton the fuck-up couldn't get the raft he promised his family. Jeton the fuck-up let his family drown even though a raft was two feet below them, hanging from the ceiling of Good Day Variety.*

Pawing and clawing, cursing, sweating, then nearly weeping, he does get the raft down. It's hard to say how long it takes. A long time. Anger helps. Fuck the rats!

Then he's in the water again, only this time, the raft is beside him, riding up on things he can't see and much heavier than he imagined it would be. He realizes that he can't get it up the stairs, much less out the window, unless it's deflated.

He pats at its surprisingly stiff hide, fingers its many recesses, traces its numerous protrusions, it is so large! Then he finds the plug—but even this resists him. Does he pull it? twist it? He feels anger burn through him like electricity boiling through a vein.

Stop, he warns himself. How would he explain to Betra and Samson that he found the raft, that he got it down, only to put a hole in it?

Gently, he pulls and twists the plug. Air wheezes, then farts, then stutters from the plug-hole. But now the huge thing is collapsing around him like the weight of a wet sail. He falls back, fighting to stay afoot, his arms enfolded in the heavy rubber hide, which he tries to punch and fold and roll, pushing the weight between his legs but careful not to let it sink too far.

It is almost too much to carry. With the bulk of it draped over his shoulders, he inches towards the stairs, feeling his way with his toes. He knows he must go slowly or risk snagging the raft on the obstacles at every turn. It takes a long time to find the stairs.

"Jeton got a raft!" Samson shouts before Jeton can wave him silent. "He's got a raft!"

Unthinking, Betra joins him in this gleeful announcement.

Soon they are surrounded by the others, so many children and curious adults. Even the goats have come, peering at him through the crowd. Jeton thought he would inflate the raft on his own, hiding on the lower roof—it is only one raft, after all—and then he and Betra, Samson, and *mama* would slip away. He knows a secret escape would be impossible now.

He has laid the big thing down on the puddled roof. It is surprising, exhilarating, how much light is up here compared to down below in the rat-filled store.

"Is this a raft?" someone asks.

"He got it by himself," Jeton's mother announces. "He could have drowned."

Others murmur their interest, many squatting for a closer look.

Jeton ignores them, pulls the raft's valve to his mouth, then begins to blow. He blows and blows. And nothing happens. He blows until he is dizzy and breathless. A finger on the valve-tip, he slumps forward to recover. The raft is too big, he realizes, much too big. It might take an entire day to inflate.

"Here, let me try," says a man whose name Jeton doesn't know. He has a big belly and maybe good wind.

He blows into the valve for five minutes, then someone else wants to try. Two hours later, they have formed a crowded circle around the raft and it is Jeton's turn again. Blowing into the valve makes his head ache. He has calculated that, big as the raft is, each family could put one person aboard. Someone who knows rafts has unfurled from the sides a tent that will keep the rain out.

"Look how big," Samson says.

"We are going to ride the raft!" Betra boasts.

When they are ready to set it in the water, Jeton asks each family to pick the person—how can he say this? the person they want to save? the person they want to send away?

"Pick one person from your family," Jeton instructs. He imagines that long ago, when a clan had to abandon an island, they were prepared—they all knew how to swim and they had dugout canoes for everyone and nobody had belongings to leave behind.

Now, from the lower roof, as he helps women and children into the raft, starting with his own Betra, Samson, and ṃaṃa, Jeton wonders if he is doing the right thing. The raft looks sturdy and reliable, bobbing, butting at the building. But a flooded island is a treacherous thing. "Stay away from the buildings," he tells the two teenagers who will paddle. "Steer for deep water, head for the lagoon. Find the boats so that they can watch over you." The boys nod dutifully. He could make them wait—until it was clear that the water was about to overtake Good Day Variety and there was no other option. But then everyone would want a place on the raft and nobody would get away.

Several men have pulled more things from Good Day variety: two paddles for the young pilots, orange life vests for Jeton's mother and three other women, and inflatable water toys for the children to wear—brightly colored dragons, sea horses, and ducks. As two men steady the raft, the children crowded into the raft-tent, the two paddlers at the front, the women behind them, it all looks ridiculously fragile, and Jeton wants to call to his mother, his brother and sister: No, get out, this will not do! The pounding rain seems to have eased. Or has Jeton simply gotten used to it? It must be near daybreak. Things will look better in the light.

Betra smiles to him from the crowd of children. "I will email you from Kwajalein," she jokes. She wears a big cartoon duck about her waist.

"Let's go!" Samson calls. The other children pick up the chant: "Go! go! go!"

The men push them off. The raft drifts back. Jeton's mother offers a timid wave, her face that *mejān* mask.

"*Mama!*" he calls, but that is all he can say, terror caught in his throat.

The boys dig in with their paddles. The children shout and whoop as if they were on a festival ride. The yellow raft jerks away slowly like a giant turtle, families calling their goodbyes from the roof, the rain too loud to make out their words clearly.

Jeton watches with the others, watches until there is only darkness and gray rain and no sounds but water—the sound of grief, he thinks, the sound of loss. Exhausted, he sits cross-legged in the wet roof gravel and weeps. They are gone. He has let them go. If he has done the wrong thing, if he has sent them to their deaths?

The goats gather around him. He smells their wet animal

stink. One nudges his head, then mouths the fingers over his face, nosing for a handout. Jeton hears someone singing a hymn in Marshallese—about room for all in the house of Jesus. Others join the singing: they make a ragged chorus, the voices poorly matched. Still, Jeton wishes he knew the words to join them.

He pushes the nudging goat away, but it stands nearby, waiting the way a dog has learned to wait—the way Jeton himself is learning to wait, now for morning and, soon, for the good things that God has promised.

* * * *

Testimony:
Felicity Tannebaum, All-World Security, USAKA

First thing I thought when I saw them—several Marshallese leaping onto the pier from a rickety boat that had pulled dockside—was That's stupid! Dangerous stupid, I mean. A second thought came just as quickly: They're breaking curfew. It was two A.M. None of the indigenous folk are allowed on our island after the last ferry takes them to Ebeye at 8:00 P.M. They return, work passes in hand, every morning at six. We're very strict about that because this is a high security installation.

Not that you'd see anything spectacular here—no missiles or giant radar and so on. You'd have fly up to Roi-Namur and Meck to see those things. And they are a sight, believe me. The radar on Roi-Namur is one of only 3 in the world, as big as a circus tent. Here on Kwajalein you have only civilian housing, mostly. It's where the brains bed down: all those mathematicians and programmers and engineers. Their families too.

Two things you should know about standing watch at Echo Pier. a) It's the worst duty on the island because nothing ever happens out there. And b) I wouldn't have been on Echo if I hadn't fucked up big time at the airport, where I missed two dangerous detections on the scanners my first week. I had plenty of good excuses but, as anyone in security work can tell you, excuses don't count. Which is why you take nothing and nobody for granted. It didn't help that I put a lot of stock into intuition.

I'm not saying I'm clairvoyant or tuned into to some otherworldly vibe. But I am blessed with, let's say, a keen vision. I was the girl who could tell at a glance that our fifth grade teacher Ms. Mallonee was pregnant, even before she knew it herself; I was the girl who knew her uncle Wallace was an embezzler just by the way he folded money into his wallet. You get the idea. Suffice it to say, I feel I've got a sharp third eye most of the time. Unfortunately, if you're among people who describe the world only according to "facts," then there's no room for intuition. My boss, Garry, was one of those people.

I'd come to the island to be with my girlfriend, Inez, a nurse at the hospital. We had recently decided to get married in Massachusetts as soon as our TODs were done and we'd saved some money. I'm talking the American Dream here. The legitimacy of lesbians? That's how fast things were changing in the world. Think about that.

But I had fucked up, as I said, and maybe couldn't hang on to my job at All-World. Inez wasn't happy about this, as you can imagine. I'd been out on Echo pier for about 3 months, trying to redeem myself. It wasn't easy staying awake. Two weeks into the pier duty, I'd started drinking coffee, even though I hate the taste of it. I took my work that seriously. When the Marshallese showed up, I thought: Finally, some action! It was raining hard. We were getting nicked by the tail of a cyclone. The lagoon was especially high that night, which made it easier for the larger boats to get dockside. But, because of the storm, the waves were whalelike swells that prevented anybody from tying up. The smaller boats risked smashing to pieces if they got caught under the pilings. Through the haze of rain, I could see the ghostly lights of boats plying nearer. Dozens of them.

The big boats would edge to the dock, bobbing dramatically, then, at just the right moment, as swell, boat, and pier were aligned, a group would leap for safety. When I aimed my spot down the pier and caught an eyeful of these very wet Marshallese tumbling and clambering onto the pier—did I see a few fall into the chasm between boat and pier?—I realized that these people were desperate.

I trotted down the pier, big spot in one hand and life preserver in the other. "Code 666," I started calling into my two-way. Yeah, some wag in the company had given us this one: the devil's number for chaos. 666 was mostly a joke, the code that meant all hell was breaking loose.

You might think, like my mother, that because I've dedicated myself to a life of security work, I'm spoiling for a fight—that I'd welcome a 666. But nothing could be further from the truth. The truly big thrill for me isn't fighting trouble, it's making things right. Maybe that's a fine distinction but, at the end of the day, we officers in the security trade want—most of all—the world to make sense.

When I got to the crowd of Marshallese, they hardly acknowledged me, they were so frantic, shouting over the roar of rain, waving caution to their friends and families still on the boats. Many of the men were shirtless, wearing soaked trousers, and most of the women wore those muumuus that look like grandmotherly nightgowns, though some had on blue jeans. Everyone was barefoot. The wind flattened their hair and made the brim of my rain hat snap and stutter.

The Marshallese are a curly haired people with chocolate complexions, wide faces, broad noses, and remarkably good teeth. Because of a diet of American junk food, they are portly, for the most part, and to most observers they don't seem very ambitious. I had never stood among them, never spoken to them, never visited their little island of Ebeye.

Now, at the back of their crowd, I felt stupid because I didn't know a word of Marshallese. I saw immediately that the single life preserver I carried was useless. There were so many heads on the water's surface—I saw five, ten, twenty? people swimming away from the pier because they were smart enough to see that the waves would knock them senseless into the pilings but, then, they would not have an easier time swimming to the island because there was no beach for half a mile, only rocks the size of compact cars piled against the shore.

Just then I had a terrible vision of the drowned floating like splintered timber in the calmed lagoon the next day, the sun bright on their backs.

"Damn it, Merino, can't you hear me?" I shouted into my two-way. "This is a 666!"

At that early hour, Merino was supposed to be manning the dispatch desk. I want to be kind to Merino but I must tell you that, ever since his boating accident, he hadn't been right. You could tell by the way his eyes drifted whenever he looked at you: the man couldn't focus. So I really wasn't surprised when he didn't respond to my call. For all I knew he was plugged into his CD player while watching cable in the lounge.

The Marshallese pilots were fearless, edging up to the dock again and again. Already there was a crowd of about 30 on the pier, waving and shouting encouragement to those on the boats. That's when the boat folk started tossing children across. They were careful about it—as careful as you can be during a driving rain with high water kicking your boat around. What made it eerie was that, unlike the adults, the kids weren't screaming or wailing: they just gave themselves over. And there they went, flying, one after the other, from boat to dock, into the open arms of friends and family.

Now, I've been trained to think clearly in an emergency. Of course thinking clearly accomplishes nothing if it doesn't lead to appropriate action. At this point, I was 40 yards from my watch box and the phone. Had I been military personnel, my course of action would have been a no-brainer because the military prides itself on following the Chain of Command: you do nothing without contacting your superior. However, the security force on Kwajalein is not military, it is the top-drawer sub-contracted All-World Security. Which meant that we had more leeway than military. Which meant that I was not bound by rigid protocol. Which meant that I did not have to sprint back to my box to call my supervisor, which would have wasted precious time.

I commandeered eight young men. "You, you, you, you, come with me," I shouted. They did as they were told. Maybe because I was wearing a uniform, maybe because the Marshallese are "compliant" people. I led them half way down the dock, to the warehouse, a big gray hangar made of corrugated steel, which the Army was always painting to keep down the rust. The warehouse was for interim holding, mostly of domestic goods: like five container-loads of toilet paper or pallets of paper towels stacked to the ceiling. There was always something in there, though I never paid much attention. My job was to watch the ship crews and make sure they did not leave the pier: if your ship stopped at Kwajalein, you got no farther than my watchbox.

On my ring of keys, I had the one to the warehouse door, which took three of us to roll open. The thing was fifteen feet high and twenty wide. The darkened warehouse exhaled a warm, pungent breath. Silly me, I thought it'd be lit up inside like Ali Baba's cave. It was noisy from the rain rattling on the tin roof. Right away I saw what I'd hope to see, if my memory served me: stacks of plastic-covered foam mattresses—274 of them brought that month by the Lucinda Maru from Manila. They were scheduled to replace the mattresses in the Coral, Surf, and Sands bachelor quarters.

My commandeered crew read my mind. They started pulling down the pads. I arranged them in a fire-line, then we pushed, hauled, and shoved the mattresses from the belly of the warehouse, across the rain-slick wood pier, and then over the side, into the loopy waves. When the first mattress hit the water, I wasn't sure it would float. Foam's not as buoyant as you might think—and these were heavy foam. But they did float, some better than others.

Was this brilliantly innovative? I'm not saying I was congratulating myself—I was too busy, standing at the pier's edge and shouting the others on. I'd lost my hat and I was soaked, both from rain and sweat, and there was too much going on in the water below. Those in the boats were instructing those in the water to latch on. It was a delicate dance, the bobbing mattresses, the flailing swimmers, the nosing boats, but it was working. That's when I thought, *This is what it's all about! this is what I've worked for!*

After doing rescue for an hour or more, and after it looked like the warehouse was empty of mattresses and most of the swimmers were hanging on, I sprinted to my watchbox and phoned Inez.

A sound sleeper, she answered on the fifth ring.

"What the hell?" she said.

I said, "Honey, this is an emergency with a capital 'E.' I've got about five hundred Marshallese on Echo Pier and many need medical attention."

"Why are there 500 Marshallese on Echo Pier?"

"It's the storm," I said. "They got washed out."

"Who else is there?"

"Just me."

"Felicity, this doesn't sound good."

"It's not good, it's not good at all. That's why I'm calling, Inez. Are you coming down here with some medical help or not?"

"Okay, I'm coming."

Then I called Garry, my supe.

"Garry, it's a 666," I said breathlessly.

"That's not funny, Gina." I could hear him yawning.

"This is for real."

"You and me joke sometimes, I know, Gina, but it's three-thirty, for cripes sake."

"The Marshallese are down here, unloading in boatloads."

I could see some on the pier edge had tossed ropes over—a dangerous move.

"Which Marshallese?" Garry asked.

"All of them. They're crowding the pier. It's like a flood."

A moment of clarity descended upon me and I knew the cause immediately. All of the criticism aimed at the Ebeye causeway project had come true: the Chinese engineers had done a sloppy job, built the causeway too high, making it inevitable that during the next big storm the rising tide, instead of finding egress through the pass, would sluice down the causeway and drown Ebeye, which is only 2-miles long and a quarter mile wide. Simple.

Garry cleared his throat. I pictured him sitting up, his baby fine hair splayed out like a misty cloud, his thin lips mouthing alarm. "You're telling me indigenous personnel have set foot on Kwajalein?"

"That's right."

"How many?"

I glanced down the pier: it looked like a gathering for a dockside revival meeting. "Maybe five hundred."

"Five—where's the Army cutter?"

"If I had to take a guess, I'd say it's run aground."

Later, I'd learn that I was right. Intuition, I'm telling you—respect it.

I could almost hear Garry's thoughts groaning on the other end. Our Commander, Captain Manning, was in Hono for a vacation, so, understandably, Garry was feeling some pressure to make the right decision.

"Garry, people are going to drown if we don't get help fast."

"I've got to call the Colonel," he said.

"Call the fucking rescue squad first."

"You call the rescue squad," he snapped. "Keep everyone in one place—use the warehouse if you have to. This may be a trick." Then he hung up.

For a moment, as I punched in the rescue squad, I felt an uneasiness. It was a combination of dismay and dread. Dismay at Garry's response, because he was so administrative, and dread that his suspicion would make trouble. What did he mean a trick? And how was I going to "keep everyone in one place"? There were 13,000 people on Ebeye.

The pier wasn't going to hold them; the warehouse wasn't going to hold them. Hell, not even Ebeye had held them very well. So I was standing in my callbox, the wind wheezing through the window seams, raindrops as big as quail eggs smashing across the plexiglass, I heard my heart beating in my ears, I was thinking of the swimmers clutching foam mattresses in the chop out there, their brothers and sisters and aunts and uncles and mothers and fathers watching helplessly from the pier, their voices lost in the noise of wind and wave, and all the small boats trying to get to the dock or to the shore without breaking up, I was thinking of all that hope and horror out there while standing in the white light of my callbox, rain dripping from ringlets of my hair, then I knew what no logic could have told me: if I waited much longer, if I waited for the "Command Group" and the "Intelligence Office" and "Host Nation Activities Office" and my own All-World Security to assemble and formulate a plan, if I waited for an *official operations protocol*, I would witness more pain and suffering than I would be able to hold in a single lifetime.

It's easy to tell the grunt in the callbox to crowd the refugees into a warehouse while the refugees' loved-ones are drowning a few yards away. I don't want to overstate my case here, so let me admit that maybe no one had drowned yet—it was early, after all. And maybe the raindrops weren't as big as quail eggs. And maybe the waves weren't the size of *whales*. Nevertheless, this was clearly a 666, clearly an extraordinary situation, clearly a threat to life and limb.

Inez arrived with an ambulance and an orderly. She was wearing her white uniform under an orange storm slicker. I love a girl in uniform. I couldn't have been more proud of her. She was all business, but had found the time to put on lipstick, I noticed. She looked at me with some concern, pecked me on the mouth, then said, "Show me the worst first."

I led her to the warehouse. Someone had figured out the lights and the place was now smarting with fluorescent glare. A dozen injured people were sitting on pallets. Inez went to them straight away. The lanky orderly, wearing a blue poncho, followed her around with a big first aid suitcase.

By the time the Rescue Squad arrived—one truck, two women, three men, flashing red lights—I had assembled a rescue protocol of my own. I'd be the first one to admit it was a very risky operation, asking life-preserved volunteers to jump back in so that they could slip the marine lines (we had looted the Marina store) around the waists of the swimmers. But I had plenty of hardy volunteers, mostly young men. And we on the pier kept a tight grip on our end of the rope so that the jumpers wouldn't get away. It wasn't ideal. Some of the swimmers got beaten against the pilings. That accounted for five broken arms and some seriously bruised legs, which kept the rescue squad busy. More than a few of the swimmers we pulled out suffered gashes from the ropes. At least two suffered concussions against the pilings. But no one had drowned yet. At least none that we could see.

While the others continued the rescue and Inez and the rescue squad ministered to the injured, I ordered the Marshallese inland. "Just knock on the doors," I instructed them, "tell them you are refugees." I made them repeat that word several times, which was really difficult, it was so noisy out there. "Tell them you need dry clothes and a place to sleep. They will help you."

If you lived on a little island in the mid-Pacific and a wet, wind-blown, bedraggled native came to your door with that story, what would you do? Never mind the natives weren't supposed to be on the island after curfew. What would you do?

* * * *

The pounding that wakes her is not thunder. It is someone at the door. Alison bolts from the couch, where she fell asleep, still wearing a T-shirt and shorts. More pounding. "Coming!" she calls. Then her hand is on the door handle. It's a flimsy aluminum door, perhaps older than she is. The rain has abated. She can hear that for sure. Flicking on the stoop light, she sees the silhouettes of several people. The wind rattles the louvered glass panes of the door's upper half. Alison pulls the door open enough to peer out, she hears the sudden suck of air, feels the wet warm rush of wind, then she sees them: an older Marshallese woman, two children down the steps, then an older man below. They are soaked and wide-eyed and frightened. Clearly frightened.

"What happened?" Alison exclaims. She opens the door all

the way.

The woman says, "*Ịọkwe*," which means "hello" and any number of other things, like "excuse me." Then, her teeth chattering, she explains in halting English that "we crash in the rain" and "we are many" and "we seek help" and "we are refugees" and "there is no Ebeye," where they live, where all of the native people live, then "the water, it drowns Ebeye and we float away" and "my son is there drowning maybe" and then she's weeping.

Alison pulls her in, the shirtless boy and the skinny girl clinging to the woman's soaked dress. The older man, who could be the woman's husband, stays outside. He says, "I gotta go." He points to the water. "The pier," he says. "We are at the pier."

The pier is a short walk away. Alison sees other Marshallese rushing through the sandy alleys between the trailers. Some are limping. Some stand at other doorsteps, knocking, and lights are flicking on inside, trailer after trailer, the wind whipping the trees, broad leaves smacking and clattering overhead, the rain coming in bursts that sound like pebbles thrown at glass.

"It's a flood," Alison explains to Doug and Stan. Both boys are shirtless, wearing their surfer shorts. Doug hesitates, stopping at the edge of the living room. He looks angry but Alison knows this is a face of fear.

Stan approaches the visitors with a grin and a big wave: "Yuk way!"

"Get some towels and pull the sheets from your beds," Alison orders. She tries to get the woman and her two children to sit. But the woman refuses. "Wet!" she says. She wipes at her eyes, her lower lip trembling.

Alison makes some tea. The landline is dead. Her cell phone does nothing. Stan and Doug find clothes for the boy and the girl. The woman won't remove her dress but wraps a sheet around herself. "The tea is hot," Alison cautions as she hands each a Styrofoam cup of it. She realizes she is talking too loudly, as if they were deaf.

"I know what hot is," the little girl says.

Alison is surprised to hear such good English but what does she know of the Marshallese? She has never talked with one, never been closer to a "native" than at the grocery store, where Marshallese women work as checkers.

"Stay here, with our guests," Alison tells Stan and Doug. "I'm going to get Gayla and Topher."

"I wanna go!" Stan says.

"It is dangerous," the girl tells him. "People drown."

"That's why I wanna go!" Stan says.

"I need you here," Alison says. She turns to Doug: "You're old enough to take care of things until I get back."

Doug nods his head solemnly.

Alison turns to her younger son: "Stan, show these two how to play Stone Deaf Death Rangers on the laptop."

Stan looks skeptically at the boy. "You know what a laptop is?"

The boy stares back with wide eyes.

The girl says, "My brother does not speak English good but I can play."

"You can play?" Stan asks doubtfully.

"Show me what you got!" the girl says. It sounds like a dare.

Then Alison is outside, jogging through the rain, past the soaking refugees who are coming in greater numbers, dark figures huddled and hurrying through the alleys. Electrified by the emergency, Alison feels a bizarre thrill as she hurries on. The night is like a Halloween that's gone wrong, carrying the menace of mischief and ugly surprise.

Gayla and Topher live in one of the triplexes, across the paved road beyond Silver City. Their living room light is on. The sight of it gives Alison a jolt of adrenaline. She doesn't bother knocking. She finds Gayla pulling on a yellow poncho just inside the door and Topher wrapping an ice pack over the knee of a middle-aged Marshallese man, who sits on the floor in a puddle of water. Two

Marshallese women are toweling off in the kitchen. Two or three children too. Somewhere a baby is crying.

"So you've heard," Alison says breathlessly.

"Alison, honey, are you and the kids are all right?"

"We have visitors too," she says. "It's happening at Echo Pier."

"I'm on my way to see what I can do. Topher will stay here and tend to these folk. You coming?"

"It's a flood," Alison says outside. They are jogging. "Though it looks like the worst of the storm has passed."

"Storm tide," says Gayla. "It could last for days."

"Then why aren't we swamped on Kwajalein?"

"Fuck if I know," says Gayla, short of breath.

"Look at this crowd!" In the hazy arc lights of the pier, Alison sees hundreds of Marshallese. And suddenly she is among them, surrounded by the cacophonous din of their chatter and shouts and commands. Nobody is in charge! Here are four men pulling a rope up from the pier side and suddenly there's a half-drowned man gasping like a landed marlin at their feet. He heaves, then spits up water, then heaves some more. His four rescuers crouch around him as if to prevent him from wriggling away but they don't touch him because he's not done fighting off the ocean's hold: he's not theirs yet. The man vomits, then pushes himself up with both arms and coughs, gasps, then in an exhalation of pain and exhaustion releases a loud groan as he collapses face-down onto the boards. At last the rescuers carry him away.

Alison looks around. Gayla is gone. Somebody bucks her and she falls back, then drops abruptly to the pier boards: the pain quakes her bones. She hears a child whimpering behind her, sees mothers rushing off with rescued babies. Someone steps over her. Then another person. Bodies pulled from the water, people puking, water pouring from their nostrils, a child flying through the air into the arms of young man as in a nightmarish acrobatic show, then a woman wailing, and all the while the nasty smack and thunk of waves brutalizing the pier posts. Alison scrambles to her feet. She realizes she is paralyzed with fear and horror. She is absolutely useless.

She runs to the broad maw of light at the nearest warehouse. Once inside, gasping as if asthmatic, she sees the wounded laid out on the concrete floor, tended by a American medicos who work with remarkable speed and precision and calm—they seem so calm!

"You," a nurse says to her. A short woman with pinched features and a commanding presence. "Come here. Press your hand like this." The nurse takes Alison's hand and lays it on a thick gauze pad at the shoulder of a teenaged Marshallese girl who looks up at her with dazed trust. "Press hard until I come back. Can you do that?"

Alison nods that she can do that. And then she presses hard. The girl moans. Alison sees a single tear streak from the corner of the girl's beautiful almond-shaped eye. Than another tear from her other eye.

With her free hand, Alison gently brushes one finger across the girl's cheeks to wipe after the second tear. At last, she finds her voice: "You're going to be all right!" She tries a smile but it feels like a grimace and the girl looks at her with alarm. Then Alison sees that the gauze pad is sopping with blood, her fingers sticky-wet with it.

"*Kommool*," the girl murmurs.

Alison nods in kind acknowledgement, then she sees that the man lying next to her is passed out or dead, a man who could be Erik's age, his mocha-colored skin drained to a putrid greenish-gray, his mouth open, his lips too pale like Erik's lips, which she knows have long been eaten like delectable worms by a thousand tiny fish, his body churned into spongy silt by their relentless gnawing, so that by now there's nothing left but his shredded wetsuit, caught up in the silty currents like the tatters of a scarecrow waving in the wind.

NINETEEN

Seasick, soaked, and exhausted, Cooper and Art float in their orange rubber pod for two days before the kicking and bucking of waves subsides and then one more before Cooper wakes from his delirium. Their escape was almost textbook perfect, really something to be proud of. After the rollover, Cooper found Art slammed upside down against the galley but conscious. The Lickety Split had surrendered to boarding waves. Water was pouring in from the cockpit. It was nearly night and the wash across the deck was greenish white with phosphorescence. Clawing forward on one crutch, Cooper slung on the backpack of supplies, yanked naked Art to his feet, then they fought their way to the stern, where Cooper pulled out the compacted raft, ripped at the cord, and voila, there it was: a four-man tented float.

After they climbed inside, zippered against the howling wind and then whirled away by a huge wave, they were sitting in a foot of phosphorescent water, amazed that they were protected and afloat. Cooper peered through the plastic window and couldn't tell whether or not the boat would crush them. In fact, he couldn't see the boat at all. Had he time, he would have put her down himself, cutting the intake lines and opening the seacocks so that she would sink properly. But there was no time. Not even time to send a "mayday" over the radio. And now the Lickety Split was ignominiously floundering and might stay adrift, capsized, for days, weeks, even months, a deep-water hazard. Cooper felt sick about that.

When he comes to, he finds his wrists bound with a bungee cord. Everything about him feels profoundly wrong: his skin burns and itches, his head throbs with the noisy pulsing of his heart, his throat scorches from thirst. The tented raft is gloomy with weird orange light. It stinks of urine, sweat, and fetid sea water.

Cooper tries to raise his head, muscles quaking. Hoarsely, he says, "What the hell, Art?"

"You've been raving for three days." Art is hoarse too. "No doubt withdrawal from your pain pills. With maybe a pinch of shock."

"Three days!"

"You were most unpleasant, son. At one point I had to sit on you."

"Why are my hands tied?"

"To keep them away from your torn-up stump. Itches, doesn't it?"

"Like I'm being eaten by ants!"

"That's the salt poultice I put on it."

He sees that Art is naked except for his PFD. "Where'd you get salt?"

"From your galley. You had a big box of it. I saw you were bleeding, so I rummaged around to see what might help."

"Smart man! What else did you take?"

"A couple of plastic plates we might use as paddles. A portable air horn—one of those things people blast at football games. And half a chocolate bar."

"Chocolate—I'm starving!"

"You and me both. Literally. You should see how bad you look."

"And thirsty!"

"We get a sip of water every four hours. Just enough to keep our kidneys from failing." He unties Cooper's wrists. "I've been catching rain in your hat."

Cooper rises slowly to his elbows, glances down at his enflamed stump, his new wound crusty brown and rimed with salt.

"Since when did you get so disciplined and resourceful?"

"I've got to see my family, Cooper."

He says this quietly, his voice cracking. Cooper feels for him—and kicks himself for being such an impulsive fool and putting the old man at risk.

"Can you open the hatch a little? It reeks in here."

When Art unzippers the door, Cooper squints into the gray glare. It's raining lightly, the sky dark with laden clouds. It could be morning or evening. Then Coopers sees them: sharks—a dozen of them—circling. He could reach out and grab a fin easily.

"What the fuck?"

"Blacktips," says Art. "They're not the worst, that is, not the most aggressive. But they travel in schools and will attack that way, swarming."

"Some look pretty fucking big."

They're clearly visible in the crystalline water, like horror movie props: dead eyes, gaping mouths, finny turns and glides. Here's one sliding past: a six-foot-long prehistoric monster with a steel-gray carapace and kitty-white belly.

"They know we're of interest," says Art. "But they're not sure what we might be."

"Will they attack the raft?"

"That would be unusual," says Art. "No, they're just waiting and watching. They know something's up. The good thing is they're reef sharks, so we might be near land."

"Not that we could get out and swim even if we saw land," says Cooper grimly.

"Don't be negative."

"Ha. You didn't lose your boat!"

"Oh, don't start with that, son. You earned your wreck in spades!"

"You're right. I'm an ass," says Cooper. "Will you forgive me?"

"I'm not a forgiving man," says Art. "Honestly, I thought of dumping you the first day. Put you out of your teeth-gnashing misery."

"But you took pity?"

"No, I thought I might eat you in the end." Art smiles.

"You asshole!" says Cooper with gratitude.

"Not quite as big an ass as you, I should say. Now tell me, Sinbad, what currents might we be in?"

"Major currents travel west just north of the Equator," says Cooper wearily. "If we can stay afloat, we'll hit land eventually. Maybe even your own atoll, Jaluit. Isn't that due west?"

Art nods his head "yes," hardly looking convinced. "What about this little gizmo?" He holds up the EPIRB, a yellow plastic rectangle the size of a bread loaf. "I thought this thing guaranteed rescue."

"You can be sure it's sending signals to the Cospas-Sarsat satellite," says Cooper. "And somebody has picked it up. But I'm not sure who wants to fetch us. Whose jurisdiction are we floating in?"

"Shit, if it's the Republic of the Marshall Islands, don't count on a fast response, especially in this weather. I don't even know if their airline is still operating. They're always in bankruptcy."

"That's grand," says Cooper. "Doesn't help their international image, does it?"

Art shakes his head in dismay. "In the eyes of Westerners, Pacific island nations are notoriously lax. 'Island time' and all that."

"And nobody knows we left Majuro on the Lickety Split!"

"We can thank you for that, can't we?"

"Didn't I say I'm an asshole?"

"You can't say it enough, as far as I'm concerned. What exactly is your problem, Cooper?"

"I've tried to be a good man, Art. But it seems I'm impulsive and thoughtless and selfish."

Art zips up the door. "You're an American, that's your problem."

"If—*when* we get rescued, you can bet it'll be the Americans who pick us up. Then you'll be singing 'God Bless America' till you're red, white, and blue in the face, my irascible friend."

"I'm done with America and its gonzo cowboy citizens waving guns and shouting for attention. America needs to take a pill and sit down. *Just sit down, America, and shut the fuck up!*"

"Then why aren't you a citizen of the Republic of the Marshall Islands?"

"They don't want me," Art says sourly. "They don't want any Americans."

"Really? I'd've thought they'd snatch us up. We've got money, don't we?"

"They've seen plenty of America's money. Money's not what they need. They need to get back what they've lost—their culture, their heritage, the folk tales their elders used to tell, the *kaṃōḷos* that brought their people together, the fishing skills that fed them, the seamanship that made them proud."

"You're dreaming, Art. *Nobody* can go back."

"Why not? Who's to say we must bind ourselves to this mindless race for everything that's new and distracting and destructive? These Marshallese kids, even my own, want cell phones. How stupid is that? They dress like L.A. gangsters. They mouth rap songs that make no sense to them. And why?"

"It makes them feel connected and powerful, Art. You know that. In my day it was punk-pop music. In your day it was, what, the Beach Boys?"

"I'm not talking about music. I'm talking about the cheapening of sensibility. And loss, Cooper, we're drowning in loss."

"You might feel differently if you had a good meal in your belly."

Art scowls. "You insult me with your smug American confidence, your glib acceptance of the status quo."

"That's where you've got me wrong, Art. I'm a sailor precisely because I don't want the status quo."

"How big a fool do you want me to believe you to be? You're

working for the military industrial complex, my addled friend. You're in the vest pocket of the status quo. If you think sailing a boat in blue water is going to change that, then your entire life is a miscalculation."

This shuts Cooper up. Art's disdain bruises him. And he fears the old man may be right. From their vantage in this stinky little life raft, Cooper's adventure seems little more than a flight of adolescent fantasy. If he really hopes to get away from the expectations that stifle him—his parents' entreaties and the plans Lillian is making for a future he doesn't even want to consider—then he'd better take another tack.

Something bumps the bottom of the raft.

"Shit," says Art.

Then another bump.

Cooper sits up dizzily. "Are they *attacking*?"

"Sharks often head butt their prey before they attack," says Art.

"Where's the knife?"

"What, Cooper, are you going to go Tarzan on me and wrestle a black tip? Can you even swim?"

"Just give me the fucking knife, Art."

Another jolt from below.

"God damn it, Cooper. I will not forgive you for this." He hands Cooper the knife.

Cooper zips open the door. He sees breakers coming at him. Sharks too. "Behind us," he gasps. "I think we're coming to shore!"

Another jolt, then one corner of the raft dips abruptly. Two more jolts and another corner dips. Water seeps into the raft but they stay afloat. The breakers shove them. The raft jerks and jerks, "What do we do?" Art croaks.

"I can hear breakers hitting the shore," says Cooper. "We might be hung up on coral."

"The minute we leave the raft, they'll be on us!"

"So glad you threw away my pistol, Art."

Cooper sees one fin, two fins, three, but not as many as before. Is this high tide or low? How far from shore? Half a mile? Quarter mile?

"Let's try to turn the raft around for a better view," he says.

Using the plastic plates Art pilfered, they lean out and dig at the water. The work makes Cooper want to vomit. He worries that he might not have the strength to swim far, if at all. A shark—carried like a body surfer on a two-foot breaker —noses up to the raft's door and Art, without thinking, slaps it with his plate. His strike makes a distinct crack!

Like an earthquake's aftershock, fear shudders down to Cooper's core: he shits his pants.

Then he sees Art pull the air horn from the backpack and thrust it into the water. The horn's blast makes a muffled *haaarrrump!* that lasts a full three seconds.

He shouts, "Back off, fuckers!"

He and Cooper paddle again with their plastic plates and finally, stubbornly, the raft turns. Then they see the shore. Just fifty yards away. Maybe less.

It's a tiny island. White sand, a stand of palms, a clutch of undergrowth, several gulls picking through flotsam in the receding wash across the beach. The island could be anywhere in the Marshalls: north, south, east, or west. One sand-dot among fifty or a hundred in the oblong ring of an atoll.

"Wait," says Cooper. He slices two swatches of material from the tent sides, then fashions booties for Art's bare feet. He secures them with bungee cords. "That might protect you from the coral."

Cooper clamps the knife between his teeth. Like a pirate. Then he and Art jump in feet-first. Maybe the air horn scared off the sharks, maybe the shallow water discouraged them. Whatever the reason, they're gone for now. Cooper is surprised at the rush of energy in his limbs as he splashes forward, propelled by the incoming waves. Gentle waves! Art is gasping and cursing. "My feet are heavy as bricks!" he shouts. The water is green-brown, roiled with sand.

Cooper's foot touches bottom. The contact is electrifying. He tries to hop but a wave knocks him forward and he's underwater, paddling like a frantic dog, stabbing at the sand with his knee and his stump until at last he's belly down on the wet beach. Then he opens his aching mouth and lets the knife drop. He hears Art noisily sloshing up behind him, sees Art's makeshift booties gushing water, then spies Art's tiny penis puckered below his heaving belly.

"OH MY GOD!" Art bellows. "OH MY GOD THANK YOU!" He drops into a sitting position on the soaking sand, his legs splayed like a child ready to build a castle.

The sun is a white blur behind fast-moving rain clouds. Soon it will break through. It's morning. Sandpipers kite low across the receding water, then touch down in a sprint, plunging their long beaks into bubbling sand here and there and here again.

Wherever Art and Cooper are, it looks like the end of the line—the last island of this atoll's lopsided ring. To one side is open water, the treacherous passage from ocean to lagoon. The pass would be deep, the currents strong and unpredictable. Had they drifted into it, they would either have been drawn into the lagoon—a good thing—or pushed out to sea.

To the other side, they see the welcome redundancy of islands extending one after the other in a long hazy line. There's no sign of habitation. No boats in the lagoon.

"Is this Jaluit?" Cooper asks. He has found a bone-white spar on the beach. It makes an excellent staff for walking.

Art gets to his feet, slaps the sand from his naked ass, then squints into the distance. "Jaluit's a big atoll. We could be at the northern end."

"How far would that put us from civilization?"

Art smirks at the word. "I don't know, 30 miles?"

"But we might run into somebody before that—there's always somebody out here doing something on these islands."

"I like an optimistic thought, Coop. Maybe we'll run into a hermit. Or one of Amelia Earhart's heirs. She disappeared out here, you know."

"*We* are NOT going to disappear," says Cooper. "We *made* it. We're *here!*" He tamps the sand with his staff.

"Then we'd better get walking. Low tide will allow us to cross from island to island."

"The EPIRB!" says Cooper. He turns around to scan the water. Their deflated raft looks like a wet blanket snagged in the shallows. "Might as well leave it. It'll be good for a while."

"Sending signals into space?" says Art with a skeptical shake of his head. "Where would we be without technology!"

"We're MIA, Art. Our families will report our absence. Soon somebody will come looking for us and the EPIRB will point the way."

Art waves one weary hand as if to say, *Whatever.* Cooper watches him walk on, Art's orange nylon booties scratch-scratchy with each slow step. Already his broad silver-haired back is pink from the sun, his scrawny ass pebbled with a rash. Cooper limps after him, determined to keep up. He understands now what he never understood, that profound pain isn't an impediment to a body moving forward. Doubt is the impediment. He must sweep all doubt from his mind and make himself a better man. For starters, he will find a way to make this up to Art. Somehow he will make it up. And then Cooper will sail again. That's foremost in his mind. After having done all of this, given so much, lost so much, he is bound to the sea. Who would dare tell him to stop now? He won't hear it, any of it, from Lillian or his parents or his brother or his therapist. Let them pine, if they must, and peer sadly after him as he sets sail. And let them heap their agonized guilt and grief upon him—he'll throw it into the hold of his new boat and use it as ballast.

As for Cooper's employers, they won't be happy. Maybe they'll send him packing. Or commit him for psychological evaluation.

He's tempted to tell them, "It's been a stunning run of bad luck," but he knows this would not be the truth. Luck is something you play at the roulette wheel. It can't explain choices you've made day after day. That said, he feels lucky today. There were sharks within hand's reach! A cyclone that killed his boat! A thousand ways he and Art could have died—and died miserably! And yet here they are, a wondrous sight, the lumbering old fat man and the peg-legging younger man, as naked as newborn chicks, trekking across the sun-blanched rim of these micro islands as if they were a couple new to this world, their backs to the dawn-yawning sky, their eyes eagerly scouting the salt-misted horizon.

* * * *

"What island is this?" Stan asks when they land in Oakland.

Doug regards him with disdain. "It's not an island, fool, it's the United States of America."

"I knew that, stupid, I was just joking."

But Alison is sure that Stan was not joking. He was only five, going on six, when they moved to Kwajalein two years ago. This huge airport, this mob of people—all of Kwajalein could fit inside this terminal—must overwhelm him.

Handsome and ever reliable, Eddie is there to meet them just past the security portal. He's holding a hand-painted sign as big as a coffee table. It says in neat block letters, "Welcome Ali, Doug, & Stan!"

He hasn't changed much in all these years, still wearing his hair short-short and still favoring a preppy retro look: white shirt with blue jeans, white socks, and scuffed penny loafers.

His partner, Cam, is a bit artier, a short broad-chested man with a barely-contained mop of frizzy auburn hair, which he has tied back with small colorful strands of red beads. He wears rectangular eyeglasses, also red, and black jeans with an untucked, but well pressed (thanks to Eddie), vintage Pendleton plaid shirt.

Alison has heard plenty about Cam and hopes that she

and the boys make a good impression. She last saw Eddie two years ago, just before they left for Kwajalein, when Eddie flew to Milwaukee to see them off. He didn't bring Cam, she suspects, because the visit was short and their parents were—and remain— uncomfortable with Eddie's "lifestyle choice." Never mind that Eddie and Cam have been together for five years.

"Look at this sign!" Alison calls as she wades through the crowd.

Eddie lowers the placard, then kisses her on both cheeks. "You're looking good, sis, though I know it was a hard flight."

"We spent the night in Hono," Doug says.

"That's short for Honolulu," Stan adds. "In Hawaii."

"Big boys!" Eddie gasps. "You were such squirts when I last saw you!" He hugs them. Half smiling, they tolerate a few fore-head kisses. "Boys, this is Cam."

"What's up, guys? I won't embarrass you with a hug." He extends his hand for a shake and they dutifully take his broad hand. "Now let's try both at once," he says. "A group shake."

Stan glances to Doug as if to say, *Is he weird or what?* But they do as he requests. The group shake, their small hands cling-ing to his, makes them laugh.

"I bet your clock's all messed up," Eddie says.

"We gained a day!" Stan says.

"He means we flew back over the International Date Line," Doug says.

"So it's like tomorrow never happened for you two?" Cam says.

This makes Stan squint in confusion.

Doug rolls his eyes at his brother and says, "You don't get it?"

The flash flood of traffic on I-85 frightens Alison. "Good God, how do you stand it?" she asks.

"It's just traffic, Ali, you remember traffic."

"I don't like it either," Cam says. He's sitting in back with the boys. "I guess I shouldn't have put you shotgun. I wasn't thinking."

"What's shotgun?" Stan asks.

Cam explains the term, adding a brief history of stage coaches. "Maybe we should watch a western this week," he says.

"What's a western?" Stan asks.

Cam says, "A western's a kind of adventure fantasy that has made people in this country do all kinds of crazy things."

"I know what a western is," says Doug impatiently.

"We'll watch one," Cam says, "and have some fun deconstructing it. I think you'll find it very funny."

Alison can tell that Stan wants to ask about deconstruction but holds back for fear of sounding, once again, too young and ignorant.

After they exit onto Ashby and drive east, toward the hills, Stan says, "It's so crowded here, you can't see the sky!"

"That's because you come from a place where there's nothing *but* sky," Eddie says. "Sky and ocean."

"Why isn't there more ocean here?" says Stan.

"Why is my brother so stupid?" Doug sighs.

"Doug, don't start," Alison warns.

"Stan is just curious," says Cam. "There's nothing wrong with asking questions." He offers Stan a reassuring smile.

"Cam is a teacher, kind of like your mom," says Eddie.

"Mom's not a teacher any more," says Doug.

"She's a alcoholic," says Stan.

"An alcoholic isn't really a job," says Cam with a sympathetic smile.

"It's a condition I will always have," Alison says quickly. "Isn't that what you mean, Stan?"

Stan grimaces.

If Alison wants her boys to be honest and strong, she can't show reluctance or fear when confronted with the truth.

Eddie glances at her, then into the rearview: "Cam teaches college."

"That's what I want to do," Stan announces. "I'm going to

teach college."

"What are you going to teach?" Doug asks with a smirk.

"Global warming," says Stan. "Everybody needs to know about that."

"The islands we came from," says Doug, "they're getting swallowed by the ocean. All the Marshallese got flooded out of their island. Some of them came to our house."

Eddie and Cam know the story because the fiasco delayed flights out of Kwajalein for a week. This was just as well because Alison needed the time to recover from the trauma of witnessing the havoc on Echo Pier. She feels shamed by her collapse—she fainted while trying to help a nurse in the improvised hospital. Her therapist assured her it was nothing short of PTSD, the flood having brought back too vividly all of her thoughts about Erik. Still, it was humiliating and Alison was eager to get out of Kwajalein before the story circulated widely.

"It's sad to hear of the flooding," says Cam.

"But they might use garbage to build up their islands," says Stan.

"That's bizarre," says Eddie. "Is it true?"

"Stranger things have happened," says Cam.

"Have they?" says Alison. "Look. That's the university where Cam teaches."

"We're going just beyond it," Eddie says. "Up the hill."

Cam and Eddie's house is a brown shingled behemoth that has a towering eucalyptus in the backyard and an expansive view of the bay from the living room window.

The place must have cost a fortune.

"This is amazing, Eddie!" Alison can't stop raving.

"Stan, Doug, up here," Cam calls from the top of the stairs. "Each of you gets your own room."

"Oh, man!" Stan says, bounding up the oak staircase.

"This is a house?" Doug asks. "Just Uncle Eddie and Cam live here?"

He's never been in anything so large.

It's an Arts and Crafts interior, parquet floor in the dining room, an oak breakfast nook just off the kitchen, dark oak wainscoting in the den, which features a stone fireplace, and brass-caged light sconces along the hallway.

"It's our dream house, Ali. I've told you about it."

"Well, not enough, apparently. I just can't believe how great it is."

"We have done a lot of work in the last few years, I have to say. But it was always a splendid house, as you can see." Eddie looks to the ceiling as if to peer through to every room. Then he turns an affectionate gaze on Alison. "You're welcome to stay as long as you like. There's plenty of room."

"I don't know what to say, don't know how to repay you," she says.

"Don't get all awkward and self-deprecating," he says. "It'd be great if you and the boys could find a place of your own nearby eventually."

"I don't know what I'm going to do for work," she says.

"You're young, Alison. What do you want to do?"

"I'll have to go back to school." Alison follows him into the kitchen. "I could get a masters in Art History. That doesn't sound very practical, does it?"

"Frankly, no, but you're still thinking things through, right?"

"You've always been so generous with me, Eddie."

He scoops some coffee beans—they smell of chocolate and vanilla—into the grinder. The counter is made of twelve-inch square tiles, glazed a lemon yellow. "A friend of mine does art therapy. Maybe you should talk to her."

"You're overwhelming me," she jokes. "All of this is over-whelming—the traffic, the beautiful houses, the—"

"Yes, the possibilities, I know. It's America, Ali. It comes with the territory. But enough." Eddie holds up one hand, reminding Alison of Gayla suddenly. "You still like your coffee black?"

Cam and the boys find them in the kitchen, Eddie grinding the beans as Alison holds her ears. Everything seems louder here too.

"The boys and I are going to drive down to the Berkeley Bowl," Cam says. "They don't believe the market is as grand as I claim it is."

"He says they have seven different kinds of oranges," says Stan skeptically.

"And fifty kinds of cereal," says Doug.

"Maybe only forty," Cam says, winking at Alison. "We'll have to count."

"Pick up some arugula, sweetie?" Eddie asks.

"Sure, babe. Alison, any requests?"

"I'm sure Stan and Doug will pick out something I'd like," she says. "Here, let me give you some money."

"No need," Cam says, shepherding them out the back door. "We've got it. See you in about an hour."

Allison watches them clamber into Eddie's green Volvo wagon.

"He's great, Eddie."

"One in a million." Eddie turns to smile at her. "I got lucky." Then as if remembering that Alison hasn't been so lucky, he adds: "So tell me about your trip. It was hard leaving, wasn't it."

"Hard," she muses. "It's been very hard. I worry about the boys, the damage done to them."

"You can't blame yourself," he says.

"Erik and I thought we were doing the right thing. It seemed like a slam dunk good choice to uproot and regroup."

Eddie starts grating one of three lemons that lie on the counter. Alison hopes that he's about to make lemon butter cookies, one of her favorites. He says, "You couldn't have known. I know you understand that."

"Intellectually, yes, I understand. But emotionally I can't shake my misgivings. It has, really, been a disaster all the way around, Eddie."

"I'm sorry, Ali. I'm really very sorry. You deserve better luck."

"Is it luck?" she asks. "I think if I were stronger, more resourceful, a better artist, even, I could have made this work. But now I'm back with nothing to show but bruises."

Eddie adds four scoops of flour, then unwraps a stick of butter and drops that in. Then the sugar. Alison can't remember when her brother learned to bake.

"I'm sorry," she says, "I'm full of self-pity, aren't I?"

"Luck isn't about magic," he says. "It's, as they say, dumb—sometimes nothing more than being in the right place at the right time."

Alison thinks of Erik, how he was in the wrong place at the wrong time. Eddie seems to see this turning in her mind. He says, "Alison, give yourself credit for the things that are in your control. Like getting sober and getting the hell out of there."

"Cutting my losses?" she says. "There it is again, self pity—I'm sorry!"

"Stop apologizing, sis!"

"I'm sorry I'm apologizing so much!" she jokes, then reaches over for a finger of batter. *Mmm, perfect: lemony tart and buttery sweet.* "When did you learn to bake?"

Eddie shrugs. In silence, she helps him dollop dough onto the baking sheet. Then he slides the laden cookie sheet into the oven and says, "Let's get you settled."

"I suppose, like the boys, I have my *own* room?"

"You've got the room with a view!"

The house is open over the staircase, a tall leaded-glass window extending from the middle landing to the ceiling, twenty feet higher. On the second floor, Alison's room is in the far corner of the house, flanked by Stan's and Doug's. She's not used to these high ceilings and all of this indirect light.

The room Eddie gives her has a canopied bed, a marble-topped washstand, an oak vanity with a tall tear-drop mirror, and a large, round hooked rug with a subtle pattern of pale red roses.

The three windows are open to Berkeley's cool summer afternoon, the curtains simple swathes of yellow muslin, which match the walls.

"I'm in heaven," Alison gushes.

"Then I am too," says Eddie. "It's good to have you back."

Alison sees that her brother is about to cry and this takes Alison by surprise because she can't remember the last time she saw tears in Eddie's eyes. "I'm all right," Alison assures him. "And so happy to be here."

Eddie wipes hastily at his eyes with one sleeve of his white shirt. "I know," he says. "Let me look after those cookies."

"They smell wonderful," Alison calls after him.

Already Eddie is down the stairs: "We have lots of time!"

Odd that he would say that, Alison thinks, because time was the one thing she didn't think she had when she was on Kwajalein. The need to find Erik was a daily deadline.

Standing at the window, she can see a portion of the bright blue-green bay many miles away. The island she sees, far out, must be Alcatraz, smaller than she imagined it would be. Eddie told her that it has become a bird sanctuary. Everything on Alcatraz will be left to ruin until the birds, roosting in every crumbling corner, take it over.

It is time, she knows, to bury Erik. Despite protests from her parents and his, she has stubbornly refused to hold a memorial service for him, as if she still expected him to show up one day with a tale of how he was picked up by a Malaysian freighter and carted twice around the world before he could return home. Now she is willing to accept what she has never accepted truly, that he may never be found. A fact of life. To accept Erik's absence finally is to accept also something she has kept secret from herself: no matter where she goes, she will see water, either in its abundance or in its absence, stream beds, lake beds, the beds of ancient oceans; and every body of water will remind her of Erik's body, the phantom warmth of his hand against her cheek, his chest against hers, his breath like her breath. This is all she's left with and this will have to be enough.

TWENTY

Jeton is quietly amazed as he watches his players beating the American team, goal after goal, on the same field where he first met Nora. It is amazing to him that he is once again back on Kwajalein, where for many months he was *persona non grata*. It is amazing that Alfred Tibribrik, the coach, accepted Jeton's request to assist him—despite Jeton's reputation as a jona. It is amazing that at the dockside checkpoint an hour ago, the Security guard hardly looked at his ID as he sauntered forward surrounded by the many children on his team. It is amazing that Jeton loves this work and is proud to help these very young players who—amazingly—respect and listen to him.

"It is no mystery," his mama told him this morning as she made him breakfast of eggs and SPAM. "God is watching over you."

His mama's new house is just like her old house. After the flood, the Americans gave the *Majel* government money to buy wood and brick and metal to rebuild Ebeye. But much of the money disappeared and nobody could decide what to build anyway because Ebeye belongs to landowners who live on other islands and the landowners did not want new buildings. In the end, the *ri-Majel* government sent a boatload of pusswood and corrugated plastic and sheet tin and the shacks went up almost overnight. Now they are painted bright colors and Ebeye looks the same as always.

Cousin Mike is working on the causeway again. He says that when the causeway is done, it will not make Ebeye flood. Jeton thinks this is bullshit but he does not say so. Cousin Stevie works with cousin Mike, doing the job Jeton was doing: blowing holes in the coral. Cousin Stevie still wants to pilot a boat like the *Irooj*. And Jeton still feels bad about this every day.

Until a couple weeks ago, Lino was visiting Jeton nightly. He would stand at Jeton's bedside and stare at him with wild drowned eyes and say, "Hey, Jeton, 'sup?" This was better than saying, "We're sinking, man!" Jeton would be polite and make small talk but it was frightening every time. He is not sure why Lino stopped coming. Maybe the flood settled the ghosts in the Baptist graveyard. In an effort to keep the peace and show respect, Jeton visits Lino's grave once a week.

He continues to volunteer at the Head Start school, where Anjua has agreed to help him pass his GED. He has decided that he will miss Anjua when she's gone. She promises to return, but Jeton does not believe her. Few *ri-Majeḷ* return after leaving.

Here is something Jeton tells no one: he has quit smoking and is running every day because he wants to try out for the national soccer team. He runs barefoot from one end of Ebeye to the other. He runs very hard and very fast. The old people think he is crazy. "Where are you going in such a hurry?" they ask. "Do you know where you are going?"

Yesterday, he could have said, "Kwajalein! I am going to Kwajalein!"

When Jeton ferried from Ebeye this morning on the new boat—a sleek white hydrofoil named Jera or "friend"—he promised himself that he would hold up his head as he walked onto Kwajalein's Echo Pier. He would not be shamed if they sent him back. But when he stepped off the ferry, no one said a word to him. It was like *anijnij*. Magic. Like he was invisible. Or maybe, as his mother believes, God has placed over him some kind of invisible cloak that makes him a *jona* no more. Maybe now he is something else.

Panting from their run, the children gather around him after scoring their fifth goal. They are eager, wide-eyed, their foreheads glistening with sweat. Like Jeton, they have no shoes. But they run faster than the American boys, who wear cleats. Jeton kneels to explain how they must stay scattered on the field. The American children forget their game, he explains, and so they crowd together on every play because each boy thinks he is going to get the ball. That is how Americans think. Every American player believes that he is more important than his teammates, that he will be the one who will win the day. The *ri-Ṃajeḷ* know that every player is important. They understand how a *kumi*, a team, must work together. The *ri-Ṃajeḷ* boys nod their understanding as Jeton talks. They will hold their positions. Each boy will get his pass.

The children share cups of water before taking the field again. Jeton notices that each child on the American team has his own plastic bottle of water. It was the same way when he was playing with Ebeye High against the boys of Kwajalein High. The Americans had "cheerleaders" and bottled waters and *power* bars. And still they lost.

He imagines that Nora will watch the soccer team at her college. And maybe she will fall in love with the goalie the way she fell in love with Jeton. The thought of this sours his stomach the way a dinner of bad fish would. But he knows that this is one of many difficult things he must learn to accept—like the death of Lino and the loss of cousin Stevie's boat, the *Irooj*. In a very short time, the world has become as hard to read as shallow water in a storm. He suspects that this is what Nora meant when she said, "We'll see things differently when we are adults."

Yes, he thinks, *everything is different now.*

"*Momān kan*," coach Alfred says—looking good!—as the children jog downfield.

When Jeton asked to be the coach's assistant, the old-man coach looked at him skeptically and said, "What have you to teach children?" Jeton answered, "I have made many mistakes." This was all the coach needed to hear. Now Jeton kneels beside the coach the way a retainer would kneel beside his *irooj*. Always the coach sits higher. Always the coach gets Jeton's undivided attention.

Jeton has promised himself that when he is old and wise, he will be on the lookout for young men who need a second chance. "You don't need a second chance," cousin Mike has joked, "you need a *tenth* chance!" In recent months Jeton has taken on as many jokes as a boat takes on barnacles. It is hard work carrying around that weight but he does not complain.

Hoarse from shouting, Jeton calls his encouragement across the grassy expanse. The old coach nods his approval. Then Jeton says what the coach says—*Momān kan!*"—to test it out because one day he will be the head coach, running the children hard, showing how they can be better than they think, even barefoot, and then laughing loud with them—shouting happiness to the blue *ri-Ṃajeḷ* sky—when they score! again and win their game.

ACKNOWLEDGEMENTS

Excerpts of this novel appeared in *West Branch*, *Crab Orchard Review*, the *Greensboro Review*, and *Short Story*.

I would like to thank the following people and institutions for their considerable support, advice, and assistance: Loyola University-Maryland, the Maryland State Arts Council, the Eastern Frontier Educational Foundation, Sewanee Writers' Conference, Pirate's Alley Faulkner Society, The National Maritime Museum (London), and the British Library (London); John A. King, M.D., and Caroline Queale for their medical expertise; Rick Boothby and John Webb for their boating expertise; Ed and Gail Radigan, my Kwajalein hosts; Charlotte Scholte, my Kwajalein guide; Newton Lajuan, Carmen Bigler, Justin DeBrum, and Wilfred Kendall on Majuro; my Majuro acquaintances Jim and Mary Abernathy, Joe Murphy, and Alan Bell; Dr. Byron Bender and Alfred Capelle for their linguistic expertise and great patience; Father Gould and the late Father Hacker; the late Rueben Rieger for a tutorial in missile defense; Bill Remick for great photos of Kwajalein; Scott Johnson and Dean Jacobson for amazing underwater photography; journal editors Jon Tribble, Allison Joseph, Jim Clark, and Paula Closson Buck; Alice McDermott and Randal Keenan for early advice; Joseph DeSalvo, Jr., Rosemary James, and Tim Gautreaux for early support; readers Jeff Miner, Lia Purpura, Ned Balbo, Scott Allen, Mark Osteen; moral support: Geoff Becker, Michael Downs, Jessica Anya Blau; further support from fabulous writers Julia Glass, Bob Shacochis, Kevin Wilson, and Joseph O'Neill. And always and forever: Jill Eicher for more than I can put words to.